Praise for *New York Times* bestselling author

# MARIA V. SNYDER

"Maria V. Snyder tantalizes readers
with another complex, masterful story set in
a magical world so convincing that
she'll have you believing that it's actually real."
—*YAReads.com* on *Storm Glass*

"[A] compelling new fantasy series."
—*SFX* magazine on *Sea Glass*

"Wonderfully complex…
Opal finally comes into her own in *Spy Glass*."
—*Fantasy Book Review*

"This is one of those rare books that will keep
readers dreaming long after they've read it."
—*Publishers Weekly*, starred review, on *Poison Study*

"Filled with Snyder's trademark sarcastic humor,
fast-paced action and creepy villainy,
*Touch of Power* is a spellbinding romantic
adventure that will leave readers salivating for
the next book in the series."
—*USA TODAY* on *Touch of Power*

"Maria V. Snyder is one of my favorite authors,
and she's done it again!"
—*New York Times* bestselling author Rachel Caine
on *Inside Out*

Also by
*New York Times* bestselling author
Maria V. Snyder

## HARLEQUIN MIRA

### *Study series*

POISON STUDY
MAGIC STUDY
FIRE STUDY

### *Glass series*

STORM GLASS
SEA GLASS
SPY GLASS

### *Healer series*

TOUCH OF POWER
SCENT OF MAGIC

## HARLEQUIN TEEN

### *Inside series*

INSIDE OUT
OUTSIDE IN

Look for Maria Snyder's next novel
TASTE OF DARKNESS
available soon from Harlequin MIRA

# MARIA V. SNYDER

# SPY
# GLASS

This Belongs To:
Molly Rose Writing

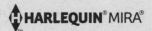

HARLEQUIN® MIRA®

Recycling programs
for this product may
not exist in your area.

ISBN-13: 978-0-7783-1468-4

SPY GLASS

Copyright © 2010 by Maria V. Snyder

**Printed in U.S.A.**

For Bob Mecoy, agent extraordinaire.

Without your encouragement and frequent feedback on this one, it never would have been finished.

# MAGICIAN'S KEEP MAP

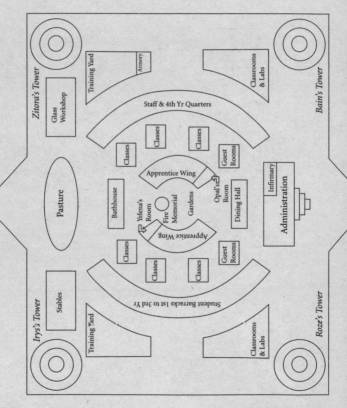

Map credit: Christopher Phillips

# IXIA AND SITIA

NORTHERN ICE SHEET

MD-2

MD-1

MD-3

SOUL
MOUNTAINS

General's House +

General's House +

General's Hovse +

SUNSET
OCEAN

THE TERRITORY OF IXIA

+ General's House

MD-8

MD-4

MD-6

+ General's House

MD-7

Commander's
Castle

MD-5

General's House +

Castletown

Lake Krystal

+ General's House

SNAKE
FOREST

Moon
Clan

Krystal
Clan

Featherstone
Clan

Owl's Hill

Mica

★ CITADEL

Finar

Ognir

THE
CLIFFS

THE
FLATS

Thunder Valley

SITIA

EMERALD
MOUNTAINS

Cloud Mist
Clan

Stormdance
Clan

♡ Blood Rock

Bloodgood
Clan

Greenblade
Clan

Rye

AVIBIAN PLAINS

Sunseed
Clan

JADE
SEA

Vein Ream

Brandy

Daviian Camps

DAVIIAN PLATEAU

Diamond Lake

Jewelrose
Clan

Cowan
Clan

Blair Market

Daviian Camps

Greenwood

Zaltana
Clan

Kohinoor

LION'S
CLAW
PENINSULA

ILLIAIS JUNGLE

1

Crouching in the darkness of the closet, I stilled as footsteps approached. My instincts screamed to run. I stared at the thin ribbon of light under the door, shadows of shoes paused. I silently urged them to walk away. All I wanted was one day of peace. One day. The knob turned. No luck. With a whoosh of fresh air, my hiding spot was exposed.

"For sand's sake, Opal, what are you doing in there?" my mother asked.

I suppressed a sigh. The truth—hiding from her—wouldn't help. "Looking for my boots?"

Her scowl deepened as she pushed back a lock of graying hair. "They're on your feet."

I straightened. "Oh…yes…well."

"Come. There are a thousand things we need to do, and you're wasting time." She shooed me through my room and downstairs to the kitchen. "Sit and read me the guest list while I cook lunch."

My gaze swept the long wooden table filled with paper, swatches of fabric, lace, sequins, sewing patterns and half-completed decorations—enough clutter to force us to eat in our formal dining room. I cursed my sister Mara under my breath. Before returning to work at the Magician's Keep's glass shop, Mara had asked our mother to plan her and Leif's wedding, trusting her with everything. Smart girl. She remained a safe five-day journey away from Mother's all-consuming new passion.

When I failed to sit at the table, she stabbed a spoon at the chair. "Guest list, Opal."

"You've been over it a hundred times."

"I want to be certain—"

"You haven't missed anyone. It's perfect. Stop worrying."

She dried her hands on her apron. The stained white fabric covered her chest and long skirt. "Do you have something better to do? Did I interrupt your moping time?"

"I'm not moping." My voice whined. Not a good sign.

"Resting, recuperating, moping, it's all the same." She hauled a kettle filled with water over to the glowing coals in the hearth.

"No it isn't. A lot has happened—"

She pished at me. My own mother!

"Stop wallowing in the past. What's done is done. Focus on the future. We only have one hundred and fifty-three days until the wedding! Then it's only a matter of time for grandchildren and maybe you and Kade…?"

Yanking the chair out with a loud scrape, I plopped on it. I snatched the list from the pile and read names aloud as my mother continued to bustle about the kitchen. She had mentioned Kade almost every day since I'd arrived. Sixty-three days of missing him, dodging her questions and being drafted to help with preparations for an event two and a half seasons away. How could one woman be so irritating? For a second I wished for another family. A sensible one without all this…stuff, like the Bloodrose Clan, living in austere isolation.

"Opal, stop making that face."

I glanced over the list, but her back was to me. Long strands of hair had sprung from the knot she had tied this morning. She rolled dough with quick efficiency.

"How did you know?"

"I'm your mother. I see all. Hear all. Know all."

I laughed. "If that's true, then why do you ask me so many questions?" Ha. Got her!

Her hands stilled. She turned to me. "Because *you* need to hear the answers."

My father's arrival saved me from a retort I didn't have. He filled the room with his large frame. Even though most of his short hair had turned gray, he still looked young. My brother, Ahir, bounded in behind him. A mirror image of our father except Ahir's thick black hair brushed his shoulders.

"Hey, mop top," I said to Ahir.

"What's up, peanut?" He smirked.

I used to tower over him, but now he was six inches taller than my own five-foot-seven-inch height.

Before I could throw another insult at him, he handed me an aqua-green glass vase. "New recipe. Look at the clarity. Sharp."

I examined the glass in the sunlight. The cold crystal felt dead in my hands. No throb of potential. No song vibrated in my chest. Nothing. My glass magic was gone. Although painfully aware of my loss, a small part of

me hoped to feel a spark every time I touched glass…
only to be disappointed each time.

"Working with this melt is pure joy," Ahir said.
"Let's go over to the factory, I'll gather a slug for you
to try."

I gave him a tight smile, letting him know I saw
through his blatant attempt to interest me in creating
with glass again. But no magic equaled no passion. Before Yelena had uncovered my abilities, I hadn't known
about the magic. It had been masked by my desire to
create. Now, the inert lump in my hand was just another
reminder of my useless existence.

"I think I'll go for a ride instead." Returning the vase
to Ahir, I left the kitchen. My mother's protests about
missing lunch followed me to the shed.

My family owned an eight-kiln glass factory, not
horses. However, when I decided to stay for a while,
my father cleaned out the shed, converting it into a
temporary stable for Quartz. The small enclosure had
room to hang my tack and saddle, and to give Quartz
shelter from bad weather. Being a Sandseed horse, she
preferred to graze in the Avibian Plains bordering our
land.

No one would dare bother a Sandseed horse in the
plains. I scanned the tall grasses. They swayed with
the wind. The reds, yellows and oranges of the cooling season had faded into the gray and brown dullness
of the cold season. I shivered, thinking of the miserable weather yet to come. Believe it or not, I had been
anticipating this time of year. The fierce storms on the
coast had abated. Kade planned to spend a few weeks
with me, until the Commander of Ixia had invited him

to demonstrate his Stormdancing powers, taming the killer blizzards blowing from the Northern Ice Sheet.

Kade had invited me along, except I hated the cold and would rather not be anywhere near the ice sheet. Plus what would I do there? I would have no job other than keeping Kade's bed warm. Well… That wouldn't be a chore at all. I smiled, but sobered. Despite my mother's intentions, my one reason for being home wasn't to help with Mara and Leif's wedding. I needed to make a decision.

Unease twisted. My bad decisions outweighed my good ones by two to one. I had a thirty-three percent chance of getting it right. Dismissing those useless thoughts, I stepped into the plains to search for Quartz.

After I traveled a hundred feet, magic pressed on my skin as if I pushed against a giant sponge. I waited for the pressure to dissipate as the protection determined I wasn't a threat. It was usually suicidal to walk into the plains without permission from the Sandseed Clan. Their defensive magic would confuse me, sending me into a panic, convinced I was lost. This time, my new immunity blocked the Sandseed's magic. I could sense it, but it registered my presence as a magical void. Nice perks, yet…

Without my glass magic, I felt as if a chunk of my soul had been sliced off. I had no regrets over my actions, sacrificing my powers had been the right choice. So if I wasn't moping, then why the ache? Why did I feel trapped in the shadow world?

All maudlin thoughts vanished when Quartz trotted into view. Considered a painted mare, her coat was a patchwork of white and auburn colors. The darker color covered her face, except for a white star between her soft brown eyes. Forgoing a saddle and bridle, I hopped onto her back and left my worries and Mother's wedding plans far behind.

Sitting in the living area later that evening, I addressed envelopes. My mother had appealed to my ego by complimenting my handwriting and had bribed my stomach by baking my favorite pie—black raspberry.

Warmth and light pulsed from the fireplace. I felt better after my ride with Quartz. Mother sat in her favorite chair, sewing Mara's veil. Ahir sprawled on the floor, snoring, and Father worked on bills. A true moment of family peace. And like all such moments, it was too good to stay true for long.

A knock on our door broke the silence. Mother glanced at me in confusion, then brightened. "It's the printer! He said he might be done with the invitations tonight, and I told him to bring them over right away."

Silk and lace filled her lap. Before she could untangle herself, I offered to answer the door. I suppressed a sigh. If the invitations were indeed here, I would have to stuff them into the envelopes, sealing them with wax. A tiresome chore.

I glanced through the peephole. Shadows covered the face of a man holding a bottle. Not the printer. He must be the local winemaker Mother commissioned to distill the special wedding wine. She spared no expense, and, for that, I was glad.

When I had sacrificed my magic, the power had transformed into diamonds. The Sitian Council had returned them all to me, and I had plenty of money to pay for all the wedding expenses—my gift to Mara and Leif.

I opened the door and froze in terror.

Valek, the Commander of Ixia's personal assassin, waited outside. Only one reason for Valek to be here.

"Hello, Opal. Sorry for the surprise visit. Is this a bad time?" he asked with a pleasant tone and quizzical smile.

It was always a bad time to die.

2

I gaped at Valek. He stood on our front step within killing distance.

"Opal." My mother's voice cut through my panic. "Don't stand there like a simpleton. Invite your guest in."

I stuttered a few words and backed up with numb legs. His smile widened as my mother approached. The need to warn her lodged under my ribs. My body's functions had disconnected, scattering my thoughts.

"You must be Opal's mother," Valek said. He shook her hand. "Your cooking skills are legendary, Mrs. Cowan. I wouldn't be surprised if the Commander invites you to cook for him in Ixia."

The wrinkles on her face disappeared as she blushed, erasing years of worry and stress. "Please, call me Vyncenza, Mr....?"

"Valek." His name erupted from my mouth. "What are you doing here?"

"Opal, don't be rude."

"Mother, this is *Valek*." I gestured. "The Commander's—"

"Security Chief," he said. "And this is one of our finest vintages of Ixian Ice Wine." He presented the bottle to my mother.

"Thank you. This is my husband, Jaymes."

My father shook his hand. Ahir woke and jumped to his feet. He grinned at Valek in awe as he pumped his arm. The whole surreal scene swirled in front of my eyes like snowflakes.

"But, Mother. Valek is—"

"Practically family. Come in. Come in. You must be hungry. Jaymes, open that cognac your brother sent us. Ahir, fetch our good glasses." She escorted Valek to the couch and hustled off to the kitchen as Ahir and my father hurried to complete their tasks.

Valek caught me staring. He smiled. "Relax, Opal. I'm not here on *official* duty."

My heart resumed beating. "Then why are you here?"

"Since I'm practically family, I thought I should meet your parents."

A stretch of truth only my mother could believe. Valek was Yelena's heart mate, and Yelena was Leif's sister; ergo, once Leif married Mara, Leif's family, including Valek, would be part of ours.

"What's the *real* reason?" I asked.

"Later," he said as my mother burst into the room carrying a tray loaded with food.

My father poured drinks and everyone settled in for a cozy chat. I listened to the small talk in amazement. Valek's infamous reputation didn't seem to bother anyone but me. And I should know better. Why would the Commander order my assassination when it was well known my glass magic was gone? Unless he knew about my immunity? Only one other person in the world could make the same claim. And he sat next to me, sipping my uncle's cognac.

But Yelena had promised not to tell anyone about my protection. Besides Kade, Zitora and Leif, no one else knew. Not my parents or siblings or friends. Not Valek. I trusted Yelena. Then why was he here? No idea. I would have to wait.

An eternity later, my mother finally stopped offering Valek our guest room when he promised to return the next day to tour the factory. I escorted him outside and down the lane to the gate.

"Spill," I ordered.

Amusement flashed in his blue eyes as a smile quirked, softening the sharp features of his face. His pale skin almost glowed in the moonlight, an obvious contrast to the mostly darker-skinned Sitians, including me. Wearing a nondescript short gray cloak and black pants, he didn't quite blend in, but he didn't stand out, either. I gathered from his lack of disguise he wasn't working undercover.

Valek scanned the empty street before he answered. "Yelena sent me to help you."

"Help me with what?"

"No idea. All she said was you needed help. Are you on a mission for the Council?"

I laughed. "No. Unless you consider wedding planning an act of espionage."

"Hmm… My napkin folding skills are renowned. I can make a swan in seconds."

"Don't tell my mother or you'll be folding napkins for days."

"Days?" Valek's left eyebrow rose.

"The guest list is up to five hundred names with more being added hourly."

"Sounds like quite the party. However it's not the reason Yelena sent me."

I suspected why, but wanted to make sure. "What were her *exact* words?"

"She said, 'Opal needs your help.'"

"That's it?"

He nodded.

"You've traveled all this way without asking her for more details?"

"Of course." His tone implied I lacked intelligence for asking such a question.

So sweet. He had absolute faith in his heart mate.

When the silence lengthened, he asked, "Does this have anything to do with losing your magic?"

I suppressed my immediate annoyance over the word "losing." Why did everyone insist on using *that* word? Losing something implied a potential to find it again. Same with "lost." So sorry you lost your magic, Opal. As if all I needed to do was search for it. No. It was gone. Never to return. Unless I used blood magic and that I wouldn't do. Besides being illegal, it was far better to be without power than be addicted to it. Than to kill for it.

"Opal?"

Valek's voice snapped me back to the problem at hand. Yelena sent him for a reason. She hadn't shared my secret with him, but she thought I should. "I need some time. Can we talk tomorrow?"

"Of course." He bade me a good-night and disappeared into the shadows.

* * *

My night was far from restful. The decision to inform the Sitian Council about my immunity to magic flipped from yes to no and back again. My past dealings with the Council were rocky at best. Magicians who graduated from the Keep usually worked for the Council, but I had broken that tradition by going out on my own. This wouldn't have been too big a problem, except I took my glass messengers with me.

The glass messengers that allowed magicians to communicate with each other over great distances in an instant. The glass messengers I no longer had the power to create, rendering a whole network of relay stations obsolete.

My new immunity could benefit the Council if they trusted me and if I trusted them. Big if. My tendency to keep certain abilities to myself had caused major trouble, resulting in the retirement of Master Magician Zitora Cowan, which left the Council with only two Master Magicians and the eleven elected members. One for each clan in Sitia.

The best course of action would be to stay far away from the Council. But what would I do? No glass magic and no desire to craft vases, bowls and tumblers. Planning Mara and Leif's wedding for the next two and a half seasons would be torture. And I would know, having had personal experience with torture.

I had to face it. I couldn't make this decision alone. Yelena had already figured it out, but why didn't *she* come to help me? She was the liaison between Ixia and Sitia—a neutral third party and my friend. Instead, she sent Valek. The most dangerous man in the world.

A strange notion popped into my head. Was I the

most dangerous woman in the world? I laughed. My few past attempts at stealth had mixed results—almost caught and almost killed. Not an impressive track record.

By morning, no sudden insight had flashed. Guess I would rely on my instincts. A truly terrifying prospect.

Valek arrived on time and was the perfect gentleman as my father showed him the factory and his laboratory. The half-completed experiments in the lab fascinated Valek. He asked many questions, and, by the end of the tour, Father helped Valek gather a slug of molten glass to play with. Wielding the metal tweezers in competent fingers, Valek shaped the slug into a lifelike daisy. I had forgotten Valek's sculpting skills with rocks.

Blue eyes lit with enthusiasm, he said, "Opal, you never told me how extraordinary glass is."

The few times we had interacted had been during crisis situations. No need to reminisce. Especially not with my parents nearby.

After my mother rushed off to prepare dinner and Father returned to puttering in his lab, Valek and I took a walk, heading in no particular direction.

"Have you thought about why Yelena sent me?" he asked.

"All night."

"That would explain the dark circles under your eyes."

Trust Valek to notice.

He paused. "But not why you look so…tired. Are you still having nightmares about *them?*"

Them, as in the seven glass prisons. Despite trapping those evil souls inside glass, their voices had haunted my dreams. The closer I had traveled to one, the louder the voice and the stronger the influence over me became. Valek had hidden them, telling no one their locations, but I could find them. Well, not anymore.

"No. Without magic my connection to them is gone," I said.

"Then why so tired?" He kept his expression neutral.

"The incident in Hubal drained me. I'm still recovering." The truth.

"I see." He continued walking with a smooth stride. "I've read the reports about Hubal. Nasty business."

"The records are supposed to be sealed. How did—"

"Because of Janco's unfortunate and illegal involvement, I had full access to them." Annoyance colored his tone.

Janco was one of Valek's second-in-commands. "He shouldn't get into trouble. I asked for his help. It's not—"

"His fault?"

I nodded.

"Asking for help isn't the problem. It never is. Janco should have brought your message to my attention, and we should have decided on the best course of action. Instead, he left without permission and without telling us where he went. Plus he made an illegal border crossing."

"But…"

Valek waited.

"I hope you didn't demote him."

"What happened to him in Hubal was punishment enough. That blood magic is extremely potent. Yelena explained how it works, but I don't fully understand why Ulrick and Tricky needed *your* blood."

I glanced at him. Was he pretending to be confused?

No way to tell. The man had the best poker face in the world.

"When I had my glass magic, if a magician attacked me, I could transform his magic into glass. Even if he didn't attack, I could siphon...steal all his powers if I so desired. But Tricky discovered that I couldn't drain him because he used *my* blood to increase his powers."

"So your blood protected them from your siphoning magic?"

"Yes. At first, but when Zitora was dying and I was desperate, I realized my blood tattooed in their skin connected us. To draw off all their powers, I had to drain my own, as well." I rubbed the scars on my arms. Not completely healed, the vertical ridges pulsed with an angry reddish-purple color, and resembled rungs on a ladder that climbed up the inside of my arms. A souvenir from Hubal.

"How much blood did they take from you?"

An odd question. And Mr. Stone Face only showed polite interest. "I don't know. I lost track of the days. But I know they came every day with a suction device. Most of the time, I passed out before they were done."

"According to Janco's report, they held you for six days." Valek's comment seemed for his benefit instead of mine.

We walked for a while in silence. "At least one good thing came from your sacrifice. No more nightmares. And since you can no longer hear the souls in the glass prisons, it would be prudent for me to collect them, and rehide them so you won't be in danger any longer."

Surprised, I said, "You'd do that? Just for me?"

"Of course, you're practically family." He smiled. "Besides, my decision to spread them all over Sitia and

Ixia was poor. With them together, I can monitor the prisons better."

I gasped in mock horror. "You? Make a bad decision?"

He laughed. "All the time. Why do you think I'm so adept at escaping sticky situations? It's because I constantly find myself in them."

He was adept at so much more. I envied his skill and confidence. "The best decision you've made is hiding Gede's prison in the snow cats' den. No one is brave or stupid enough to go in there."

Valek snorted with amusement. "So which one am I? Brave or stupid?"

"I didn't mean—"

"No worries, Opal. Actually it was easy to place that one in the den. I left a fresh-killed steer a half mile upwind and waited for the cats to leave." He crossed his arms and tapped a finger. "I'll need a better location for all seven prisons."

I tried to imagine the perfect hiding spot, but couldn't think of one. Our aimless route led us into the Avibian Plains, and I scanned the area for Quartz.

"Let's get back to our original subject," Valek said. "Why Yelena sent me. Any ideas?"

Logic warned me not to tell him, yet my heart yearned to trust him. "I think Yelena sent you here to help me make a decision."

"Emerald green."

"What?"

"You should wear an emerald-green-colored dress for your sister's wedding."

"Valek, I'm *serious*."

"So am I. With your dark hair and eyes, you would look stunning in that color."

We had traveled far enough into the plains to trigger the Sandseeds' magical protection.

Valek studied me as the power swelled then died. I hadn't decided what I should tell him, but it seemed my unconscious mind chose for me.

He waited. When the magic didn't cause me to panic and insist we were lost, he asked, "Are you related to the Sandseed Clan?"

"Not yet." Once Mara married Leif, a distant cousin to the Sandseeds, I would be connected to them if they considered marriage a legitimate relationship. Or perhaps not. In that case and with enough time, everyone in Sitia would be allowed to roam the plains at will. "I don't think so."

He chased the logic. "Do you have special permission to travel the plains?"

"Without Quartz, no."

"I see." His gaze turned inward. "Does the Sitian Council know?"

"Nope."

Understanding flashed on his face. "Ah…the reason for Yelena's request. Who else knows?"

"Zitora, Leif and Kade."

"My advice, don't tell the Council about your immunity. Instead, come work for me."

3

Work for Valek? A complete shock and *not* a course of action I had ever considered. Stunned silence built, but I couldn't form a coherent response. He remained serious and he seemed in no hurry for a reply.

My emotions thawed from surprised to flattered that he had asked me to be a part of his corp. Curious, I asked, "What would I do for you? Spy on Sitia?"

"No. That's my job." He grinned. "I would like you to protect the Commander from magical attacks when I'm away. And to help with any incidents that are tainted with magic."

"That's rather vague."

He shrugged. "Dealing with magic is unpredictable, and each time it's been an…education. It also doesn't match my schedule, so magical problems tend to arrive when I'm out of town, leaving Ari and Janco to handle them."

I laughed at Valek's queasy grimace. Janco hated anything magical. I became his new best friend the minute I could no longer access the blanket of power that surrounded our world and gave magicians their abilities.

"Is the Commander attacked often?" I asked.

"No. He hasn't been in years, but I still worry. And you know the old cliché. Better safe…"

Than sorry. A good motto. One I should heed more often. While Valek's offer tempted me, I knew deep down in my heart my new immunity should benefit Sitia. My home. And despite my troubles with the Council, their goals to keep Sitia safe matched mine.

Valek watched me. "You've made a decision."

"I'm honored for the invitation, but will have to decline."

He nodded as if expecting my answer. "If you change your mind, let me know. There is no time limit."

Good to know. "Thank you."

"What are you going to do then?"

"Tell Master Bloodgood and see what he recommends."

"He'll inform the Council and it could go one of two ways," Valek said. "They'll debate for seasons or they'll quickly figure out how useful you are and put you right to work. Either way—" mischief danced in his eyes "—I may request your special help from time to time. Through Liaison Yelena of course. Wouldn't want to upset the Council…for your sake."

"As in you'd gladly upset them for another reason?"

"Of course. I like it when they're buzzing in concern and arguing with each other. Don't tell Yelena that or I'll be in trouble." He winked.

"Don't worry. I'll keep it to myself."

We turned around, heading back to the house. Halfway there, he asked, "Are you planning to tell your family and friends about your immunity?"

I considered. "I'd need to minimize the number of

people who know in order to be more effective when I help the Council."

"It's a valid strategy, but as soon as you interact with a magician, he will learn of your immunity. Inevitably the word will spread. If you remain in Booruby, then you can probably keep your secret. Another thing to think about is, if you get sick or are injured, a healer can't help you."

The downside.

Valek crossed his arms and drummed his fingers. "I would suggest you send me a message if you're in really bad shape. If you can."

"Why?"

"I'll send a medic down to help you. They are quite competent in healing without magic. Your healers are useless if their magic doesn't work."

His comment drove a point home. Because the Commander had forbidden magic in Ixia, the Ixians studied medicine in a way my own people didn't. I hadn't fully contemplated my new situation. "What else should I be aware of?" I asked.

He scanned the horizon. The rolling terrain of the plains covered the landscape like a blanket. Quartz grazed, munching on the long stalks of grass. Every so often she would glance at us, but she remained on the hillock as if she sensed I didn't need her.

"Frustration." Valek finally answered my question. "Knowing magic is being aimed at me, but not knowing what type drives me crazy."

"Why?"

"In a few situations, I didn't know if a magician was trying to kill me, warn me off or trying to help. It's important for deciding on my response. Sometimes it's obvious what they're attempting. If the person next to you suddenly freezes, it's not hard to figure out. It's when I'm alone that it's harder. Another frustrating aspect is not being able to pick up *where* the magic is coming from. Unless the magician is in the room, I can't determine a source. Perhaps you'll have better luck."

Doubtful. "Any other problems?"

"It can be exhausting when powerful magic is directed at you. It's like trudging through syrup. It sticks to you and pulls on your muscles. It's hard to move and to breathe." He placed a comforting hand on my shoulder. "There're benefits, too. You'll know who is a magician and who isn't. You won't be fooled by an illusion or be physically or mentally controlled by another. No one can read your thoughts. Although—" he smiled "—to truly take advantage, you're going to have to work on keeping your feelings from showing on your face."

"That bad?"

"To me, yes. You could play poker until you stop losing, or perhaps a few acting lessons would help you. Especially since pretending you're affected by magic can be to your advantage. When you return to the Citadel, talk to Fisk, he'll find you the perfect teacher."

Even Valek knew Fisk, the beggar boy turned leader of the Citadel's Helper's Guild. I remembered I owed him a...special visit for the ambush he had set up. He had been working for Master Bloodgood at the time, but I still wanted to talk to him. Guess helping shoppers bargain for goods had lost its appeal.

"Any more advice?" I asked.

"Ask me to keep your secret."

I stopped. "Why?"

"Otherwise, I'll tell the Commander."

"You'll tell him anyway."

"Only if he *needs* to know."

"Oh. All right. Valek, will you please keep the knowledge of my immunity to yourself?"

"Yes. And I'll ask you to keep the *reason* we're immune to magic a secret."

According to Yelena, when I had drained Tricky and Ulrick of their blood magic, I had pulled their null shield to me, but hadn't been able to purge the shield as I had all the other magic, including my own. She also claimed a traumatic experience in Valek's life caused him to pull in a null shield that bonded with his soul. Kade, Leif and Zitora knew about the immunity, but not the null shield.

Another quirk of the null shield being kept from the Council and Sitians was its ability to be woven with fabric. I had argued against keeping the information from them—if they didn't know about it they couldn't guard against it. But the Master Magicians and Yelena had overruled me.

"Does the Commander know why you're immune?" I asked.

"No. Only the three of us, and I like it to *stay* that way."

In the past, keeping secrets had led me into trouble. "I won't tell anyone unless he or she *needs* to know."

"Could you give me an example?"

I reviewed the events that had caused my current situation. If Zitora had known null shields could be attached to various objects, like nets, walls and clothes, she wouldn't have entered the glass factory and almost died.

"I don't want to be bound by a promise in a life-threatening situation. Or if I need to tell Kade why I'm immune, I will."

"Fair enough," Valek agreed.

When we returned to the house, my mother insisted Valek remain for dinner. She tried to embarrass me by reciting stories of my youthful misadventures. While I heard her voice, I ceased listening. My mind replayed the conversation I had with Valek.

Something he had said—a word or comment—nagged at me, but I couldn't pinpoint the exact phrase. Not until hours later. After Valek left and my family had all gone to sleep. When I woke in the middle of the night with my heart slamming in my chest and my nightclothes soaked with sweat, the reason finally clicked in my head.

Tricky had bled me every day for six days. More blood than would be used in that short amount of time. Only a small portion is mixed with the tattoo ink. Valek had even said blood magic was extremely potent.

What happened to all my blood? Spilled? Spoiled or had it been preserved and hidden away? Or given to another for safekeeping? Did Valek suspect there was more out there? Was he hunting it? Would Yelena know what Valek was up to? Or even where my blood was? Perhaps.

Tricky would know. But he was in a Fulgor prison along with his three goons and Ulrick while they waited for the Council to decide their fate. Doubtful any one of them would tell me, unless...

I spent the remainder of the night planning. Instead of traveling to the Citadel to tell Master Bloodgood about my immunity, I would make a detour. Guessing and hoping wouldn't work this time. I needed to act. If vials of my blood existed, I would find them. First stop—Fulgor.

"You just arrived. Why are you rushing off?" my mother asked for the fourth time.

"Mother, I've been here for two months." Sixty-five days of wedding plans to be exact. I was surprised I lasted that long. "Since I'm not helping Father in the factory—"

"Doesn't matter. You're helping me."

I shoved another shirt into my pack and glanced at her. She stood in the doorway of my bedroom, fidgeting with her apron. Mara had the same nervous habit. "What's really the matter?"

She fisted the white fabric, then smoothed it. "This past year has been difficult on you. Kidnapped, tortured…" Her gaze dropped to the floor. "Do you think you're ready? You don't even have magic to protect you."

I debated. The temptation to inform her about my immunity pulsed in my chest. However, I knew she wouldn't be comforted by the news. It would give her another reason to fret. I had confided in my father last night, and he had promised to keep it quiet, understanding the need for secrecy.

"You'll worry even if I stayed here a hundred days," I said. "I'm just going to the Keep." I lied to my mother and lightning didn't strike me. At least, not yet. "There are plenty of travelers on the road, and I do know how to defend myself. You watched me dump Ahir in the mud." I grinned at the memory. The big oaf thought he could overpower me with his strength and size. Ha!

"Plus I have Quartz. If we run into trouble, we'll duck into the plains. No one would follow us in there." The majority of the route to the Citadel followed the edge of the Avibian Plains.

She softened a bit. Time for the winning card.

"And I'll be seeing Mara. I can take a few swatches along to show her." Eventually.

Delight replaced concern. She rushed off to gather the wedding samples, letting me finish packing. Leaving most of my possessions behind, I carried my saddlebags to the shed. No sense bringing everything when I didn't know where I would end up.

Quartz trotted over as soon as I arrived, as if she'd been waiting for me. I wondered if the presence of the saddlebags tipped her off, or if she sensed I planned to leave.

I had worried about my connection to Quartz after my powers were gone. Sandseed horses were picky. The Stable Master at the Keep called them spoiled rotten. The breed didn't allow many people to ride them. But Quartz treated me the same—to my vast relief.

After enduring a round of goodbyes, and finding room for my mother's bulging packages of food and fabric samples, I guided Quartz through Booruby, heading north to keep the illusion of my trip to the Citadel. The temptation to cut northeast through the Avibian Plains pulsed in my heart. Quartz's desire matched mine. She leaned toward home as she galloped. I decided to wait a few days before turning toward Fulgor.

The nastiness with Ulrick and Tricky had happened in Hubal. But the small town lacked a jail and the six men had been incarcerated in Fulgor, the capital of the Moon Clan's lands. I would send my mother and Kade a message after I arrived, informing them of my change in plans. A coward's action, but I didn't want to endure another lecture on safety from my mother.

A small hum of excitement buzzed in my chest as the miles passed under Quartz's hooves. The outcome of this trip could go either way, but there was, at least, one positive result so far. I had stopped moping. Not that I ever would admit I had been moping in the first place. Especially *not* to my mother.

After two days on the main north-south road to the Citadel, I turned northeast into the plains. The terrain seemed to undulate as a damp breeze rippled the grasses. Farther in, the sandy soil would transform the landscape. Scrub grass and clumps of stunted pine trees would cling to the ground. Dry firewood would be hard to find and rocks would dominate the area.

Good thing I wouldn't be in the plains for long. I touched Quartz's shoulder with my finger and my world blurred. Colors streaked by, dragging long blazing tails and the air thickened, carrying me and Quartz aloft as if her hooves no longer touched the ground.

The Sandseeds called this phenomenon the gust-of-wind gait. When gusting, Quartz could cover twice the distance that she could at her normal gallop. Only Sandseed horses had this magical ability, and only when they were inside the Avibian Plains.

Before, Quartz's gust-of-wind gait felt like flying—fast and light. Since magic had become tangible to me, the experience reminded me of sinking into a muddy river and being pushed downstream by the thick current. An odd sensation, but I wasn't going to complain. If we had stayed on the main roads, the trip to Fulgor would have taken ten days. By cutting through the plains and gusting, we arrived at Fulgor's main business district in six.

Weaving through the busy downtown quarter, I searched for a reputable inn. The sun teetered on the edge of the western horizon, casting our thin shadows far ahead. Vendors emptied their stands, and shops closed their doors. Everyone would return to their homes and eat supper before returning to sell goods to the evening crowd.

I scanned the streets without focusing on any one person or place. My thoughts dwelled on past events. This town held no cheerful memories for me. I wondered if fate kept sending me here so I could... What? Could get it right? Except what was "it"?

Perhaps I was supposed to leave this town without being duped, tricked or incarcerated. At least this trip, everyone smiled at me and laughed with their companions. No strained and worried glances. The last time I had arrived here the townspeople hurried fearfully through the half-empty streets, staring at the ground.

Interesting how the citizens hadn't been able to pinpoint the reason for their unease in those days, but they had instinctively known something had been wrong. What I'd discovered was their Councilor had been kidnapped by her sister, Akako, and, with the aid of Devlen's blood magic, Tama Moon's soul was switched with Akako's. While Akako pretended to be the Councilor, she locked the real Tama in a cell in Hubal about twenty miles away.

Devlen then switched his soul with Ulrick and pretended to be my boyfriend to trick me into finding his mentor. At least that didn't work as he had planned. I smiled sourly. By draining Devlen of magic, I stopped him from finishing the Kirakawa ritual and becoming a master-level magician.

He claimed I saved him. No longer addicted to blood magic, he tried to make amends. During the incident in Hubal, he had refused to hurt me. And after, I had watched him surrender to the town's guards to begin a five-year prison sentence.

I rubbed a fingertip along my lower lip, remembering the light kiss he'd given me before turning himself in to the authorities. Had he really changed? From Daviian Warper to repentant citizen? Yelena had read his soul and supported him. She had spoken on his behalf and, combined with the fact he had saved Master Magician Zitora Cowan's life, the Council had cut his prison time in half.

Quartz snorted, jerking me from my thoughts. She stood in front of a stable. I blinked at the stable boy.

"Want me to rub her down?" he asked.

"No thanks, I'll do it." I dismounted. Quartz had picked an inn. The stable's wide walkways, clean stalls and the fresh scent of sweet hay boded well for the rest of the place. "You're spoiled rotten," I said, scratching her behind the ears.

"Excuse me?" the boy asked. He hovered nearby.

"Here." I handed him her bridle. "Hang it up in her stall please."

When he returned, he helped me remove her saddle and settled her in for the night. I fed her milk oats before searching for the innkeeper. I paused outside the main entrance and laughed. Quartz had a warped sense of humor. Or perhaps she could read my mind? Either way, I hoped the Second Chance Inn had a vacancy.

The next morning, I woke at dawn. The town's soldiers trained every morning to keep in shape, and I planned to join them. I wrapped my heavy cloak around my shoulders as I hurried to the guards' headquarters. Located right next to the Councilor's Hall, the station also housed criminals before they were processed.

When I arrived, I scanned the sweaty faces of the guards. Even in the cold morning air, most of them had tossed their long-sleeved tunics over the fence, training in short sleeves. The sight made me shiver. Steam puffed from their mouths as they heckled each other. More men than women worked on sword drills and self-defense, which made it easy for me to spot Eve.

Although she matched my height, she looked tiny compared to her partner, Nic. A brute of a man, who had made a bad first impression when we met. He recognized me and beamed. When he wrapped me in a bear hug, I had to admit, it wasn't his fault our first encounter hadn't gone well. After all, I had been arrested for disobeying the Council's orders. He had just been doing his job.

Pressed against his damp shirt, I breathed in his rank scent and coughed. "Phew, Nic." I pulled away. "You stink."

"Hello to you, too," he said with a growl. But couldn't hold it for long. Wrinkles emanated from his big puppy-dog brown eyes which contrasted with his sharp too-many-times broken nose.

"By the end of the cold season, we use him as a weapon," Eve said.

She gave me a quick hug of welcome. Her short strawberry-blond hair tickled my cheek. Intelligence and humor danced in her light blue eyes.

"All right, I'll bite. A weapon?" I asked.

"He hates bathing during the cold season. So by the end he reeks so bad, we'll send him into places we know criminals are hiding, and, within minutes, they pour out like rats escaping a burning building. Works better than a stink bomb."

"Ha, ha," Nic deadpanned. "You certainly don't smell like roses after you've been working out. Besides, I hate being wet and cold."

"Me, too," I said. We launched into stories of woe, trying to outdo each other on who had been wetter and colder during our various adventures.

"No way the Northern Ice Sheet is colder than Briney Lake," Nic said. "One time, I broke through the ice, sinking up to my thighs—"

"Nic, that's enough. I'm sure Opal didn't come to talk about your wet feet," Eve said. Her gaze focused on me and she crossed her arms, reminding me of her powerful build. "What's the trouble?"

"Can't I come visit two friends without—"

"No," Nic interrupted. "It's too soon. You should be with your family or that boyfriend of yours, resting and recuperating."

"Kade's in Ixia, and my mother's…wedding preparations drove me away," I said.

"Why didn't you go to the Magician's Keep?" Eve asked. "Doesn't your sister live there?"

"She lives there with Leif." When they failed to react, I added, "Have you seen those two together? I'm queasy just thinking about it."

They shared a glance.

"Why here?" Eve asked.

"Why not? I'm not surrounded by magicians here. Besides, I need something to do. Are you hiring?"

Nic laughed, but Eve punched him on the arm. "She's serious."

He sobered. "Come on, Opal. It's us."

Trying to keep secrets had gotten me into trouble before. I was supposed to be smarter now. I glanced around the training yard. "Not here. Later, when you're off duty."

"Okay, come back for the late-afternoon training session. Bring your sais. After *we* work out, we'll grab supper at the Pen," Nic said.

"The Pen?"

Eve grinned. "The Pig Pen. Nic's brother owns it. Best stew in town."

After talking to Nic and Eve, I sent an overland message to my parents and one to Kade, explaining my whereabouts. Then I spent the rest of the day studying Fulgor's prison. Located in the far northwest quadrant of the city, it occupied a huge area, extending five blocks wide by eight blocks deep. Its sheer outer walls were topped with coils of barbed wire. Glints of sunlight reflected off glass shards that had been cemented into the top third of the wall, acting as an effective and low-cost device to cut climbing ropes.

Watchtowers perched above the four corners of the massive building. I walked around the structure, noting only two well-guarded entrances. The place appeared to be impenetrable. Sneaking into the prison was out of the question. Escape also seemed impossible.

I found a hidden spot to observe the entrance. Not a lot of movement either in or out. I had hoped a shift change would create a flurry of activity, but the shifts must have been staggered. Every two hours, some officers went in and three or four would leave. Even delivery wagons were few and far between.

Janco would be delighted by the challenge, but I wouldn't ask him for help. He was in enough trouble because of me. There had to be another way inside.

Cold and stiff from my day-long surveillance, I arrived at the guards' afternoon session with my sais and wearing my training uniform. A long-sleeved tunic tied with a belt, and a pair of loose-fitting pants. Both garments were dark brown to hide the bloodstains and dirt. I wore my softest pair of leather boots, also brown with black rubber soles.

I joined Nic and Eve, and it wasn't long before my stamina waned. My bouts with my brother Ahir hadn't been enough to get me back into shape. Huffing and puffing with effort, I swung and blocked Nic's sword a few times before he unarmed me.

He tsked. "*Someone* hasn't been keeping up with her training."

"The man's a genius," I said between gulps of air. "What are your next words of wisdom, Oh Smart One? Water is wet?"

"*Someone* gets grumpy when she's outmatched."

I responded by triggering my switchblade.

Nic sheathed his sword, and pulled a dagger. "Street fight." He lunged.

Not quite a fair match. His longer weapon kept me at

arm's length, but I used a few nasty moves Janco taught me. Even so, Nic disarmed me again.

At the end of the training session, my arms ached and I couldn't lift a sword let alone defend myself. All my hard work to reach a competent level had been undone by one season of light activity.

Eve bumped my shoulder with hers. "Don't worry. The skills are there. And you're looking a lot better than the last time we saw you."

"Loads better," Nic said. "Then I could have blown you over with my breath."

I met Eve's gaze. He had given me the perfect opening.

"Too easy," she said, shaking her head. "Trust me, you'll have plenty of opportunities to slam him."

"When?" I asked her.

"Twice a day, every day as long as you're in Fulgor."

Nic put a sweaty arm around my shoulders. "We'll get you into fighting shape in no time."

"Great," I said, and held my breath until Nic released me. "Does his brother have the same hygiene?" I asked Eve. "Is that why the place is called the Pig Pen?"

Her sly smile failed to reassure me.

My first impression of the tavern was utter disbelief. The place smelled of spiced beef and fresh-baked bread. Patrons filled all the tables and a bright fire warmed the room. Nic led us through the crowd. A bunch of people gathered in front of the bar. All the stools should have been occupied, but two remained empty.

Nic and Eve headed straight toward them. Eve slid onto hers as Nic called to the bartender. He settled in his stool, and before I could move, a ripple flowed along the bar and an empty stool appeared next to Nic. He gestured for me to claim it.

Amazed, I sat. No squawk of protest. No murmurs of complaint. Instead the room buzzed with conversation, and laughter punctuated the general hum. The dark wood of the bar gleamed with care. Clean glasses lined the shelves behind the counter.

The bartender placed steaming bowls of stew and mugs of ale in front of us, but before he could wait on another customer, Nic introduced me to his brother, Ian.

I shook his hand and studied Ian. His dark hair touched the top of his shoulders, and he was slimmer than Nic. No scars like the one Nic had along his jaw. Ian also wore fitted clothes that matched compared to Nic's ad hoc pants and shirt. Other than those differences, the men looked identical.

"Twin brother?" I asked Nic.

He grinned, brushing a hand over the bristle on his head. "I thought the hair would throw you."

"I used to be an artist. It takes more than a different hairstyle to fool me."

"Good to know." Nic dug into his stew with abandon, dripping gravy onto the bar. Ian rolled his eyes and wiped up the mess.

"Pig pen?" I asked Ian.

"Family joke. Growing up, our mother had trouble keeping track of who was who. She used certain clues to help her, and when we figured out what she was using, we would switch. For example, Nic's half of the room was always a mess, so when Mother would come in to say good-night, she expected Nic to be in the messy bed, but I was there instead."

"So when she comes into a tavern named Pig Pen,

she expects Nic to be behind the bar because he's still a slob, but you're there."

"Right."

"Hey!" Nic wiped his mouth on his sleeve. "I think I've been insulted."

"Not insulted. *Identified*." Ian laughed and returned to work.

"That's it. I'm tired of being picked on," Nic said. "I'm never coming here again."

"Where will you go?" Eve asked. "All the other taverns will make you *pay* for your meal."

"Are you calling me cheap?" Nic demanded.

"Not cheap. Spoiled."

"That would explain the smell," I said.

Eve choked on her ale as Nic growled.

We spent the rest of the evening catching up on news and gossip. The stew was better than my mother's, although I wouldn't admit it out loud. No one mentioned my real reason for coming to Fulgor until Nic and Eve walked me back to the inn despite my protests.

"After your sorry performance this afternoon, you should have a bodyguard until you get in shape," Nic said. "I'm hoping your plans in Fulgor don't involve any danger." His comment sounded like a query.

My first instinct was to dodge the question, but I needed their help. Might as well take the direct approach. "Can you get me a job in the prison?"

They skidded to a stop and gaped at me. Eve recovered first. "If you're worried about those men who hurt you, they're in the SMU."

"SMU?"

"Special Management Unit. In a place that is isolated from the regular prison population."

"Good to know, but that's not the reason," I said.

"Then why?" she asked.

"To obtain information."

"Wow," Nic said. "That's seriously vague."

"I'd rather not give you details at this time, but it is important."

Nic chewed on his lip. "You're not going to do something illegal, are you? Like help a prisoner escape?"

"Of course not."

"You'll give us details later?" Eve asked.

Later could be years from now. "Yes. I promise. Will you help me?"

"Depends," Nic said.

"On what?"

"Do you need a position at Wirral or Dawnwood?"

I hadn't realized there were two in Fulgor. "What's the difference?"

"Wirral is a maximum-security facility. Dawnwood is low-security."

"Maximum-security."

"We can't help you," Eve said.

"Why not?"

"We don't have any contacts at Wirral. They recruit people straight from the academy and train them for another year."

"Yeah, if you wanted a post at Dawnwood, we could pull some strings," Nic said.

I tried to hide my disappointment. "Do you know anyone who has a friend at Wirral?"

Eve shook her head. We continued the rest of the way to the Second Chance in silence.

Before I could say good-night, Nic groaned and slapped himself on the forehead. "How could I forget?"

"Do you want a list or should I just summarize?" Eve quipped.

"Ha. Ha. We don't have any connections to Wirral, but *you* do, Opal."

"Me?"

"Damn. He's right. I'm sure *she* would help you."

"Who?" Partners could be so annoying!

"Councilor Moon."

# 4

The Councilor's Hall teemed with guards. Four times as many as the last time I had been here. I couldn't just sign in and find my own way. No. Instead, I had to surrender my sais and switchblade, endure being frisked and interrogated about my reasons for coming to the Hall. Then I was assigned an escort.

My companion was a friendlier version of the entrance soldiers. He didn't carry the full complement of weapons around his waist. I guessed these half guards were an attempt to downplay the overwhelming tension that vibrated in the air. It didn't work.

As I followed him across the black-and-white checkerboard tiles of the Hall's lobby, my skin crawled with the feeling of many gazes watching my every move. Strident sounds echoed in the large open space. The ceiling with its grand glass chandelier hung ten stories above my head. On the opposite side of the lobby, an elaborate wooden staircase wound up the floors, giving access to the rest of the building where the Moon Clan's administrative staff had offices and suites.

When we reached the bottom step, a bubble of magic

engulfed us. My escort continued to climb the stairs, but I glanced around, looking for the magician. The press of power disappeared. Since no one caught my eye, I hurried to catch up.

Councilor Tama Moon's office suite was located on the first floor. The long hallway to her elaborate double doors had been decorated with art from various clan members. I noticed all of Gressa's glass pieces were gone. Not surprising. She had helped Akako take possession of Tama's body. I wondered which prison Gressa had been sent to—Wirral or Dawnwood.

When we entered Tama's expansive reception area, my escort said for the fifth time, "She won't see you today, and it's doubtful she'll even let you make an appointment."

The woman sitting behind the desk frowned and appeared to steel herself for an argument. Considering what had happened to her, I understood Tama's precautions, but the whole atmosphere reeked of paranoia.

"She knows me, and if I have to wait a few days to see her, that's fine," I said.

However, the heavy tread of boots behind me wasn't fine. I turned and two wide guards tackled me to the floor. My breath whooshed out with the impact. In a heartbeat, they yanked off my cloak, pulled my arms back and manacled my wrists.

Voices yelled and confusion reigned for a moment. Jerked to my feet, I swayed as dizziness obscured my vision. A hot metallic taste filled my mouth. I probed teeth and lips with my tongue, seeking damage. A split lip so far.

The commotion drew Councilor Moon from her office.

"What's going on?" she asked.

Good question.

"Zebb said she has a null shield," the guy clutching my left arm said.

Why would they think—? Oh. The bubble of magic couldn't sense anything from me, therefore I must be shielded.

Tama stepped closer. The men increased the pressure as if I would try to attack her. I almost laughed at the ridiculousness of the situation until I saw the strain in her face. Hollow cheeked and with dark smudges under her eyes, she gaped at me in fear.

"Opal?" she asked.

Not trusting my voice, I nodded.

"Why are you here?" She hugged her arms to her chest as if to keep herself from falling apart.

"To visit you."

She blinked. "Why are you shielded, I thought…"

Stunned, I watched this brittle shell of a woman as she struggled to make sense of the situation. Her blond hair hung limp and greasy; she had aged years in the span of one season and stains covered her white silk tunic.

Her gaze snapped to me with a sudden intensity. "You lost your magic. Are you afraid someone is going to attack you, too?"

"No. I'm not shielded." But I began to understand. Magic once again surrounded me, seeking. I guessed the magician wanted an update.

My escort spoke for the first time, and I wondered if he could feel the power, as well. "Maybe I should fetch Zebb?"

"No. Absolutely not. He is not allowed up here,"

Tama said. "Why did that magician think you've erected a null shield?"

She spat the word *magician*. Coming here had been a bad idea; I wondered if Nic and Eve were aware of the change in the Councilor.

"He must be mistaken," I said. "You know I have no magical powers. Why would I come here to harm you? I helped rescue you."

The viselike grip on my arms relaxed from crushing to bruising. Tama melted. She covered her face with her hands, either embarrassed by her overreaction or relieved.

"What's this all about?" another female voice demanded.

I glanced over my shoulder and recognized Faith Moon, the Councilor's First Adviser. Light reflected off her glasses as she scanned our little group, assessing the situation. The Adviser's short brown hair was tucked behind her ears. Her mouth dropped open when she spotted me wedged between the two guards.

"Release Opal immediately," she ordered. "Dari, bring some tea for our guest." The woman behind the desk shot to her feet and bolted from the room.

The guards didn't move. "Councilor?" Left Arm asked.

Tama dropped her hands as if overcome by pure exhaustion. "Yes, of course. Let her go."

Right Arm unlocked the manacles. I rubbed my wrists. My skin crawled as if I had walked through a sticky spiderweb. Threads of invisible magic clung, but I couldn't wipe them away. Or could I?

"Opal, please forgive me. I...I don't...know..." The Councilor spread her hands out in a vague gesture.

Faith wrapped a supportive arm around Tama's shoulders. "Let's go back to your office. Opal, please come with us." She scowled at the three men. "Gentlemen, you can return to your duties." She guided Tama into a comfortable armchair near the door.

I stood to the side, feeling awkward. The magician stopped trying to reach me. The bands of magic fell away and I sucked in a relieved breath. When Dari returned with a tray of tea, Faith grabbed it from her and shooed the woman out. Two guards bookended the entrance, but remained in the outer office. Faith closed the office door with her hip and set the tray on a table.

Serving the Councilor first, Faith then handed me a steaming cup. "I'm glad you're here. Please sit down."

I sank into a chair opposite Tama and sipped my tea. I didn't know what I should say or do. "If this is a bad time…" I tried, but they ignored me.

Faith knelt next to Tama and clasped her hand. "Talk to Opal. She might be able to help you. She's been harmed by magic and by Warpers. She's been betrayed." Faith gestured to me. "Yet, here she is. And without any magic to defend herself."

Tama shrank into the cushions, shaking her head. "She wouldn't understand."

"Not completely, but you *need* to tell her what you won't tell me." Faith squeezed her hand, shot me an encouraging look and left the room.

The click of the door vibrated in my chest. An awkward silence grew.

Tama finally said, "Did the Council send you?"

"No. I'm here on my own."

"Why are you in Fulgor? Can I help you with something?"

I would have welcomed her attempt to change the subject and the opportunity to ask for a favor, but not now. Not when she held herself as if she would shatter at the next harsh word. I had no idea how to help her, but I had to try.

I dredged my memories, disturbing the painful emotions that had settled to the deepest layer of my mind. They swirled and polluted my thoughts.

"It was horrible to be betrayed." I met her wary gaze. "It felt like my heart was rotting in my chest and every breath burned with the knowledge I had been fooled. It was difficult to trust after that. The rot spread throughout my body, leaving behind so many doubts, I stopped trusting myself."

Tama leaned forward. "How did you conquer it?"

"I didn't. I survived it. Endured by realizing my friends and family can always be trusted no matter what. And when I feel the rot creeping back, I grab on to one of them and hold on until it goes away."

She snagged her lower lip with her teeth. "But you have a large family and friends. I don't. I have Faith." A weak smile touched her lips at the play of words.

"What about Dari?"

Tama waved her hand in a dismissive gesture. "New. My sister killed all my loyal people."

"So this place is filled with strangers?"

"Yes."

"Then get rid of them. You don't need all those guards. They're tripping over themselves."

"But who…"

"Will protect you?"

She nodded.

"Do you trust me?" I asked.

"Yes."

I pulled in a deep breath. My plans to find my blood would have to wait. This was more important. I had to finish rescuing Tama first. "*I* will protect you. Hire me as your new assistant, and I'll find you the right people."

"But what about magic? It can influence anybody. Force them to do horrible things. And magicians can be corrupted by all that power. That magician downstairs has been spying on me." She shuddered so hard her teacup rattled.

Which explained the paranoia I had sensed earlier. "We can ask Master Bloodgood to assign you another magician. One who can surround you with a null shield. Then you won't have to worry about being spied on or attacked."

"No. I don't want anyone who has magic near me!"

I backed off. One problem at a time.

We summoned Faith and I outlined my plans to her. She glanced at Tama. A little color had returned to the Councilor's face and she leaned forward, listening to my strategy.

"Did you check employment history before hiring the new staff?" I asked Faith.

"We didn't have time. Everything was so chaotic."

"First order of business is to reduce security. We'll keep the best ones on staff."

"How do you know who is trustworthy?" Tama asked.

"I don't. But I trust two people who do."

"Wow." Nic whistled. "You went in search of a job as a correctional officer, and became the Councilor's new assistant. How did you manage that?" He propped his elbows on the edge of my massive desk. He rested his square jaw on his hands.

We were in the Councilor's reception area. I had claimed Dari's work space and Nic and Eve sat opposite me.

"I impressed her with my amazing filing skills. I can alphabetize in seconds." I snapped my fingers.

"In seconds? You're my new hero." Nic batted his eyelashes at me.

Eve punched him in the arm. "Knock it off." She turned to me in concern. "What's going on?"

Only a few people knew all the details of what had happened in Hubal. The whole city of Fulgor believed the Councilor had been under the influence of her sister. That Akako used magic to control Tama. Close enough.

I explained Tama's fears.

It didn't take Eve long to sort through the information. "What do you need from us?"

"The Councilor needs two bodyguards with her all the time. How many teammates do you have?"

"Our team has twelve. I'll talk to Captain Alden about our short-term reassignment, and I'll work up a watch schedule."

Nic groaned. "Don't put me on night shift or I'll die of boredom."

"What's next?" Eve asked, ignoring her partner. Just like her fighting style, she didn't waste energy or time.

"Weeding out the security staff. Can you do a little digging into their histories? Find out who's trustworthy?"

"I can get rid of half of them for you right now," Nic said. "When the Councilor returned, she wanted this place full of soldiers. We couldn't provide the manpower, so they hired people with no training or previous experience just to have warm bodies here."

"Great. Make me a list," I said.

"Captain Alden can investigate the rest for you," Eve said.

Nic tapped his finger on the chair's arm. "I hope you realize you're not going to be popular once word spreads."

"I'm not here to make friends," I said. "Besides, I'm temporary. Once we have the right people in place, we can all go back to normal." Except, I didn't know what normal would be. Since my sister Tula had been kidnapped and murdered over six years ago, nothing in my life had been normal.

Dari and the Councilor's personal bodyguards were the first to go. Nic and Eve returned for the night shift and handed me a list of names.

"Good or bad?" I asked.

"The riffraff," Nic said. "Can I give them the boot? I always wanted to be in charge."

I scanned the names, but didn't recognize any. "No. Faith Moon will handle that unpleasant task." I glanced up from the paper. "Are you ready to be reacquainted with the Councilor?"

"I showered," Nic said.

"Did you put on clean undergarments?" I asked.

"Yep. Got my best pair on. No holes. Do you think she'll want to check?" He grinned with wolfish delight.

"Eve, I think you should do all the talking."

"Yes, sir."

I knocked and waited for Tama's faint response before entering. The Councilor's back was to us as she pulled employee files from a drawer, sorting them. Her office was long and thin. Narrow stained-glass windows striped the side walls and stretched up to the ceiling two stories above our heads. The sitting area was near the door and across from an oval conference table. Opposite the entrance, her U-shaped desk faced a wide picture window.

The sunlight faded, reminding me of the need to light the lanterns. My stomach grumbled. I hadn't eaten since this morning. When Tama reached a stopping point, she turned and faced us.

I introduced the soldiers, emphasizing their help in Hubal. Her stiff demeanor relaxed, and she smiled at them when I explained they would be guarding her tonight.

"Finally," she said. "A good night's rest!"

While they talked, I lit the lanterns. The cold season's nights arrived fast, dropping a curtain of darkness with little warning. When I passed my friends, I brushed against magic. I paused and stood behind them. Trying not to be obvious, I rested my hands on the backs of their chairs. The hairs on my arms pricked. A web of power surrounded them. Her magician must be eavesdropping, but I couldn't be sure. I now understood Valek's frustration.

Not wanting to upset Tama, I kept quiet as Nic and Eve left to take up position outside her office door.

"Make sure you introduce them to Faith," Tama said. "She's the only person I allow in my private suite. I keep Council business and my personal life separate, but with living in the Hall…" She wrapped her arms around her waist, turning to stare out the window.

I wondered if she looked at her flickering reflection

or the blackness of the night. My image stood beside her, but it didn't waver. Odd.

She turned to me. "Where are you staying?"

"At the Second Chance Inn."

"You can live in the assistant's apartment on the ninth floor once Dari leaves."

"I'd rather not."

She tried to hide her disappointment.

I rushed to explain. "Eventually, we'll find you a permanent assistant. And I should be out there—" I pointed to the window "—listening to the tavern gossip, getting a feel for the citizens' moods and complaints for you. If I stayed here, I'd never leave and we'd miss the opportunity to connect with the townspeople."

"That's smart, Opal. Your experiences have made you stronger and more confident. While I'm a mess. I can't make decisions and I'm terrified another magician will…"

"No magician will hurt you. The man who switched your soul with Akako was a Warper. He used blood magic. And the Warpers who know how to use it are all locked up in your prison. The magician downstairs… Zebb?"

She cringed, then nodded.

"Was he sent by Master Bloodgood?" I asked.

"Yes. Bain assigned every Council member a magician capable of erecting a null shield around them for protection."

"And Bain would only send a trustworthy person. You're a Councilor. One of only eleven and all critical to Sitia. Your safety is of the utmost importance."

"Really?" Tama shot back. "Then how come not *one* of them, Master Magician or Councilor—the same people I've known and worked with for years. *None* of them even questioned Akako when she attended Council sessions in my stolen body. When she voted on policy and laws. Not one!"

"She was protected by a null shield," I tried to explain.

"That only blocks magical attacks. We have different personalities. How could they not suspect something was wrong?"

I swallowed the huge knot in my throat. "They knew something wasn't right. They probably worried about it, and they also probably found logical explanations for all your new quirks."

Tama remained doubtful. "Come on. They're intelligent men and women."

"You called me smart. Do you believe it?"

"Of course."

"I wasn't smart enough to figure out Devlen's soul was in Ulrick's body, and I was dating Ulrick." I told her my story. "He was bolder, more confident, and there were other clues, as well. But I didn't even question him. I justified each and every one. Try not to be so hard on the Council and Master Magicians. I'm sure they feel horrible, and I'd bet my sister's favorite skirt that Bain sent you the finest protector."

Her lips parted, but no words escaped. I couldn't tell if she thought I was an idiot or if she pitied me. Good thing I didn't tell her that Devlen had managed to do what Ulrick couldn't while we dated. Sleep with me.

"I'll have to think about it," she said.

"That's a start." I said good-night and moved to leave.

"Opal?" She touched my shoulder.

I stifled a yelp as magic burned through the fabric of my shirt.

"Thanks for sharing your story."

I nodded because if I opened my mouth I would cry out.

"See you tomorrow." She pulled her hand away.

I left her office and waved to Nic and Eve as I hurried through the reception area. Once I reached the deserted hallway, I sagged against the wall, and rubbed my shoulder. Magic coated Tama's skin. Since she wasn't a magician, it had to be Zebb's. If he protected her, she'd be surrounded by a null shield. He was either trying to manipulate her or spy on her. Either way I just lost Mara's favorite skirt.

Exhaustion soaked into my bones. I couldn't deal with this magician right now. I pushed away from the wall and descended to the lobby. Plenty of guards milled about, but most of the staff had gone for the day. I signed out.

The lamplighters had lit the streets of Fulgor. Soft yellow light flickered. Shadows danced. Groups of townspeople talked and laughed as they headed toward taverns or their homes. I should stop at the Pig Pen for a late supper and to listen to the gossip, but fatigue dragged on my body.

I would visit the taverns tomorrow as well as join the soldiers for their early-morning training. When I arrived at the Second Chance Inn, I checked on Quartz. She munched on hay, but poked her head over the stall door so I could scratch behind her ears. With eyes half-closed, she groaned in contentment. Then she moved, presenting other areas for me to scratch until I dug my nails into her hindquarters. Spoiled horse.

"A Sandseed horse. Figures," a man said with a sneering tone.

I turned. A tall man leaned against one of the stable's support beams. His crossed arms and relaxed posture the exact opposite of the strain in his voice.

"Excuse me?" I grabbed the handles of my sais. Magic enveloped me for a moment then receded. I stayed still despite the desire to bash him on the head with the shaft of my weapon.

"Some people get all the luck," the magician said. "Sandseed horses and special treatment even when they're no longer special."

He appeared to be unarmed, but his combative tone set off warning signals. I drew my weapons, keeping them down by my side. "My mother believes I'm special."

He snorted. "She would."

I'd had enough. "Is there a point to this conversation? Otherwise, you're wasting my time."

"I want to know what you're doing here."

"I'm checking on my horse."

"Cute. Let me rephrase the question. Why are you bothering Councilor Moon?"

Bothering. Interesting word choice. "It's none of your business."

"It is my business. I've been assigned to protect her."

Ah. Zebb. "Then go ask her."

He straightened and stepped toward me. A tingle of fear swept my body. He wore a short cloak over dark pants and knee-high boots. No visible weapons.

"I already know the lies you fed her. Came to visit

and stayed to help. What a sweet little girl," he mocked. "Except I know there is nothing sweet about you. You destroyed the entire communications network in Sitia. You're persona non grata with the Council, the Master Magicians and most of Sitia. Let me ask you again. Why are you here? *Who* sent you?"

"I'm not a threat to Tama, so it's still none of your business."

"I disagree."

I shrugged, trying to project a casualness I didn't feel.

"Doesn't matter. You're going to tell me."

I braced for a magical attack, but nothing happened. "Why would I?"

He held up one of my glass messengers. The ugly goat reflected the weak lantern light. I could no longer see if the interior of the goat glowed with magic or not. The glass no longer sang to me. Emptiness filled my chest.

"Because if you don't tell me, I'm going to broadcast the news of your immunity to every magician who still has one of these, which includes the Master Magicians and all the Councilors' bodyguards." He brandished the messenger in my face.

"I was going to tell them eventually. You'd be saving me the trouble." I kept my voice even.

"Trouble is what you're going to be in when I tell them you came here to assassinate Councilor Moon."

5

"That's a lie," I said, letting my outrage color my tone.

"Too bad there are only a few precious glass messengers left," Zebb said. "Otherwise, you could tell them the fast way. But a message sent by courier will take five days. And, really, who would believe you over a magician assigned by Master Bloodgood?"

I assessed the magician. Sandy brown hair fell in layers around his face and the tip of his nose looked as if someone had pushed it down toward his upper lip. He wasn't bluffing.

"That's blackmail," I said.

"No. I'm protecting the Councilor."

I huffed in frustration. "No one sent me. As you pointed out, I'm not very popular with the Council or the Master Magicians right now. I came to ask Tama for a job, but when I saw how…fragile she had become, I wanted to help her instead." The truth. When he failed to reply, I added, "Besides, I had planned to convince her of your…good intentions? Maybe I need to rethink that. Unless you'd rather she not trust you enough to let you be in the same room with her?"

His stance relaxed a smidge.

I pressed my advantage. "And I'm positive her view of magicians wouldn't improve if I told her you'd been using magic to spy on her."

"I'm not spying. I'm doing my job."

"Then why isn't she surrounded by a null shield? That would have protected her."

"Not from you." He gestured to me. "You could have attacked her with your sais. Magic isn't the only weapon."

"But she's surrounded by guards at all times."

"Guards you selected."

"They're Fulgor soldiers. They're more loyal to her than *you*," I shot back.

He crossed his arms again. This conversation had gone nowhere. I returned my sais to the holder hanging around my waist. Long slits in my cloak allowed me to access them without getting tangled in the fabric.

"How about a truce?" I asked.

"I'm listening."

"I believe Tama can sense your magic on an unconscious level." I held up my hand when he opened his mouth. "Hear me out. In order to help her over her fear of magicians, I need you to stop the protective magic. If you feel she's in danger, you can surround her with a null shield. And in return, I will keep you updated on her progress."

He considered my offer. "Not you. I want the Councilor's First Adviser to give me twice daily reports."

So he could read Faith's mind to ensure we didn't lie to him. "Fine."

"And you have to answer two questions."

Wary, I asked, "What questions?"

"Why didn't you tell Master Bloodgood about your immunity?"

He couldn't use magic to determine if I lied, but he studied me with a strong intensity. Remembering what Valek had said about my poor acting skills, I kept as close to the truth as possible.

"At first, I hoped my powers would return after I healed. They didn't. Now, since the Council and Bain are dealing with the consequences of the soon-to-be-extinct glass messengers, I wanted to keep a low profile until things settled to a point where I can tell Bain and he'll be more receptive to figuring out a way my immunity can help Sitia." I waited, hoping that last bit wasn't too much.

"Why did you come looking for a job in Fulgor?" Zebb asked.

"Obviously, I can't go to the Citadel and my hometown, Booruby, is filled with glass factories." I lowered my gaze, not having to pretend to be upset. The hot, sweet smell of molten glass fogged the streets, and the glint of sunlight from shops displaying glasswares pierced the air. It was impossible to avoid the reminders of what I had sacrificed.

"I have a few friends in Fulgor. It seemed like a good place to start," I said.

He agreed to the truce, but also puffed out his chest and threatened to tell the Council about my immunity if I failed to keep him informed. I ignored his bluster. What concerned me more was I still didn't know why Zebb failed to erect a null shield around Tama. Until then, I wouldn't trust him.

\* \* \*

Tama Moon's confidence crept back over the next twenty days. We had weeded out the inexperienced guards and assembled a group of seasoned veterans with flawless service records. Nic's team remained her personal bodyguards, but her distrust of magicians failed to abate despite my assurances and the lack of magic.

The taverns buzzed with general rumblings from the citizens over the mass firings of the guards, but otherwise their biggest concern was over why their Councilor hadn't returned to the Citadel.

Sipping wine at the bar of the Pig Pen, I overheard bits of a conversation from a few people talking nearby.

"...they're making resolutions without her."

"...we need someone to speak for our clan."

"First Akako and now this...maybe we should demand her resignation."

"The Council could assign someone..."

"...they take forever to make a decision."

When they turned to another subject, I stopped listening. Their accurate comment about the Sitian Council and the slow pace of decisions snagged on one of my own worries. What if the Council decided to execute Ulrick, Tricky and his goons before I had a chance to find out where they hid my blood? A slight risk, but still a possibility. Perhaps it was time to resume my own project.

I had planned to ask Tama to arrange a visit with Ulrick for me, but no visitors were allowed inside Wirral. And I couldn't find any exceptions—like by order of the Councilor—to that rule. I needed an alternative plan.

* * *

"Faith, do you have a minute?" I asked from the threshold of her office.

"Sure, come in."

Sunlight streamed in from the large glass windows behind her. I suppressed the memory of being here when Gressa had occupied the First Adviser's position. Then I had been manacled and considered a criminal. Instead, I noted the lush carpet and rich furniture. Her office was as ornate as the Councilor's, but smaller.

I settled into a comfortable chair in front of Faith's desk. When she smiled at me, a prick of guilt jabbed me. Squashing all such feelings, I stayed pleasant as we exchanged small talk. Eventually, she asked what I needed.

"Tama has improved so much over the last twenty-five days, but she is still terrified of Zebb," I said.

"That's understandable," Faith said.

"I know, but the townspeople are worried about her missing Council sessions and if she doesn't return soon, there could be a call for her resignation."

Faith tsked. "There are always naysayers out there. You can't please everyone."

"True, but I have an idea that might help."

Her eyebrows arched as she waited for me to continue.

"I'm assuming her sister, Akako, and Gressa are in the maximum security prison?"

"Yes, they are both in the SMU along with those other men."

"Do you know the correctional officers who work in the SMU?" I asked.

"Not personally. They're a specially trained elite

unit. In fact, there are only a handful of people allowed in the SMU."

"Do the officers live there?" That seemed extreme.

"No." She tapped her fingertips together. It was an unconscious habit that she displayed whenever the logic in a conversation didn't quite add up; as if she could push all the illogical pieces together and build something she could understand. I'd spent more time with her than I realized. Tama had made an excellent choice when she appointed the practical and sensible Faith as her First Adviser.

"Do you have the names of those in the elite unit?" I asked.

"How is this related to Tama's fear of Zebb?"

Time for a little creative reasoning. "We did background checks on all the guards in the Council Hall and Tama has relaxed. She's afraid of a magical attack. So I thought if we did some digging into the backgrounds of the unit, she would feel better, knowing the men and women guarding those who know blood magic are trustworthy. I know I would sleep better with that information. And I think we should check into Zebb's history, as well."

Faith's hands stilled and she pressed her steepled index fingers to her lips. "Why don't you just ask Tama for their names?"

"She would want to know why I was interested. And it's more complicated than with the Hall's guards. Then we were just weeding out the inexperienced and those of questionable repute. The unit has been with these prisoners for over a season. What if we discover a real problem? Akako could have assigned moles in the prison just in case her plans failed. You know Tama requests daily updates, and I can't lie to her. She would be terrified by the notion. I'd rather wait and tell her good news once we assess the situation." I held my breath.

"A reasonable plan, and I agree we shouldn't tell the Councilor. At least not yet." Faith opened a drawer in her desk, pulling out a sheet of paper. "I'll send a request to Wirral's warden."

Uh-oh. I hoped to keep the number of people involved to two. "Don't you have that information here?"

"No. Grogan Moon is in charge of all Wirral's personnel."

"Is his office in the Hall?"

"No. It's at the prison where he spends most of his time. He comes here for meetings with the Councilor and other clan business." She dipped her quill into ink and wrote the request.

After she folded the paper and sealed it with wax, I jumped to my feet. "I'll deliver the message."

She hesitated.

"I want to make sure it reaches the warden and not some underling. Besides, I think it'll be helpful if *I* take a look around."

As soon as I entered, the solid mass of the prison's stone walls bore down on my shoulders. The air thickened and I fought to draw a breath. I clutched Faith's request in my hands, which were pressed against my chest as if it were a shield.

With each step, I sank deeper into the bowels of Wirral. My escort held a torch, illuminating his aggrieved scowl. Most messengers delivered their communications to the officers at the gate, but I had insisted on handing the missive to the warden himself.

After an intense debate, an order to disarm and a thorough search of my body, I had been permitted to enter. I'd regretted my insistence as soon as the first set of steel doors slammed behind me. The harsh clang reverberated off the stone walls, and matched the tremor of panic in my heart. More sets of locked gates followed until I lost all track of time or location.

Rank and putrid smells emanated from dark hallways. Shrieks of pain, curses and taunting cries pierced the air. We didn't pass any cells. Thank fate. I had no wish to view the conditions nor the poor souls trapped in here.

Eventually, the officer led me up a spiral staircase so narrow my shoulders brushed both walls. The acrid odors disappeared and the oily blackness lightened. Dizzy with relief and the fast pace, I paused for a moment by the only window we encountered. Drinking in the crisp breeze, I looked down on an exercise yard. Completely surrounded by the prison, the packed dirt of the square at least allowed the prisoners some fresh air and sunlight.

My escort growled at me to hurry, and I rushed to catch up. The top of the staircase ended at another steel door. After a series of complicated knocks from both sides of the door, it swung open, revealing two officers wedged in a small vestibule. Another round of explanations followed another pat down.

Yep. This had been a bad idea. One of my worst.

I was finally admitted to the warden's office. Windows ringed the large circular room. A stone hearth blazed with heat in the center, and behind a semicircle-shaped desk sat the warden.

My first impression—big bald head. Second—an immaculate uniform cut so tight wrinkles would be impossible. Another man lounged in a chair next to the desk. He also wore a correctional officer's uniform, but instead of the standard blue, his shirt and pants were deep navy and no weapons or keys hung from his belt. He eyed me with keen interest.

My escort waited for the warden to acknowledge our presence before approaching the desk. I lagged behind and tried not to duck my head when the warden turned his irritation on me. Steel-gray eyes appraised me, and I stifled the need to scuff my foot and fidget like a small child. He stood and held out his hand. His movements were so precise and rigid, I wondered if his bones had been replaced by metal rods and his flesh petrified by years spent inside this stone prison.

"The message?" His voice matched his demeanor. Rough and sharp.

I handed him the request. He snatched it, ripped it open, scanned the words and tossed it on his desk. "Go," he ordered.

"But—"

"What? Am I supposed to hand *you* the information?" His tone implied yes would be the wrong answer.

"Er…" Wonderful retort. Opal, the superspy.

"Am I supposed to stop everything I'm doing to give *you* classified documents?"

"Um…"

"Go now."

I used to believe a powerful Daviian Warper addicted to blood magic was the scariest person I'd ever encounter. Not anymore.

Outside and several blocks away from Wirral, I sucked in huge gulps of air, trying to expel the fetid taint of the prison inside me. My gasps turned to hiccupy giggles as I imagined going through with my original plan to work undercover as a correctional officer. Light-headed and unable to draw in a decent breath, I reached for a lantern post as my head spun. I missed and toppled to the ground. Dazed, I waited for the spinning to stop.

"Hey! Are you all right?" a man asked. He peered down at me in concern.

"Fine. Fine." I waved him away. "Just lost my balance."

He knelt next to me. "It's brutal the first time."

I squinted at him. "What?"

"You were in Wirral. I thought you looked…shaky."

Recognizing the man from the warden's office, I pushed to my elbow in alarm. "You followed me?"

"Of course. Your face was whiter than a full moon, your eyes were bugged out and you wobbled when you left. What was I suppose to do? Let you fall and crack your head open?"

"No…sorry. I'm just… That was horrible!"

"It's a punishment. It's not supposed to be fun."

"But it seemed…cruel."

"What did?"

Was he teasing me? A cool humor lurked behind his grayish-green eyes, but it didn't spoil his genuine interest in my answer.

"The smells, the shrieks, the darkness, the…"

He waited. When I didn't continue, he said, "Did you actually see anything cruel?"

"No, but—"

"Your imagination filled in the details."

I wanted to correct him. Not my imagination, but my experience.

"I won't lie to you. It is bad, but not cruel. They're fed, given water, exercise and fresh air. No one is tortured or harmed by the COs. And considering what most of them have done to others, it's more than they deserve. Here…"

He hooked his arm under mine and helped me to my feet. I swayed, but regained my balance, trying to remember the last time I ate.

"What are COs?"

"Short for correctional officers. We abbreviate everything."

The man still held my arm.

"Thanks for the help," I said, trying and failing to subtly break his strong grip. "I'll be fine."

He gave me a skeptical look. "You need a drink, and I know just the place."

Instinctively, I gauged his skill level. About six inches taller than me, he had a lean, wiry build. Buzzed black hair showed a few scars. I guessed he was five or six years older than me. Long, thin face that could easily get lost in a crowd, but those hazel eyes… Amusement filled them, and a slanted smile transformed him from common to unusual.

"Think you can take me?" he asked.

I laughed. "That obvious?"

"Yes."

"Can you blame me? I don't know you, and shouldn't

you be returning to work?" I pointed in the direction of the prison.

"My name is Finn. I'm off duty. And I'm wearing a lieutenant's uniform and not a prison jumpsuit. Shouldn't that be enough to trust me?"

"No."

He laughed. Letting go of my arm, he stepped away with his hands up by his shoulders. "Smart lady. No wonder the Councilor hired you as her assistant."

Alarm flashed through me. "How do you know?"

"COs like to gossip. Besides, I was consulted before they'd let you in."

"But I had a message."

"Doesn't matter. No one enters. No visitors. No messengers. No deliverymen. Not even Councilor Moon can visit her sister, and for their safety, the Councilor and First Adviser are not even allowed inside. Authorized personnel *only*."

"And you authorized me?"

"Yes. Now are you going to stand here all day, or are you going to let me buy you a drink?"

Finn must have quite a bit of power within the prison. I chose the drink. He led me to a tavern a few blocks away. Called the Spotted Dog, the utilitarian decor lacked warmth, but the patrons didn't seem to mind. They generated their own coziness, acting like one big family. It made sense since almost all of them worked at the prison.

My arrival with Finn sent a ripple through the tavern. The hum of conversation died for an awkward moment before spiking back to life. In that time, appraising glances, surprised stares and hostile glares were aimed at me. A few women mingled with the men. A couple of the women wore uniforms, but the rest were in civilian garb. Finn and I sat at a table away from the general crowd.

If this group learned to trust me, then I'd hit the jackpot. Finn had said the COs liked to gossip, and since I had no idea whether the warden would deliver the names to Faith or not, perhaps I would overhear information about the SMU or discover the names of the elite officers. Big if.

Would I be welcomed here without Finn? Doubtful. How much did Finn know about me? Did he know about Kade? And was I really considering using him to obtain the information I needed? How different was this from the story I spun for Faith? I was sure these questions didn't bother Valek and his corp. Perhaps I should wait for the warden.

But the thought of waiting any longer sent nervous darts of fear through my body. The desire to find my blood before... What? My imagination created all kinds of scenarios. Spilled. Used. Lost. Hidden. Far better to be proactive than not.

"How long have you been working at the prison?" I asked Finn.

He swallowed a gulp of ale and flashed me his slanted smile. "Feels like forever. Actually, I recently transferred in from a Bloodgood prison."

"Do you plan to stay?"

"This move was a promotion and I'm hoping to work my way to be a warden someday."

A strange gleam shone in his eyes, and I couldn't tell if he joked or teased or if he told the truth. "You seem too nice to be a warden. And I can't imagine anyone ousting Grogan." I shuddered, remembering his fierce demeanor.

"It's not a matter of usurping the man." Finn leaned forward. "It's a matter of *outliving* him."

The Lieutenant was serious. Yikes. "That bad? I thought Wirral is a maximum security prison."

"It is. You've seen the fortifications. However, we house the worst offenders from all over Sitia. And some of those guys are amazingly creative and intelligent. It doesn't happen very often, but in Wirral's long history, there have been a few escapes and riots and warden assassinations."

Icy dread climbed up my throat. "Even from the SMU?" Tricky had escaped from Ixia—an almost impossible task. Would this prison be easier?

My obvious unease caused Finn to rush to assure me. "SMU is escape-proof. See those guys?" He pointed his mug toward a trio sitting at a far table.

They kept a distance from the others. Absorbed in conversation, the average-sized men didn't evoke any warm feelings of safety in me. Plus I had learned words like *impossible* and *escape-proof* never worked. Someone, somewhere, at some time would prove it wrong.

"They're the best of the best," he said. "When we finish our training, we're all locked inside the prison for thirty days. Those of us who escape or manage to outwit the COs in some way are given another year of training and assigned to the SMU."

Impressive. "Thirty days inside must have been—"

"Not fun. And since I transferred in, I still had to do thirty days in Wirral despite my other time behind bars."

"And?"

"I managed. And with my prior experience, I was assigned to the SMU." He relaxed back in his seat. "So don't worry. No one's escaping on my watch."

Finn asked me a few questions about my life and from them I learned he knew I had been involved with Councilor Moon's rescue, but not all the details. Good.

As we talked, I kept an eye on the other SMU officers, trying to memorize their faces. At one point during our conversation, magic brushed me. A light inquisitive touch. I scanned the crowd, but, besides the two drunken soldiers glaring at me, no one paid me any attention. The drunks' hostility didn't match the magic, but making eye contact with them was a mistake. They approached us.

Finn stiffened and said, "Don't say a word."

Anger radiated from them. A sheen of alcohol and malice glazed their eyes. And they kept their hands on the hilts of their swords. They were a mirror image of each other, except the bruiser on the left had braided his hair into rows along his scalp and his companion's lank hair hung straight to his shoulders.

"Hey, LT, do you know who you're cozying with?" Braids asked Finn in a loud voice. "That's the Councilor's new assistant."

"Why 'ja bring the bitch here?" Lank asked, slurring his words.

Finn placed his hand on my arm. A not too subtle hint to keep calm. His gaze never left the men.

"She fired my cousin, LT," Braids said.

The tavern quieted.

Braids, sensing he had a larger audience, raised his voice and addressed the room. "She put my cousin and at least a dozen others out of work."

Lank said, "And why 'ja think she was sniffing around the prison? How many of us are gonna be fired?"

Not good. I glanced around. Others nodded in agreement, siding with the drunks. No stopping it now. This was probably going to turn ugly.

My recent streak of bad decisions continued. What had I been thinking when I agreed to a drink with one of the prison officers? The rumblings of discontent over my presence in the Spotted Dog tavern increased. A couple men moved closer to the two drunks who had started this confrontation, and one of the elite officers joined the growing mob.

Tossed out would be the best scenario for me. Beaten to a pulp the worst.

"She cleaned out the riffraff," Finn said to the two in my defense. "Did us a favor, and you know it. Besides, you hate your cousin, Cole. Said he couldn't guard a baby."

Not the right thing to say. Braids…Cole drew his sword. "You takin' her side, LT?"

Finn stood in one fluid motion. The tension thickened the air, making it hard to draw a breath.

I rose to my feet, being careful not to make any sudden moves. "Gentlemen, Councilor Moon has no intention of changing anything at the prison. I was merely delivering a message for her. I'm sorry about your cousin, Cole. If you tell me his name, I can try to find him another job."

He blinked at me as if trying to make sense of my words. Before he could respond, Finn said, "The government will be hiring construction workers to build an addition to HQ when the weather's warmer. Lots of jobs then."

The friction eased. A voice announced that a barrel of special ale was open and most of the crowd disbursed. When a few more COs entered the tavern, cheerful calls to a rookie hotshot erupted. Knowing a good distraction when I saw one, I grabbed Finn's hand and headed toward the door.

I didn't release my hold until we were a few blocks away. The setting sun cast long shadows along the street.

"Sorry, I didn't think anyone would recognize you," Finn said.

Confused, I asked, "Why not? You did."

"I'm naturally nosy." He quirked a smile. "Actually, knowing who is who in town is part of my job. A new arrival might mean someone is trying to aid a prisoner."

"To escape?"

"Escape, or just to smuggle in supplies. Trading goods inside is very lucrative and every single item in there has two different uses at least. I keep track of all the merchants and delivery people. If I see a new face, I'm automatically suspicious. When I heard the Councilor hired a new assistant, I made sure to get a good look at you."

"I hadn't realized there was so much involved with your job."

"A common misconception. Everyone thinks we just

stand around. But we have to be one step ahead of the prisoners or risk being surprised by a weapon made of crushed glass mixed in feces."

I stopped. "You're not serious. Are you?"

His queasy grimace didn't change.

"Yuck. At least you have one more person who has a greater appreciation of what you do. Thanks for the drink. I'd better get back before the Councilor worries."

"I'll escort you."

I opened my mouth to protest, but Finn was my only link to Wirral. "Okay," I agreed. He could be my way inside.

We walked for a while in silence.

I mulled over what he had told me. "Do all the different areas of the prison have specific titles like SMU?" I asked.

"Yes. There are a ton of official designations, but we have nicknames for almost all of them."

"Where does a rookie hotshot work?"

He laughed. "That's the new guy in the SMU. The nickname for us is the *hotshots*. And rookies are the ones either newly graduated from training or new to the prison. I was called the rookie LT until he arrived."

"Here you go." Faith dropped a thick file folder on my desk. "Delivered this morning."

Her amused tone drew my attention. I glanced at her. She stood with one hand resting on her cocked hip. Her short hair was tucked behind her ears as always, but she smirked.

Oh no. "What's the catch?" I asked.

"The warden wasn't…happy with your interruption two days ago."

"And?"

"And you're barred from entering his prison again."

I shuddered, remembering the conditions. "That's fine by me. So why so smug?"

"You've met the man. Not much upsets him, but our request plus your *audacity*—his word, not mine—in not trusting him or his people has galled him. He has issued *you* a challenge." Faith was downright gleeful.

"Why me? You wrote the request," I grumbled.

"Come on, Opal. The warden isn't an idiot."

"Since you're dying to tell me, go on."

"He challenged you to find anything, *anything* wrong with his correctional officers or his prison."

"He's that confident?"

She nodded.

Nothing was perfect. "Tell him I accept his challenge."

Faith whistled. "Bold."

"What's bold?" Tama Moon asked from behind Faith.

The First Adviser jumped a foot. "Don't scare me like that!"

"Sorry." But the Councilor didn't appear apologetic. In fact, her eyebrows were pinched close, puckering the skin on her forehead. "What are you two plotting?"

I noted her word choice. Plotting. Paranoid vibes wafted from her.

Quicker to respond, Faith said, "Nothing." However, she couldn't lie convincingly, which added to Tama's suspicions.

"Nothing important," I said. "Nic challenged me to spar with him. My sais against his sword, and I not only accepted but claimed I would win."

Tama released a breath and her shoulders eased down

a fraction. "That is bold." Her frown remained. She shoved a stack of files at Faith. "Here, I need you to check the payroll numbers and send them down to accounting."

Faith clutched the packet to her chest and shot me a worried glance before hurrying away.

"Opal, I need to speak to you in my office."

I studied her as I followed. Uncombed white-blond hair hung in clumps as if she just rolled out of bed. Her hands hugged her arms. When we reached her desk, she snatched a paper from the surface and waved it at me.

"What is this?" she asked.

I reached for the sheet and touched magic. A thick bubble resisted my hand, but I pushed through and took the paper from Tama. Damn it, Zebb. We had a deal. I squashed my desire to find him and crack his head open with my sais. He had just undone weeks of improvement, sending Tama back to where we started.

Instead, I kept my face neutral as I scanned the letter. When a person was convicted and sentenced to prison, all his assets were turned over to the Sitian government to put toward the cost of his incarceration. The letter was a standard reversal of assets to the Moon Clan and not something that would need the Councilor's approval. Except in this case, the prisoner was Akako, Tama's sister. Akako's signature meant she agreed to the terms stated in the letter, and it was countersigned by Tama.

Confused, I tried to determine what she was really asking. "You approved the transfer."

"I know that! Look here." She stabbed her finger at a line of text below her signature.

I squinted at the fine print. "You also waived your right to purchase her assets. Is that bad?"

"Of course it's bad. She owned my parents' house! I want to buy it. It's a good thing I found that before it went to the realty office." She rounded on me. "How did you do it, Opal? Stick it in the middle of a bunch of papers so I wouldn't see it when I signed it?"

Her accusation took a moment to sink in. She believed I had tricked her into signing away her rights. "I didn't—"

"Don't lie to me." She snatched the paper from my hands. "This is an act of espionage."

"Why would I do that? What would I gain?" I tried to reason with her, but she wouldn't listen.

When she called for her guards to arrest me, I realized the magic must be influencing her. Zebb's way of getting rid of me? Seemed complicated, but I could have underestimated him.

The two guards rushed over. Nic and Eve were off duty. Bad timing for me, but not for the magician. With panic building in my chest, I touched Tama's wrist, hoping my immunity to magic would somehow cover her and break the spell. No luck.

She shrieked and yanked her arm back. The guards grabbed my shoulders, pulling me away. My mind raced through my five years of magical instruction at the Magician's Keep, searching for something, anything that would help.

"Wait," I said to the guards. "She's being influenced by magic. If we don't break it, it'll be just like before when Akako took control of the clan."

They hesitated.

"Trust me." I snagged an idea. "Don't let go of me. Keep hold, but let's walk in a circle around the Councilor. We don't have to get close to her. She'll be in no danger."

"No. Arrest her for espionage and for attacking me," Tama ordered.

"You've been guarding her for half a season. Something isn't right. Trust yourselves," I said.

"Once around and then down to the cells," the guard on my left said.

"No tricks," the other said.

Wedged between them, I stepped to the side, keeping the Councilor in front of me. I reviewed my plan. Magicians pulled threads of magic from the blanket of power surrounding the world. They aimed these strings of power at people or objects. Since the magic around Tama wasn't from anyone in the room, I needed to find the direction of power. After that, it would be pure guesswork.

She glared at us as she turned to follow our progress. I hoped the magician wouldn't spread his influence to the guards. In that case, I would be screwed.

Three-quarters of the way around, I started to worry. What if the magician was in the room above or below? And when did I decide it wasn't Zebb?

After a few more steps, I entered a stream of magic. It pushed against my back. I stopped.

Confusion spread on her face. She reached toward me. "Opal? What…"

The magic moved and she jerked. "Get her out of here!" she yelled. "She's a spy and should be locked up."

"I blocked it for a moment," I said. "You saw her change! I need to get closer." I dragged the guards three feet and I stepped left and right, searching for the stream. Once again the magic slammed into my back.

The Councilor sagged into her desk chair. "Listen to Opal," she said in a weak voice.

When the magic moved, I stayed with it. "Get Zebb," I ordered the guards as I shrugged them off. "Hurry!"

I expected Tama to protest, but she pulled her knees to her chest and hugged them, making herself into a smaller target either by instinct or intelligence. It didn't matter. By this time, I stood close to her and shielded her with my body.

The magical pressure increased and I used every bit of energy to keep from being flattened. Where was Zebb? Gasping for breath, I strained against the attack. My calf muscles burned with the effort. Sweat stung my eyes.

When the door banged, I yelled, "Null shield!" without bothering to see if it was Zebb.

Two things happened at once. The onslaught stopped, and Zebb's magic pushed me away from Tama. I staggered and dropped to the floor, panting with relief.

"What the hell was that?" Zebb asked.

I let the guards explain.

"This is *exactly* why I need to be near the Councilor at all times," Zebb said. "I knew you'd endanger her."

He continued to rant about her safety, but I tuned him out. I wondered again if the magician had been after her or me.

When I felt stronger, I climbed to my feet. "Zebb, shut up." I resisted smirking when he listened to me. See? I could be mature. "Can you sense another magician nearby?"

"No, but I was on the first floor."

"How about when you entered the room?"

He shook his head.

I sighed. "Help me out here. Where would a magician need to be to reach her?"

"It depends on how strong he is."

I noted his pronoun choice. Habit or did he know more than he was telling me? "Can we narrow it down to inside or outside the building?" I asked in exasperation.

"Outside. No one with powers can get by me."

Ignoring his boast, I asked, "Can you take a few guards out to search?"

He sneered. "I know you're used to hanging out with the Master Magicians and the Soulfinder. They can walk the streets and sniff out any magicians. The rest of us can't."

"But you just said—"

"Line of sight. Everyone coming into the Council Hall has to pass by me. If I can reach their thoughts, they don't have any power."

I thought it through. "Then the magician who attacked the Councilor is stronger than average. He didn't need line of sight."

His lips parted in surprise. "But he would have to know she was in her office."

We both turned to the picture window at the end of her office. Sunlight streamed through the large pane of glass. Tama had located her U-shaped desk close enough to it so she could enjoy the view while she worked.

I moved closer, looking outside. Her first-floor office was a mere twelve feet above the street. Below, townspeople strolled or hustled by either on horseback or on foot. Wagons bounced along the cobblestones. From this distance, I could see clearly. No one seemed interested in the window. No one lurked in the shadows. At least not now.

Zebb joined me.

"Would curtains help protect her?" I asked.

"To some extent. The magician would have to guess if the Councilor was here. Or risk alerting me by sweeping the building. We could move her desk to make it harder for him."

"No curtains," Tama said. Her first words since the incident. A touch of color had returned to her pallid cheeks.

"But—"

She cut Zebb off. "I understand your concerns. How about a compromise?" She swiped the hair sticking to her face. "No curtains and I'll let Zebb and his null shield stay with me."

"Finally," Zebb said. "It's what I've wanted from the beginning!"

Not a diplomatic response and uncertainty filled her eyes.

"You've made a smart decision," I said. "Zebb may be a pompous ass, but he's trustworthy." The background check on him hadn't found anything.

Faith rushed in before he could retort.

"Tama, are you all right?" She gathered the Councilor in her arms. Tama leaned into her.

"What happened?" Faith demanded.

I let Zebb handle the explanation while I mulled over a possible reason for the attack.

When he finished addressing all her questions, I asked Tama about her enemies. "Any other relatives that might be trying to usurp you?"

Faith answered for her. "No. Akako is her only sister.

Her parents died years ago and she has one aunt and a couple of cousins on her father's side. They live in the Krystal lands and she's never even met them."

Tama pulled away. "My father was from the Krystal Clan. He met my mother while here on business." Her colorless lips formed a wan smile. "He claimed love at first sight, but it took him a few seasons to convince her. The clan wasn't happy about their heir marrying an outsider. But he won them over just like he did with my mother. Everyone loved my father."

A sweet story, but no help for our current problem. "Can you think of anyone who might be after you? Or a reason someone wanted to control you?" I asked.

"Perhaps we missed one of Akako's people," Faith said. "Only Tama can release Akako from prison."

"Then why did he force me to arrest Opal?" the Councilor asked. "I was convinced she was a spy and I'd only be safe once she was secured in Wirral."

"Basic strategy," Zebb said. "Eliminate the person's supporters so no one protests when the person changes her behavior."

A logical argument, yet an uneasy chill swirled. Being incarcerated in Wirral would be a waking nightmare.

For now, at least the null shield protected Tama, and I had my immunity. Faith declared she would go over Akako's files, searching for any insurgents who may have been missed.

I returned to my desk and the thick file on the hotshots in the SMU. Perhaps Akako had managed to bribe one of them or one could already be loyal to her. I would have laughed at the irony if I had the energy. The creative reasoning that netted me the file in the first place might lead to an answer and to something to prove to the warden that his prison wasn't perfect.

I read through the files until I was cross-eyed with fatigue. After spending the entire afternoon studying the information on the hotshots, I had nothing to show for it. Finn's matched his story. Complete background checks with confirmations from two different sources had been attached to each CO's dossier. Even the rookie Lamar's papers had been included. His letter of recommendation from the Iolite Prison's warden had been verified twice.

When the words swam together, I stopped for the day. Tama had retreated to her suite for the night, but Faith remained in her office. I debated. Should I skip supper and get a few extra hours of sleep or go to the Pig Pen for a bowl of stew?

Preoccupied, I left the Hall and paused. The black sky meant I had missed the late-afternoon training again. Nic and Eve would harass me about it.

"Working late?" a voice asked from behind me.

I drew my sais, whipping around. Finn leaned on the Councilor's Hall. He spread his hands. "Easy there."

"Sorry." I slid my weapons back under my cloak.

"Are you always this jumpy?" he asked.

"No. It's been a long day." I gathered my scattered wits. "What are you doing here?"

"Waiting for you."

"Why?" The question popped out without censure.

Finn laughed. A nice rumble. "I enjoyed our conversation the other day and wanted to continue it."

"Oh." My tired brain finally caught up. This was good. Right? I wanted to get closer to him and find out more about the prison. Kade would understand. I was working undercover. But what if our roles were reversed? How would I feel if he had to seduce another woman? Horrible. I shook my head. Ridiculous speculation. I didn't plan to seduce Finn.

"Would you like to have dinner with me?" he asked in an uncertain tone.

"Of course. I'm sorry. I'm tired and—"

"We can go another time then."

"I didn't mean that. I'm famished. How about I pick the place this time? I know a tavern with the best stew in town."

He flashed me his slanted smile. "Any angry officers?"

"We shouldn't need a distraction in order to leave."

He swept his arm out. "Lead on."

The jumble of voices reached us before we entered the Pig Pen. Nic's brother served drinks, and Nic and Eve sat at their usual places. Not good. I thought they were on duty. Fulgor soldiers filled every table and people crowded the bar. I was about to retreat to another tavern when Ian waved me over. He snapped his fingers a few times and two stools next to my friends emptied. So much for a quiet conversation.

Finn whistled. "Wow. You must be a good customer." He nodded to a couple of people as we claimed the stools. I made sure to sit between Finn and Nic.

"Have you been here before?" I asked him.

"No, but I know a few of Fulgor's security forces. All part of the job."

Hoping Nic and Eve wouldn't blow my cover by mentioning Kade, I introduced them to Finn. Nic sized him up and gave me a questioning look before Eve elbowed him in the ribs. If Finn noticed he didn't react. Two bowls of stew appeared in front of us, and I turned Finn's attention to Ian. When Finn made the connection between the brothers, I felt a strange sense of pride.

"Is he the reason you've missed four training sessions?" Nic asked me.

"I've been busy with work."

"No excuses," Nic said. "It's too important. Does Kad— Ow!"

"Time to go," Eve said, standing. She pulled Nic off the stool. "Nice meeting you, Finn. We'd love to stay and chat, but we're on duty tonight. Opal, we'll see *you* in the morning." Her pointed gaze warned me she would question me thoroughly.

Eve hustled Nic out the door. Confusion creased his face, but he followed his partner.

Finn and I ate our stew. He pushed his empty bowl aside and drank his ale. "You're right. It is the best in town."

The food revived me, and cleared my mind. "It's better than my mother's, but don't tell anyone I said that or she'll disown me."

"Your secret is safe with me. Although I could blackmail you with it."

I smiled at his teasing tone. "You could try."

"You never did answer my question."

"Which one?"

"If you think you can beat me with those sais of yours?" He touched my arm, resting his warm fingers on my forearm. "Think about it. You did miss a few training sessions."

"How much training have you had?" I asked.

"Ten years."

I had gotten serious about improving my own skills only a year ago. "I doubt I could win a match against you." Unless I cheated and used those pressure points Devlen had inadvertently taught me.

"You may surprise yourself. From what I hear, you're rather resourceful."

"What have you heard?"

"There wasn't much information in the gossip loop, and you didn't give me a whole lot, either."

"I hardly know you." Yet I didn't pull my arm away.

"True. But you're in a powerful position, working so close with the Councilor and the First Adviser."

I couldn't argue with him without telling him why I took the job. "And?"

"And I knew someone in security *had* to know something." He leaned his elbow on the bar with a smug casualness.

"Who ratted me out?"

"Do you know a Captain Alden?" He gestured to the still-empty stools. "Your friends' boss?"

"I've met him once or twice." Nic and Eve had reported everything they witnessed in Hubal to him. Their report had lacked a few important details. "How do you know him?"

"Friend of a friend."

"Are you proud of yourself?"

"Of course. Plus I feel better knowing *you* are with the Councilor, and I can tell the warden good things about you."

"The warden asks you because…?"

"I know everyone in town."

"You didn't know Alden."

"Miss Logical. I see you're going to keep me on my toes. I didn't know Alden personally, but if I passed him on the street, I could tell you his name, rank and his position on Fulgor's security force."

We talked about random things until I steered the conversation to the SMU and the hotshots.

Finn leaned close. "I know why you're so interested in them."

"You do?" My mouth felt dry, and I resisted the urge to gulp my ale.

"No one is escaping from the SMU, Opal. No one. Stop worrying. Those men who stole your magic won't hurt you ever again."

Covering my face with the mug of ale, I tipped it up and took a long drink. Did he know about the file on my desk? I decided to tone down my focus on the hotshots in Finn's presence for now, and pretend he had guessed everything right.

I placed my hand over his and gave it a light squeeze. "Thanks."

Our conversation returned to more mundane topics. When I couldn't stifle a yawn, Finn stood. "Time to go. I have an early day tomorrow."

"Me, too." I grimaced. Nic would be extra hard on me and Eve would pepper me with questions. Ugh.

Finn grasped my hand when we reached the street. Our footsteps echoed along the empty road. I hadn't realized how late it had gotten.

"The day after tomorrow is my day off," he said. "Would you like to go riding with me?"

I hesitated. Quartz would love the exercise, and I hadn't taken any time off since I arrived.

"There's a pretty little waterfall in the forest north of the city," he said.

"Sounds fun." But guilt welled. I tried to rationalize my actions by reminding myself of my goal—finding my blood. If Finn's feelings were hurt in the process then I would apologize and move on.

"Great. I'll meet you at the inn's stables *after* your morning training."

That would make Nic happy. Finn escorted me home, but I started to worry when we drew closer to the inn. Would he want a kiss good-night? What would I do? Being undercover was harder than I'd thought.

The kissing issue turned out to be a needless concern.

One block from the inn, magic brushed my shoulder, warning me a split second before four armed men surrounded us.

# 7

My hands grasped the handles of my sais, but I didn't pull them. Not yet. I studied the men. Ordinary in appearance, wearing nondescript dark clothing and lacking any distinguishing features, the four men could easily blend into a crowd—except for the short swords and daggers in their hands.

Finn stepped in front of me. "Do you gentlemen have a problem?"

"Not with you," the man in the middle said. "We'd like a word with your companion."

Why wasn't I surprised? Firing those guards was about to get me killed. I flexed my muscles. Four against one, suicide for me, but with Finn, we'd have a better chance.

"In private," Middle Man said.

"Not happening." Finn drew his sword. Before his blade cleared his scabbard, two of the goons rushed him.

I yanked my sais free of my cloak. Middle Man and the remaining goon advanced. I managed to land a few bruising blows, but they disarmed me in seconds. Stronger than they looked, two of them clamped on to my upper arms and countered my attempts to kick them. A suspicion that these men weren't the average goons for hire rose along with the bile in my throat.

Finn lasted longer than I did, but the scuffle ended when one of the men struck Finn's temple with the hilt of his dagger. He collapsed to the ground.

Middle Man glanced up and down the street. "This way."

Leaving Finn, they dragged me a number of blocks south then west until we stopped in a small side street without lanterns. With a surge of fear-induced energy, I broke their hold. The snick of a switchblade sounded before I even stepped away. Cold steel pressed against my throat. I froze. An arm snaked around my chest, pulling me close to the owner of the knife.

"Relax," Middle Man said. "We just want to ask you a few questions."

"Make an appointment," I said, but he ignored me.

"Why are you in Fulgor?" he asked.

I considered a smart remark, but the sharp blade convinced me not to be too hasty. "To find a job."

"Why here?"

"The people are so friendly." I couldn't resist the sarcasm, but I regretted it as soon as the words left my mouth.

Middle Man's gaze cut to his buddy standing on my right. Motion registered a second before pain exploded in my ribs. I slammed into the man behind me. He kept me on my feet. The switchblade remained in his hand, but it no longer touched my throat. Progress.

They waited for me to recover. Nice of them.

"Why here?" Middle Man asked again.

Time to name drop. "I have friends here. Guards on Fulgor's security force."

"You're close to the Councilor. Who sent you to cozy up to her?"

"No one."

Even anticipating the blow, I still couldn't block it. This one landed higher, causing a sharp jab of pain with every breath.

"Who are you working for?"

"Councilor Moon." I puffed.

Buddy moved to my left and now both sides of my lower rib cage burned.

"Are you working for the Master Magicians?"

"No."

Another blow. My sides felt tenderized. Time for a cookout.

"Did the Council send you?"

"No."

"Harder," Middle Man ordered.

"I'm telling the truth!"

Didn't seem to matter. Another two rounds of "who are you working for" were followed by precision blows. Hard enough to hurt, but not break my bones.

Before Buddy could land another, Finn appeared. He latched on to the wrist holding the switchblade, yanking the weapon down. They fought for control as the other three tried to pull Finn away. Boots pounded on the street and strident voices ordered the men to stop.

Middle Man said, "Security." And they bolted.

By the time the guards reached us, the men were out of sight, but they chased after them. Finn's opponent had abandoned his switchblade. I leaned against the wall. The muscles in my legs trembled and I slid to the ground.

Finn knelt next to me. "Are you okay?"

"I'm fine." I held still and tried not to breathe in too deep. "How about you?" Blood oozed from a small gash on his temple.

"Just a cut. You don't look fine. I'll fetch the healer."

I grabbed his arm before he could stand. "No."

"But your ribs—"

"Aren't broken, just bruised. They were professionals. Just give me a minute." All the muscles in my upper body ached.

He settled next to me. "What did they want?"

I repeated their questions. "They think I have a hidden agenda."

"You have worked for the Masters in the past," Finn said. "What did you tell them?"

"The truth. I'm here on my own. Although I don't know why a bunch of fired guards would care if my orders came from the Council or not."

The soldiers returned. Scowls creased their faces.

The guard on the left said to Finn, "They've disappeared. Why didn't you stay behind us as requested?"

"You weren't fast enough," Finn said. "I couldn't let them hit Opal again."

The soldiers grumbled, but didn't argue.

Finn helped me stand. His concern was evident in the gentle way he pulled me to my feet. "I'm sorry for not protecting you."

"Don't be silly. We were outnumbered and those guys…" Reminded me of Valek and his corp. "Even with my sais… Damn. They took my sais."

"At least they didn't take your life," Finn said.

"Thanks to you. How did you find me so quickly?"

"Pure luck. When I woke up, I flagged down a couple guards. We were on the way to the station to organize search teams and we passed this street."

Nice of luck to go my way for once. Finn insisted on coming along as the guards escorted me to the closest station house.

It turned out to be HQ, and every soul on duty descended on me the instant I arrived. Finn stayed beside me as I reported the attack. We remembered a few vague details about the men, but couldn't provide any usable information. As for a motive, I speculated on the recent security changes at the Council Hall.

The ache in my ribs combined with my fatigue, and I fought to keep my eyes open. Finn noticed and offered to walk me home. However, the guards felt one protector was inadequate and I ended up with six escorts.

Before the group would allow me to enter my room at the inn, I had to promise not to go outside without protectors. At this point, I agreed. Finn shot me his slanted smile and mimed riding a horse, reminding me of our…date?…the following day. I nodded and hurried inside. With only a few hours left until dawn, I didn't waste any time changing my clothes. Careful of my sore ribs and wishing for Leif's pain-relieving wet dog potion, I slid into bed.

I'd just finished my breakfast when Nic and Eve joined me at my table in the common room.

"What a stroke of luck," Nic said. "Meeting you here this morning. A happy coincidence."

I peered at him. "Yeah, right. Does this mean we'll be having more of these coincidences?"

He scratched the stubble on his chin. "You liked being beat up? I thought you were smarter than that."

"Yeah, but it was late and—"

"Strength in numbers. Eve, explain it to her while we're walking." He stood.

"You can't walk and talk?" Eve asked him.

"I'd like to stay focused on other…things."

As we strode over to headquarters, Eve said, "After last night's attack, the Captain arranged for you to be escorted at all times."

"All? You know I'm protected in the Councilor's Hall and at the inn."

"I meant on the streets. We are to make sure you arrive at your various destinations without incident," Eve said.

"What about tomorrow? I'm going riding with Finn."

I shouldn't have mentioned his name. Nic's attention snapped to me. "Riding with Finn? What about Kade?"

"Shouldn't you be focusing on the shadows or something? There might be another attack." I appealed to Eve, but she wouldn't help me. "Finn works at Wirral."

Nic's scowl eased. "Part of your secret mission?"

"It's not…" Secret mission sounded so…deceitful. "I'm trying to find information."

"Uh-uh." Nic remained unconvinced.

"And you're romancing it from Finn," Eve said.

I didn't like that word choice, either, but couldn't think of a better replacement. "And it's not very romantic with escorts. Besides, I'll have Quartz with me."

Eve conferred with Nic and they agreed I would be accompanied to the stables, but once I was with Quartz, I wouldn't need their protection.

My sides still ached and I begged off training.

"Not that you need practice or anything," Nic remarked. His voice heavy with sarcasm.

In response, I lifted my shirt up and showed him my torso.

Nic whistled. "Wow. Every shade of red and purple. Colorful."

"Painful," I corrected. "And one jab to my ribs and I'll be screaming."

"So? Don't let me get past your blocks."

"I'm not worried about you," I said.

Eve laughed. "Point for Opal."

Nic remained silent the rest of the way to the Councilor's Hall. When I reached my desk, I read through the file on the hotshots who worked in the SMU at Wirral, looking for any bit of oddness. I reviewed the rookie's... Lamar's paperwork. The only thing that stood out was the verification for him. The letter took fourteen days to travel to Iolite Prison and fifteen days to return. An extra day. Which could be explained by many reasons— weather, problems with the horse, sickness. Except two letters had been sent at different times, and each one took a day longer to return.

As I read through all thirty-six hotshots' records again, I noted their performance on the locked-up challenge. Eighteen had managed to escape their cells, but not the prison. Six had successfully started a black market inside the prison, bringing in contraband goods to sell. Ten had built complex weapons from the standard items available to prisoners. Only two had escaped the prison.

Flipping through the paperwork, I found the names of the two. Finn and Lamar. Finn had been very modest when he'd said he managed. Lamar's file noted he had escaped in three days—the fastest in the history of the prison. Finn had taken seven. Interesting.

When Tama and Zebb entered the reception area, I put the files away. Color had returned to her face and she fired off a list of things she needed me to accomplish for the day. I asked her about taking tomorrow off.

She bit her lip as panic flashed in her eyes. "Come in my office, please," she said. Then Tama turned to Zebb. "You can maintain my null shield from out here, right?"

He hesitated. "Yes, but—"

"Wonderful. Opal, when we're done, have another desk brought up here for Zebb." She entered her office.

I ducked Zebb's glare as I followed her and closed the door behind me. Tama stood near the window, hugging her arms.

"Magic can't reach you now," I said. "You're safe."

"I don't feel protected." She rubbed her hands along her white silk shirt. "I only feel safe when you're nearby."

"But I was here yesterday, and that magician—"

She cut me off. "Yes, I know. I've been thinking about the attack all night, trying to deduce a motive for it. Nothing made sense until I remembered the magician's strong desire to lock you away."

"I'm not very popular with the guards we fired." I debated telling her about the attack, but she had enough to worry about without me adding more.

"This was…different. And *you* saved me. Blocked the magic. How did you do it? You have no powers and you sent for Zebb to build a null shield."

I had hoped she wouldn't recall any of the details of my "rescue." Should I formulate a creative explanation or should I tell her the truth? Tama held herself as if my words could knock her over. She had been lied to, betrayed and ill-used. I would undo all the good progress if she discovered I hadn't been frank with her. She needed to trust.

"I'm immune to magic. That's how I was able to block the attack. But I can't shield you. Remember when I touched your wrist?"

"Yes."

"It didn't work, so my efforts were a temporary fix until Zebb arrived. If the magician had been prepared for my interference, I wouldn't have saved you."

"Why didn't you tell me this before?"

I sighed and explained my reasons. She sank into her chair as I talked.

"And Zebb knows?"

"He figured it out the first day."

"Why didn't he tell me?"

"Because I asked him not to." Before she could respond, I added, "I wanted to keep the knowledge of my immunity from the Council until I decide what I want to do with it. His primary concern is keeping you safe. Since my immunity wouldn't harm you, he respected my request."

"You do plan to tell the Council. Right?"

"Yes. It's inevitable. Anytime I interact with a magician, he or she will figure it out. I'm just waiting for the Council to...settle down and be a little more receptive to listening to me."

She laughed. "You've been hanging around here too long. That was very diplomatic." Tama paused for a moment. "At least my instincts are still reliable. When you asked for a day off, I sensed your presence was linked to my feelings of safety."

"But—"

"I know, I know." She waved me off. "Feelings are not logical, Opal. And I'm not going to let my fears stop you from taking a day off. You need it. No offense, but you look terrible."

"Gee thanks."

"Why don't you take today off, as well?"

"I'm fine." When she didn't appear convinced, I added, "Your list of tasks won't take long. I'll leave early. Okay?"

"Good."

I turned to go, but she asked me to wait. She scooted her chair closer to her desk and stacked a few papers. "Can you take these to the realty office?" She held out the sheets.

"Sure." I reached for the papers and hit an invisible wall. My fingers bent back as I tried to pierce it. The barrier felt solid and hard. Not magic. Magic moved like thick syrup, and I could put my hand in and swirl it around.

"Opal, what's wrong?"

"I think…" I leaned my weight on the invisible barrier. "I think—"

Zebb burst into the room with Tama's two body-guards right behind him. "She's being attacked," he cried as he rushed over to us.

"Relax, Zebb," I said. "It's just me. I got too close."

"Oh." He dismissed the guards, and waited for my explanation.

When the door closed, I said, "The shield must have reacted to my immunity." I thought it through and fol-lowed the logic. My immunity was created by magic. A null shield blocked magic. I couldn't reach Tama through the shield. Another interesting quirk to my new status. Another thing to keep quiet.

As I saddled Quartz early the next morning, Finn arrived on the back of a beautiful golden quarter horse. Her blond mane and tail had been braided and her legs had white socks.

I couldn't resist running my hand along her long neck. "What's her name?" I asked him.

"Sun Ray."

"Perfect." I tightened Quartz's girth strap. Anxious to go, she fidgeted.

"Is she a Sandseed horse?" Finn asked.

I looked over. "Yes."

"I thought they're rare, and only given to..."

I finished for him. "Councilors, Master Magicians and powerful people like the Soulfinder?"

He remained neutral. "Yeah."

"They are." I let him figure it out. When I swung up into the saddle, I was eye level with Finn.

He changed the subject. "Is that a jumping saddle?"

"Yep." I grinned. "Quartz loves to jump. I hope you can keep up."

"That won't be a problem, because you won't catch me." He spurred Sun Ray into a gallop.

To be fair, I waited a few seconds before giving Quartz the signal. Then we gave chase.

My ribs protested the motion, but the pure joy of riding banished my aches, worries and problems. I concentrated on my connection with Quartz and soon we moved as one, flying over fences, chewing up the miles and drinking the wind. We transformed into a combined mass of energy and power, free to go anywhere. Exhilarating.

We caught up to Finn and Sun Ray. He pointed to a forest in the distance. Our destination. With a burst of speed, we passed them and bolted for the forest. Once at the edge of the woods, we slowed and returned to horse and rider. I dismounted and walked beside Quartz, letting her cool down.

Holding Sun Ray's reins, Finn joined us, leading her beside us as she puffed for breath. Her golden coat gleamed with sweat. "I always thought the stories about the Sandseed horses had been exaggerated. Now I'm thinking they didn't quite explain the—" he searched for the proper word "—splendor of the horse. Not just physical attractiveness, but the whole way she moved as if she embodied the tangible essence of pure beauty." He looked a bit chagrined. "Sorry. I didn't mean to gush."

"As long as it doesn't go to her head. She's already spoiled, but she'd be impossible to live with if she developed an overinflated ego."

We entered the forest, following a trail through the bare branches and crunching dead leaves under our boots. A few evergreens saved the landscape from being outright creepy. Only a few days remained in the cold season, but full greenery wouldn't arrive until the end of the warming season.

The gurgle of water reached me before we entered a rocky clearing. A stream cut through the middle, snaking around the bigger rocks. Finn tied his horse to a nearby tree, but I pulled Quartz's bridle off and let her explore.

"Aren't you worried she'll run away?" he asked.

"No. Although, if she chooses to leave, I'd be devastated."

Quartz snorted and flicked me with her tail. Finn peered at me as if my skin had turned another color.

"With Sandseed horses, the horse picks the rider. And if she decides she wants to return to the Avibian Plains, there's nothing I could do to stop her. Well…I could tempt her with milk oats."

She raised her head at the mention of her favorite treat, but returned to drinking from the stream when I failed to produce them.

I scanned the clearing. "Where's the waterfall?"

"Upstream." He removed a sack from Sun Ray's saddlebags and slung it over his shoulder. "Come on."

We hiked along the bank, hopping from rock to rock to avoid the mud and water. A light shushing filled the air and a moisture-rich breeze fanned our faces. The sound grew louder and the stream widened as we continued. Up ahead, a bend blocked my view, but a thin mist floated low over the water.

Anxious, I increased my pace and rounded the corner. I stopped. The waterfall was three feet high.

Finn shot me his slanted smile. "I did say it was a pretty *little* waterfall."

He opened the sack and drew out cheese, bread, two flasks, two cups, a variety of small sandwiches and a blanket. Arranging them on the top of a large flat boulder, he smoothed out the blanket and invited me to sit next to him.

For a moment I stood in stunned silence. This was a date. An actual date. I'd never been on one before. Ulrick and I had started as friends and then took the next step. And Kade… Our initial meeting hadn't gone well, but the relationship grew over time and crises. We never had a peaceful moment. Not even a picnic on the beach.

I suddenly wished Kade and not Finn waited for me to join him. Settling on the ground, I turned my attention to him. We talked about nothing in particular as we ate, but at the first natural segue, I steered the conversation to Wirral. Because this shouldn't be a real date. I needed to learn everything I could about the prison.

Finn answered a few questions, but the gleam in his eyes meant he saw right through me. Eventually he asked, "Is your interest in the prison linked to the attack last night?"

"No. I was just curious."

He leaned back on one elbow. "Even if I hadn't been trained to spot one, you're not a good liar. Your questions about security at Wirral combined with the attack last night, mean you're up to something. You're on a mission."

I tried to protest, but he shook his head. "Don't bother denying it. Since I doubt you're up to no good, why don't you tell me what's going on so I can help you?"

I hesitated. He straightened and said, "I have sources all over Fulgor." He leaned toward me. "What if you're attacked again? If I know what's going on, I can better protect you."

Sticking to the truth, I said, "I'm on a mission for myself. No one sent me. You know I'm not popular among the guards. Remember the drunks at the Spotted Dog?"

"What's the mission?"

"I'd rather not say. Don't worry. It doesn't involve helping any of the prisoners at Wirral."

"Good. Do you expect to be ambushed again?"

"Not with my escorts following me around Fulgor."

Finn gave me a wry smile. "They care about you. And…" He reached for one of the flasks, twisting off the cap. He poured wine into one of the cups and handed it to me. He filled the other and fiddled with it.

Unsure of what to do with the cup, I prompted, "And?"

"And, I'm beginning to care about you, too." He brushed a stray strand of hair from my face. His warm fingers stroked my cheek and lingered under my chin, drawing me closer. He kissed me.

My heart broke into a gallop. In order to maintain the ruse, I kissed him back. After…I don't know… seconds?…minutes?…he drew back and gave me that slanted grin. He raised his cup and stopped as a twig snapped.

We both turned. The four men who had attacked us before stood a few feet downstream. My heart increased its pace to a full-out canter.

"How romantic," Middle Man said. "I hope we're interrupting."

Finn stood and pulled his sword. I cursed myself for not replacing my sais. Instead, I grabbed my switchblade and triggered it as I positioned myself next to Finn.

He glanced at me and asked, "Are you certain these goons aren't here about your mission?"

"Yes," I said.

The four men advanced.

"This isn't going to be pretty. Any chance we can talk our way out of this?" he asked.

I called to the men. "What do you want?"

"You already know, Opal. Don't go acting like you're surprised," Middle Man said.

Finn asked, "Any chance you could just tell them or give them what they want?"

"I'm not working for anyone," I shouted at the men. "Why don't you believe me?"

"Then why are you in Fulgor?" Middle Man asked.

"I told you. For a job. My friends." I almost screamed in frustration.

The men paused and exchanged a glance with Finn. He lowered his weapon and turned to me. "You're either incredibly smart or unbelievably stupid."

A chill raced over my skin. "Excuse me?"

"Somehow you blocked my magic, so I can't read your intentions." He gestured to the goons. "We couldn't scare the information from you, and I couldn't romance it from you, either." A wild gleam lit his eyes. He sheathed his weapon.

I backed away, pointing my knife at his chest. "What are you saying?"

"The game's been fun. And it just galls me to resort to the old-fashioned ways, but, sweetheart, you're one tough nut to crack."

8

My mind reeled as I backed away from Finn, trying to connect him to the four smiling goons. The realization that I was an amateur caught in a professional's game lodged in my throat. And even though my heart pumped for all it was worth, my legs refused to run.

Upstream remained the only direction open. Since Finn had arranged this whole surprise, he probably already had it covered. He matched me step for step until I reached the edge of the boulder. My knife was all that separated us.

Finn moved without warning. Pain flared in my wrist, and he held my switchblade.

"Are you going to cooperate and tell us what your mission is?" he asked.

"I told you—"

"Nothing. No matter. You will."

"Why don't you believe me?"

"I deal with prisoners all day so I don't believe anyone. And, I've told you before, it's part of my job to find out why you're in town. The warden has also given me permission to make sure your keen interest in the

SMU isn't because you're up to no good." He reached into his pocket.

I jumped off the boulder, landing hard on the uneven ground. I spun, intent on running, when a dart pricked my neck. Finn grabbed my arm before I could yank it out. I marveled at his reflexes as my world liquefied. He picked me up as if I weighed nothing.

How could he hold me when my body was a puddle? He poured me back onto the boulder. I sloshed at the edges and stared in amazement at the drippy trees and his gooey face.

Finn settled next to me. "Isn't this better than torture?"

The forest spun around my boulder. His men stretched into long lines of color. "Anything's better than torture." The intense rush of the waterfall overwhelmed my senses.

"Plus you've proven to be very resistant to torture."

I giggled. In a minuscule section of my mind, a tiny Opal was appalled by my behavior. Miniature Opal screamed at me to stop being ridiculous. This was a serious situation. But big Opal was completely at Finn's mercy.

"Tell me," he commanded.

And I couldn't resist. The words gushed up my throat and poured from my mouth, filling the forest until I drowned in them.

When I woke, I couldn't remember what Finn had asked me or what I had told him. My stomach heaved and I rolled over and expelled the picnic lunch onto the ground. Only spotty details of the afternoon remained.

I glanced around, expecting to see Finn and his goons gloating, but the forest was empty.

I lay back as relief then fear then anger consumed me. Did he expect me to ignore what happened? And why did he go to all that trouble? Why did he and the warden care about my reason for being in Fulgor? Did they really think I would try to help one of the inmates escape? The answers eluded me.

Should I tell the Councilor? The thought pumped ice through my veins. His magic couldn't hurt me, but that meant nothing. This guy was out of my league. He reminded me of Valek. Perhaps it was time for me to call in that favor. After the Warper Battle six years ago, Valek had offered me his assistance. Anytime and anywhere, he had said. I hoped he meant it.

I staggered from the boulder. A moldy smell clung to my clothes, and I wondered how long I had been out of it. By the time I found Quartz, the sun hovered over the horizon. Having no energy to face anyone, I headed straight for the inn. I wouldn't tell anyone about Finn. Not yet. He had the warden's permission. Plus he had claimed he was doing his job—my questions about the SMU worried him, but his methods sent warning signals. This time I wasn't going to waste effort trying to solve this one on my own.

In the middle of the night, I woke, convinced Finn hovered over me. I jolted upright, and scanned the shadows. No one. A shudder rattled my teeth as I realized how easy it had been for Finn to fool me and how quickly he'd trapped me. I was defenseless against him.

I doubted Finn could get that close to Valek. Worry panged. Maybe I should deal with Finn myself? Stop it,

Opal, I chided myself. Young and inexperienced Opal would have reported him to the Councilor and tried to convince her of his misdeeds.

Older and smarter Opal called for help right away. This concerned Valek just as much as me. Finn had illegally obtained private information about both of us.

I mentally checked Finn off my to-do list. He had to know I wasn't here to help anyone escape from the SMU. If I avoided him, I should be fine until Valek arrived. I would concentrate all my effort on finding my blood. Then it hit me. I had to assume Finn knew all about my mission. Damn.

My sore muscles protested as I pushed the blankets from my legs. I hopped down and paced the room. I needed a new strategy and fast. Finn could decide to find my blood and use it, or sell it, or dump it on the ground for a laugh.

I reviewed all that I had learned since arriving in Fulgor. The warden, Finn and the hotshots. I sorted through my memories. As the sky lightened with the dawn, I formed the only plan that had a chance of working. I would sneak into Wirral and ask Ulrick myself.

When I arrived at work in the morning, Zebb sat at his desk. For better or for worse, Zebb was part of the team. My background search on him had uncovered an exemplary service record. We still didn't like each other, but we tolerated each other's presence.

"Zebb, do you still have that glass messenger?"

He straightened, instantly wary. "Yeah. Why?"

"I need you to contact Leif Zaltana for me."

Huffing at my audacity, he said, "Sorry, it's for emergencies and Council business only."

"This is Council business. I have an idea about who may have attacked the Councilor, but I need more information."

He hesitated.

"Should I bother the Councilor for permission?"

"No." He yanked the goat from his pocket and peered into its depths. "Leif better have one," he grumbled.

"He does." I had always given him extras.

Zebb concentrated and then asked in a distracted voice, "What do you want to know?"

"Ask him if a Finn Bloodgood was ever a student at the Keep." I waited.

Eventually Zebb put the goat down. "He doesn't recognize the name, but he said he'll find out and get back to me. Do you think this Finn is involved in the attack?"

"It's possible, and I'd like to know how strong he is."

"Anything else?" Zebb asked. His flippant tone indicated he didn't think I would request any more.

He was wrong.

"Yes. Can you contact Yelena Zaltana?"

"The Soulfinder?" He seemed a bit shocked.

"Unless you know another Yelena?"

When he didn't respond, I said, "You made that snide comment about my hanging out with Master Magicians and the Soulfinder, so why are you surprised?"

"I thought you weren't…"

"Important enough to really know the Soulfinder?"

At least he wasn't tactless enough to agree with me. Progress. Instead he raised the glass goat. "I can't believe I'm doing this."

After a few moments he smiled. First genuine smile I'd seen from him.

"She wants to know what you're doing in Fulgor," Zebb said.

"Tell her I'm assisting a friend, and ask her to contact Ghost for me. I need his help."

"Ghost? Who's that?"

"A mutual friend." Ghost was Kiki's name for Valek. Yelena could communicate with her horse, and Kiki had special horse names for everyone. Leif's was Sad Man, and Janco's was Rabbit. I never did find out mine.

Zebb returned the goat to his pocket.

"Well?" I prompted.

"She said he's already on his way."

I should have known. Perhaps our immunity connected us and he sensed when I really needed him.

"Do you think this Ghost can find the magician?" Zebb asked.

"Oh yes. No doubt."

Later that day, Zebb told me Leif didn't see Finn's name listed in the Keep's records. I wasn't surprised. Not all magicians attended the Keep. The Sandseed Story Weavers taught their own children and new Stormdancers learned from the experienced dancers.

Before leaving, I carried a box of old documents down to the Councilor's record room. I had waited until most of the workers left for the evening. Since this area only housed Tama Moon's documents, it wasn't staffed. The rest of the Moon Clan's records filled up its own building and employed five people to keep it organized.

I added my box to a stack before searching for design plans. Long sheets of parchment rolled into tubes lined the back wall, but after going through them, I realized they were blueprints for various buildings throughout Fulgor and not ones for the important structures like security headquarters, the Councilor's Hall and the prisons.

After five such visits, I finally discovered a long metal cabinet hidden under a sheet and under piles of boxes. Its long drawers were only a few inches deep— the perfect size for blueprints. They were also locked.

I pulled my lock picks from the hem of my shirt. Using a diamond pick and my tension wrench, I unlocked the cabinet. Buried beneath detailed maps of Fulgor, I found the blueprints for Wirral. Each level of the prison had its own sheet. I gathered all ten oversize pages and folded them to resemble a stack of papers, which I shoved into a file folder. If Finn spotted me leaving the Councilor's Hall with rolls of paper, my intentions would be obvious.

However, it appeared as if Finn had lost interest in me. He had gotten what he wanted—my reason for being in Fulgor. I hadn't seen him in days, but again, with someone like him it didn't mean he wasn't watching my every move. At least, I still had my escorts and I kept my guard up, determined not to relax.

With all the information and documents I had collected on my excursions, I outgrew my tiny room at the Second Chance Inn. Time for a bigger place with more privacy.

I hadn't planned to buy it. My intentions had been to find an apartment or small cottage to rent. But when I passed the building with its bright For Sale sign hanging in the window, I couldn't resist.

I didn't need it, didn't know what I would do with all that space and equipment and couldn't form a good enough explanation as to why I bought it. So much had happened there, and I had no fond memories of the place. Yet I couldn't walk away and let someone else, probably a saner and more logical someone else, purchase Gressa's glass factory. Mine now. I waited for the feelings of panic and buyer's remorse to overwhelm me. Nothing.

The two-story brick building was at the end of a long row of stores. Its narrow front masked the depth of the structure. Unlocking the door, I entered the salesroom. Dust-covered shelves lined the walls and display cases dotted the floor. All of Gressa's glass pieces had been sold. Since this room would no longer be used as a store, I made a note to buy curtains for the large front windows.

The door into the factory was behind the register. The Employees Only sign remained, but the knob turned under my hand. I paused and viewed the four kilns and various glassmaking paraphernalia. Familiar feelings bubbled, not because I had worked here before, but because the silent cold kilns and abandoned equipment matched my soul.

No hum, no warmth and no magic.

I would eventually need to sell the machinery, but for now I explored the office. Colored glass sheets hung on the walls, and the clear glass desk, tables and chairs remained, but Gressa's personal things and documents were gone.

The upstairs apartment had also been stripped of Gressa's belongings. However, there was furniture in the six rooms, and no one had removed the beautiful stained-glass murals. Their intricate swirls of color captured and reflected the weak afternoon sunlight. Truly talented, Gressa had wasted her gift, letting her ego drive her actions.

Cobwebs and dust coated every surface, and the linens would need to be replaced. I left my saddlebags in the one bedroom and spread out my notes and files on the prison in the upstairs office.

Living here would take a while to get used to, and I needed to change the locks and buy an extensive list of items, yet I felt…comfortable. Strange.

It was seven days into the warming season, and instead of meeting me at the inn per our routine, I had asked Nic and Eve to come to the factory in the morning. They were unhappy with my new location.

"Do you like being an easy target?" Nic asked. "There are too many points of entry, it's too big to guard effectively and the neighborhood is too deserted at night."

"You're right," I said and laughed at his shocked expression. "But I'm not moving. Can you make it safer for me?"

He grumbled and hedged and finally agreed to try. We walked to HQ and joined in with the morning training. While we practiced, a large group of men and a few women arrived. They bustled about the west end of the building, carrying shovels and pushing wheelbarrows.

"Construction crew for the expansion," Eve said.

And jobs for the fired guards. I scanned the workers, looking for Cole's cousin. Even though the prison guard at the Spotted Dog hadn't taken me up on my offer, I had located his cousin, securing him a position with the crew. "Who are the people in the blue jumpers?" I asked.

"Prisoners," Eve said.

"From Wirral?"

"That would be unwise. And I'm starting to think you've been hanging around Nic too long."

"What's that supposed to mean?" Nic asked her.

"It's called thinking before speaking. You ought to try it sometime. It'll reduce the number of bar fights I have to break up."

Before they could launch into an exchange of insults, I stepped between them. "Prisoners from the low security prison?"

"Yes, from Dawnwood," she said. "The ones who have gained a certain amount of trust, and it's also a way for them to give back to the community."

I spotted a few correctional officers. Instead of helping with the construction, the COs watched the blue jumpers. Although they were armed, they were also outnumbered. "Aren't they worried the prisoners will try to escape?"

"A few have tried over the years, but they earn points for good behavior and for volunteering for these work details. If they accumulate enough points, then their sentences can be reduced."

We finished out the practice time with a few self-defense moves, breaking a front choke hold, an arm grab and a rear choke hold. Even though I had broken these holds a thousand times, the response to an attack needed to be automatic, almost instinctual, and the only way to achieve that was by mind-numbing repetition.

Nic and Eve filed into HQ with the others to change and report for work. Since HQ was across the street from the Council Hall, they trusted me to arrive there without trouble.

I picked up my cloak. Instead of leaving, I ambled over to the construction site and stood to the side. At this point, there wasn't much to see. Workers shoveled dirt into wheelbarrows which were dumped in a back corner of the training yard. Others strung ropes to mark future walls.

Bored, I turned to leave and a familiar voice called my name. I grabbed the handles of my new sais and spun around, stepping into a fighting stance.

My heart lurched when I met his blue-eyed gaze.

Devlen.

# 9

"What are you doing here?" we asked in unison. He laughed. I didn't.

"I thought you were in Wirral," I said.

He set the wheelbarrow he had been pushing down. "I thought I would be, too, but they sent me to Dawn-wood for five years."

When I thought of all he had done while addicted to blood magic, five years wasn't near enough. But after I had stolen his magic, he tried to make amends, claiming his obsession for power had driven him to do those vile deeds. He had saved Zitora's life and helped in capturing Ulrick and Tricky. But still...

"Why are you here?" he asked.

The strong features of his face had haunted my night-mares. Just a glance at his powerful build and the scar on his neck had sent me into a panic. Those cold, killer eyes had burned into me despite the distance from him.

Yet, that same face smiled at me, pleased. Humor and kindness radiated from between those long eyelashes and softened his sharp nose. He had pulled his long black hair into a braid. Sudden warmth pulsed through me when I remembered his goodbye kiss.

I snapped back to reality. "I'm training with the guards, keeping in shape."

"I meant here in Fulgor."

I debated, and decided to tell him part of the truth. "I'm helping Councilor Moon."

"As an Adviser?"

"No. Her assistant."

I expected him to chuckle at my new job, but the humor dropped from his face. "You're better than that, Opal. You should be—"

"What? I have no magic. The Council has no use for me." My tone sounded harsher than I wanted. "I'm needed here."

"The Councilors are idiots. Just because you have lost your magic doesn't mean you are no longer valuable," he said.

"I stole your magic and here you are, moving dirt." I gestured to the full wheelbarrow.

"You see it as moving dirt. I see it as a worthy project. A way to help atone for my misdeeds."

"Even after you've spent time in prison?"

"More so, because I would rather be here than sitting in my cell with nothing to do."

I pished. Silver lining and all that nonsense—he could deceive himself. I preferred to look at my situation more realistically.

"Back to work, Devlen," a big guard called as he hustled over.

"Come on, Pellow. She's a friend," Devlen said.

"You know the rules. Go on or I'll report you." He rested his hand on the hilt of his sword.

Devlen turned to me. "He's all bluster, but I don't want him to get into trouble." He grabbed the handles of the wheelbarrow, then shot me a look I had never seen on his face before—vulnerable. "Visit me?"

Unable to speak, I nodded. He beamed and delivered his load of dirt to the growing pile.

"Ma'am, you're not allowed to fraternize with the prisoners. It's against the rules," Pellow said.

I glanced at the guard. As tall as Devlen, his over-size muscles strained the seams of his uniform, but his doughy face contrasted with his solid build. I wondered if the Dawnwood COs had nicknames for their positions, as well. Would Pellow be called a babysitter?

A hardness in his gaze belied his pleasantness. "And it's dangerous. We're not in a controlled environment."

"Is any environment truly controlled?" I asked him.

Pellow conceded the point. "Better to stay away altogether."

Sound advice, yet as I moved through my day, my mind kept returning to Devlen. The shock of seeing him wore off by nightfall, and then I realized my stupidity. I could have questioned him about my blood. He had been with Tricky and Ulrick, he might know if they had saved a vial.

Guess I would visit him after all.

Not quite a strip search, but the female CO ran her hands all over my body—an unpleasant experience. I had already surrendered my weapons, and my identity had been verified. Dawnwood's prison walls didn't press down as hard on my shoulders as Wirral's, and I could breathe in here. The brightness and cleanliness masked the buildings true purpose for a little while, but the double sets of solid doors still slammed with a tone of finality.

Visiting hours spanned late afternoon to early evening each day. After completing my tasks for the Councilor, I had practiced with Nic and Eve and walked home with them. I had waited until they were out of sight before heading to the prison.

Once through security, I was escorted into a visiting room. Iron bars separated the square space into two sections. On my side, an uncomfortable-looking chair faced the bars. But on the opposite side, a sturdy metal chair had been bolted to the floor.

My escort ordered me to sit and said in a monotone, "Do not approach the bars. No touching and no inappropriate language or topics of conversation. Any of these things will result in your immediate ejection from Dawnwood. You have ten minutes." He stood by the door with his arms crossed and his face devoid of emotion. His bored demeanor an act to make me relax and forget he existed so I might blab something important.

The door across the room opened and Devlen entered, followed by Pellow. Devlen's hands were manacled behind his back, but he smiled at me. Pellow unlocked the cuffs, pushed Devlen into the chair and then shackled him to the chair's arms. The guard stationed himself behind Devlen.

"I thought this was low security," I said.

"It is. But you're my first visitor, and they don't know how I'll react. Better safe than sorry."

His first visitor? A pang bounced in my chest. He wore another short-sleeved blue jumper and black boots. A number had been printed across the front of the shirt with Dawnwood written underneath. I noted he'd kept in shape. The uniform clung to his powerful frame.

Pulling my thoughts to the present, I asked, "So if you play nice, then you won't be cuffed to the chair next time?"

"Yes. I earn points for being well behaved." He tilted his head. "I told you back in Hubal I'd cooperate fully."

"I was still having trust issues."

"And now?"

"It's better, but it will take me a long time."

"I'll be patient."

Another oddity about him struck me. "What happened to your Sandseed accent?"

"Gone for now. I already stand out in here so I don't need another…quirk." He leaned forward. "Now, tell me why you're *really* here in Fulgor?"

"My answer hasn't changed since this morning."

"What about your Stormdancer? Does he know why?"

"Of course. Kade is in Ixia. The Commander has agreed to allow him to harvest the blizzards." I spotted the next question in his eyes and explained why I wasn't with Kade. "Cold season. Northern Ice Sheet. Icy wind."

He nodded. "You hate the cold. You use to shiver at night and I'd—"

"Don't go there. Working on trust, remember?" Memories of my time with him when I had thought he was Ulrick threatened to bubble to the surface. I squashed them deep down where they belonged.

"Sorry."

We kept on safe subjects for a few minutes, catching up on news. He leaned back in his chair, looking relaxed despite his situation. And happy. Robbed of his freedom for the next four and a half years, his magic gone and yet he seemed at peace. Was it his Sandseed heritage?

"How do you do it?" I blurted, interrupting his description of lights-out.

"Do what?"

I searched for the proper words. "Be so…calm… so…" I waved my hands as if trying to pull what I wanted to say from the air and shove it into my brain. "Be so…content without your magic?"

He considered my question. "I've lived a year now without magic. A…difficult year. At first, I was furious, and I vented my anger on you. That's one difference between us. You sacrificed your magic. No one stole it. So you believe you have no one to be mad at but yourself."

"But—"

"Listen. How could you be angry at yourself when you did the right thing? You can't. Instead, you swallowed that resentment, and are pretending to be fine. However, that emotion is smoldering inside you, burning a hole in your soul."

"You're an expert now? Do you do group therapy for your fellow prisoners?" Sarcasm laced my voice. How could he know how I felt?

"I trained as a Sandseed Story Weaver. Magic was but one of the many tools we learned to help others."

"That was long ago, before you turned into an evil Daviian Warper who tortured me." A small part of my mind was shocked by my cruel words, another part cheered me on.

But he remained calm. "There's your anger. Good. Now direct it at the proper place. I said you believe you have no one to blame but yourself because of the person you are."

"According to you, I'm a nice, accommodating doormat." I spat his words back at him. No reaction.

"You're tenacious, intelligent and kind, but you're hard on yourself. You believe there was something you could have done better or smarter at Hubal. If you had only been quicker, you wouldn't have had to make your sacrifice."

I sucked in a breath, feeling as if I had been slapped.

"You need to realize you did your best in an extremely difficult situation. Most people wouldn't have survived at all. Your anger is valid and needs to be directed at the men who *forced* you to make a sacrifice."

"Time's up," my CO said.

Devlen said in a rush, "Allow yourself to be furious at Ulrick and Tricky. Purge it from your soul and come back to see me."

"Why?" I stood before the CO could grab my arm.

"Because I will help you take the next step and fill the emptiness inside you."

"How?"

"Like I have. *You* motivated me to be a better person and in the process the emptiness filled. We need to find something or someone who will encourage you to move past it."

The correctional officer hustled me from the room. With my thoughts on my visit, I had no memory of the trip through the darkening streets of Fulgor. Devlen's words swirled in my mind. He had always been an expert at twisting logic and playing with my emotions. If I repeated our conversation enough times, the flaw in his argument would appear.

*Maria V. Snyder*

He had been right about one thing. One thing only. I hadn't been clever enough in Hubal.

By the time I reached home, I failed to find the gap in his logic, and I realized I had forgotten to ask him about my blood. Idiot.

After unlocking the four complicated locks Nic had insisted on installing, I entered the front room. Lighting a lantern against the increasing gloom, I spotted my first surprise. A letter had been slipped under my door. I carried it upstairs to read and encountered my second surprise.

Valek sat at my kitchen table, eating a bowl of stew.

The aroma of ginger and garlic hung in the air. Valek was eating Ian's beef stew, which meant he had been following me and had already visited the Pig Pen.

"How long have you been here?" I asked.

"Hello to you, too," he said. He pointed to a second bowl. "Sit. Eat. You must be starving."

I joined him at the table. He had lit all the lanterns and the room glowed with a cozy yellow light. Heat radiated from the meat, yet the coals in my hearth remained banked. He must have arrived only a short time before me. We finished the meal in silence.

When he leaned back, I asked him again, "How long have you been in Fulgor?"

"Long enough to confirm what you're trying to do."

I acted nonchalant. "Good, then I don't have to explain anything."

An eyebrow quirked. He had darkened his pale skin and was unshaven. His plain and stained clothing resembled those worn by the construction workers.

"Nice try. What I don't know is why you called for help."

"Then why did Yelena tell me you were already on the way?"

"Good timing. I heard you traveled to Fulgor after our chat and guessed the reason you came here. I figured you would encounter trouble."

Annoyed, I asked, "Are you sure you guessed right?"

"Unless collecting blueprints of Wirral is a new hobby of yours?"

I slouched in my chair. "You're right. I encountered trouble. Again."

"It's the nature of this business," he said.

When I failed to perk up from his "pep" talk, he asked, "Remember when I told you I make mistakes?"

"Yes."

"This—" he swept his hand out, indicating the room "—is all due to my mistake in underestimating you."

"Go on."

"I thought I was being subtle when I asked you about your blood. I must be losing my touch." He gave me a wry smile.

"If it makes you feel any better, it took me several hours to put it together."

"I'll hold off on my retirement then." He waited.

I sighed. "When exactly did you arrive in town?"

"First day of the warming season."

I made a quick mental calculation. "A few days before then, I had a humbling encounter." I detailed my experiences with Finn and his pack. "I have to assume he knows the reason for our immunity, about blood magic…everything. I'd like to know what game he's playing, but I can't touch him. You, on the other hand, won't have any problems getting to him." I grinned in anticipation. Finn was in for a nasty surprise.

Valek had remained silent as I talked, staring into the distance. He played with his spoon, spinning it around and around on the tabletop. "I agree. Finn must be dealt with, but not by me." He met my gaze.

"You don't need to worry. He's not in your league," I said.

"Thanks for the vote of confidence. I've no doubt he's a classic overgrown bully. But he's not mine to deal with." His flat tone revealed no emotion. "He's yours."

# 10

"Did I hear you right?" I leaned on the table, propping my elbows near the edge. "Me? Weren't you listening when I described Finn's speed and his goons and that serum? I can't fight him."

"Then why are you in Fulgor?" Valek asked.

"I told you."

"How committed are you?"

"I'm here. And I have blueprints of the prison, files on all the hotshots—"

"That isn't what I asked."

"Very committed."

"Then why are you helping Councilor Moon? Why did you purchase this building? Why are you hanging out with your friends?"

I didn't answer.

"Halfhearted spies tend to die, Opal. In fact, you're lucky Finn decided you weren't a danger to him or the prison. Otherwise, you'd be dead by now."

"I'm making progress. Being Councilor Moon's aide gives me access to data I wouldn't normally have. It's just spying, lying and deceiving others go against my nature."

"Then I'll ask again. Why are you here?" His matter-of-fact tone irritated me, but he continued as if having a pleasant conversation. "Why not ask someone to find the information for you?"

"I'm being smart. I can't handle Finn—"

Valek raised his eyebrow. I hadn't answered his question.

"It is too important to trust anyone else," I said.

"Now we're making progress."

I groaned and rested my forehead in my hands, closing my eyes. Was it lecture Opal day? First Devlen, now Valek. Did I miss the announcement? All I needed was my mother to pop up and berate me for not delivering the wedding samples to Mara for the mess to be complete.

Valek said, "And you're right."

I was right? I glanced up.

"It is too vital to send another in your place, but you lack the skills for this type of occupation. Being able to work undercover and hide your intentions and emotions doesn't happen overnight. You can't just rush off and jump right in." He snorted with amusement. "Well, you can and you did, but that's the fastest way to blow your mission."

"I recognized my inexperience and sent for help," I said. Which brought us back to the beginning. "I wanted you to keep Finn occupied, while I talked to Ulrick."

"A reasonable plan."

"But?"

"Think about it in glassmaking terms. You're given the task of producing a complicated sculpture for the

Sitian Council Hall. It's a difficult job and you're going to need an assistant. Who would you rather have helping you? Your father or me?"

My father. Why? He had over thirty years of glassmaking experience, while Valek had spent one day playing with the glass. So who would Valek sneak around a maximum security prison with? One of his corp, like Janco, or me?

I mulled over his comments. His question about my commitment now made sense. I'd been pretending, playing dress up, and in the process sacrificed my magic and gotten Janco into trouble. In order to do it right, I needed to know things—things only Valek could teach me.

Valek watched me.

"Will you teach me?" I asked.

"You're willing to give everything up?"

I swallowed, thinking of Kade. "Everything?"

"For now. The rest of your life is on hold."

"How long?"

"Four months. Maybe less. You did pretty well so far, considering you're a rookie."

"Then, yes. I'm in one hundred percent."

Valek smiled. "Good. First, send Kade a reply, asking him not to come." He pointed at the unopened letter on the table.

I had forgotten about it. Sealed with wax, the message appeared to be secured.

Valek shrugged. "I was bored."

"Second?"

"We'll review your visit to Devlen, and decide what to ask him next."

"And the rest of the time?"

"Spy training." He grinned.

"You don't really call it that, do you?"
"No."


Kade's sweet letter almost broke my resolve. He had planned to stop in Fulgor on his way back to his home in the Stormdance lands, spending the rest of the warming season with me. In my carefully worded reply, I asked him not to come. Instead, I told him I would meet up with him at the end of the warm season for Mara and Leif's wedding in Booruby.

One half of me expected an angry reply, the other waited for him to show up on my doorstep.

Valek moved into my spare bedroom. We boarded up all the windows on the ground floor for security and privacy, and Valek converted a window on the ground floor into a hidden exit to the alley behind the building. He also rigged a way for us to descend from the second story.

"Always have alternate escape routes. The more, the merrier," he had said.

He brought in various gadgets and weapons and equipment for training, filling the ground floor with them. He even ordered me to fire up a kiln and return to working with glass, insisting the effort of creating would enhance my training.

I asked Faith to begin interviewing new assistants for the Councilor. In the meantime, I continued to help Tama and I joined Nic and Eve every morning. Evenings I worked with Valek, sometimes late into the night.

After reviewing my conversation with Devlen, Valek sent me to Dawnwood for another chat. It was three weeks into the warming season and the late-afternoon sun warmed my shoulders. Fourteen days had passed since my previous visit. Even though Devlen worked on the construction site next to the training yard, I hadn't talked to him.

And since Finn and his goons hadn't shown up at all, my security escorts had stopped. Although I was quite sure Valek tailed me just in case.

A strange little sensation bubbled in my chest as I headed toward the prison. Expectation? Dread? Worry? None of them. It was more like pleasant anticipation. Oh joy.

Some experiences you just don't get used to; being searched was one of them. After doing the entrance dance, a correctional officer led me to a visiting room. I jerked to a stop. No bars. A square table with two chairs had been placed in the center of the small room.

"Twenty minutes," the CO said and left.

Surprised, I scanned the room. The bare white walls appeared to be solid. Except for the door on the opposite wall, nobody could see in. Devlen entered with Pellow a step behind.

Devlen sat at the table and Pellow remained by the door.

I pulled out the other seat and perched on the edge. "New room?"

"More trust," he said. Devlen rested his arms on the table, leaning forward. "You look tired. You shouldn't work so hard."

"How do you know I haven't been hitting the taverns at night?"

He flashed me a grin. "Give me a little credit. First, you're not the type and second, I think you've been playing with Gressa's toys. Have you fired up one of her, or more accurately, one of *your* kilns yet?"

Alarmed, I asked, "How did you know?"

"The construction workers like to gossip. A lot. Their incessant chatter is a nice diversion from the mindless labor." Devlen waited for an answer.

"I just started."

"Good. It'll help you heal."

"Are you going to turn all Story Weaver on me? If so, then I have other things to do."

"No."

"Thank fate." I drew a breath. "I wanted to ask you about...Hubal."

He stiffened for a second then relaxed. "Go on."

I glanced at the CO, then met Devlen's concerned gaze. "I was a...guest for a number of days, and I'd like to know if there were any...extras left." Too cryptic?

A ridge of flesh puckered between his eyebrows as he tried to follow my hint.

"Since I donated so much...money to my host, I wonder if he spent it all or had some left over." In other words, what had Tricky done with all my blood?

Understanding lit his face followed by chagrin. "Unfortunately our host didn't trust me with his plans. He hadn't since I left him behind in Thunder Valley. Remember?"

"I'll never forget." I had thought Tricky, Devlen and the others had been safely locked away when Devlen ambushed me. I rubbed my thighs. Scars from his sword still marked them and my upper arms.

Sadness pulled the corners of his mouth down. "And when he offered me some of your money and I declined, he became even more suspicious of my intentions." He cupped his chin in his hand as he visited the past.

He would figure it out soon. That was the problem

with asking him about my blood. Devlen claimed to be on my side. This would be a test.

Dropping his hand, he said with a sudden eagerness, "That is why you're in Fulgor. If there's money left over, you could—"

"Don't say it." The possibility of me regaining my magic was slim to none. No sense getting my hopes up for a tiny chance. "Besides, I may not have any *legal* right to it, and what if I start desiring more? That's too high a price to pay." Using my blood to gain power could have the same influence over me as blood magic.

"It's a shame you don't have any powerful friends to help you. One that has both magical and political influence would be ideal in this situation," he teased.

I slapped the table. Yelena! She could monitor me and ensure I didn't become addicted by pulling the blood from me if I did. But then I sobered. Since it was my own blood, would the magic work the same? Would I have to inject it into my skin or into my bloodstream?

Devlen rested his warm hand on my fingers. "See? I'm helping you. Maybe you won't wait so long to visit me again." He squeezed.

Fire sizzled up my arm. I jerked my hand away in surprise.

"Sorry," he said, as Pellow stepped forward and yanked Devlen from the chair.

"Time's up, Dev. You know the rules," Pellow said. "No touching."

Devlen resisted for a moment, looking at me in pain. "I thought you were no longer afraid of me."

I shot to my feet. "I'm not. I…"

Pellow shoved Devlen through the door. The CO

glanced at me over his shoulder. "The rules are to protect you, ma'am."

The door slammed shut. My thoughts whirled as the skin on my right hand tingled. What the hell was that? He probably just hit one of those pressure points by accident. I dismissed it.

Since Devlen had no knowledge about the location of my blood, I had, at least, accomplished my task. No need to visit him anymore. I knocked on the other entrance and my CO escorted me from the prison.

On the way home, I felt out of sorts and not happy with the way our session had ended. I wanted to reassure him. Me? Reassure Devlen? I almost laughed out loud, except another part of my brain planned to visit him again.

Unfortunately, time was a precious commodity. I kept my daily routine so I didn't draw suspicion, but Valek kept me busy every spare minute.

He taught me about balance. We performed endless numbers of hand-eye coordination drills. He hounded me about my reflexes until I reacted to the slightest movement. I learned how to use a blowpipe, how to pick complex locks and how to climb walls, repeating exercises to a point where they ran together and my muscles shook with fatigue.

I discovered this type of clandestine operation involved the tools of an assassin. Poisons, curare and drugs like the one Finn had used on me. The goal was to enter and leave without being seen. Too bulky and heavy, my sais would be left behind. Instead, I practiced my aim with throwing knives and darts. Valek drilled me in knife fighting. I added a dagger to my arsenal, since a longer blade would be impractical.

We discussed strategy and tactics until my throat burned. Then he led me into the streets where I learned the language of the lie—the slight glance down, the tension in the lips, the tiny shrug of the shoulders, the hand that tapped nervously against a belt. Body language, verbal cues, and clues—I struggled to keep from laughing when the lies were so clear. Everything I learned to spot, I learned to hide.

During our early forays into secured buildings, my nerves buzzed with excitement and fear. My heart performed acrobatics in my chest. But repetition was the key. Eventually, my body stilled and I could think and strategize without panicking.

A few skills were harder to perfect, and after a particularly frustrating session trying to lie convincingly to him, I asked Valek why he bothered with me.

"Don't you miss Yelena? Don't you have better things to do?" I asked. I could think of a million other tasks I'd rather do. First I would find Kade. It had been four weeks, and he hadn't replied or arrived in Fulgor. I worried about him and about his reaction to my message.

"Of course I miss her. She's in Ixia with the Commander while I'm here," Valek said, leaning his "stick" against the wall.

He used the wretched pointer to tap me at the location my body or my face revealed a lie. The middle of my forehead ached from multiple pokes.

"Isn't being away all the time hard on your relationship?" I asked.

"No amount of time or distance can break us apart.

Besides, Yelena would kill me if I allow you to go on a mission you aren't prepared for."

"Two seasons isn't much time." I sighed. Our goal was to be done with this business before Mara and Leif's wedding at the end of the warm season. And the constant worry about something happening to my blood before I could find it rubbed on my nerves.

"You're making excellent progress. And I must confess I have ulterior motives."

"Really?"

"I'm hoping all this training will be put to good use."

I smiled. "As in, I'll enjoy sneaking around and playing spy so much that I'll agree to work for you?"

"Exactly. Now tell me you love me." He picked up his stick.

"I do love you, Valek."

He gawked. "You do?"

I laughed. "Of course, you're practically family."

He relaxed.

"But that also means I hate you, too. It's part of being in a family."

"I see."

"And right now, I'm leaning more toward hate. Because if you poke me with that horrid stick one more time, I'm going to take it from you and whack you over the head with it."

He slid his feet into a fighting stance. "You can try."

"Gotcha!" I smirked. "You believed me!"

"Well done. Take tomorrow night off. You earned it."

I started to protest, but clamped my lips together. Needing a break, I mulled over the possibilities. I could visit Devlen, or have dinner at the Pig Pen with

Nic and Eve, or take Quartz for a long ride. Interesting how I listed Devlen first.

"I'm glad you came back," Devlen said.

We sat in the same visiting room with the table and chairs, but this time Pellow cuffed Devlen's wrists to the chair's arms.

"I wanted to be here sooner," I said.

He brightened. "You did?"

"I wanted to explain—"

"No need. I understand. After all the pain I caused you…" He grimaced. "I still haven't done enough for you. I don't know if I'll ever do enough to compensate for my actions."

I shook my head. "You don't understand. You surprised me, that's all." Which was true. I didn't need to mention the fire.

"I've been thinking of ways to help you with your… money problem." He turned to Pellow. "Can you give us a minute?"

The CO's face creased into a mixture of amusement and shock.

"I broke up that fight yesterday and saved Sewer's job," Devlen said to him. "You can let me have one minute."

Pellow hesitated a moment more, then nodded. He said to me, "Yell if you need me. I'll be on the other side of this door." Then he left.

"Sewer?" I asked.

"One of the officers. He smells awful." Devlen lowered his voice. "That's not important. Finding your blood is. Here's my idea. I lose points every time I break the rules, and if I become a problem, I'll be sent to Wirral. Once there, I can—"

"No." He wanted to be transferred so he could talk to Tricky and Ulrick. "No. Do *not* become a problem." Why not? I had complained over his light sentence.

"But—"

"They didn't trust you on the outside, why would they talk to you in prison? Besides, I have another way." I could see he wasn't convinced, but the thought of him inside Wirral upset me. "Promise me you won't cause trouble."

"Why not? I can help you. I *want* to help you."

"I need you here." I almost smiled at his puzzlement.

"Why?"

Good question. "Because I can't visit my Story Weaver if he's incarcerated in Wirral."

His confusion turned into utter astonishment. I couldn't erase my statement, and I suspected I had gotten myself in deeper with Devlen. I hoped I wouldn't regret it.

Pellow entered, announcing the end of our session. He unlocked Devlen's wrists from the chair.

"Promise me," I said before they could leave.

Devlen grinned. "You have my word."

His word. When had I started accepting it? Perhaps all those lessons in body language had given me more of an insight. Or not. If I could learn how to lie with conviction, Devlen could, as well. I stopped second-guessing myself. Nothing but a headache to be gained for it.

After I left the prison, I headed toward Justamere Farm. Located on the western edge of Fulgor, the boarding and training stable was within walking distance of my new home. Quartz greeted me at the pasture's fence. A shy Thoroughbred stood next to her. She had made a friend.

I loved the stable. Clean, neat and in good repair, the buildings housed a number of horses and an indoor training ring as well as one outside. With another hour of sunlight left in the day, I decided to saddle Quartz and do a few practice jumps.

If Devlen was my Story Weaver, then Quartz was my best friend. Spending time with her, I let all my worries and frustrations melt away. A creature of power and energy, she flew over the hurdles with ease. I needed to imagine dealing with my own problems the same way. Stay on task, keep a steady pace, launch at just the right time and land without upsetting your stride.

By the time I met up with Nic and Eve at the Pig Pen, the evening rush had subsided.

"'Bout time," Nic complained.

Eve plucked a horse hair from my cloak. "She's been hanging out at the stables." She peered at me. "What else have you been doing at nights?"

"Breaking and entering, petty theft, shoplifting and drunk and disorderly until I pass out," I said. All true except the D and D, and I returned everything I stole.

"Funny," Nic said, but he didn't smile. "Maybe we should switch our schedule and start working nights. Sounds like quite the party."

"I thought you did work nights," I said.

"Not anymore." Eve shook her head. "You've been distracted during our morning training. Nic gave you three good openings to slam him yesterday, but you missed them. Obviously you're not paying as close attention at work as well. Councilor Moon has her own guards now. All trustworthy and with excellent records." She swigged her ale. "We're assuming your attention is focused on something more important. Your side project?"

"Sorry I've been distracted."

"Should we be worried?" Nic asked.

"No. Everything's progressing well." I waved Ian over and ordered a meal. "What are you doing now? Patrolling the streets?"

"Sometimes," Eve said. "Our unit tends to fill in where needed, depending on what's going on."

"Today we got to watch prisoners build a wall at HQ. Here's to another thrilling day on the job." Nic raised his mug as if making a toast. "One inmate actually tried to talk to me. Gasp."

Despite the sarcasm, I sensed another current under Nic's words. "What did he want?"

"He asked about you, Opal. Seemed concerned about your welfare."

Devlen. "That's was nice," I tried.

"Yeah, downright decent of him. Something you don't see too often in convicted criminals."

"Okay, Nic. Spit it out," I ordered. "What's really the matter?"

He bunched up his napkin and tossed it onto the bar. "I don't like being kept out of the loop, and when I meet a prisoner who knows more than I do about someone who is *supposed* to be my friend, I get a little testy."

"He does know more about me than you, Nic. Probably more than anyone except Kade." And Valek. There was no hiding with Valek. Yelena may be the Soulfinder, but he was the Soulseer. "That prisoner was one of the men at Hubal."

Nic looked surprised. "What's he doing in Dawnwood? He should be at Wirral."

"It's complicated, but he redeemed himself in the end."

"Is that why you've been visiting him?" Eve asked.

Alarmed, I asked, "Have you been following me?"

"No need." A half smile played on her lips.

I groaned. "The gossip network strikes again. I forgot you have friends who work at Dawnwood."

"And it upsets them when the Councilor's assistant starts visiting a prisoner," Nic added. "I suggest you stop."

An unpalatable thought. "I can't."

"Why not?" Eve seemed curious, but Nic glared.

"He's the only one who understands how it feels to suddenly be without magic."

"We understand. We don't have magic—"

"And you never did. It's different, Nic." I sighed. He didn't quite comprehend. "Look at it this way. You're a strong man. You can lift heavy things and swing that hunk of metal you call a sword with one hand. What if I took away your strength? You can't carry a barrel of water on your shoulder or draw your sword to defend yourself. Who would you identify with? Your brother, who can still heft a casket of wine, or Eve, who never could, or me, who also lost it?"

The lines on his face smoothed. "All right. I see your point. I still feel like I'm out of the loop. Like one of those neighbors."

My turn to be confused. "What neighbors?"

"The people who live next to a crazy psychopath

and tell us, 'He was such a good neighbor. Quiet. No trouble,'" Nic said in a high squeaky voice.

"How about if I promise to tell you about the bodies buried under my factory *before* security digs them up? Will that make you happy?"

"Ecstatic," he deadpanned.

Eve changed the subject and we were soon laughing and joking. As the evening drew to a close, they walked me home.

"Are you watching prisoners tomorrow?" I asked.

"Sort of," Eve said. "We're escorting a trio from the Greenblade Clan from our holding cells to Wirral."

"Best part is seeing them gape in horror when they realize what their future holds," Nic said. "Some break down and bawl."

"I'd cry, too," I said as a chill zipped along my spine.

"Don't feel too bad about those three. They discovered a way to extract the venom from Greenblade bees. They sold the poison to others. At first, the murders appeared to be accidents. Poor man, stung by a lethal bee." He tsked.

"How did they catch them?" I asked.

"Greed and stupidity," Eve said. "They sold the venom to anyone who could afford the price, without thought to where the murder would be committed. After the second bee sting in the middle of the city where there are no bees, the authorities became suspicious."

"Greed and stupidity are our friends," Nic said. "It's amazing how creative and inventive criminals can be, but eventually greed, sheer stupidity or both will bring them down."

* * *

The next month passed in a blur. At one point, while clinging to the side of a building in the middle of the night, I wondered what the hell I had been thinking to agree to this training.

One positive thing Valek had been right about was working with the glass. It helped me focus my mind. When the kiln had been hot enough to melt sand, soda ash and lime into glass, I gathered a slug of molten glass on a pontil iron and basked in the bright glow. Such potential locked inside just waiting for me.

The orange light pulsed as if beckoning me. *Come on, Opal. Mold me, shape me,* it cooed. *I've been a constant throughout your entire life. I've never betrayed or harmed you.*

Even though I hadn't touched glass in seasons, my skills returned as if there hadn't been a gap. Being able to thumb a bubble for the first time in my life, I crafted a few small and delicate vases. Then I made glass flowers to set inside it. A tiny spark of joy returned to my soul as I experimented with my rediscovered talent.

I also admitted to myself that my mother had been right. My refusal to work with the glass had been moping.

Eventually, my glass pieces filled my shelves and I crafted gifts for others. I made a paperweight for Tama's messy desk. I shaped a fist-sized ball, then filled the inside with a bunch of small bubbles. It resembled boiling water that had been frozen. Satisfied with the paperweight, I cut in a jack line and cracked it off into the annealing oven to cool.

"Solved all your problems yet?" Valek asked as I cleaned up.

"No. But I decided what I want for dinner," I said.
"It's a start."

As we continued training, fatigue settled into my tired muscles, and each exercise sucked more energy from me. At this rate, I wouldn't have the strength to accomplish the mission. And the sense of time running out loomed over me. Each day spent preparing was one day lost. And another day for something bad to happen to my blood.

With only forty-five days remaining until Mara's wedding, my impatience boiled over. "Look, all I need are the basics," I said to Valek that evening. "Once I find my blood, I won't be doing all this sneaky stuff."

He sat at my kitchen table. The prison's blueprints had been spread out in front of him. Valek displayed no emotion. Which wasn't a good thing. I had learned to correlate his annoyance level to his lack of sentiment. The greater his ire, the flatter his tone.

"And what will you be doing instead?" he asked.

I hesitated. "Probably helping the Council."

"In what capacity?"

"I don't know. Whatever they need, I guess." Wrong answer.

"Then I should bill the Council for your training. Because they will not hesitate to take advantage of your immunity, and assign you to jobs that require you to sneak around."

I opened my mouth, but closed it as his stony gaze fixed on me.

"I suggest you decide what *exactly* you are going to do. Indecisive *probablys* usually lead to trouble." He returned to studying the blueprints, ignoring me.

Sitting in a chair opposite him, I considered his comments. If I dug deep enough, I would find the nugget of hope that I would reclaim my blood and my powers. Then I could return to making glass messengers and being able to help a wild magician to avoid flaming out. And if I didn't? My thoughts shied from that scenario.

Valek and I spent another seven days training, watching Wirral and poring over the blueprints. We donned disguises and followed the correctional officers home from the prison. The effort netted us names to match faces, and I identified Finn's goons—Erik, Carrl and Lamar. No surprise that all were hotshots.

As the days passed, Valek tested me on spotting a disguise. It was one skill that came easily to me. With my artistic background, I held the advantage. Even though confidence in my abilities grew, I still worried about the amount of time we used. My sister's wedding was thirty-eight days away and I needed at least eight to travel home. I feared thirty days wouldn't be enough.

My fears turned into reality when Valek threw his quill across the table. I looked at him.

He crossed his arms. "I never thought I would say this, but it's impossible."

My stomach flipped. "What is?"

"Getting into Wirral. There isn't a way in without being caught. We're done."

# 11

"What about the plan to disguise ourselves as correctional officers?" I asked Valek, hoping the last seventy-plus days of training hadn't been for nothing.

"Think about the information we've collected these past couple weeks," Valek said.

I huffed in annoyance. He had all the answers, but he wanted me to puzzle it out myself. Sorting through everything, I recalled a conversation Valek had overheard at the Spotted Dog. "We can't go in as COs because there are too many checkpoints, and they change the password daily," I said. "Someone before us must have tried that trick."

"What about bribing a hotshot to ask Ulrick?" Valek asked.

"Won't work. They're an elite unit. It's doubtful they'll take a bribe, and they're all terrified of Finn." I tried to see past Valek's blank mask. Was this all a test? A ruse to get me to use the strategy I had learned.

"Bribe one of the other COs to get in?"

"No way. They're all terrified of the warden." I didn't blame them. "We could transfer in from another prison.

That would save us having to join the force in Fulgor and advance through to the elite unit." And save years.

Valek suppressed a smile. "That might work. Although the paperwork would have to be forged. It will take a couple weeks to set it up." He glanced at the windows. "It's late. Maybe a better solution will come to us in the morning."

When I woke the next day, no sudden insight into our dilemma occurred. I dressed in my training clothes and joined Nic and Eve for our morning session. I worked self-defense drills with Eve and sparred Nic.

"Damn, girl," Nic said after I slipped past his block and scored a hit. "You've improved big-time, and I don't think it's because of us."

"And you have more confidence about your fighting skills," Eve added. She arched an eyebrow at me. "Night school?"

"I've been working with you for almost two seasons," I said. "Give yourself some credit."

They exchanged a look, and I braced for another round of questions.

But Nic shrugged. "Doesn't matter. It's working and I like seeing this part of you. Reminds me of the Opal from before."

"Before when?" I asked.

Eve shot her partner a warning look, but he ignored her. "Before you lost your magic. When you came to Fulgor with fire in your eyes."

"And it ended badly."

"No it didn't. No one died and you stopped a dangerous plot. I get that you have battle scars and need time to heal. I'm just glad you are finally moving past it. The fire is coming back."

Eve and I stared at Nic in astonishment.

He reddened. "What? I do work in law enforcement. I know people."

Smiling, Eve patted his shoulder. "We know. You're just not usually so…eloquent about it."

Nic preened as he and Eve filed into HQ with the other guards to report for duty. I remained in the yard. The construction crew arrived and buzzed around the half-completed extension. Masons laid bricks and the prisoners mixed mortar, delivering wheelbarrows full of the gray-colored mud.

The sun had burned off the cool morning fog. Devlen and a few others had pulled down the top of their prison jumpers and tied them around their waists. His skin had darkened from being outside, but pale scars on his back stood out.

I realized I knew nothing about his life before he became a Warper. Did he have siblings? What were his parents like? I hadn't even seen him without a shirt. When his soul had occupied Ulrick's body, I'd been intimate with him. But in his own body, he hadn't tried to seduce me, just use me.

This confused my memories of being with who I thought had been Ulrick. Could I claim he raped me when I willingly slept with him? I thought he was Ulrick, but Devlen said he never pretended about his feelings toward me, even disguised as Ulrick. It had been his addiction to blood magic that had driven him to force me to search for his mentor.

*Confused* wasn't a strong enough term for how I felt about him now. To avoid a headache, I returned my thoughts to the present. My gaze once again sought Devlen among the workers. He pushed the wheelbarrow around as if it was a toy, and he towered over most of the other prisoners. He had allowed his black hair to grow long. It reached past his shoulder blades.

I was about to go when Devlen caught me staring and smiled. Glancing around, he wheeled the barrow toward me. I scanned the COs, looking for his ever-present watchdog, but didn't see Pellow's broad shape.

"Opal, is something wrong?" he asked.

"No. Why would you think that?"

"You never stay after the soldiers leave for their shift. Did the Councilor give you the day off?"

"I wish."

He waited.

"I'm just thinking. Something I've been working on isn't panning out like I had hoped, and I need to figure another way." I shrugged, trying to downplay my concern.

He wasn't fooled by my act. Putting the wheelbarrow down, he stepped closer to me. "All I need to do is escape. Easy enough out here." He gestured. No one paid us any attention. "I'll let them catch me and they'll transfer me to Wirral. I'll get close to—"

"No."

"I can help."

"Ulrick won't talk to you. I need to get inside."

The shock on his face lasted a second before he grabbed my shoulders. He pulled me toward him so we were almost touching. "No, don't. I *won't* let you." Real fear filled his eyes.

"You can't—"

"I have heard horror stories about the conditions and

the prisoners. The COs threaten us with it to keep us in line. No. I'll go and *force* Ulrick to tell me. You know he'll crack."

I shook my head. "I *need* to go, Devlen." When I realized he wasn't backing down, I said, "I can handle myself." And it was the truth. With Valek's training, I had an edge.

He closed his eyes as if enduring a surge of pain, then pulled me into a hug. Startled, I froze for a moment before wrapping my arms around his bare torso. I inhaled his familiar scent—a mix of spice and sun. The same smell I remembered from when I had lain with him after... But he had been in Ulrick's body then. Odd.

Devlen drew back to meet my gaze. "Promise me you'll be careful?"

"I promise." When he failed to look reassured, I added, "Don't worry. I have help. I'm not going in alone."

"Who? Your annoying Ixian friend?"

"Yes." I didn't lie. Valek matched the description. He was Ixian and quite annoying at times.

"Hey, Dev, are you going to share?" a male voice asked. "I could use a hug, too."

We broke apart as a group of prisoners approached us—five men with strong arms from working at the construction site. Not a CO was in sight. Figured.

"Go back to work," Devlen said. "Or you'll get into trouble."

"The COs are busy," the biggest of the men said. "Fight broke out inside." He inclined his bald head toward the new wing.

I pulled my sais.

"I didn't mean from the COs." Devlen's voice held a warning.

"From you?" The men laughed.

Devlen stepped away from me. "She's the one you need to worry about."

More chuckles.

He met my gaze, and I knew in a flash what he would do next. I flipped my sais up into an attack position, flourishing the weapons to distract the men. Devlen moved, stepping in close to the big man and striking his throat with the edge of his palm.

Reversing my weapons so the weighted knob on top led, I shuffled forward, ramming the knobs into the closest prisoner's solar plexus. A cheap shot, but it was effective for disabling an opponent without causing serious injury. I turned to the next guy in time to duck his swing, and repeated my move.

In a matter of seconds we had all five men gasping for breath. Devlen's strike to the neck caused a temporary and painful swelling to the windpipe. If his hit had been harder, it would have crushed the windpipe, killing them.

The group stumbled away.

"Will they report you?" I asked Devlen.

"No. But I'll have to watch out for them."

The image of them ambushing Devlen inside Dawnwood caused my heart to race. Unlike the scuffle, which I hadn't even broken a sweat for. "Maybe you should inform the COs or tell Pellow?"

"No need." He dismissed my concerns.

"Can you handle all five?"

He turned to me. "Opal, worry about your own plans.

Not me. If I get attacked…" he shrugged "…it's all part of being in prison."

Which he deserved. Which I kept forgetting.

"You'll keep me informed of your progress?" he asked.

"I'll try." First I needed to figure a way to get inside.

He studied me as if memorizing my face. Those blue eyes with their thick eyelashes used to scare me, but now his intense gaze sent a surge of heat through my body. We had fought well together. Without thought, I stepped close and kissed him. Stunned, he froze, then returned the kiss with passion.

Coming to my senses, I jerked away. "You should go before you get into trouble." Or I do.

"Opal, I'm—"

"Don't apologize. I started it."

"True."

"And don't go all Story Weaver on me, either."

"Wouldn't think of it." He flashed a grin and pushed the wheelbarrow toward the construction site.

Dizzy with confusion and disbelief over what I had just done, I remained rooted in place until I reined in my out-of-control emotions. Didn't anyone see us? I scanned the workers. They appeared to be oblivious, and the COs counted heads, making sure no one ran off while they were preoccupied. All except Pellow. He nodded at me before returning to his post. Damn.

When Nic and Eve left HQ escorting a prisoner, I ducked behind the fence so they wouldn't see me. Did I kiss Devlen because Kade still hadn't sent me a message? And why was I hiding from my friends?

I waited until they were out of sight before I headed toward the Councilor's Hall. My mind swirled with questions with no real answers, replaying the intense conversation with Devlen. He really cared for me. It hadn't been an act. No glib words or sweet talk. He would have gone to Wirral for me.

Then the worries started. What about Kade? I loved him. So why was I kissing Devlen? Would Pellow gossip about our kiss to the other COs? I hoped my friends didn't find out. I'd never live it down. Nic and Eve would—

And then from the chaos of my thoughts an astonishing idea sparked. I had the answer to how Valek and I would get into the maximum security prison.

I reported to work and assisted Councilor Moon with interviews. We had been searching for another person to take over my duties. Now that I had a way to get inside Wirral, hiring a new person and training him or her became critical. Tama wasn't happy, but she understood. She had made such progress in trusting others, but, at times, I found her clutching the glass paperweight I had made for her.

Tama claimed my gift steadied her and gave her strength. "It reminds me of you," she said after the last interviewee had left. "I remember what you have done despite—" she swept an arm out "—everything. If you can face your fears, then I can, too."

Glad she found comfort from my paperweight, I swallowed my doubt that I faced my fears. Seeking my blood felt more like avoiding the fear of being without magic forever.

Later in the afternoon, I ran errands for Faith. Just like every day, I delivered various papers and forms to the other offices in the Hall. Except today I failed to hand over one form. Instead, I slipped it into my satchel. One day's delay wouldn't be noticed. I hoped.

After I finished my tasks for the Councilor, I raced home. When I entered the ground floor, I paused. The lantern we kept lit in the glass factory was dark. It was either out of oil or someone had extinguished the flame.

I put my bag and cloak down. Sliding my sais from the holder around my waist, I left them with my cloak and palmed my switchblade. I stepped to the side, keeping my back against the wall. I waited for my eyes to adjust to the semidarkness. Slivers of sunlight cut through the cracks in the boards covering the windows.

As I strained to hear any sounds over the hum of the kiln, two possible scenarios came to mind if the lantern had been snuffed. One ambusher or more than one. The second possibility jacked up my heart rate.

Remaining with my back to the wall, I moved to the left, stopping after each step to listen. When I reached the corner of the room one of the slivers of light flickered as a shadow passed. Inside or outside? Valek's voice lectured in my mind—assume the worst. Inside then.

I had no desire to leave the corner, but I could be here all night if I didn't check the lantern. The out-of-oil scenario hadn't been dismissed yet. I ghosted along the long wall of the factory. The lantern sat in a stone alcove at the midway point. I reached it.

Before I could check the oil level, the shadow returned, and I dived toward it before it could move. I slammed into a person. Knocking the ambusher down, I pinned the man to the ground. With a move I had practiced a thousand times, I triggered my switchblade and pressed the tip to flesh.

He stopped struggling in an instant.

"Talk or die," I ordered.

He laughed.

I groaned and pushed to my feet. "Did I pass your test, Valek?"

"With flying colors. I especially liked your ultimatum," he said.

"Is this a new twist to our training? Am I going to have to be on guard all the time?"

"You should be on guard all the time, regardless." He lit the lantern. The yellow glow illuminated his amusement. "Practice and repetition sharpen your reflexes to a point where you move without thinking. However, the element of fear is hard to replicate during training. Which is why I make you pick locks on real houses with the occupants sleeping inside and why I will test you from time to time."

"Wonderful," I muttered.

I collected my satchel and cloak and followed him upstairs. When he pulled a chair up to the table full of blueprints, I remembered my epiphany.

Feeling smug, I withdrew the form and slapped it down in front of him. "Here's our way into Wirral."

He scanned the page. "Well done."

"Was it a test, too? Pretending it was impossible?"

"No. It had been impossible for you to get inside the prison." He paused.

I took the bait. "Me? But not you?"

"Correct. I can get inside without donning a disguise or doing any of those other tricks. You would need a few more years of experience and training to do the same."

"Years?" My future life flashed before me—creeping around in the dark, being away from my family and friends—not appealing.

"Yes. And you've been assessing the mission under a false assumption. One I hesitated to correct you about."

I braced for his revelation. "Go on."

"I'm not going with you. This is your mission, not mine."

Two seasons ago, I would have been terrified by his statement. Instead, only a nauseous anxiety swirled. I pointed to the form on the table. "What if I get caught?"

"Mission over. You'll have to deal with the consequences."

Meaning no rescue. More than enough incentive to avoid capture. I tapped the paper. "I don't have the resources to forge that document or the men to—"

"My people will assist you. Just because you're going in alone, doesn't mean I'm not still helping." He smiled.

My muscles relaxed and I sagged into a chair.

Valek drummed his fingers on the table as he considered. "Will you be able to handle the role? You've had some awful experiences."

"I can do it," I assured him and myself. I had to do it. No other options remained.

"Good. You have completed the first level of spy training." He pulled a small box from his pocket and handed it to me. "Go on, open it."

Unwrapping the package with care, I half expected the contents to be another one of his tests. Nestled inside the box was a black cylinder. It was only a few inches long and as round as a coin. A glass ball filled one end and the other was hollow and had a slight lip.

Seeing my confusion, Valek plucked the object from

my hand and pulled on the lip. The cylinder extended into a foot-long tube.

"It's a spyglass." He held the hollow end up to his right eye and closed the other eye. "It brings distant objects closer." Valek gave it back to me. "Consider it a graduation present."

I pointed the glass at a lantern and squinted through the tube. "Incredible. Thanks." I lowered the gift. "Do you give these to all your students?"

"No. Each person is unique. I enjoy finding something that matches each one's personality."

"And how does a spyglass fit me?"

"You're living in the present. It's a reminder that you can see the future if you just point the glass in the right direction."


During the next five days, I checked off my to-do list. Councilor Moon hired a new assistant and I trained her. I submitted the forged paperwork. And after one of our morning training sessions, I told Nic and Eve I would be traveling to Hubal for a few weeks. No surprise Nic grumped at me, and when it was time for them to report to work, I touched Eve's sleeve and asked her to stay behind as the other guards went inside.

"Something wrong?" she asked.

"No, but I wanted to ask a favor."

Eve grinned conspiratorially. "One you don't want Nic to know about?"

"Exactly." I summoned my courage and handed her a sealed letter. "If I don't return from Hubal by midseason, can you deliver this to First Adviser Moon?"

She peered at the envelope. I had worded the letter with care just in case Eve or Nic decided to read it before giving it to Faith. If I was caught, then all of Fulgor would hear the news. However, if Finn discovered me first, I could become a permanent occupant of the prison without anyone the wiser. I hoped it would be my insurance.

"I wish you would trust us," she finally said.

I gestured to the letter. "I am. And I trust you to do your jobs. I never wanted to compromise your positions on Fulgor's security force. That's not being a friend."

"But we want to help you. We don't mind breaking the rules for a good reason."

"Eve, if it was critical to Sitia or was to protect the Councilor then I would have included you right from the start. This is a selfish mission, benefiting only myself. No reason to risk your jobs."

She frowned and opened her mouth as if to argue, but snapped it closed and nodded. "You better be back by midseason," she ordered.

I gave her a mock salute. "Yes, sir!"

Eve hurried to HQ. The empty yard matched the feeling in my chest. Last time I had gone on a mission by myself, I had gone about it the wrong way. This time I would do it right. My plan was based on strategy and planning with the best spy in Ixia and Sitia. I had confidence in my abilities. I hadn't lied to Eve. I needed her and Nic to do their jobs.

So why couldn't I be content? Why the worry? Why couldn't I be like Valek and focus on the logic? No emotion needed. Perhaps it was my lack of experience or the personal nature of the mission.

I pushed those thoughts aside and waited for the construction crew. It didn't take Devlen long to find me.

"You're leaving," he stated.

No surprise he could read my mood. As I had told Nic, he knew me inside and out. He reached. I stepped. Devlen wrapped me in his arms. Resting my head on his chest, I listened to his strong heartbeat.

"If you don't return, I'll come for you," he said.

"Wait until the heating season. I have another plan in place, but it could fall through."

"That's alarming."

I leaned back. "Alarming?"

"It's the first time you agreed with me. You must be worried."

"I'm being smart."

"Good. When you find your blood, you'll need me."

And if I didn't, I'd need him. No one else would understand.

He followed my thoughts. "I'll be here. Regardless." Then he kissed me. Devlen drew away, trailing his fingers along my arms.

Goose bumps raced along my skin, sending a shiver up my spine.

"Do you remember the pressure points?" he asked.

The pleasant tingle fled, replaced by a sudden wariness. "Why?"

A slight cringe creased his brow at my tone, but he gestured to his torso. "If you run into trouble, there is a point that you can reach when your hands are manacled behind your back." Grabbing my hand, he placed my fingers on a spot near his waist. "If you jab here with two stiff fingers, the person's stomach muscles will cramp bad enough to cause them to bend over in pain. It lasts a few seconds. Long enough to follow up with another strike or to run away."

I moved my fingers, trying to memorize the location.

"It's about two inches to the left of the belly button," Devlen said. "Practice if you have time."

"Thanks."

He squeezed my hand. "I'm already missing you." With a slight wave, he returned to the construction site.

Again no one appeared to notice except Pellow. Since Nic hadn't lectured me about my illegal visits with Devlen, I assumed Pellow hadn't been gossiping. I wondered why as I hurried home.

Quartz and I left for Hubal the next morning. Bright sunlight lit the countryside. The cool temperature was just right for Quartz. She stretched her muscles and jumped anything she could find, including a sleeping cow. The half day's ride ended too soon as we approached the small town by early afternoon.

Slowing Quartz to a walk, we navigated the streets of downtown. I waited for my unpleasant memories to attack. The scars on my arms itched, but once I reached the Dolomite Inn, my mind filled with recollections of the generous innkeeper instead. He had endured the invasion of my family and friends for half a season, and had allowed my mother to take over his kitchen.

He greeted me with a wide smile and open arms. After Quartz was settled in the inn's stables, I joined him in the common room. He looked the same. His bushy white eyebrows were the only hair above his big ears.

"There was such a to-do after you left," he said. He flagged down one of the servers. "Bring Miss Opal a bowl of our marble soup," he ordered.

"Yes, Mister Paul," she said.

"Marble soup?" I asked.

He chuckled. "The masons like it when I name dishes after the stones they carve. It brings in more customers and doesn't cost me a thing!"

The waitress delivered a bowl filled with a steaming white liquid. The unmistakable scent of oysters reached me. I stirred the soup with a spoon and discovered long green strings. The soup resembled the white marble streaked with green veins that was mined in Hubal. Every government building in Sitia had been built with that particular marble.

I tasted a spoonful. The fishy flavor dominated. "What's the green stuff?"

Mister Paul wheezed with humor. "Seaweed. But don't tell anyone."

"You're far from the sea. This must be expensive soup."

"Not too bad. There's an outfit down along the Bloodgood coast that found an abundance of oysters and they hooked up with some magician so they can ship the seafood without it going bad."

When I had traveled along the coastline, there had been a number of depressed towns fading into ruins. I hoped one of them had hit the oyster jackpot.

"How do they ship it?" I asked between slurps of my soup.

"Cold glass."

I almost dropped the spoon. "Really?" My voice squeaked.

"Yeah. It's strange stuff. The food is packed into these glass jars. They're cold to the touch, but as soon as you open the jar, the cold disappears." He shrugged. "Took my wife a bit to get used to it, but it works."

"Can I see one?"

"Sure." He sent another server to the kitchen.

The soup felt as though it turned to stone in my stomach as I waited. The woman carried a jar coated with frost and handed it to me. Magic clung to it, but I couldn't figure out what it was doing to keep the contents frozen. A rose design had been stamped into the lid.

"Do you know who is providing these?" I asked.

"The merchant is a Bloodgood. Said his name was Fallon. Why?"

"Just curious." The name sounded familiar, but I couldn't place it. I examined the jar. The cold numbed my hands, but I didn't see anything unusual. The server returned it to the kitchen. I would have to investigate after my business with Ulrick was completed.

"How long are you staying?" Mister Paul asked.

"One night."

His ears seemed to droop in disappointment. I suppressed a smile.

"You mentioned a big to-do after I left. What happened?" I asked.

"Nothing bad. Just lots of visitors and officials and questions. Lots of customers!" He beamed. "They took that Donner place apart. A Master Magician and the Soulfinder stayed in my inn." Pride puffed his chest.

With Irys and Yelena on hand during the search, I was certain they hadn't found a vial full of blood in the Donner factory. Otherwise Valek wouldn't have been asking me questions about it.

"What happened to the factory after everyone left?" I asked.

"Closed up. It's for sale, but no one is interested."

* * *

The next day, I headed north, aiming for the boarding stables Valek had mentioned. Odd for the stables to be so far from any towns. When I arrived at the tiny barn with one stable lad and one black horse, I guessed this place wasn't on any of the official Sitian maps.

When Valek came out of the modest farmhouse to greet me, I asked, "I thought Yelena discouraged these Ixian safe havens?"

"She does. But they are vital to me. And until she has a better reason than promoting goodwill between Sitia and Ixia, I'm keeping them." He glanced at the sky. "Come on in. We have much to do and we're on a schedule."

He led me to a room filled with clothing, wigs, props and makeup. If I didn't know any better, I would've thought I was backstage at the Citadel's theater.

"Sit." Valek pointed to a stool in front of a mirror. He poured water into a bowl and mixed a yellow paste. Turning me so I faced my reflection, he gathered my long brown hair in his hands.

"Sorry, Opal. But—"

"A person's hair is one of the most recognizable features." I repeated his lesson. "Go ahead. Get it over with." I closed my eyes as his scissors sliced through the locks.

As Valck cut and dyed my hair, I avoided looking in the mirror. With my hair wet and wrapped in a towel, he handed me the bowl of dye, a brush, comb and a robe.

He gestured to the washroom, but didn't meet my gaze. "You'll be searched. And…um…your hair color needs to match. You know?" He squirmed in embarrassment.

I laughed when I understood. What else could I do? Cry?

Inside the washroom, I followed his instructions and dyed my pubic hair blond. It would be interesting to explain *that* to Kade. Although... I hadn't received a letter from him, so it might not be a problem. Pain flared in my chest, but I squelched it. This wasn't a good time. I needed to focus.

When I finished, I joined Valek. "Blond? I always wanted to be a redhead."

He smiled. "Red would draw attention. Better to go with a dirty blond...I mean a...darker blond color... closer to light brown." Now he looked panicked.

"You're blushing!"

Huffing, he stabbed a finger at the stool. "Sit." He rummaged for another bowl. This one contained a flesh-colored goo. He then transformed me from Opal Cowan into Rhea Jewelrose.

I believed I was both physically and mentally ready for the mission. But when the wagon pulled to a stop in front of the small farmhouse late that evening, a rush of cold fear swept through me, leaving me weak. I wobbled.

"Rhea, are you all right?" Valek asked. He had called me by my new name since putting the finishing touches on my disguise.

"Fine." I inhaled deeply, pulling in the cool night air and releasing it.

I nodded at the two men who drove the team of horses. One stepped down and unlocked the wagon. It was more like a metal box on wheels. At least the two small windows let in air through the bars. It was empty.

"The makeup will stay fresh for a few days. Don't get it wet. Get in and get out as fast as possible," Valek said.

"Yes, sir," I said.

"And don't get caught. Yelena will kill me," he joked.

"I'll be careful for your sake."

"Good. See you on the other side."

My "companions" wore guard uniforms from the Jewelrose Clan. I studied their builds and looked for the clues Valek had taught me to see through a disguise, but didn't recognize them. A part of me had hoped Valek would use Ari and Janco as my escorts.

I climbed inside, reviewing the plan in my mind to keep from screaming. The door clanged shut and the lock clicked into place.

After a few moments, the convicted murderer named Rhea Jewelrose was on her way to start her prison sentence at Wirral.

# 12

"Transfer papers?" the bored receptionist asked.

I stood between my escorts. They had manacled my wrists behind my back before we arrived at Fulgor's security HQ. Valek's people had forged the paperwork and I hoped no one would discover the fakes.

"Collin," the receptionist called over his shoulder. "Take her down to cell five."

A Fulgor guard arrived and one of my escorts removed my manacles.

"She's all yours," he said as they left.

I bit my lip and rubbed my wrists, waiting.

"Come on," Collin said. He swept his arm out, indicating I should go first.

I glanced at his weapon belt, spotting a pair of manacles.

He chuckled. "I don't think we need them. You're not going to cause trouble, are you?"

"No, sir."

"Good." He put his hand on my shoulder and guided me to the prison cells below HQ.

Unfortunately, I'd been here before. I would count the

number of different cells I'd been in over the last year, but didn't want to start… What? Crying? Or laughing hysterically? Both seemed possible at this moment. I swallowed the knot of emotion.

I spent the night in cell number five. When my prison escorts arrived the next morning, my disguise and training were put to the ultimate test. I tucked a strand of my dirty-blond hair behind my ear. No hair ties were allowed and with the chin-length style, my hair tended to fall into my face which itched from the putty. I now had full cheeks and a pudgy nose compliments of Valek.

"Another killer?" Nic asked Eve.

They stood on the other side of the bars. Eve consulted a clipboard. "Yep. Killed her husband in a fit of jealous rage."

"Really?" He peered at me in confusion. "She doesn't look the type."

"I'm not. It was a horrible accident," I said, pitching my voice a little higher than normal. "I'm innocent."

Nic glanced at Eve.

"He fell on her knife fourteen times. A real klutz," she said.

He snorted. "What is it about the cold season? We get twice the number of murders during those two months." He shook his head and unlocked the door. "Stand back."

I moved away and he entered, grabbing the manacles from his belt. A powerful and dizzying sense of déjà vu hit me and I swayed.

"Easy there," he said, touching my arm to steady me.

I blinked. Just when I thought I understood him, Nic was being…nice? Unexpected.

He manacled my hands behind me and guided me from the cell, resting his hand on my back. I guessed it was safer to have a prisoner in front where you could see them.

As we walked through Fulgor's streets, fear simmered. To distract myself from my impending ordeal, I said, "I can tell you why there are more murders during the cold season."

"Is this a confession?" Nic asked.

"No." One thing Valek had stressed—criminals *always* proclaimed their innocence.

"The cold's the reason," Eve said. "Her husband warmed himself in another woman's bed."

"Not quite," I said.

"Oh?" Eve asked.

"He was in *our* bed when he had his...mishap."

"That *is* cold," Nic said.

"But that's not the reason you have more murders," I said.

"Do tell," Nic said. His voice was edged with sarcasm.

I ignored his tone. "Sunlight. Or rather the lack of sunlight. It turns everything gray. It's depressing and makes you crazy. You'll do anything for a bit of color." I had remembered Kade commenting on this phenomenon.

"I don't think bright red blood is a nice change of pace, but then again my partner insists I'm color-blind," Nic said.

"You *are* color-blind. No one but you would ever match lime-green pants with an orange shirt," Eve quipped.

We remained silent until we reached the outer gates of Wirral. Even though I had been there before, the prison's presence hit me like a physical blow to my guts. I blanched and skidded to a stop.

"I hope you're not one of those people who go crazy with a lack of sunlight," Nic said. "Because there's no sunlight in there." He studied me.

No need to act, I let my fear show. "He killed himself," I whispered.

Eve raised an eyebrow. "Fourteen times?"

"He had bad aim."

Nic laughed. "First time I've heard that one!" He tugged me into motion.

As we drew closer, I asked Nic, "Is everyone in there for life?"

"No. But some are serving life on the installment plan." He noticed my confusion. "They keep getting into trouble and coming back."

The officers at the gate scanned the papers Eve handed them. One of them scrawled a signature and I was officially delivered to Wirral.

"Good luck, Rhea. I hope you survive," Nic said as a female CO led me inside.

I thought I was scared before, but entering the prison created a whole new level of panic and fear. It had been easy to plan this when I was comfortable and free. Valek had been right, actual experience was another story entirely.

Taken to a bare room, the CO unlocked the manacles and ordered me to strip. She stayed and watched. Her face remained impassive as I removed the jumper.

"Undergarments, too," she ordered.

I added them to the pile. She kicked them aside. "Turn around, lean on the wall with your hands on the blue prints and your feet on the yellow prints on the floor. That position is called Secured. Remember it. The guards will frequently order you to assume it."

The blue prints were above my head and the yellow foot-shaped ones were spread far apart. When I did as instructed, I felt more vulnerable and helpless than when Devlen had chained me up. At least then, I had clothes on. And I would rather endure the pain of a pressure point than be strip-searched ever again. The woman's rough hands left no part of my body untouched. Her fingers found holes and creases I didn't even know I had, and thoroughly explored the ones I was well aware of until they ached.

A knock stopped the search. Thank fate.

"Don't move," she ordered.

Voices and a bang. Then another set of hands was on me, rougher than the first. Alarmed, I looked over my shoulder and protested. "She already—"

"Shut up and listen." Her fingers dug into my skin. "We're in charge. You have no rights. You gave all that up when you murdered your husband. So if we want to recheck a search, you'll stand there until we're satisfied. Even if it takes us twenty times."

I bit my lip as I was searched again. When she finished, she tossed a gray prison jumper at me. "Get dressed."

All my own clothes were gone. My lock picks and few other tools hidden inside the fabric gone with them. She hadn't given me undergarments and I was smart enough not to ask.

When I finished, she studied me. Her light brown hair had been twisted back into a knot. She had dark brown eyes and a lean build.

"I'm Lieutenant Cicek. You've been assigned to my

block. This means I decide everything for you. When you eat, when you sleep, when you work and when you get fresh air. Keep me happy and you'll do well. Cause trouble and you'll end up in the SMU with Lieutenant Finn. I'm an indulgent mother compared to him."

The LT led me through a maze of doors and lantern-lit corridors until we reached a set of metal doors. She unlocked them with a flourish and revealed a long block of cells. "Welcome to the Black Widows' Wing. Your home for the rest of your life." Nodding to the correctional officer who sat at a utilitarian metal desk, Cicek pulled me along.

The dank smell of body odor and fear hung in the air and clung to me as I followed the LT down the row. The other prisoners watched me through their bars but didn't make a sound.

"We like it quiet in here," the LT explained. "Outside this wing you can scream all you want, but if you want the privilege of fresh air, you'll keep your mouth shut."

She stopped and opened the fourth cell on the right. Pushing me inside, she slammed the door. After the metallic echoes died, the silence rushed in.

I needed to endure the rest of the day to orient myself and plan. Valek and I had chosen my crime with care. Murderers were housed in two adjacent wings—one for men, the other for women—and one floor above the SMU. However, with all the turns and stairs to arrive at my cell, I needed to be certain they hadn't changed the location. And I needed to make sure the COs' shifts remained the same. Hopefully, the LT would leave tonight. Cicek appeared way too competent for my comfort.

Lunch was the first time I was allowed to leave my

cell. LT Cicek and two other COs escorted all of us—a dozen Black Widows—to the dining hall. The place reeked with an unidentifiable stench that overpowered my senses and made me gag. I forced myself to eat to keep up my strength.

After the meal, we were marched down four flights of stairs to the exercise yard. I scanned the square space. It was nestled in the center of the prison. Almost sheer walls surrounded it. High above, a patch of blue sky let dim sunlight reflect down, casting shadows on what appeared to be a training course with obstacles, weights, a running track and an open area.

As my fellow Black Widows hurried to meet up with friends, Cicek pointed out the armed COs standing up on the third floor balconies. "They have crossbows and tend to shoot first and don't bother to ask questions."

I noticed COs stationed in the yard didn't have any weapons. And now that I thought about it, the LT was unarmed, as well. I asked her why.

Her face hardened. "Even though it's unlikely, there's a slim chance one of the inmates could take our weapons. We're trained to handle ourselves without weapons. Remember that."

Her gaze drilled into me until I nodded. She waved over one of the COs in the yard. His dark skin resembled the Sandseed Clan members, and his bald head reminded me of Moon Man, Yelena's Story Weaver. Moon Man had died during the Warper Battle. A sudden wish for Devlen's comforting presence washed over me.

"This is the Black Sergeant. He's in charge of the yard," the LT said.

He nodded.

"Behave and follow the rules," Cicek told me.

"What are the rules?" I asked.

"Depends on my mood," the Black Sergeant said.

I would have laughed except he didn't look like he was joking. Cicek left and the Black Sergeant returned to his post, leaving me. I glanced at the inmates. All females and only a few used the training equipment. The others preferred to gather into groups.

Leaning against the far wall, I watched the activity. The first sign of trouble was the glances. A large cluster of women kept looking at me. When they spread out and approached, I prepared an escape plan. The Black Sergeant kept an eye on us, but he didn't appear too concerned.

"Hey, new girl," the one woman called. Slightly broader than the others, she was also a step ahead of them. "Did you enjoy killing your husband?"

I smiled despite my rapid pulse. "I think you're mistaking me for someone else. I didn't kill anyone."

"You can quit the innocence act. We know better," she said in an unfriendly tone. She came closer.

Valek's patient instructions replayed in my head, calming my heartbeat. I examined my opponent. A classic bully intent on making a point. Talking my way out of this wouldn't work.

"You know nothing." I pushed off the wall and strode toward her, stopping mere inches away. I confronted her. "Go away before you get hurt."

Her gang members laughed, but she didn't. Perhaps it was because she read the intent on my face.

"Big talk."

As she reached into her pocket, I moved. Poking her torso with two fingers, I stepped to the side as she hunched over in pain. She pulled a weapon. I grabbed her wrist and squeezed. With a shriek, she dropped the shank, and I increased the pressure, forcing her to her knees.

My attack lasted seconds. By the time her gang recovered from their surprise, she was at my mercy.

"Keep your distance or I'll break her arm," I ordered.

They hesitated. Without their leader, they didn't know what to do. I met the Black Sergeant's gaze. He nodded.

"I'll make this simple," I said to the others. "Stay away from me or you'll end up like her." Pinching my finger and thumb, I sent a fresh wave of agony up her arm.

She screamed and writhed on the ground. I waited until she passed out, then released my grip. Standing over her prone form, I made eye contact with each woman. No one challenged me.

Satisfied, I picked up the shank and joined the Black Sergeant. He hadn't moved from his post. I handed him the weapon.

"Impressive," he said. "Too bad those moves won't work for you tomorrow."

I hoped I wouldn't be here then. Because he was right.

Back in my cell, I waited. It occurred to me that most of the time needed to carry out a mission involved waiting. And the inactivity wore on my nerves. Finally, after confirming the LT's departure for the evening and listening for the midnight check to finish, I prepared for my foray into the SMU. Even though I had lost the tools and weapons in my clothes, I still had a few tricks up my sleeve. Well… Not quite my sleeve.

I pulled my jumpsuit down and dug my fingernails into the skin on the outside of my right thigh, peeling away the strange putty Valek used to cover the lock picks glued there. He had matched my coloring so well, two strip searches hadn't discovered it.

On my left thigh, I uncovered a few other surprises. Once all my goodies were in their proper places, I lay on the bed, or rather the metal shelf covered with a thin mat, and sang one of my favorite songs off-key. Happy my voice didn't warble with the nervous fear humming in my blood, I belted out the lyrics.

"All right, songbird, quit the concert," the CO ordered through the bars.

"No." I started the second verse.

She grumbled something about teaching the new girl as she unlocked the door and entered my cell. "Stand up."

I noticed she kept her distance. The Black Sergeant must have told her about my use of the pressure points in the yard. I stood and faced her.

She gestured to the back wall. "Secured position. Now."

"No."

The officer's foot kicked toward my ribs, but I dodged to the side and trapped her leg. I jabbed a dart into her calf and depressed the little plunger, squirting liquid into her body.

She yelped and jerked her leg free, staring at me in horror. "What the…?" Her confusion softened.

She staggered and I caught her before she hit the floor. I dragged the now-sleeping woman over to the bed and undressed her. Pulling clothes off an unresponsive body was harder than I imagined. I tugged and swore under my breath, wasting precious time. The next check would be in an hour.

Once I finished, I changed into her uniform, smoothed my hair and locked the CO in my cell. I stopped at her desk, rummaging for a piece of paper. Folding it in half, I used the CO's keys to access the stairs and headed down to the SMU.

After another set of doors, I approached the main entrance to the wing. A single CO sat behind a gray metal desk. As soon as he spotted me, he jumped to his feet. Suspicion creased his face.

I waved the paper. "Message from the warden."

"At this hour?"

I feigned shock. "Haven't you heard?"

"Heard what?"

"Rioters attacked the Councilor's Hall. They're holding the Councilor for ransom."

A slight hesitation. "And?"

"The Fulgor security force is worried they will demand certain prisoners to be released. The details are all here..." I stepped closer.

He reached for the paper and I pricked him with a dart.

"Hey!" Grabbing my arms, he dragged me toward him. "What did...?" He swayed.

I steadied him. "Sit down before you fall down."

He plopped into the chair and slumped over the desk, sound asleep. I silently thanked Valek's fast-acting sleeping juice. The last barrier between me and Ulrick remained. This would be difficult.

The steel gates into the SMU could only be opened from inside. I pounded on them. After a few moments, a small panel slid to the side.

A hotshot peered through the opening. "What?"

Relief that it wasn't Finn or one of his goons spread through me as I pointed to the side. "Your man is sick, and he can't go to the infirmary by himself. I'd take him for you, but he won't leave his post unmanned."

"What are you doing up here?"

"Delivering a message." I held up my paper and explained about the Councilor.

"What's the word?" he asked.

"Scratched." One of the benefits of the silence rule in the Black Widows' wing—learning today's password.

The panel slid back into place. I crossed my fingers as my heart did calisthenics. A series of snaps and clicks sounded before the gate swung out. The hotshot nodded to another behind him and glanced at the sleeping man. He sighed. "Deggan, stay in the unit. I'll cover until a replacement shows." He cleared the threshold. "Let me see the message."

When I handed the paper to him, I poked a dart into his hand. He flinched.

"Sorry, my ring must have—"

He turned away. "Deggan, lock down!" he yelled before collapsing onto the floor.

Damn. I jumped over him and rushed Deggan, who tried to close the gate. Tackling him to the ground, I jabbed his leg. Not the smoothest move, but it worked. He remained still. Another victim of Valek's juice. Two darts left.

I tried to drag the men into the SMU wing to hide them, but they were too heavy. Plus the lack of time. Once my CO was discovered missing, escaping the prison would be impossible. Right now, I had a fifty-fifty chance.

The cells in this wing had no bars. They had solid metal walls, and steel doors with slots for food trays and a window like the one on the gate. Only a couple lanterns had been lit.

Hurrying through the wing, I counted cells. From various overheard conversations, Valek had determined Ulrick's location. Although, considering his recent comment about being able to get into the prison, I wondered if he'd already been inside.

I skidded to a stop in front of number ten. Sliding back the cover on the window, I peered into the cell. Darkness spilled out between bars. I would have to trust Valek.

"Ulrick," I whispered through the opening. Nothing. "Ulrick, it's me, Opal," I called louder.

A rustling sound reached me and Ulrick appeared. "Opal?"

He met my gaze and I gasped. Haggard, hollow-eyed and looking years older, he blinked at me without emotion. The fire gone from his green eyes.

"Nice try, Finn," he said. "But you don't even look like her." He sighed. "Which means you lied about seeing her in Fulgor." He turned away.

"Wait! It's me. I'm disguised as a CO."

Returning to the window, he said, "That's a new one. At least you got the voice right."

"Ask me something only I would know."

"Nope. Not playing your games anymore, Finn."

Frustrated, I peeled the putty from my face, yanking off the padding around my nose. "It's me!"

He considered. "What are seeds?"

"Bubbles in the glass."

"Too easy. What killed the leader of the Storm Thieves?"

"I did."

An incredulous laugh burst from his lips. "It *is* you! Only Opal would blame herself and not the Greenblade bee for his death." Then he sobered. "Why are you here? Did you come to gloat?"

"Of course not. I need information."

His eyes narrowed. "Why would I tell you anything? You're the reason I'm here."

Sudden fury welled. "No, I'm not," I snapped. "Your own selfish actions led you here."

"You stole my magic!"

"It wasn't all yours. Most of it was mine, and you left me with no other choice than to suck us both dry!" Anger burned through me and I didn't care if I shouted. "Take responsibility for your own actions, Ulrick. Admit your mistakes and make amends."

"Like Devlen? Don't tell me he's still conning you? How stupid can you be?"

"I'm smart enough to avoid the lure of blood magic. It made you greedy for power." Nic's comment about greed and stupidity being the downfall of many criminals replayed in my mind.

"You think you can resist blood magic? Overcome the addiction?" Ulrick asked.

"Of course. And I don't have the time to argue with you. I need—"

"I know what you came for, Opal. What do I get in return?"

"I can appeal to Councilor Moon and the rest of the Sitian Council to *not* execute you." My offer had an unexpected effect.

Instead of looking relieved, Ulrick blanched. "No deal. I'd rather die than be in this hell for the rest of my life."

After spending a day here, I understood. "How about if I promise to inform the Councilor about the horrid conditions?"

"Can you kill Finn for me?"

"Tempting, but no. I could try to get him fired."

"Not enough." He considered. "And Miss Goody-Goody wouldn't help me escape. Would she?"

"No."

"You don't have much to offer." He stared at me a moment. "I wasn't planning on telling you, but I changed my mind. Since Miss High and Mighty thinks she can resist the lure of blood magic, I'm going to tell you where you can find your blood." Ulrick explained where he hid it. "The rules still apply whether the blood is yours or not. You'd better talk to the Councilor about the conditions in here before you become an inmate. See you later, Opal." Ulrick retreated into the darkness of his cell.

I slid the window shut as a variety of emotions twirled in my chest. Relief mixed with fear—he could be right about becoming addicted even if I'd use my own blood. I shoved my concerns aside. It was time to escape.

A good plan, except a sizzling whoosh sounded as all the lanterns blazed at once. Squinting into the sudden brightness, I froze.

Finn and his goons—Erik, Carrl and Lamar—stood between me and freedom.

# 13

Not waiting for Finn to make the first move, I threw a dart at him, aiming for his neck. He deflected the weapon with his magic, sending it skittering along the wall before it landed on the ground.

He advanced. "What a lovely reunion. I think I might cry." Finn mimed wiping tears as he sniffed. "I knew that rat would squeal to you. He resisted my torture and my tricks, guarding his precious little secret. Even my truth serum failed to work. Unfortunately it's a hit-or-miss type of drug. You babbled on and on about searching for your blood and about your immunity to magic, but I couldn't get you to tell me *how* you managed to become immune."

"Why do you care about my blood?" I asked.

"It's very valuable. Gentlemen, please escort Miss Rhea Jewelrose back to her cell."

In the narrow hallway, only two men could rush me. Though they were skilled fighters, I jabbed Erik with my last dart and held off Carrl with a flurry of palm heel strikes until Lamar joined in. Even with my intensive training, the two of them overpowered me. Held between them, I struggled to no avail. They anticipated all my self-defense techniques, rendering them useless.

"Someone's been practicing. Bravo," Finn said. He picked the dart from the floor. "A sleeping potion?" he asked me, but didn't wait for an answer. "I must say I'm impressed with your efforts. When you left Fulgor, I set a watch for you, but I expected you to get caught sneaking in."

"Councilor Moon knows I'm here."

He smiled, but the humor failed to reach his eyes. "No she doesn't. Nor will she. Whatever insurance you left behind will be intercepted before it arrives. Didn't her new assistant seem too qualified?"

"But her background—"

"Impeccable." He cocked his head. "Are you going to cooperate or do I need to incapacitate you?" Finn raised the dart.

Horror swept through me at the thought of being unconscious. "No need for that."

"Secure her hands," Finn ordered.

On my right, Lamar released his grip. With Finn aiming the dart only a few feet away, I couldn't resist. Lamar pulled my arms behind me and nausea bubbled in my throat. He snapped the cuffs on my wrists, but he didn't tighten them. Then he slipped a round object into my palm. Trying to keep the surprise from showing on my face, I automatically fisted it, recognizing the shape.

Finn stepped to the side as my escorts guided me past. They would never be this close again. It was now or never. I held my breath, yanked my arm from the loose cuff and from Lamar's weak grip and flung the glass ball to the floor.

It shattered on impact, releasing a bright flash and

a noxious gas. Finn and Carrl coughed and sputtered and were soon prone. It was one of Valek's toys, but it had been too big to conceal on my body. I met Lamar's cocky gaze. Despite the gas, he remained standing.

Several clues clicked together and I groaned. "I shouldn't have worried," I said, being careful not to breathe in. "It was a classic damsel-in-distress situation. Who else would save me?"

He grinned. "Better hurry, Opal. I can't reveal myself. This guy is brutal." He nodded at Finn. "And hard to figure."

"Thanks, Janco. Guess you shouldn't have pissed Valek off or you would have gotten Pellow's—or should I say—Ari's cushy job at Dawnwood."

"And be bored? No thanks." He shooed me away and crouched in the fumes, inhaling deep breaths. By the time I reached the door, he was unconscious, as well.

The outer entrance to the wing was quiet, but when I slipped into the stairwell, the shouts and pounding of boots echoed below. My exit route was blocked. I had spent too much time with Ulrick and Finn. Panic rolled through me. I allowed the fear to crash and settle before reviewing my options. It was time for my backup plan.

With no way to get past the commotion below, I went up instead. I reached the warden's office without incident. The lack of COs meant the warden wasn't inside. Good. Using my lock picks on the four complex locks, I eventually let myself into his office and re-locked the door.

Exhausted, I collapsed on his desk chair, wondering how long it would take the COs to inform the warden of my escape. I lounged back and put my feet on his desk to appear casual. My heart, though, didn't get the whole acting relaxed order and insisted on knocking against my breastbone.

When the distinct sound of a key shoved into a lock reached me, my heart jumped. I chanted the word *relax* in my mind, but I still froze with fear when the warden entered his office. His diatribe trailed off as he noticed me. The COs who had been enduring a dressing-down gasped.

For a moment we all just stared at each other. Then the officers moved toward me, splitting up to go around each side of the desk.

"Stop," the warden ordered.

They halted mere feet from me. Furious glares promised I would pay dearly for my escape.

"Is this the prisoner you seek?" the warden asked.

"Yes, sir," the guard on the left said.

"You're certainly a bold one," the warden said to me.

"I just did what you wanted, Grogan."

He glowered, and I suppressed the urge to sink under the desk.

"Explain," he ordered.

"You issued me a challenge to find anything wrong with your officers or prison. I sneaked in disguised as a prisoner and escaped. I'd say that qualifies as something wrong."

"You didn't fully escape," he said.

"Doesn't matter. You said anything." I leaned back in his chair, exaggerating the motion. "Besides, if I wanted to leave, I could have ambushed you when you entered your office and used you to escape."

He laughed. "Wouldn't work. We all know our lives are forfeit if we're taken hostage."

I shrugged. "I still managed to get into the SMU before coming up here. And I found other problems."

As I talked, color rushed into his face. "Get Finn. Now," he ordered the COs.

They bolted.

Not good. I swallowed. "Finn isn't reliable. He's been torturing the SMU prisoners."

"He's my right-hand man. I'm sure he can explain your allegations."

I stood. "They're not allegations. They're facts."

We glared at each other until one of the COs burst into the room, panting.

"He's…gone, sir." The guard motioned to me with his hand. "She was…in the wing…knocked every… one out."

Lamar and Carrl entered behind the guards. The gas in the glass ball didn't last near as long as the sleeping juice.

Grogan aimed his anger at them. Carrl blanched, but Lamar…Janco kept his face neutral. Although a spark of humor flashed in his eyes when he met my gaze.

"Where is Finn?" the warden asked them.

"She must have done something to him," Carrl said.

"I'm impressed that you think I'm strong enough to move an unconscious man."

"When we woke, sir, Finn was not among us," Janco said. "I believe he was working here under false pretenses."

And then it hit me. Finn had overheard Ulrick and knew where to find my blood. I caught Janco's attention. He understood my sudden need to leave.

"Why wasn't I informed?" Grogan bellowed.

"Truthfully, sir, Finn is scarier than you," Janco said.

Carrl nodded in agreement, but he still appeared nervous. "Do you think he's gone for good?"

"If not, he will be," Grogan promised.

I edged toward the door.

"Should I escort our…guest out?" Janco asked.

"Not until you get details on how she managed this…" He swung his arm wide, indicating me and the room. "I want a full report on my desk in one hour."

"Yes, sir," Janco snapped.

He held my arm and we left. The warden's loud orders to Carrl followed us until the door closed.

Janco and I raced down the stairs.

"Think you'll have time for that report?" I asked.

"Doubtful. Too bad, I *live* to write reports."

Unfortunately, we were stopped a few times by COs. Janco informed them the prisoner had been captured and to return to their regular duties. Even though I wore a CO uniform, a few squinted at me with suspicion, but Janco was a hotshot and therefore outranked them. Handy.

We reached the street and ran to the nearest stables.

"How long?" I asked.

"Finn has about an hour head start."

Damn. We arrived at the stables and roused the owner, renting his two fastest horses. The man would have an interesting tale to tell.

As the horses chewed up the miles to Hubal, the sun rose. We didn't slow when we reached the downtown. People scattered and cursed at us. The trip to Ulrick's glass factory located in the woods passed in a blur. We rushed around the back of the building and dismounted. The sandpile had been removed, but evidence of where it had been remained along with more recent activity.

My world tilted and I sank to my knees. Dirt piled next to a fresh hole in the ground. My blood was gone.

Janco crouched near the hole. He scooped a handful of dirt and sniffed it. Scenting the wind as if he were a dog, he scanned the area. He put a finger to his lips and drew a dagger from his boot.

I jumped to my feet and followed him toward the abandoned factory. The back door was locked. Janco pointed and I popped the lock in a few seconds with my picks. Impressed, he raised his eyebrows. My speed had improved while working with Valek.

Turning the knob, I eased open the door. Janco rushed in without making a sound. I stayed right behind him. We stopped in the main area. Finn stood in the middle of the empty room with a sword in his right hand and a large glass bottle filled with a bright red liquid in his left. They had drained more blood than I thought. From the color, I knew the blood had been preserved by magic.

"Lamar, how very unexpected," Finn said with a disapproving tone.

Magic brushed us. Janco flinched, but held steady.

"Even now I can't sense your deception. No matter. We've already proven you're no match for me."

Janco grinned. "It's never wise to beat your boss. Good thing you're not my boss anymore."

I stifled a laugh. Not only had he used the word *wise,* but Janco's current position in Ixia had been gained by beating a succession of his superior officers.

"Give Opal her bottle," Janco said.

"No. Someone is willing to pay an outrageous amount of gold for this."

"Who?" I asked.

"Someone who hates you very much."

Janco glanced at me. "That narrows it down to half of Sitia."

"Not funny." Because if I considered the people who were upset and inconvenienced due to the loss of my glass messengers, he might be right. "Hand it over, Finn."

"Seems we're at an impasse," Finn said. "If we fight, or if you use one of your darts or that nifty gas ball, I might drop the bottle, spilling your blood. You'll have to decide if you want to risk it or not."

"All right. How much?" I asked.

Finn jerked with surprise, but recovered. "You can't afford it."

"Try me."

He peered at me as if assessing my net worth. "Did the Council let you keep the diamonds from here?" He pointed down.

"Yep. I'm richer than Vasko Cloud Mist."

Finn flinched at the name. "Doubtful."

"How much?" I asked again. Would I be willing to give him all my money for that bottle? Yes.

He hesitated.

"Despite his claims, Finn's not doing this for the money, Opal," Janco said.

Janco was right. Better to spill my blood than for it to get into the wrong hands. "Janco, why don't you entertain Finn with one of your rhymes?"

"My pleas—" Janco froze.

I reached and encountered a bubble of magic around him.

"I'm not in the mood for a fight," Finn said. He

sheathed his sword and yanked out a blowgun. Loading the pipe without rushing, he was confident I wouldn't be a problem.

"Too bad," I said as I snatched Janco's dagger.

Finn blocked my first attack with the blowgun. I parried and my blade hacked chunks from the wooden tube as he used it to protect himself. He backed up as I advanced, pressing my advantage.

"Well done, Opal," he said when the dagger sliced his blowgun into two.

I stepped closer and he chopped my wrist. He used this move before to the same effect, stunning my hand with the edge of his palm and taking the weapon from me. At least this time, I saw it happening. Didn't help, but it was progress.

Finn touched the tip of the dagger to my neck. "I'm growing quite fond of you. My patron paid for your blood, but I imagine you would bring a higher price. Or perhaps you would pay me to release you?"

Oh no. Not this again. I leaned back away from the blade and kicked forward, hitting him in the ribs. Not hard, as I was unbalanced, but enough to distract him while I shuffled out of reach. He surrounded me with a thick bubble of magic. It weighed me down and slowed my movements. Holding a dart, Finn stalked me.

Frantic, I splayed my hands and without piercing the bubble of magic I pushed it away from me before Finn could aim. It moved. I did it again until I was free.

"Unbelievable," Finn said. The bubble dissolved. "You have an affinity with magic, but it can't affect you…I wonder if your immunity is fueled by magic."

I rushed him to keep him from making that last logical connection and slammed into an invisible barrier.

Too late. He figured it out and erected a null shield. Magic couldn't pierce it. Stunned, I blinked at an ecstatic Finn. He held his hand out and the barrier forced me back until the shield trapped me in a corner.

"A null shield," Finn said in amazement. "I love the irony! This is going to make my life so much easier." He threw the dart.

I couldn't move my arms to block it. Hitting my shoulder, the drug worked fast. The room spun into darkness.

"Opal?"

An ungentle nudge. I swatted at the disturbance.

"Wake up, or I'm leaving you here," Janco grumped.

I groaned. My head ached and the floor swayed.

"Killer hangover, isn't it? Finn used the hard stuff." Janco pulled on my arm. "Come on. It's getting dark."

He helped me to my feet. I glanced around the abandoned factory and I remembered. "Finn? My blood?" Relief spiked as I realized he hadn't taken me.

Janco grimaced. "Gone. After he knocked you out someone called from outside. He jabbed me and left. When I woke, I tracked him to the road, but once he reached it, I've no idea which way he went." He gestured to the windows. "We were asleep for hours and he stole one of our horses. I had to chase down the other."

We trudged to the Dolomite Inn, leading the remaining horse. Even Mister Paul's delighted welcome couldn't dispel the gloom that had settled on us. The thought of oyster soup turned my stomach, but Janco enjoyed it while I ate bread and a few mouthfuls of beef.

My thoughts lingered on my failure. All those

months of training, planning and sacrifice for naught. Nothing for me. Finn made out well. I scowled.

"Something wrong with your dinner?" Janco asked. He had removed his disguise, revealing his thin face and scarred ear.

"The food's fine. My companion needs to start explaining why I had to endure the whole prisoner experience when he was already one of the hotshots?"

"Think about it, Opal. You already know the answer," Valek said from behind me. He and Ari joined us.

"Wonderful," I muttered. "The gang's all here." I eyed Ari's white-blond hair. He'd also ditched his disguise. "Won't Devlen miss his buddy, Pellow?"

Ari shrugged. "He's made friends with half the COs in the joint."

I wanted to savor my foul mood, to let it ferment and turn into an all-out temper tantrum. But these men didn't act without a plan and I should focus on the positive.

"Finn's truth serum didn't work, and Janco couldn't get Ulrick to talk? So you needed me," I said.

Valek nodded in encouragement.

"Why didn't you tell me he was there?" I asked. No one answered, letting me puzzle it out on my own. I could have been captured and forced to expose Janco, ruining months of undercover work. Plus my actions in the prison might have been different if I knew Janco was there. Working under the impression I was on my own, I couldn't relax or be lazy. I grudgingly agreed with his strategy.

As Ari ordered enough food to feed the whole table, I reviewed all that I had learned. I should have spotted Janco when I read through the hotshots' files. Who else would escape from Wirral in record time? He even beat a magician.

After the server left an array of steaming plates, I said, "You had Janco in place before talking to me about my blood back in Booruby. Why?"

"They used blood magic," Valek said. "And could again. I didn't trust the Sitian Council to deal with them properly or in a timely manner."

"You were going to assassinate them?" I gaped at Valek. "Until you found out about my blood, then decided not to."

"It is always a good idea to wait and watch. Unless Yelena is around at the time of death, it's hard to interrogate someone once he's dead."

I looked at Janco. He didn't strike me as the assassin type. "Could you…?"

"No," Valek answered for him. "That's *my* job. He was there to gather information only."

Which reminded me. "How did he manage to fool Finn? He's a powerful magician."

Janco pulled a necklace from under his shirt. A large round pendant hung from the chain. He took it off and handed it to me. The white circle was sticky with magic.

"Ivory?" I asked.

"No. Bone." Janco looked queasy.

"Animal?"

His grimace answered my question. Not animal. Human. I set the pendant down carefully. "How?"

"Yelena found a…volunteer, willing to help disguise Janco's real thoughts," Valek said.

"A soul." I swallowed. Yelena had channeled a person's soul into the bone pendant. It was amazing and creepy at the same time.

"Lamar Krystal died in the line of duty," Janco recited as if from memory. "A prisoner in Compton killed him with a shank. Yelena found him wandering in the shadow world unable to find peace."

I studied my friend. Janco hated magic and yet he had lived with a soul near his heart for seasons.

"And the poor guy hasn't found much peace hanging out with Janco," Ari said, breaking the sober mood.

"If he'd been with you, he'd have been bored to death," Janco countered.

"That's impossible. He's already dead," Ari said.

"Souls can cease to exist, and therefore die," Janco said.

Ari laughed. "That's ridiculous."

I tuned out their argument over dying souls. My thoughts returned to Valek's earlier comment about assassination being his job. Even though the mission hadn't gone as planned, Ulrick had revealed the location of my blood.

Cold fingers of realization touched me. There was no reason for Valek to wait any longer to go through with his original strategy to assassinate them.

I met Valek's flat gaze. He'd watched me while I had sorted through the information.

"Wait. Please," I said to him. My response surprised me.

He didn't react. "By the time the Council decides to do the right thing, more damage could be done."

"But—"

"We've shown the prison is easily infiltrated."

"But—"

"The officers can be compromised."

"But—"

"We were lucky Finn only desired your blood and didn't want to learn how to perform blood magic. We won't be so lucky next time."

"It's not your decision," I shouted.

Ari and Janco ceased their bickering.

Unperturbed, Valek said, "I disagree."

"Besides," I said into the ensuing silence, "they'll need to be incarcerated in glass like the Warpers from before. You'll need Yelena."

"No they won't. They have no magic. The Warpers still had the magic they were born with. If you had discovered your siphoning powers back then, we wouldn't have needed those glass prisons at all."

I wilted. Valek's argument made sense when viewed with cold logic, but on the emotional level, it was all wrong. Then horror swept through me.

"What about Devlen? Him, too?" I asked.

Valek glanced at Ari.

"No," Ari said. "He's committed to making amends."

I inhaled as powerful relief welled. "So could Ulrick and the others. You need to give them a chance."

Just as fast as it had come, the feeling of respite fled when the three men exchanged a look. I stood on shaky legs. "It's too late. Isn't it?"

"Your escapades in Wirral provided the perfect distraction," Valek said. "They didn't suffer, and I left evidence pointing to Finn as the assassin."

As all sensation fled my body, I gaped at Valek. "All of them?"

"No reason to kill Gressa and Akako. They don't know how to use blood magic."

A minor concession. My mind couldn't steer away from the knowledge Valek had used me to kill five men.

My escapades had allowed him to... Grief flooded. Poor Ulrick. I had hoped he would... What? See the error of his ways?

"Come on, Opal." Janco stood and hooked his arm in mine. "You're exhausted. I'll escort you to your room."

"You just don't want me having a fit in public."

"Of course. I've a reputation to maintain." He shot me a grin, but it died just as quick. "Almost forgot." He picked up the necklace and put it on. Tucking the pendant under his shirt, he tapped the slight bump it made. "I promised Yelena I would keep Lamar safe." He looked at me with a very un-Janco expression. "We all make sacrifices for what is right. And you've experienced firsthand the horrors caused by blood magic. To be truly safe, we should assassinate Devlen regardless of his efforts to redeem himself."

I clutched his arm to keep from shouting the words. "Then why didn't you?"

Ari said, "Because of you."

"Me?"

The big man shifted in his seat, appearing uncomfortable. "Do you really believe we would eliminate someone you're in love with?"

I sputtered. "I'm not—"

Ari held up a hand. "He's helping you, then. That's important to us."

Staring at him in shock, I finally asked, "Love trumps logic?"

"Every time," Valek said. "Plus he's being watched. One move toward his old habits and *I'll* pay him a visit."

Overwhelmed, I let Janco pull me away from the table. On the way to my room on the second floor, I sorted through the conversation. How could Ari think

I was in love with Devlen? We'd kissed a few times. That was all. No big deal.

After I said good-night to Janco, I locked the door and faced my empty room. At least it matched the hollowness in my chest. No blood. No magic. No Kade.

Kade had stayed away just like I asked. Finn planned to sell my blood to someone who hates me. And magic... Not my friend. The happy discovery that I could move it had been countered by Finn's effective use of the null shield to trap me. My immunity to magic was no longer an asset.

All in all, a horrible day.

The next morning the four of us headed north to Valek's small stable. Once there, we discussed options on how to find Finn.

"I'll alert my network throughout Sitia. Someone will spot him," Valek said with confidence. "Once we pick up his trail, I'll have a chat with him."

Annoyance flared. "I thought you said Finn was my problem."

"As an obstruction to your goal, he was. But now we know he has a different agenda."

Still unhappy, I grumped. "If you'd taken care of him in the beginning, we wouldn't have this *different* agenda."

Unfazed, Valek cocked his head. "Then we wouldn't know about this other player. The one who is willing to spend a lot of gold for a vial of your blood."

Player. Interesting word choice. This wasn't a game to me. In a foul mood, I left the three of them to plan.

I visited Quartz. Just seeing her warm brown eyes melted my frustration. Not bothering with a saddle,

I hopped onto her back and let her choose our path. The landscape streaked by, and I released all my tension. Concentrating on the movement of her powerful muscles against my legs, I became an extension of her.

When she slowed to a walk, I returned to my problems. I didn't doubt Valek would find Finn. As for recovering my blood, at this point I gave us a fifty percent chance.

After rubbing Quartz down and filling her water bucket, I sought Valek. If he planned to confront Finn, he needed to know about the null shields. I found him in the kitchen, bent over a map of Sitia.

He might keep his secrets, but I believed in full disclosure. "Valek, have you ever encountered a null shield?"

He glanced at me with a frown. "I don't think so. Why?"

I explained about Finn's attack. "I moved the magic around me and Finn followed the logic."

He straightened. "That is concerning."

Trust Valek to downplay it. "It can trap you."

"Perhaps. But your immunity seems to be different than mine. I can't move magic."

"Have you tried?" I asked and covered my grin when surprise flashed on his face.

"No. It always feels like syrup. I assumed it moved like a viscous fluid and would ooze."

"That's how it feels to me, too. But when I panicked, I spread my hands and pushed."

"Interesting." He drummed his fingers on the table. "Can a weapon pierce a null shield?"

"Yes. Anything but magic can. You can defend yourself as long as your arms aren't pinned."

"I guess we'll need to experiment when we have some time." Valek tapped the map. "First we need to find Finn. The three of us are going to split up, and search all the cities we can reach between here and Booruby."

"Three? Booruby?"

"You need to go home to help your mother." He slowed his words as my confusion continued. "And we're going to meet you there for the wedding."

"Mara!"

Valek laughed. "Even spies take time off for weddings."

I groaned aloud. "I don't have a gown or a date. I asked Kade. But he never replied, so I'm guessing it's a no. How am I going to explain his absence to my mother?"

The humor dropped from his face and an emotion I've never seen on him replaced it. Guilt? Chagrin? Hard to tell with Valek.

He pulled a letter from his pocket. "Been meaning to give you this. It's from Kade."

# 14

I snatched the letter from his hand. Folded multiple times, its worn edges looked as if it had been in his pocket for a while.

When I frowned at him, he said, "Er…it came a while ago. I didn't want to distract you from your training."

"You're evil. Did you know that?"

"So I've been told."

Instead of wrapping my hands around his neck, I left the kitchen to find a private place to read Kade's letter. I returned to my room and sat on the edge of the bed. Unfolding the paper, I braced for anger, sarcasm, rejection or perhaps all three. He had the right to be upset. But there was no hint of any of them.

What melted my heart was his sadness. He wanted to understand why I ran off to Fulgor and why I asked him not to join me there, but he couldn't. If I really wished for him to be at Mara and Leif's wedding, I needed to explain my reasons in person. He would wait for me at his parents' indigo farm until the heating season. Then he would be on the coast to harvest the storms blowing in from the sea.

Reading between the lines, I realized if I didn't go, our relationship would be over. The thought of not being with Kade struck me like a hard slap to my cheek. It cleared my head. I didn't want to lose him.

Calculating how long I had until the wedding, I rushed to gather my things. Twenty-five days until the nuptials. I needed ten days to reach the heart of Storm-dancer lands, leaving me fifteen days to talk to Kade and arrive in Booruby with enough time to avoid giving my mother a heart attack. It would be close.

As I raced to pack my saddlebags, I wondered exactly what I would say to Kade. At least I had ten days to think it over.

After a hurried goodbye to Valek, Ari and Janco, I saddled Quartz and spurred her into a gallop. All the things I left undone in Fulgor would have to wait. I owed Nic and Eve an explanation. Councilor Moon should be informed about Wirral and her new assistant. Devlen… Unlike my feelings for Kade, confusion about him twisted inside me. I planned to unknot my emotions and sort it out on the way to Kade's.

As I traveled around Fulgor, I sent a message to Nic and Eve. I assured them I was fine, informed them that Tama's assistant worked for Finn and asked them to tell Devlen I was okay.


I discovered traveling by yourself for an extended period of time was lonely and it was easy to lapse into bouts of self-pity. Stopping at inns along the way, I listened to the gossip in the common room, hoping for some useful information. Perhaps even a clue to Finn's location.

The major complaints centered on the Council's inability to deal with the glass messenger crisis. I almost choked on my food when a man sitting nearby used the word *crisis*. They thought a Sitia-wide search for another glass magician should be launched and they grumbled over having to go back to the old way of doing things.

Good thing no one recognized me with my short, dirty-blond hair or I would be worried for my safety. Janco's comment about half of Sitia hating me replayed in my mind. And who hated me enough to pay so much for my blood? During the trip, I couldn't name anyone. Well…anyone alive.

I also couldn't prepare for what I needed to say to Kade. And I failed to decide about Devlen. Without them with me, I couldn't make a connection. Logic said one thing, but being in their presence had a different effect. I hoped I would find the proper words.

After ten long days on the road, I found the lane to Kade's parents' farm. The two-story wooden house had been painted blue at one point. The roof sagged in the middle and rocking chairs filled a large wrap-around porch.

Fields of indigo plants spread from the house on both sides, and what appeared to be a workshop or factory sat behind it. The place felt deserted, but as I guided Quartz to the porch, a woman stepped out.

Tall and lean, her resemblance to Kade was undeniable. She dried her hands on her apron, which covered a pair of dark brown pants. Her tan shirt was peppered with blue stains.

"Can I help you?" she asked.

I dismounted and approached. "I'm looking for Kade.

You must be his mother. I'm Opal Cowan." I smiled and held out my hand.

"Uh-huh." She glanced at Quartz. "I see you have one of those fancy Sandseed horses, too. Something wrong with a dependable and hardworking Stormdance horse?" She didn't wait for an answer. Hooking a thumb, she indicated the field to the right. "He's out harvesting with his father." Without another word, she returned to the house.

I lowered my hand, wondering what Kade had told her about me. Scanning the field, I saw no signs of Kade or his father, but the land rose in the distance and then dropped from sight. I mounted Quartz and patted her neck. Then I asked her to find Kade.

Since she was a fancy Sandseed horse, she had no trouble understanding me and finding Kade by his smell. He hunched over a tall green plant, cutting leaves off. His shirt lay on the ground in a heap and sweat shone on his back. His skin had tanned in the sun to a deep golden color.

Another nice perk with a fancy Sandseed horse, she didn't make any noise when walking on dirt so neither Kade nor his father heard us approach.

I hesitated to call to him. After his mother's cold reception, I worried he would frown or ignore me. But Quartz wasn't shy. She neighed a loud hello. Both men stopped and turned around in surprise. I held my breath as Kade squinted into the sunlight in confusion. I tugged at the short strands of my hair. Would he even recognize me?

Moonlight whinnied and ran up to us, happy to see Quartz. I dismounted and removed her saddle so she could spend time with the big black horse—another Sandseed.

And then Kade smiled. My world brightened and I didn't hesitate this time, rushing to him. He pressed me to his chest for a moment, then tried to pry me off, claiming his sweat would stain my shirt, but I clung a little longer, breathing in his scent. Even this far inland he smelled like the sea.

"I'm guessing this is Opal," his father said.

I finally stepped away to greet Kade's father. Shorter than Kade, he had a full beard streaked with white, and a mess of white hair that fell to his shoulders. His stocky build was the opposite of his son's thinner frame.

Kade said, "Opal, meet my father, Igarian."

"Call me Ink." He shook my hand. "Everyone else does."

"Why?" I asked.

He swept a hand out, indicating the plants. "Because of my job."

Kade coughed. "He's being modest. He's known for the quality of his indigo. Most of his fellow farmers claim he has ink in his veins instead of blood."

Ink dismissed Kade's comments. "My boy likes to exaggerate. It's easy to raise indigo when it always rains just when the soil dries out." He beamed at Kade with a proud smile. "Now, if you'll excuse me, I need to get these leaves into the shed."

When Kade moved to help, Ink shooed him away. "I can do it, boy. Spend some time with your friend. Give her a tour of the farm." Ink whistled for Moonlight. The horse trotted over and let him hitch the cart full of leaves onto his harness.

My opinion of Ink rose. Moonlight liked so few people. He drove the Keep's Stable Master crazy by refusing all the students. So far, he tolerated Janco and Ulrick, before Ulrick became addicted to blood magic. And, I realized Devlen had also been able to ride him when his soul was in Ulrick's body. I wondered if Moonlight would let Devlen ride him now.

Quartz followed Moonlight as he headed back toward the house. I watched her until she was gone from view. Without Ink and the horses, an awkward silence formed between us.

"I didn't think you'd come," Kade said.

"I would have come sooner…" Would I? "Your letter was…delayed."

He wiped his brow with a rag and shrugged his shirt on. "Delayed how?" he asked.

"It's a long, complicated story."

"Will it explain your hair?"

"Yes."

"Then we'll take the extended tour." A hint of a smile quirked and humor flashed in his amber-colored eyes.

Relieved by his reception, I returned his smile. The sunlight glinted from the gold and red highlights in his brown hair. It had grown long enough to be pulled into a ponytail.

As we walked through the indigo fields, I told Kade of my adventures in Fulgor and at the prison, including Valek's and Janco's involvement and about visiting Devlen, but not about kissing Devlen.

Kade had remained silent during the whole story. "Opal, why do you want to reclaim your magic? It has given you nothing but trouble."

He had a point. "I'm lost without it," I admitted. "I feel useless."

"Your immunity—"

"Is worthless."

"Only Finn knows this. And besides, don't you think you've done enough? You almost died and those who know how to use blood magic are gone." He took my hand in his. "After Mara's wedding, stay with me. Come to the coast and make orbs with Helen. We'll take long walks on the beach. I know a few isolated coves."

Tempting. "What about Finn?"

"Let Valek and his people hunt him down."

"I can't. I need to be involved. At least until I know if I can either reclaim my magic or not."

"And then?"

"I don't know," I said. Seeing the pain in his eyes, I stopped and faced him. "You said I came into your life like a hot season squall. Do you really think I'd be content to take long walks on the beach?"

"If we are to be together, Opal, I want to *be* with you, spending as much time with you as possible."

I thought of Valek and Yelena. He had said no amount of time or distance could break them apart. Was it too much to expect the same from Kade? Then there was Mara and Leif. They kept together for most of the year.

"Why?"

"You ground me. When I'm on the coast—" he gestured to the western horizon "—and dancing, I can easily lose myself in the storm's energy and personality. I wanted to do just that after my sister died, but you kept me connected. You give me a reason to come back."

Kade tucked an errant strand of hair behind my ear. "You're kind, smart and tenacious, and I love the way you're so quick to help others. And there lies the problem. You rush off to solve Sitia's problems and you don't need my help. But I want to be selfish, keeping you safe with me."

"But I wasn't rushing off for Sitia this time. I was the one being selfish."

"An exception. What about next time?"

"Valek could teach—"

"I already have a job. I'd like a home and a family. Do you?"

"Eventually, I guess."

"Guess?" An eyebrow spiked.

"I can't see past this...uncertainty with my blood." And while it was nice to think my spyglass would show me the future if I found the right focus point, I didn't believe it.

"Whether or not you reclaim your magic, some decisions won't change."

He had a point. Yet, deep inside, I equated planning my future to giving up; if I agreed to stay with Kade and work for the Council, I was admitting defeat.

Kade watched me. "You're conflicted about more than your blood. What's wrong?"

Time for full disclosure. I resumed walking, but the beautiful scenery didn't even register in my mind.

Matching my pace, Kade stayed next to me. After a few moments, he asked, "How bad is it?"

"Bad."

"Have you and Janco decided to run away to Ixia together?" Kade joked.

He surprised a laugh from me. "I'd kill Janco before we reach the border." Then all my humor drained away. "You're not going to like this."

"Just tell me, Opal."

So I did. The words rushed out.

Kade stopped in disbelief. "Devlen? You *kissed* Devlen?"

Feeling miserable, I nodded.

"But he… How could…?"

"I don't know why. Maybe because he understands what I'm going through right now."

"I—"

"Can't understand. I'm sorry it happened, but I can't erase the past. I love you. I do, but I need him right now. The search for my blood had given me a purpose. Devlen gives me hope that if I don't find it, I'll be able to get on with my life."

"With me?"

"I'm here."

"What does that mean?" he asked.

"I knew that if I didn't come here, we'd no longer be together. I don't want to lose you, and I don't want to lie to you, either. Can you just *be* with me for now?"

"I need to think about it," he said. "The house is over there." Kade pointed. "I'll meet you later." He strode away.

I hovered near the back porch of the house, feeling lost and heartsick. The unmistakable sounds of an argument reached me. I didn't want to eavesdrop on Kade's parents, so I let their voices flow past me. Instead I counted the number of clotheslines strung next to the shed—more than I would expect for three people. I was up to ten when my name was mentioned. Unable to avoid the now-loud conversation, I sank to the steps and rested my elbows on my knees.

"…took her sweet time," Kade's mother said.

A muttered reply from Ink. I covered my face with my hands.

"...don't care... She's nothing but trouble."

At least she had that right. The door squeaked and I glanced up.

Ink leaned on the frame. "Where's Kade?" he asked.

"He said he'd meet me here."

"Don't sit out in the sun. Come in." Ink pushed the door wider.

I entered a workroom. Kegs of ink rested on a long table. Bolts of cloth littered the floor and open barrels of liquid lined the walls. I had known Kade worked on his family's farm during the off-season, but had no idea exactly what they did with the ink.

Ink didn't give me time to ask as he led me into the kitchen to introduce me to his wife. She stirred a pot heating on the hearth.

"Sarrah, this is—"

"Met her already," she said without looking up. "Go wash up before supper."

"Be nice. Opal's our guest." He shooed me from the kitchen and into the living room. He played host, telling me to sit down, fetching me a drink and asking how long I planned to visit.

"Not long," I said. "My sister is getting married in fifteen days and I need to be home in time to help."

Sarrah came out to set the formal table, setting down the plates with extra force. The bangs punctuated her ill humor.

"Can I help with supper?" I asked her.

"No."

To break the awkward silence I asked Ink about his

work. Before he could speak, Sarrah grumped. "She knows nothing about us."

"Of course she doesn't," Ink said. "Opal's been busy. Without her, they never would have fixed those orbs."

"Tell that to Nisha and Kamlesh. I'm sure they would rather have their children home with them, than for all of them to be murdered."

I missed a major connection between fixed orbs to murdered children. Ink rubbed his temples as if this were an old argument. I caught his eye and raised my eyebrows in question.

"Nisha and Kamlesh are Indra, Varun and Nodin's parents. Or were." Ink hunched over the table.

Grief welled. The three glassmakers had been killed by Sir and Tricky for the Stormdancers' secret orb recipe—the special sand mixture used for the glass orbs. I also had the recipe, but when Sir couldn't force it from me, he turned to them.

"I would like to visit them before I leave. Do they live nearby?" I asked Ink.

"Don't bother them," Sarrah said. "They have no wish to see you. Believe me."

Lovely. Kade's mother blamed me for their deaths. I wondered if Nisha and Kamlesh did, as well. At least Sarrah couldn't pin her daughter Kaya's death on me. It was one of the reasons I had become involved with discovering who had sabotaged the orbs. Through that mission I had met Kade.

As Sarrah bustled around, I studied her. She had lost a child a little over a year ago. My mother had been devastated when Tula had died, but I couldn't remember if she had been angry, as well. The man who had killed my sister had been caught, and so had the people responsible for Kaya's death. Kade had helped capture them. Did Sarrah also think I was responsible for getting him involved? He had been caught and forced to harvest the energy from the blizzards in Ixia. I shied away from thinking about my role during that time.

I remembered Kade had been just as walled off as his mother. But he had found a little peace since his sister's death. Why? I sorted through my memories. Kaya's soul had been trapped in a glass orb, existing with a storm's energy. After escaping Sir and Tricky, Kade had set her free. He had said goodbye.

"Did you have a good harvest this year?" I asked Ink.

Once again Sarrah jumped in. "Why do you care? Look at those drab-colored clothes you're wearing. We only produce vibrant and beautiful ink here."

I bit my tongue before I could make a nasty comment about her brown pants and tan shirt. I really, really didn't want to argue. Since anything I said would be misconstrued by Sarrah, I kept quiet.

Kade returned. He wouldn't look at me, and he didn't notice the tension in the room.

Supper was painful and I almost wished to be back at Wirral. Almost. Sarrah steered the conversation and I kept my temper in check. She reminisced over Kade's and Kaya's childhoods. I noted the lack of embarrassing stories. Lucky Kade.

He, on the other hand, hardly said a word.

"They did everything together," Sarrah said. "Even school. Kaya hated to be in the younger class, so she studied hard and was promoted to Kade's group."

Finally Ink managed to change the subject. "You mentioned your sister, Opal. Who's the lucky man?"

"Leif Zaltana."

Ink glanced at his son. "Is he the one who ate your mother's entire cobbler by himself?"

"Sounds like him," I said, smiling despite myself.

"Yes. He stopped by for a visit on his way back to the Citadel," Kade said.

"A powerful magician," Sarrah said. "He should marry another Zaltana. Concentrate the power for his children. When people marry outside their clans, it dilutes the blood."

Did she say that on purpose? If I had hackles they would be up. "Leif is marrying Mara for the right reason. Love."

She dismissed my comment. "Silly sentiment. Sitia needs more magicians. We've lost two Master Magicians and you gave your magic away. Love is nice, but it's selfish."

I sputtered. Gave mine away? Before I could say something I'd regret, I excused myself from the table and bolted outside. Once there, I inhaled deep breaths to calm the fury. Was she trying to get a reaction from me? Why did she dislike me so much? My guilty conscience replied that she sensed I'd hurt her son. At least I kept my temper. Fighting with Kade's mother would only upset him further.

By the time I returned to his parents' house, Ink and Sarrah sat in the living room. Lanterns blazed, pushing the darkness to the far corners. Sarrah kept sewing, ignoring me. Ink glanced up from his paper. A pair of reading glasses was perched on the end of his nose.

I stood awkwardly in the threshold. Kade wasn't in sight. "Where's Kade?" I asked Ink.

"Checking on the horses."

Sarrah tsked. "He wastes too much time with that

animal. Doesn't he know as soon as a dignitary from Ixia visits, or the Council realizes their mistake, they'll take that Sandseed horse back?"

Her tone of voice clearly indicated that she didn't want an answer, but I stepped into the room to give her one regardless. "No one can take Moonlight from Kade. No one."

She wouldn't look at me so I moved closer. "*Moonlight* decides who he stays with."

"He doesn't need a horse. He was fine without one."

"Moonlight's been a big help around here," Ink said then ducked his head when his wife glowered at him. "Er…sit down, Opal. I'll go make up Kaya's bed—"

"Absolutely not," Sarrah said. She jabbed her needle at me. Panic flared in her eyes. "She can sleep on the couch. She's not allowed in Kaya's room."

And then all the clues clicked into place. Sarrah was afraid Kade had replaced his love for his sister with me. At least she would be happy when Kade tells me it's over.

Ink started to protest, but I touched his arm. "The couch is fine. After ten days on the road, anything soft will do."

Kade still hadn't returned by the time Ink and Sarrah retired for the night. I squirmed into a semicomfortable position on the couch. The pale moonlight slipped in through the small gap in the windows. Shadows from the curtains flickered on the floor's wooden beams.

Unable to sleep, I watched the fabric billow and sway with the cool night breeze. After a few minutes the curtains would settle and then blow in and part as if announcing the arrival of the wind.

A squeak woke me from a light doze. Kade's shadow crossed the floor. He paused and I waited. Then the steps groaned with his weight as he climbed the stairs.

# 15

I couldn't blame him for giving up on me. I'd lost Kade. Despite the wrenching inside my chest, I ruminated on the word *lost* as I stared at the ceiling. Lost his love, not the man since he slept upstairs. I had planned to leave early in the morning if Kade couldn't stay with me. Why wait? I wouldn't be able to sleep. Not now. Quartz enjoyed traveling at night and she had all day to rest.

But I needed to say goodbye. Tiptoeing upstairs, I paused on the landing. Three closed doors ringed the short hallway. Which one was his?

I stood in front of each door as I decided. A slight draft caressed my bare toes from under the door on the right, but air blasted my feet from the left one. Only Kade would have his window wide-open.

Biting my lip, I tapped on the door before turning the knob and peeking in. If he was asleep...

"I'm awake," Kade said.

With no shirt on and wearing only short pants, he lay on top of the bedspread. A knot formed under my ribs and I shivered.

"I understand your decision. I'm leaving tonight and wanted to say goodbye."

He gazed out the window. And I studied his face, committing the strong line of his jaw and his smooth skin to memory. The consequences of my quest had been very high. I turned to go.

"Where are you going?" he asked.

"Home for Mara's wedding."

"You can't leave so soon. If I'm going to spend time with your family, it's only fair you spend a few more days with mine."

I spun around.

He pushed up on his elbow. "I don't want to give up on us. This thing with Devlen isn't love, is it?"

"No. He's like my Story Weaver."

"And he'll help you?"

"Yes."

Kade drew in a deep breath. "You know what I want and need. And you love me." He quirked a smile. "I can be happy with that for now. After the wedding, you know where I'll be." He patted the bed and I slid in with him. He settled back and I snuggled in close.

"Although," he said, "you'll have to deal with my mother for the next couple of days."

Dealing with his mother seemed a mere inconvenience. I'd been given a second chance with Kade and I wasn't going to blow it. My thoughts returned to my earlier assessment of Sarrah. "I think I know why she hates me so much."

"After one day?"

"I've learned a great deal about human nature from Valek."

"Go on."

"She needs to know you still love your sister. Your father already knows you're not trying to replace her with me. When you released Kaya's soul on the Northern Ice Sheet, you had a moment with her that your parents missed. You said goodbye, and even I experienced her joy at finding peace. They didn't. I think if you tell them what happened, your mother might feel better about us."

"Once I decided to let her go, I never considered waiting. So wrapped up in my own grief, I had forgotten my parents' pain." He looked at me. "It was a very selfish thing to do."

"At that time, you couldn't see past your own pain."

"Sounds like you have some experience with this."

It would explain my actions with Devlen. "Yes I do, and it usually leads to trouble."

When I woke the next morning, Kade was gone. I stretched and felt a rare moment of contentment before getting up to find him. Halfway down the steps, his mother's voice reached me. I slowed.

"Sounds like wishful thinking—harvesting Kaya's soul. Honestly, Kade, you're a Stormdancer not a Soulfinder. You didn't have these delusions about your abilities before you met that girl or got that horse. All this running around, for what? Nothing."

I cringed for Kade. Deeper issues lay between him and his mother, and I might have made it worse. His reply was too quiet for me to decipher.

"Why can't you pick someone like Helen? She's beautiful, talented…"

Unable to endure any more, I hurried through the living room and out the front door. When had she met

Helen? I thought the Stormdancer's new orb maker worked in Thunder Valley during the off-season, selling her glasswares.

Helen was pretty and her glass statues were unparalleled works of art. And she was sweet. And she spent three full seasons working with Kade. I stopped that line of thought. Despite all the pain I caused, he had stayed with me. Love trumps logic.

I found Quartz and Moonlight grazing behind the shed. Her copper-and-white coat looked fuzzy and unkempt. Shedding season. I retrieved a shedding blade from my saddlebags and pulled the thin metal loop through her thick cold season coat. Hair rained to the ground, piling around her hooves like drifts of snow.

Kade arrived. He groaned with annoyance. "I combed her last night." He gestured to the piles of hair. "Not that you would know it."

Moonlight snuffled Kade's hair and sneezed.

"Ugh." Kade wiped his face on his sleeve. "Good morning to you, too." He scratched the horse behind his ears and then sighed when he noticed the black hairs sticking to his hand. "Now he's shedding."

I ducked behind Quartz to hide my smile, but Kade joined me. "I'll finish grooming Quartz. You need to get cleaned up." He wiped horsehair off my chin.

"For what?"

"Shopping with my mother," he deadpanned.

"But she—"

"Agreed to spend time with you for my sake."

"But I heard…"

He tilted his head, waiting.

"Er…I only caught a sentence or two, but I don't think my idea to tell her about Kaya worked."

"Nothing's a quick fix, Opal. But it was a step in the right direction. After I reminded her about her own often-repeated advice to not jump to conclusions about new people, she thought a day in town with you would be acceptable."

"But, I don't need anything."

"Really? I thought you needed a dress for Mara's wedding."

It was my turn to groan. Dress shopping with Kade's mother. Kill me now. The alternative—arriving home without a gown—was equally unappealing.

"Okay, but I'm taking my switchblade along."

"To defend yourself against my mother?" he asked with an incredulous tone.

"No. To slit my throat if the day goes badly."

He laughed. "Make sure you don't bleed in front of her. She faints at the sight of blood."

"I'm *so* glad you have your priorities straight," I said. My voice dripped with sarcasm.

Unaffected, he pushed me toward the house. "You'll have… Well, you'll have an interesting day at least. And you should listen to my mother. She has an excellent eye for color."

Sarrah eyed my short locks as we walked to town. "First stop, the hairdresser. Those dark roots look awful."

I sucked in a breath and held it for a moment. It was going to be a very long afternoon. When we arrived in the town of Cumulus, I followed Kade's instruction and listened to Sarrah, letting the hairdresser return my hair to its natural color. I tried to ask Sarrah questions about her life in an effort to get to know her better, but she either ignored me or gave me a vague answer that implied that I really didn't want to know so why should she bother.

The dress shop was busy. Sales staff hustled, and the seamstress fretted over her customers with a measuring ribbon. I didn't have time for a custom-made gown, so we searched through the racks of finished pieces.

When I moved to the back row, Sarrah stopped me. "Kade can't afford those. They're silk. If we can't find something here, we can ask if they have any other cheap or rejected gowns."

I blinked at her a moment. Did she just say Kade? Did she actually think I would let Kade pay for my gown? Or I needed him to pay for it? Her opinion of me was worse than I imagined. I endured her abuse for two reasons guilt over Devlen and keeping the peace for Kade. No longer.

"Outside," I said. "Now."

She fussed about wasting time as she followed me. Surrounded by indigo fields, Cumulus's entire downtown area fit within a two-block radius. I stopped at the edge of town and turned to her.

"I get it. You don't like me. That's fine. But you're making the wrong assumptions about me and that *isn't* fine. Kade and I are together. We're not going to change because you don't like it. And I'm no longer ignoring all your snide comments. If you don't have anything constructive to say, then keep your mouth shut."

"Or what?" She crossed her arms, daring me.

"Or I'll leave and I'll take Kade with me. He wants us to spend more time together, but if you're going to continue to be nasty, then it won't be here with you."

"Finally!"

Not the reaction I expected. "Excuse me?"

"I don't like you, Opal. But weak people who don't defend themselves I like even less. Come on." She hurried down the street.

I rushed to catch up. We passed the dress shop. She cut down an alley and knocked on the back entrance of a residence. When the door opened, a young lady peeked out. Laughter, shrieks and wails of children sounded behind her. A mane of blond hair framed her round face and she wore old clothes. A row of straight pins had been stuck in her shirt.

She smiled and greeted Sarrah as if they were old friends, then invited us in. The comfortable living area had been invaded by romping children. We bypassed the troops and she led us to a quieter sewing room.

Sarrah introduced us. "Tori, this is Opal, Kade's... friend. She needs a gown right away. Do you still have the one you made for Anya?"

Tori frowned. "Yes. After all that work, she changed her mind and wouldn't pay for it! And you had mixed me such a gorgeous color."

"I think Opal is her size."

She scanned me and squealed, dashing for a closet. After sorting through it, Tori pulled out a gorgeous emerald-green gown. Simple and elegant, the sleeveless V-neck bodice was lined with lace and crystals. From the waist down, layers of silk overlapped with crystals sewn along the ends of each layer.

Tori handed me the gown. "Try it on in there." She pointed to a curtain.

Behind the material, I found a small changing room with a bench and mirror. Careful not to rip the fabric,

I squirmed into it. The cool caress of silk touched my skin. I loved it.

When I came out, Tori squealed again.

Sarrah said, "It's a little big."

"Minor adjustments," Tori said as she tugged and pulled. "I'll take it in around the waist and shorten the straps. A few hours at most." She used the straight pins in her shirt to mark the changes. "Oh my."

The rows of scars on my arms had caught her attention. Sarrah also noticed. Great.

Tori patted my shoulder. "No problem. I have a pair of long white gloves and some extra dye. Plus I can dye a pair of shoes to match. Can you wait until tomorrow?"

"Yes."

She quoted a price and I paid her without looking at Kade's mother. It was the most expensive garment I ever bought, but it was worth every extra silver.

Mission accomplished, we walked back to Sarrah's house. We didn't talk, but it was a comfortable silence. When we arrived at the kitchen door, I thanked her for taking me to Tori's.

She nodded. "It's the perfect color for you." Then she went inside.

Her comment reminded me of a similar one from Valek three seasons ago. He was going to be smug and all I-told-you-so when he saw me in emerald green. I still hated him and thought he was evil, but the man did have an eye for color.

Early the next morning Heli visited. At seventeen, she was the youngest Stormdancer, and her enthusiasm for life was contagious. Bounding into the kitchen with a wide smile, her energy spread to all of us in the room, including Sarrah. I marveled at the first sign of happiness from Kade's mother.

"Opal," Heli cried, spotting me sitting at the table. "Good to see you! Are you why Kade sent me a message?"

I glanced at Kade.

He flipped sweet cakes. "One of the reasons," he said.

Sarrah set another place at the table. "Stay for breakfast." She tsked at Heli. "So thin! You need to eat more."

Heli plopped into the chair next to mine and rolled her eyes. "You sound just like my mother."

"At least no one nags you on the coast," I said.

"I wish." Heli sighed dramatically. "If Kade isn't fussing at me about something, Raiden thinks he's my surrogate father. It's why I spend so much time on the beach."

"So you don't really like hunting for treasures from the sea?" I asked.

She slapped the table. "That reminds me! Remember that sea glass I found?"

Hard to forget the glass that had caused everyone to fight over it. A magical compulsion had been attached to it by an uncontrolled young magician named Quinn. I wondered if he could purposely attach magic to glass now that he should have control over his power. Then I recalled the cold glass Mister Paul had in Hubal. The two bits of information linked and I felt as if I'd been smacked. If Quinn made the cold glass, he might be able to do more.

"Opal? It wasn't that hard a question," Heli said.

I pulled my thoughts back.

Heli waited for my answer.

"Sorry. What was the question?" I asked.

"Sea glass?"

"Of course. What about it?"

"I'm this close to deciphering the message scratched on the pieces." Heli held up her finger and thumb with a half-inch gap between them.

"But the markings were just a way for Quinn to keep track of his collection."

"Did he tell you that?" she asked.

"I don't remember."

"From your description of the Bloodrose family, I think the glass was a call for help."

I shook my head. "Heli, the family was... All right, they were creepy, but I didn't see anything illegal going on. They're just oyster farmers who don't want to be bothered by outsiders."

Kade served the sweet cakes. "That sea glass already caused enough trouble, Heli. Just leave it alone."

She snapped her mouth shut, but the gleam in her eyes gave away her intentions to continue despite Kade's order. Ah. Youth.

After breakfast, Sarrah and Ink went to the shed, and I cleaned up while Kade and Heli discussed the upcoming storm season.

When she shrieked with delight, I looked over. Kade wore his sternest frown, but Heli practically bounced in her seat.

"It's a huge responsibility," Kade said. "Their safety is in *your* hands. If anything should happen—"

"Don't worry. Nothing's going to happen. I've got it covered. Thanks, Kade. Have a great trip!" She hugged him around the neck, waved goodbye to me and dashed off.

"That may have been a mistake," Kade said.

"What?"

"I've put her in charge of the Stormdancers until I arrive on the coast."

The other three dancers were older and more experienced. "Why?"

"She's the strongest of the four, and when it comes to unpredictable storms, brute strength can be more valuable than experience."

"At least it's the heating season." The storms were milder in comparison to the cooling season. "She'll be fine." Then I grinned.

"Should I even ask?"

"You may have an…interesting reception when you return. I'm sure Prin and Raiden will not be happy about the new boss."

He laughed. "She'll drive them crazy. Good. Maybe they'll appreciate me more."

Kade and I left the next morning for Booruby. Fitting a silk gown into my packs wouldn't work, so I had to tie the box to Quartz's saddle. There were twelve days until Mara's wedding and it would take us seven to reach my house, leaving five days for me to help my mother. I was in big trouble.

I set a quick pace. When we arrived at my family's home, I paused before pushing through the gate. The house seemed quiet. White smoke billowed from the glass factory's chimneys. No one was in sight. Our courtyard had been transformed for the wedding ceremony and reception. Large arches decorated the space, tables and chairs had been set up and a fabric ceiling hung above the yard to protect everything from the rain.

Leading Quartz and Moonlight to the shed/stable, I realized Kade had never been here before. I pointed out the various buildings. We removed the horses' saddles and rubbed them down. As soon as we finished, they trotted into the Avibian Plains. The grasses in the plains had returned to green and their long stalks rippled in the breeze.

When I could delay no longer, I headed toward the house. It was time to face my mother's wrath.

"Perhaps I should wait outside," Kade said.

"Oh no." I grabbed his hand. "She can't kill me if there is a witness."

"I think you're exaggerating. It won't be that bad."

I steeled myself and stepped into the kitchen—also known as wedding central. My mother bustled about the hearth, stirring pots and baking pies. I called a hello.

She turned and gave me a cold stare. "Can I help you, miss?"

"Mom—"

"Excuse me? You must be mistaken. I'm *not* your mother. No. Because *my* daughter wouldn't be so inconsiderate as to arrive so late for her own sister's wedding. Especially when she knows how much work is involved. No. I'm afraid my daughter is lying dead in a ditch somewhere."

# 16

I expected my mother to be mad at me for arriving so close to the wedding, but I didn't think she'd be so melodramatic. "Mom, I'm—"

"Hello, Kade," she said, ignoring me to give him a welcoming hug. "I'm sorry about Opal's tragic demise, but I'm sure you'll find someone more reliable and considerate. Perhaps one of Mara's friends—"

"Mother!"

She didn't miss a beat. "—would suit you. She invited all of them, and some are still single and quite pretty. There is an extra bed in Ahir's room for you. Make yourself at home. Supper will be ready in a few hours." With that, she returned to her cooking.

She didn't murder me, but I wanted to either die or kill her. Hard to tell. "Five days is plenty of time, Mom. Mara and Leif aren't even here yet," I said to her back.

Glancing over her shoulder, she said, "Kade, by the time you're settled, Leif should be back with the tablecloths. Could you help him? Mara is busy helping her father make the centerpieces in the factory."

He looked a little queasy. "Uh…sure."

Giving up, I showed Kade my brother's room. There were two extra beds wedged in with Ahir's. I recognized Leif's saddlebags on one of them. Kade dropped his pack onto the other. I showed him my room. It used to be mine and Tula's. A sudden sadness pierced my heart and I sank to my bed. Tula would have loved planning for Mara's wedding. She would have been chosen as the Bride's Maid of Honor and I would have been happy to be a regular Bride's Maid.

Kade moved around the beds, looking at my childhood knickknacks, but there wasn't much space. Two extra beds plus Tula's occupied the room. It appeared Mara would sleep in Tula's and we would have two more guests. That meant Mara's room was also being used for visitors. Despite her complaints of all the extra work, my mother loved having a house full of people. If she hadn't married my father, she would probably be a very contented innkeeper.

I sighed. Kade sat next to me and put his arm around my shoulder. I leaned into him.

"Don't worry. Your mother can't stay mad at you forever," he said.

"She'll make me suffer first. But that's not it."

"Then what is it?"

How to put my swirling thoughts into words? "After the wedding, everyone has jobs to return to. You're needed on the coast. Mara and Leif will eventually return to the Magician's Keep. Yelena, Valek and even Ari and Janco all have a purpose. I don't."

"You've given up on finding your blood?"

"By now it could be anywhere. Finding it would be like picking out one particular raindrop in a storm."

"Don't start."

I batted my eyes, faking innocence. "With what?"

"The defeated attitude. Ha! You thought I was going to say the weather analogies. Didn't you?"

"Yeah."

"Well it's not as important as your attitude. You can't give up. This is something you need to do and I understand that. Valek has his people searching. From all I've heard about them, success is likely."

"There's still nothing I can do, but wait."

"Really?"

"I tried thinking of who hates me enough to want my blood."

"And?"

"No luck."

"You haven't thought hard enough."

"You sound like Valek!"

He acted as if I had given him a compliment.

"I hate Valek," I said, but it didn't burst his bubble.

"You just need to dig deep enough," Kade said. "I can think of two people who may be after you."

"Ziven and Zetta, which are probably not their real names." I shook my head. "They were hired assassins. Gressa paid them."

"Paid them to do a job, which they failed to complete."

Thanks to Kade's quick thinking. If he hadn't created that cushion of air, I would have died. Remembering the attack, I realized the assassins had put a great deal of faith in Kade. "They were supposed to fail. It gave Akako a reason to have guards watching me all the time."

"Maybe they don't like failing, and want to finish the job?"

"But why take my blood? To use as bait? It's not like I'm in hiding. They should be able to find me."

"It's just a possibility. You need to think it through for the various people you dealt with this last year, including Devlen." His arm tensed.

I glanced up at Kade, but he stared at the wall.

"He has a good reason to hate you," he said. "Cooperating with the authorities and helping you could all be an act."

Before my training with Valek, I would have conceded the possibility, but not after. Plus he had plenty of opportunities to get to me before. No. Not Devlen.

"All right, I'll dig deeper. Perhaps I'll unearth a playmate from long ago bent on revenge," I said.

He relaxed. "From your mother's stories, it's a wonder you lived through your childhood at all."

"Hey!" I pushed him away. "My mother loves to exaggerate." Then a notion struck me. "Since I'm dead in a ditch, maybe she won't tell her embarrassing stories."

Within an hour, I wished my mother would switch to the humiliating stories. But no luck. Even though she continued to ignore me, she told Kade about all the times poor dead Opal had disappointed her.

When Leif arrived with the tablecloths, I ran from the house. "Thank fate, you're here! One more minute with that woman…"

Leif chuckled. "Suck it up, Opal. You're the one who decided to show up late."

"I didn't decide…never mind." The reasons would take too long to explain.

"So how's my favorite glass wizard…er…my favorite soon-to-be sister-in-law?" he asked.

He had the decency to squirm when I didn't answer. "Well…er… Kade!" Leif rushed over to say hello.

Next to the tall Stormdancer, Leif seemed shorter than he was. His stocky build was due to thick muscles and not fat. What he lacked in speed he compensated with his strength when he wielded his machete. Despite his tactless greeting, he was dependable and grounded. A good man in a storm. Well…not as good as Kade, because of the whole Stormdancing thing. But someone reliable to fight beside. Mara had found a mate who suited her perfectly.

Leif's horse, Rusalka, shifted her weight in impatience. She was another fancy Sandseed horse. Her saddle bulged with tablecloths. I untied the packages and removed her tack. She nuzzled my ear before taking off to find Quartz and Moonlight.

Leaving the saddle for Leif to put away, I carried the large bundle of tablecloths into the house. Kade and Leif followed. I dumped them on the kitchen table, and Mother tsked over the wrinkled material.

She sighed. "If only poor dead Opal were here to iron these."

Shocked, Leif looked from my mother to me and back. "Wow. That's…that's… Wow."

Kade ginned. "Leif is speechless. Amazing. If only poor dead Opal were here to enjoy it."

I swatted him. "Don't you start." And before Leif could add a comment, I ordered him outside. "Go, pick up your saddle and take Kade with you."

In high spirits, they left. They *could* be jolly. They didn't have to iron a stack of linen tablecloths. My mother was well aware of my aversion to ironing. I set up the board and started the first of—no doubt, many—punishments from my mother.

"What did you do to your hair?" Mara asked.

"Nice to see you, too," I grumped. "I'm sure your hair wouldn't look any better after bending over a hot iron all afternoon." I eyed her golden curls. Even sweaty and dirty from working in the glass factory with our father, she still looked radiant.

I waited for the familiar tug of jealousy. My straight hair and dark brown eyes were no comparison to her beauty. My athletic build almost boylike next to her curves. However, the envy failed to poke me. Instead a sense of pride spread through me. This lovely lady was *my* sister. I realized she had never made me feel ugly. It had always been my own lack of confidence.

"I can still work with that length," she said as if I hadn't just growled at her. "It won't ruin my special surprise."

I couldn't stay annoyed with her for long. Never could. Besides, all this preparation and work was for her and I shouldn't be difficult. After I finished with the ironing, my mother set the dining room table for supper. I helped with the silverware and noticed she miscounted the place settings. One short. I skidded to a halt when I realized she had done it on purpose. Poor dead Opal didn't need a plate.

Closing my eyes for a moment, I debated if I should just eat in the kitchen. But I had endured much worse than my mother's cold shoulder, and I could get through the next few days. I added another plate.

Ahir and my father arrived just as the hot dishes were

ready to be served. Their sense of timing never failed, and I wondered if they smelled dinner in the factory.

Details about the wedding dominated the conversation. I embraced the comforting flow of voices, content to listen to the plans and Leif's appreciative noises over the roasted duck. It was delicious as always.

"…hope the weather holds out," Mara said. "Rain would turn the courtyard into a muddy mess and ruin our day."

"We could have the wedding in the factory," my father offered. "I'll move the gaffer's benches—"

"Don't be ridiculous, Jaymes," Mother said. "I have more of that oiled cloth. We'll make sides like a tent and keep the rain out."

"Don't worry about the weather," Kade said. "You'll have a sunny day. I guarantee it."

"Oh! I forgot!" Mara laughed.

"You didn't think I'd come without a wedding gift, did you?" Kade asked.

"I knew you'd eventually be useful, Kade," Leif joked. "We could have used you that night the Storm Thieves ambushed us. Remember, Opal?"

"Er…" I shot Leif a significant look, but he prattled on, telling the story with relish. Already in trouble, he just dug me in deeper. My mother's face paled as dismay filled her eyes. I hadn't told her about that night for two reasons. I didn't want her to worry about me any more than she already did, and wanted to avoid upsetting her by letting her know her youngest daughter was capable of murder.

When Leif finished the story, my mother met my gaze for the first time since I had arrived. I looked away. Her horror and censure were too painful to bear.

\* \* \*

Over the next four days, my mother not only ignored me, but she avoided me, as well. I helped Mara when needed, and showed Kade how to gather and work with molten glass since we had the time now. Unlike during the storm seasons. He proved to be a deft student.

Visitors and guests arrived, filling the house with laughter. Cousins I hadn't seen in years shared my room. We gossiped late into the night. Many others stayed in the local inns and stopped by during the day.

Yelena and Valek's arrival created a buzz of excitement and anxiety. I hugged Yelena in genuine delight, but when I pulled away she held on to my arms and her green eyes drilled a hole into me. "What's wrong?"

"Nothing."

She shot Valek a nasty look before focusing on me again. "You're a much better liar, but you can't fool me. What's going on?"

"My mother's mad at me for being late." Now it was my turn to glare at him. "It's not a big deal."

"We'll talk later," she promised.

Unaffected by my sour mood, Valek greeted me with a smile. He nodded at Kade, who entertained a gaggle of kids with a tiny dust devil he had created. "And you were worried he wouldn't come."

"He almost didn't."

Yelena pursed her lips. "I believe I haven't been told the whole story."

"No time, love. I wasn't going to waste my first night with you in seasons on talk."

She blushed, but his comment hit me like a physical force, knocking me off my snit. He had spent so much time training and helping me—time away from Yelena.

It drove me crazy how he flipped from kind to killer and back again without batting an eye.

They both watched me.

I returned Valek's smile and changed the subject. "Were you serious about your napkin-folding skills?"

"Yes."

"Could you teach me? My mother would be thrilled."

"When are the tables being set up?" he asked.

"Tonight."

"Swans or flowers?"

"Swans."

"Consider it done."

"But—"

"You have enough to do, Opal," Yelena said. "We'll talk after the wedding."

It sounded like an order. "Yes, sir."

Hand in hand they went in search of my mother. She squealed in delight and hugged them both. I wondered if she would be as happy to see Valek if she connected him to Ulrick's death. A few of the local guests had mentioned his murder. Everyone assumed another prisoner had done the deed.

When the sun rose on Mara and Leif's wedding day, it illuminated a brilliant blue and cloudless sky. No breeze stirred the tablecloths. According to Kade the morning chill would burn off in a matter of hours. The ceremony was scheduled to start in the early afternoon, followed by a meal and dancing.

Our houseguests ohhed and ahhed over the swan-shaped napkins sitting on every plate. Speculation over the midnight artist buzzed during breakfast. I kept quiet—it was more fun to hear their inventive guesses.

Last-minute preparations were completed and the wedding guests arrived. I retreated to my room to help Mara with her gown. By the time I wove through all the people in the living room and joined her, she already had the garment on.

She turned when I shut the door. I gasped.

"What's wrong? Is there a stain?" Mara spun to the mirror.

"Nothing's wrong. You are perfect."

She pished at me. "You need to zip me up, and I still have to fix my hair."

Mara continued with her list, but her actual words failed to reach me. I had meant what I said, and I hadn't been referring to her big beautiful eyes or heart-shaped face or gorgeous cream-colored silk gown.

She had captured joy in her heart and it shone from every pore on her skin. A passion burned within her. I hoped it never died.

I zipped, primped, fluffed, pinned and brushed, fulfilling my Maid of Honor duties.

When I finished, I examined my handiwork. "No one is going to notice your dress. They'll be captivated by your eyes."

Which she rolled. "Get dressed, Opal. Leif's Man of Honor will be here to escort you soon."

And then the mystery will be solved. Traditionally, the people chosen as the Maid and Man of Honor were kept secret. I didn't know why, and half the time everyone could guess. Mara's choice would not be a surprise to anyone sitting in the courtyard below. Leif's, though, was harder to determine.

I hurried into my own gown. Mara fussed with my hair. She tsked over the short length, but managed to

sweep it up into an elegant twist which she secured
with a set of combs. Sparks of green flashed from the
jewels in the combs. I leaned toward the mirror to see
them better.

"They're magnificent," I said. "Are they—"

"Emeralds. Of course. Nothing but the best for my
little sis." She kissed my cheek.

I gestured to my dress. "How did you know I'd wear
green?"

She gave me a don't-be-stupid look. "Sisters, remember? Besides it's Tula's favorite color."

I had forgotten! How could I? I swallowed the knot
in my throat. "Thank you for the gift. I'm sorry I didn't
have time to get you anything special."

"You paid for the wedding. And by the stack of bills
Mother has collected, you might regret your generosity."

"I won't." I had plenty of diamonds. More than
enough, even after I bought the factory.

"I'm not going to be able to get rid of you, am I?"
I asked.

"I'm family, Opal. And a colleague," Valek said.

Which reminded me. "Have you found—"

"No business talk today. I promised Yelena." His
gaze swept me. "Killer dress. I told you emerald was
your color."

"Yes. You were right."

"Do you really think you need your switchblade?"
Amusement sparked in his eyes.

"That obvious?"

"Only to me." Valek extended his elbow, inviting me
to link my arm in his.

I wasn't too surprised Leif chose Valek as his Man

of Honor. He wore his Ixian dress uniform with all his medals glinting from his chest. An impressive amount had been pinned to the black jacket.

Holding on to Valek's arm for balance, I navigated the stairs without falling on my face. "New shoes," I said. I used the word *shoe* loosely. Torture device would be a better term. The heels had to be at least four inches high. Sarrah's doing, no doubt.

Arm in arm, Valek and I walked down the aisle. My attention switched from my feet to the assembled guests. So many happy faces beamed at us and we were just the honored couple. I grinned, thinking of how Mara and Leif would be received.

Kade caught my eye. He oozed dignity in his formal Stormdancer attire—a gray long tunic with black piping that reached to his midthigh and cinched around his waist with a black leather belt studded with silver. Black leggings and knee-high black boots completed his clothing. He had a silver lightning bolt pinned to his shirt. Best of all he smiled at me.

Past Kade, I spotted Ari and Janco, both fidgeting in their Ixian dress uniforms, making their medals flash in the sunlight. But they froze when they saw me. Janco's lower jaw dropped open, and I glanced behind me to see if Mara had already started. Not yet.

Standing with my parents in the front row, Irys Jewelrose winked at me. The Second Magician had arrived late last night, looking exhausted. But today she wore an elegant copper dress and showed no signs of weariness.

Next to Irys, my brother looked debonair in his formal clothes. He had actually combed his hair away from his eyes. Who knew he could appear to be a handsome young man? Not me.

After we reached our designated places, Mara and Leif entered. The gasps and ohhs and ahhs thrilled me. Leif wore black pants, a cream shirt and a black vest all made of silk. Jungle vines had been embroidered on the vest and accented with pearls, matching the pearls on Mara's gown.

The wedding ritual passed by in a blur. During the reception, I hardly tasted my food before the dancing started. All the work and preparation for just a few hours. I think I would prefer to have a simple ritual with a few guests. Perhaps on the beach. Or perhaps not. Yelena and Valek hadn't made a formal commitment, but they were devoted to each other—true heart mates. Could they say the same about Kade and me? Could I?

Before I could answer, another song started and Kade pulled me to my unsteady feet to dance. One good thing about four-inch heels, they brought me closer to his eye level. And being wobbly had its advantages. Kade held me tight.

"I'll have to thank my mother," he said.

"Why?"

"For helping you pick out that dress."

"You like it?"

"Yes. In fact, I'd love to see it off you," he whispered in my ear.

His lips brushed my neck, sending a sizzle along my skin. "So you can examine the stitchery up close?" I teased.

He bit my earlobe playfully before drawing back. "No. So I can get a good look at your shoes."

I laughed.

As the evening progressed, I also danced with Valek, my father and Leif. I traded insults with my brother.

Near the end, Ari and Janco found me taking a break from the party behind the factory.

"Damn, Opal," Janco said. "I didn't know you could look *that* good!"

"Nice." I swatted him on the shoulder. "How did you find me?"

"I tracked you. Ari didn't think I could," Janco said.

"I didn't doubt you," Ari replied.

"But you gave me *that* look."

"Which one? The exasperated one? When I'm with you *that's* my normal expression."

"Really? I thought your standard for tonight was surly. *You* managed to scare off all those who may have been brave enough to talk to us," Janco said.

"It was the uniforms, genius. At least *I* didn't squirm like a little kid in his father's dress clothes."

I interrupted their argument, otherwise we would have been there until dawn. "I think Janco looks—dare I say it?—dashing in his uniform."

Janco preened, flashing Ari a superior smirk.

"You shouldn't have dared," Ari said.

"You're equally distinguished, Ari," I said. "What is it about uniforms that make men so…"

"Irresistible?" Janco asked. "Yummy? Hot?"

"Respectable," I said.

"Boring! No man wants to be called respectable by a woman who is *not* a mother or old or married."

"Some women find respectable to be very appealing," I said.

Janco pished.

Ari, however, peered at me with interest. "Are you one of them? Because someone like Devlen has a long way to go to be respectable."

Annoyed, I snapped, "I'm with Kade. Devlen was just a...moment of weakness during a difficult time. That won't happen ever again."

"Uh-huh," Ari said.

I crossed my arms. "Are you two here for a reason? I have to return to the party."

"We thought we'd update you on our efforts," Ari said.

Mollified, I nodded for him to continue.

"With the limited time, we only searched Owl's Hill, and all the towns between Fulgor and here. Valek went farther west, past the Citadel."

"And?" A tingle of hope bloomed.

"So far nothing."

Hope died again.

Ari noticed. "Don't worry. We're bound to pick up the trail. It's only a matter of time before we find your blood."

"I know a way we could go faster," Janco said, perking up.

"How?" I asked.

"We could use a Bloodhound."

Ari and I groaned in unison.

"What? It's a good idea," Janco whined.

"It's ridiculous," Ari said. "Just because the breed—"

"I think I hear someone calling me. Gotta go." I hurried off, leaving them to argue.

When I returned, I noticed my mother had cornered Kade. Not good. I debated rescuing him, but decided against upsetting my mother again. Coward? Who, me?

Instead, I found an empty table and soaked in the revelry. My peace didn't last long. Yelena joined me. She wore a red gown and had left her long black hair

down. It flowed over her bare shoulders and matched
the butterfly pendant at her throat.

"Talk to me," she said.

"There's nothing to talk about. My mother's still
mad, my magic's still gone and Kade and I are fine."
For now.

She studied me and I fought the urge to squirm. I
imagined she examined my soul and saw a black stain
of self-pity spreading on it. Would she be disgusted?

Without any obvious censure, she asked, "Why is
your mother angry with you?"

"I've told—"

"The *real* reason."

"Leif's Storm Thieves story—"

"No. Think."

I swallowed a groan. "I already have a Story Weaver.
I don't need another."

Yelena didn't blink. "And you've talked about this
with him?"

"He's part of the problem!" Then it hit me. "Wait.
How did you know my Story Weaver was a he? Are you
reading my mind?"

"Opal, relax." Yelena reached and cupped my face
with her hands. "I can't read your mind or soul. But
it docsn't takc a magician to know you're conflicted.
You need to talk it out either with your Story Weaver,
a friend or a relative."

Yelena met two of the three requirements. Plus she
also had a Story Weaver named Moon Man, but he
died during the Warper Battle. And she was right. I
needed to untangle this mess inside my heart. Pulling
her hands down, I held them in my own and let my worries, concerns and cringe-inducing behavior pour from

my mouth. I told her about Devlen, the events at the prison and the difficulties with Kade's and my mother, leaving nothing unsaid. Breathing easier, I slouched in my chair.

She listened to the whole thing without interruption. "I can't tell you what to do, but I can offer three bits of advice." Her lips quirked into a wry smile. "Moon Man would be proud. First, the mothers." Yelena let go of my hands to poke a finger into the air. "You managed to see why Kade's mother was so hostile to you, which is a good start. Do the same with your own mother."

"But—" The warning in her eyes stopped me.

"Second, your magic. Don't give up hope, but at the same time formulate a backup plan. Where do you see yourself next year? What will you be doing in five years? And don't be afraid to talk to Devlen. He's been through it." She glanced at Kade. He laughed at something Janco said. Ari's don't-encourage-the-boy scowl didn't affect Kade's humor.

"He should understand," Yelena said.

"He does, otherwise he wouldn't be here."

"Good."

"And third?" I asked.

"Stop being so hard on yourself about Ulrick. Valek would have gotten to him regardless of your distraction. In fact, I approved the assassination."

I gaped at her. But before I could recover, Irys Jewelrose approached us.

"Sorry to bother you, but it's important," the Master Magician said. "Yelena, can I borrow Kiki? I need to get to the Citadel as fast as possible."

Yelena stood. "What happened?"

The explanation rushed out. "It's this very young

magician we'd been keeping an eye on. He's resisted all our help and Bain finally sent a few magicians to bring him to the Keep before he flamed out and killed himself. But he just pulled a dangerous amount of power to protect himself from them."

"Why do you need Kiki?" I asked.

"To cut through the plains and get to the Citadel faster," she snapped in impatience.

"But if the boy is protected and Bain can't get close, why do you think you can?" Yelena asked.

"The boy is terrified of Bain. He doesn't like me, but at least he's not afraid of me. And I have to try," she said.

"Take Valek," Yelena said. "His immunity—"

"A good idea, except the boy is scared of men. He's a runaway."

"How about Fisk?" I asked. He had been homeless, but now he was the leader of the Helper's Guild, which gave beggars and runaways jobs.

"Tried him already. Didn't work." Irys turned her hands up in a helpless gesture. "I'm open to suggestions."

"A curare-laced dart shot with a blowgun," Yelena said.

"The boy's built a barrier that repels objects and people. No one can get close to him."

"Valek could disguise himself as a woman," Yelena said.

Irys considered. "The boy's pretty smart. He might see through the disguise."

"And what happens when the boy discovers he's been tricked?" I asked. "It won't help with his trust issues."

"That doesn't matter right now. Saving his life and

the power blanket is the most important. If we had your…"

She didn't need to say my glass magic. If I had it, this situation wouldn't be a problem at all. Then I closed my eyes as I realized I'd been an idiot. When I opened them, I met Yelena's questioning gaze and nodded.

"Irys," I said, "*I'm* coming with you."

# 17

"You have what?" Irys asked in outrage.

I explained to her about my immunity.

"Why didn't you tell me before?" Her loud question caused several guests to stop their conversations and glance our way.

"Many reasons. I promise I'll tell you everything en route to the Citadel," I said, getting to my feet.

Sensing something was wrong, Kade and Valek joined us.

"Can you be ready to leave in an hour?" Irys asked me.

"Yes." I kicked off my shoes and grabbed them.

Kade opened his mouth, but I pulled him along with me as I hurried to my room. Changing into travel clothes and packing a few things, I summarized the crisis for Kade. "I know. I'm rushing off again. But how can I not?"

"You can't."

"Moonlight's a Sandseed horse. Come with me?" I asked.

"I won't be much help. And I'm needed on the coast," he said.

Although I expected his answer, regret touched me. "I get credit for asking you. Remember that." I poked him on the shoulder to emphasize my point. He latched on to my wrist and drew me in close.

"And I want a rain check on that dress." He kissed me with a fierce passion that left me dizzy. He stepped back. "Remember that."

My lips tingled. "Won't be a problem."

When I finished gathering my travel gear, I paused for a moment to collect my thoughts. "Please make my apologies to my family. My mother's going to be livid."

"I'll explain it to her," Kade said.

"I'm glad you understand."

He gave me a sad smile. "I do. Yet inside—" he pointed to his chest "—I'd rather you were coming with me to the coast."


We joined Irys, Yelena and Valek by the horses. Both Kiki and Quartz had been saddled and were ready to go.

A slight brush of magic touched me as Yelena communicated with Kiki. When she finished, I asked her what name the horses had given me.

She chewed on her lower lip. "They aren't very imaginative."

"Glass Lady?" I guessed.

"No." Yelena cocked her head, studying me. "I'm not going to tell you."

"Why not?"

"You haven't reclaimed it yet."

"That doesn't make sense. How complicated can it be? You just said they're not imaginative."

"If I told you, you wouldn't believe why they chose that name. When you're ready, I will tell you." End of discussion.

Before I could protest, Valek said, "We'll send word if we find anything." He was referring to my blood.

"Thanks." I hopped up on Quartz.

Irys and I said a final round of goodbyes and then turned the horses toward the Avibian Plains. When we reached the tall grasses, Irys spurred Kiki into the gust-of-wind gait and Quartz followed. The plains distorted around us as we sailed over the ground.

For the next two days, Kiki and Quartz set the pace. They stopped when they were tired, and nudged us when they wished to go. Their efforts brought us to the Citadel three days earlier than a normal horse would have.

We arrived in the early morning, shot through the south entrance gate and turned west. The Citadel's streets flowed under Quartz's hooves. Surprised shouts followed as she dodged pedestrians. Amazed at Quartz's speed and agility after two days of hard riding, I hung on to her mane.

Zigzagging through the intricate maze of the residential quarters, I hoped we would arrive in time to save the boy.

Kiki and Quartz stopped near an entrance to an alley too narrow for them to fit.

Irys jumped to the ground. "Come on. This way."

I hopped down. Stains and graffiti marred the white marble walls, and weeds grew through the sidewalk's cracks. Grime coated everything. I hesitated, wondering what to do about the horses. Quartz pushed me forward. They would be fine.

As I followed Irys through the alley, the stench of rot

filled my nose. I avoided the puddles of muck and heaps of trash. The passageway ended in a small courtyard. A group of people huddled on the far side.

I recognized Fisk, Master Bain Bloodgood and a few magicians from the Keep. They turned to us. Fisk transformed from worried to confused, but Bain scowled at me in displeasure. I wondered if Irys had communicated with him regarding my immunity. During the trip to the Citadel, I had explained my reasons for keeping it a secret to Irys.

"Why is Opal here?" Fisk asked. His voice had deepened since I last talked with him. He had cut his light brown hair short, and was now as tall as my brother.

The Master Magicians ignored his question.

"Status?" Irys asked Bain.

"The boy inside this dwelling is on the verge of flaming out," Bain said. "He has pulled a huge amount of power to him, blocking anyone, including me, from getting close."

"Doesn't that mean he has control of his power?" I asked.

"No. The barrier he made is out of fear and it is about to rip apart."

A disaster for magicians. Their magic came from the blanket of power that surrounded the world. If one of them yanked too hard, it would bunch and warp, creating havoc for the magicians, and killing the person responsible.

"How can I help?" I asked.

"You need to go in there and talk to him. Teach him to slowly release the magic back into the source," Irys said.

Apprehension crawled like little spider legs over skin. "Teach him how? I don't have any magic."

Fisk said, "She can't get in there. Let me try to talk to him again."

"He's losing it." Irys's face paled. "Think of the magic as a balloon filled with air. Get rid of the air without popping the balloon. Go now!"

In a panic, I ran to the doorway and bounced off a curtain of magic. After a second to recover my senses, I found the magical barrier. Pushing my hands and arms into the power, I leaned my weight forward and shoved my way into the building. I felt as if I swam in invisible mud. Every step was an effort. I fought to draw a breath. Could I drown in magic?

Struggling against the thickness, I searched the house. Damaged tables, chairs without legs and soiled bedding littered the floor. Cobwebs hung, dust motes floated and broken glass crunched under my boots. Not a home, but a shelter for those without homes. It explained Fisk's presence.

My muscles protested the abuse. My lungs seemed to fill with magic, expanding in my chest and wheezing through my throat. I kept checking rooms until I found the boy huddled in a corner. Although I wouldn't use the word *boy* to describe the wild creature who gawked at me with an exhausted terror.

His tangled, greasy hair reached the floor. Bony knees poked through tattered pants. The rest of his ragged clothes were inadequate for the cold weather. I guessed his age to be around thirteen.

He trembled and sweat dripped from his jaw. I held my hands wide, showing him I was unarmed before I crouched to his level.

"I'm here to help." I kept my voice even, suppressing the desire to pant.

A wary, doubtful look replaced his fear. His lips whitened as he pressed them together, matching his sickly pallor. He clutched what appeared to be an apron and a teapot to his upper body.

"You're not in trouble. You have grabbed a huge amount of magic. Can you feel it?"

He nodded.

The panic in my heart eased a bit. "Don't let go. You need to hold on to it a little longer. Can you do that?"

This time he hesitated.

"It's important."

His gaze slid to a battered sleeping mat next to him. A bedraggled stuffed dog with a stained pink bow around its neck lay on a dirty pillow.

I played a hunch. "If you let go, who will take care of her?"

Alarm flashed on his face.

"Hold on for her, okay?"

This time he responded with a determined nod, tightening his grip on the items in his arms. The gesture gave me an idea.

"Imagine that the magic around us is tea, and it has filled your teapot. If you don't pour the tea out, it will break the pot."

"Too much tea," he agreed with a strained high-pitched voice.

"You need to send the tea slowly through the spout, releasing it back to the sky. When the pot is empty, everyone will be safe." I hoped.

He closed his eyes. The magic thickened. It pushed me over, clogged my nose and pressed me flat to the floor. Fear spread inside me. Could I survive a flame-out at this distance? My lungs heaved, burning with the effort to draw in air.

Black-and-white spots swirled in my vision like ashes above a dead fire. The room spun and the world ceased to be for a while. Awareness of my surroundings crept in. With each blink of my eyes, the blackness faded and pale colors returned, turning into harsh brightness. Without magic blocking my nose, the powerful acidic smell of urine invaded. I sat up.

The boy was slumped over. His teapot had rolled away, but appeared to be intact. I touched his neck, searching for a pulse. Nothing. Poor kid. I covered my face with my hands, letting regret flow through me.

Eventually, I lifted my head. I had survived a flame-out, and the building remained intact. I always imagined major destruction whenever a magician talked about losing control. My visions of collapsed walls and piles of rubble had been way off the mark.

Irys rushed into the room with Fisk right behind her. She slid to a stop next to the boy and laid a hand on his head. He moaned and I jumped at the sound.

"Holy snow cats! Is he alive?" A stupid question, but my wits had scattered.

"Of course. He's just exhausted." Irys frowned. "And malnourished, and probably sick." She scooped him up with ease. "I need to get him to the infirmary." She aimed for the door.

"I'm so glad he lived through a flameout."

Irys paused at the threshold. "He never lost control. Thanks to you." She swept from the room.

I rocked back on my heels, letting the information register. I glanced at Fisk. He stood in the middle of the squalor, peering around with pain. His eyes shone with unshed tears.

"I didn't know about this place," he said. "I could have helped them, but they probably scattered when Master Bloodgood and his magicians arrived."

"Won't they come back?" I gestured to the piles of possessions.

"Maybe." He swiped his eyes. "I'll post a few watchers and if they return, we'll offer them better shelter and jobs."

I picked up the boy's apron and teapot, figuring he would want them when he woke.

Fisk nodded with approval. "They're probably his mother's. My guess is she's either dead or has abandoned him, leaving him at the mercy of his abusive father. Which would explain his fear of men."

I pointed to the stuffed dog. "I think he might have a sister."

"If she shows up here, I'll make sure she knows where he is."

Without the distraction of magic, the horrible living conditions and filth assaulted my senses. As we left, I asked, "Fisk, how does this happen? Aren't there agencies in the Citadel to help these people?"

"There is one. And they are so overwhelmed it's ridiculous." He sighed. "Believe it or not, some of these people choose to live this way. They refuse all help. Others just don't know where to go."

"You've done a lot."

"As you can see, not near enough. I tried spreading the word, but there are these little groups who stay isolated. Plus I'm dealing with vicious rumors."

"Really? I've heard nothing but praise."

"That's in your world. This world—" he stabbed a finger toward the ground "—views us differently. They're either jealous, afraid or spiteful."

"What are they afraid of? You're helping people."

"They listen to the rumors and the wild stories of us selling kids as slaves, smuggling drugs, organizing prostitution and kids being forced to work for me," he said in frustration. "It's hard to reason with a frightened child." He stepped toward the door, being careful not to crush anything under his feet.

I followed his example. Concentrating on where I walked, I bumped right into him. He had stopped. I met his intense gaze.

A thin ribbon of fear curled in my chest. "What?"

"*You* reasoned with a terrified kid. Saved him and the blanket of power." Fisk gestured to the sleeping mats. "These people don't trust *anyone*. Did you use magic on him? No...you don't have any..."

I waited as he chased the logic. It didn't take him long.

"How did you get in? Even the Master Magicians couldn't break through the barrier."

Again, I let him put the pieces together. It was sort of fun. With the way he tilted his head and his inward gaze, I imagined faint clicks echoing in his mind until he figured it out with one loud snap.

Fisk grabbed my shoulders. "Magic doesn't work on you." His eyes danced with excitement. "Like Valek. And you feel magic, too. That's why you looked like you were fighting a strong wind. Holy snow cats is right!"

"Fisk, I—"

"That's why you came."

"You need—"

*Maria V. Snyder*

"Wow. The Council's going to be thrilled. Why haven't you told them?"

I sighed. "It's complicated. Besides, they'll know soon enough since both Masters are now informed. Can you keep it quiet for a while? I don't want it to become public knowledge."

A shrewd look slid across his face. "I can for a price."

"Scoundrel. How much?"

He touched his chest as if I had offended him. "Not money. I may need your…special skills in the future to aid my Helper's Guild members, and it would be comforting to know I can engage your services."

Smooth. I guessed he was sixteen years old, but his obvious intelligence and experience from growing up on the streets made him appear older. With his long eyelashes, he was going to be popular with the girls if he wasn't already.

"Agreed," I said.

When we exited the building, two of his members appeared. Fisk assigned them the task of watching for the missing residents. During the discussion, I studied their faces. The kids seemed eager, serious and confident, but I wondered if they played or had fun. I examined the teapot in my hands. Fine cracks ran through the pattern of roses. Chips lined the handle and the lid was missing. Did the children in the Helper's Guild feel loved?

He finished and the two hurried off. I worried they would be on their own tonight. I huffed, but not with humor, more like self-disgust. First time I ever wondered about them. Or cared, to be brutally honest. Fisk had mentioned this world versus my world. And I agreed.

My world didn't include rancid bedding and filth. My

world didn't have children without homes and caring parents. My world included warmth, food and love. But our worlds did have one thing in common—bad people.

Quartz and I headed toward the Magician's Keep in the northeast corner of the Citadel. The white marble walls reflected the sunlight and bounced traffic noise, creating echoes. I avoided the crowded market in the center of the Citadel. Instead I bypassed it to the south and cut through the Sitian government complex, which filled the southeast quarter.

The sight of the Master Magicians' towers rising above the other buildings sent a wave of memories crashing over me. I waded through them, avoiding the awful ones and focusing on the pleasant ones from my five years as a student.

At the entrance to the Keep, the guard stopped me.

"Master Bloodgood wants to see you in his office," he said.

"Please tell him I'll be there after I settle Quartz into the stables."

Along with the guards, at least one magician worked at the gate at all times for safety and to relay messages to the magicians inside.

"No. Now," the guard said. "Your horse can find her way there without you."

Annoyed, I snapped. "And get chewed out by the Stable Master? No thank you. Have someone take her or I will."

After a bit of discussion, a stable hand appeared to escort Quartz. Satisfied, I crossed to the Keep's administration building. Imposing marble steps led up to the main entrance. The rectangular-shaped structure consisted of offices and conference rooms for the managerial staff as well as offices for the Master Magicians.

A feeling of being home touched me for a brief moment. As I navigated the well-known hallways, I encountered pools of magic. A few graduates from the Keep's program worked in various positions in administration. The random touch of power sent chills along my skin. I remembered Janco's nickname for the place. Creepy Keepy.

"Come in," First Magician Bain Bloodgood called through his office door.

I entered and smiled. As usual, clutter filled the room. Heaps of books strained the shelves. Odd devices and half-completed experiments littered his worktable. Piles of paper threatened to spill onto his desk. The messy office matched his wild gray hair, and the long navy robe reminded me of all the times I had sat opposite him, discussing Sitian history with him. His face would all but glow with pride when I had remembered an arcane bit of knowledge he had taught me.

I approached his desk. He glanced up from the book spread open before him. A stranger met my gaze. His appraisal lacked kindness or curiosity. The wrinkles around his mouth deepened with his annoyed frown. Dark smudges stood out against the pale, paper-thin skin clinging to his face.

"Why didn't you tell us?" he demanded.

Taken aback, I scrambled for a reply. "I told Irys—"

"She told me your pathetic excuses. What I want to know is why you kept such a valuable skill secret from us when you had created such a crisis in Sitia?"

"Crisis?"

"The crisis due to your sacrifice. Giving up your

magic has ground communications to a halt. It's as if we have all gone suddenly deaf. Your glass messengers were vital to commerce and to my network of magicians. The Council doesn't even want to hear your name."

The ground dissolved under my feet. I groped for the chair, afraid I would fall. "But what about now? I saved a boy today and protected the power source."

Bain's anger deflated a bit. "You did an excellent job today. Once the boy is recovered, he will be enrolled in the Keep to learn how to control his magic. However, even saving the boy's life won't be enough to sway the Council's opinion."

"What do you mean?"

"I'm afraid if I inform the Council about your immunity now, they'll be afraid."

Confused, I gripped the armchair. "Why?"

"The whole nasty business with Akako has them on edge. So much that I had to assign every Councilor a magician to protect them. A magician would not be able to stop you."

"That's extreme. I wouldn't—"

"I know, but as I said, they're not acting rational. Wait awhile, Opal," Bain said. "I will tell the Council when they're ready. I'm hopeful everyone will relax soon. With Councilor Moon returning to the sessions this week, I'm sure it won't be long. For now, Irys and I will keep you busy."

Bain stood and walked around his desk. My head spun as if I was falling from a great height. Before I could reply, his arm settled on my shoulders and he guided me to the hallway.

"You look exhausted, child. You're welcome to stay

in the Keep's guest quarters as long as you like. Get some sleep." Bain closed the door.

I mulled over our conversation. Was I supposed to hang around the Keep waiting for Bain or Irys to give me something to do? Working for the Council didn't appeal to me, but I would help the Master Magicians.

However, I wasn't going to remain idle. Finn was a magician. And I suspected he had been Keep trained. I would use my time here to learn more about him.

It wasn't until I stood in the formal garden in the middle of the Keep's campus that I realized I had wandered without a destination in mind. The apprentice wings bookended me and the Fire Memorial glinted with reds and yellows in the afternoon sunlight. Having no desire to reminisce about the past, I averted my gaze from the statue.

Magic collected in parts of the campus like stationary clouds of dust. Without warning, I would walk into one, stumbling on the sudden thickness of the air. A feeling of unease crept through my bones as if these pools of magic waited to ambush me. Janco nailed it. Creepy Keepy.

Shaking off my disquiet, I pondered my present situation. I could return home and smooth the relationship with my mother. Or I could travel to the coast and stay with Kade. Or I could return to Fulgor to work in my factory and be close to my friends. And visit Devlen? I refused to answer that question. I also could stay here a few days and ask around. Perhaps Finn had come through the Citadel on his way to sell my blood. It was more appealing than waiting for an assignment from Bain.

Feeling better, I stopped by the guest room manager's

office to secure a room. My possessions had already been delivered. He handed me a key. Then I checked on Quartz. She grazed in the small pasture located along the back wall of the Keep, looking healthy and content. She trotted over and nuzzled me.

The Keep's glass shop was to the east of the pasture. Mara was the shop's manager. Light gray clouds puffed from the kiln's chimney. The hot, sweet smell of burning white coal filled the air, and a faint hum reached me. In the past, the scent alone would have drawn me in.

Instead, I passed the shop and found the Weapons Master drilling first-year students in self-defense. They worked in the training yard next to the armory, sweating in the warm sun.

A wide smile spread across Captain Marrok's face. "Opal! Good to see you." He shook my hand. "When did you get back?"

"This morning."

"Have you been keeping up with your training?" he asked.

I laughed. The seasoned soldier didn't waste time on pleasantries. His reputation as the best Weapons Master in years had been well earned. His gray hair bristled from his scalp, matching the short commands he shouted to the students. Long ropes of muscle covered his arms and his roughened hands sported a spider's web of scars.

"I'm keeping fit," I said. If he counted Valek's special training, then I was in good shape.

"Yeah? Care to prove it to me?"

"Not today, I've only had a few hours' sleep last night."

"Tomorrow then. Right after breakfast."

"Yes, sir!"

With a mock salute, he returned to work, encouraging students and demonstrating moves. I stayed by the fence until the session ended. Students gathered practice swords and milled about.

Deep down, I recognized my procrastination. Why was I avoiding the glass shop? I had designed it. I had ordered all the equipment. I had helped get the kiln running. A lot of memories resided in there. The answer to my question snapped in my mind. I worried those recollections would ambush me and I wasn't strong enough to fight my way through them.

Utter nonsense. Determined, I walked toward the building, focusing on the good times, remembering when Piecov had spilled a wheelbarrow full of lime, coating everything with white powder.

"Um. Excuse me," a boy called from behind me.

I turned. One of the first-year students hustled closer. He skidded to a stop about an arm's length away. Uncertainty filled his gaze. I guessed his age to be around fourteen.

"Are you Opal Cowan?" he asked. His voice cracked midsentence.

"Yes. Can I help you?"

Sudden resolve hardened his features. His hand dipped into his pocket, and the distinctive snick of a switchblade sounded. "Yes. You can die!"

# 18

I stepped back, keeping my hands in sight as the student advanced. He held the switchblade in front of him, signaling his unfamiliarity with the weapon. When he stabbed it toward my neck, I blocked his arm so the blade missed. Then I grabbed his wrist with both my hands while turning to the side, yanking him off balance. Now I had control of his weapon and his arm. Basic knife defense.

Finding a point on his wrist, I applied a little pressure. He yelped and the switchblade dropped to the ground. I pulled his thumb back and he went down on his knees in pain.

"Why did you attack me?" I asked him.

No answer. However, a strong bubble of magic bloomed from him, pushing me. Expecting this attack, I leaned into the power. He sent another robust swell before stopping. Impressive.

"You're out of options, Puppy Dog. Talk to me." I suppressed a groan. I couldn't believe I just quoted Janco.

Silence.

I increased the tension in his hand. "Hard to finish class assignments with a broken thumb. Last time. Why?"

Pure hatred beamed from his blue eyes. His cheekbones reminded me of another regal face, which had sneered at me in disdain and contempt through most of my years at the Keep. Understanding dawned. I scooped up his weapon, then pushed Pazia Cloud Mist's little brother away from me. He sprawled on the ground for a mere second before hopping to his feet. Ah, youth.

I stood in a fighting stance, holding the knife close to my body, while keeping my free arm extended in front. "Didn't Captain Marrok teach you not to attack with a weapon until you learned how to fight with it? 'Cause now you're unarmed and I'm not."

"I don't care," he said. "You ruined my family."

"How?"

He sputtered. With his face reddening, he charged me. I sidestepped and tripped him as he lunged past. He slid into a bush. Once he regained his feet, he wheeled around and rushed. I faked a dodge, tricking him to veer left where I clotheslined him. He fell onto his back. But this time I followed him down, pressing my forearm on his windpipe. Struggling, he tried to push me away. I intensified the pressure, pinching off his air.

All color drained from his face. Panic and fear replaced his anger.

When he stilled, I eased up and said, "While this is fun, I have more important things to do. So listen up, Puppy Dog. Your family is *not* ruined. Last time I checked, everyone was healthy, wealthy and schmoozing with the political elite. Pazia and I are both responsible for what happened to her. We worked it out and are friends.

"Obviously, you're not happy with our arrangement. You can ambush and attack me again, except the next time I *will* hurt you. Or you can learn how to fight, and then challenge me to a match with a referee, witnesses…the works." I stood and extended my hand, offering to help him up.

He rubbed his neck, staring at me. "You'd honor a challenge?"

"Yes."

"What if I challenged you now?"

"Then my opinion of your stupidity would be supported. Otherwise, I'd agree to the match. It's a guaranteed win for me."

A balloon of his magic spread over me. It popped. "Do you have a null shield around you?"

"I'm not inclined to tell you, Puppy Dog." Keeping my immunity a secret wasn't going to last long at the Keep.

Ignoring my hand, he sprang to his feet. He straightened and puffed out his chest. "My name is Walker Vasko Cloud Mist the Second. Expect my challenge."

"Aww… You're cute when you're trying to be haughty, Puppy Dog. I look forward to our match. In the meantime, don't flash this around until you know how to use it." I tossed him his switchblade, gave him a jaunty wave and continued toward the glass shop.

His challenge didn't concern me too much, but I wondered if Pazia's father, Vasko, was Finn's client. As one of the richest men in Sitia, he had plenty of gold. As for the hate, he never gave me an indication when I had met him. He had even offered to support me with

the production of my glass messengers. But the friend-
liness could have been an act, and he really believed I
was fully responsible for his daughter's situation.

I considered Pazia. We had become friends despite
everything. And unlike Devlen and me, she retained
a small bit of her magic. It had been a blow for her to
go from potential master-level to basically a one-trick
magician.

Adding research into the Vasko family to my to-do
list, I entered the glass shop; the heat from the kiln
wrapped me in warmth. I hadn't even broken a sweat
fighting Puppy Dog. Standing near the door, I scanned
the room as the roar from the kilns vibrated through my
boots. Kilns? Mara had added another one along with
two more annealing ovens. I toured the shop, searching for more additions. She had designed a water system and installed a drying rack to evaporate the water
inside of the blowpipes.

Students worked at gaffer benches, turning molten
glass slugs into a variety of items. A few acknowledged
me, but the others concentrated on their tasks. One of
the new first-year students dipped a long thin rod—a
pontil iron—into the kiln's cauldron. Squinting into the
bright orange light, she rushed the gather, dripping hot
glass onto the lip of the cauldron and down onto the
floor. The long strings hardened and broke, making a
mess. Plus the lip was now sticky. Mara would be upset
by the sloppy effort.

I helped the newbie clean up and demonstrated the
proper way to gather. "You need to dip into the liquid
glass, like this." I opened the kiln's door a crack, sliding the iron over the lip. Raising my end up, I pushed
the tip into the mixture and spun the rod with my fin-

gers as if wrapping thread around a spool. "Then you push forward and pull up, but keep the rod spinning. See how it sticks like taffy?" I drew the slug from the hot kiln and closed the door with my hip. The molten glass flickered with an orange heartbeat.

I kept the iron parallel with the floor, spinning it. "Big angles mean big trouble. See what happens when I hold the end up? The glass coats the iron and there is nothing hanging off the end to work with. And when I tip it down…" Glass bulged, and would have dropped to the floor if I kept that angle. "Even if you do keep it level, if you don't keep spinning the rod…" I stopped and the glass dripped.

Scraping glass off the floor, I dumped the bits into the cullet barrel to be remelted, and stuck the glass-covered end of the iron into a bucket of water. I grabbed a clean rod and handed it to the girl. "Your turn."

She rushed through it again. Hard not to, with the twenty-three-hundred-degree heat and searing light pouring from the kiln. I admired her determination as she kept trying. And I celebrated with her when she gathered a perfect round slug.

"Now what?" she asked. Her young face peered at me with excitement.

A brief memory of my first gather flashed through my mind, bringing back the pride and feelings of accomplishment. Feelings I needed to acknowledge more often in my own life. Despite the result, getting into and out of Wirral was a heck of a feat.

"To the colored glass powder!" I shouted. "Everyone's first project is always a paperweight."

I helped her shape her molten blob into a multicolored—and a bit lumpy—paperweight, instructing her how to break it off the rod and into the annealing oven. Glass had to cool slowly or the finished piece would crack.

A passion burned in her eyes. She had caught glass fever. "What's next?"

"I'll show you how to thumb a bubble." I pulled a blowpipe from the heater and blew through the hollow pipe, making sure it wasn't blocked. After gathering a slug, I sent a puff of air into the pipe and covered the hole with my thumb. A bubble of air grew inside the slug. I still marveled at my ability to produce the round shape. Before losing my magic, I would blow through the pipe, but, instead of air, magic would be trapped inside the glass. The interior would glow, but the glass wouldn't expand at all.

"You can puff and blow to start one, but thumbing is easier," I said. "And once you have a starter bubble, it's not hard to expand it." Working with the glass, I created a dolphin.

"How do you make a vase?"

"You need to transfer the piece to another rod. It's more complicated and you're not ready yet."

"How do I get ready?"

Oh yes, she had the fever. "Practice, practice and more practice. Make sure you keep your first efforts. You'll be amazed how much you improve in only half a season."

"Then you'll show me the next step?"

I hedged. "If I'm around."

"Great! Thanks for your help." She extended her hand. "I'm Keelin."

I shook it. "Opal." I hurried away before she could recover from her shock. The story of my adventures in Hubal had reached the Keep via the lightning-fast gossip network. According to Mara, the students had marveled over my "ultimate" sacrifice and the topic had been endlessly debated.

After a full night's rest, I ate breakfast and joined Captain Marrok in the training yard on the east side of the Keep. Dark clouds covered the sky, threatening rain. Marrok had a difficult time beating me during our match, but he still claimed my skills had lost their edge. He assigned Sarn as my sparring partner for the rest of the gray morning.

I was glad to see a familiar face, but Sarn could wrestle a couple of bulls and win. He was in his fourth year of study and his magic could move objects and people.

"Hiya, Opal!" He beamed. "I missed you."

"Tired of picking on first-years already?" I teased.

"Yeah. They're no fun. Not a single one of them can break my hold." He shrugged his massive shoulders. Muscles wrapped around his thick arms and legs. Despite all his bulk, he was flexible.

But not fast. I could outrun him if I escaped. Big if. "Can anyone in the Keep break your hold?"

"Only one."

"Just one? Who?"

Sarn's eyes about popped out. "Did losing your magic mean you lost your memory?"

I thought back to my last bout with Sarn. "You can't count that. It was cheating." I had used a pressure point on him.

"Oh no, it wasn't. It was a perfect move. How many other defenses leave no bruises or stop hurting immediately? None. It's great for fending off drunks who pick fights, and people you don't want to injure, but you want to warn them you *could* hurt them."

Except if a person kept the pressure on the point, it was unbearable torture. With my firsthand experience, I had learned almost all the sensitive places on a body.

"I found one of the spots," Sarn said.

Great. Yet another one of my mistakes coming back to bite me. "Have you taught it to anyone?"

"Not yet." He peered at me in confusion. "What's wrong with teaching it? You used it on that Cloud Mist whelp the other day."

Interesting how I hadn't even hesitated to use the move on Puppy Dog or the guard in the prison, and I had felt no remorse. Not like the time I had broken Sarn's grip. Then I had been upset.

Before, pressure points and Devlen equaled evil. Now. Not so much.

"Sarn, what happens when that defensive move is learned by the wrong people?"

"I wouldn't use it in a real fight."

"Why not?"

"Come on, Opal. Basic self-defense. Hit and git. I'm not going to play nice with an opponent who wants to hurt me. When I hit him, my plan is to knock him down so he can't get up and chase me when I git."

"Using pressure points is playing nice?"

"Yep."

"I'll remember that when we're sparring."

He grinned. "I don't intend to let you get that close." Staying true to his promise, Sarn launched an in-and-out attack.

His speed had improved in a year. Outrunning him was no longer an option.

After the grueling workout with Sarn, I aimed my bruised body toward the bathhouse. Soaking in the warm water, I enjoyed a moment of peace. The students were attending their second morning session so the place was empty. I didn't miss going to class at all. But I missed Kade. We had so little time together.

Six days remained in the warm season. Then Kade would be busy with the heating season's storms. And what would I do if I traveled to the coast? Keep Kade company, search the beach for treasures with Heli and help Helen with the glass orbs?

I longed to talk to Devlen, as well. Changing into clean clothes, I headed to the market.

"Lovely lady, can I assist you with your shopping today?" A thin boy, who looked to be ten years old but acted more like twenty, asked.

"No, thank you. But can you deliver a message to Fisk for me?" I slipped the boy a copper.

He flashed a smile. "I can, but I can't guarantee an answer."

"Fair enough. Please tell Fisk, Opal is in need of his *special* services."

He saluted and disappeared into the Citadel market's crowd. I marveled at the bustling stands and shops. Even though rain dripped onto shoppers, no one seemed to mind. Members of the Helper's Guild carried armfuls of packages, haggled with stand owners, or dashed from place to place, leading confused customers to the perfect store.

The market was located in the exact center of the Citadel. Businesses and factories ringed the vast space, emanating out in concentric circles like ripples on a pond. Packed full of sellers hawking their wares, the market breathed as if alive.

The best way to navigate the various stores and craftsmen was to hire a Helper's Guild member. They knew the honest sellers, competent workers and the good deals. Without them, a buyer could be conned out of a lot of money. Hiring them also kept the poor and homeless children fed and clothed. Fisk recruited them to work for him, giving them a place to stay and money to live on.

"Lovely Opal. So nice to see you again," Fisk said in his new baritone. He held a clipboard in his oversize hands. "How is the boy?"

"About the same." When I had checked on him, he hadn't regained consciousness.

"How can I help you?"

I chose my words with care. "I need to find a person who has something of mine."

"You'll have to be a little more specific." Amusement lit his brown eyes.

I explained about Finn and my blood, guessing if Finn had been hired in the Citadel, Fisk might have heard about it.

He tapped his fingers on the board. "An odd request. And I don't normally deal with people who perform illicit deeds. However, I have a few contacts and can make some inquiries for you."

"A few contacts?"

"Just in case. I like to be prepared for all customers. Anything else?" Fisk asked.

I couldn't stay in the guest quarters of the Creepy Keepy much longer. With all the magic there, it suffocated me. Whichever way my future unrolled, I would probably spend at least half the year in the Citadel.

"I need a place to live. Small, private and secure enough I don't have to worry about it when I'm away. Is that part of your services?" I asked. I had been in the western section of the Citadel where the majority of residences were located. The maze of streets, buildings and courtyards confused me, and the sheer density of them packed together overwhelmed me.

"Of course. For the right price, I can be—"

"A prince. I remember."

We were interrupted by one of Fisk's guild members. The young lady stood on tiptoe and leaned close to his ear, whispering to him. Fisk frowned then nodded to her. She dashed away.

His gaze turned speculative. "Opal, do you remember when those fake diamonds flooded the black market last year?"

"Yes." I had helped find the source.

"Do you know anything about pearls?"

"I know oysters make them, and where they're harvested." I suppressed a shudder, recalling the emotionless Bloodrose family. They lived in isolation at the tip of Lion's Claw Peninsula, exchanging pearls for other supplies. I wondered about the cold glass. Walsh Bloodrose, the clan's patriarch, was a magician. Perhaps he invented it.

"Could you tell a fake from a real pearl?"

"Not anymore." Without my magic, I couldn't determine if those diamonds were real or fake.

"You're still an artist. You might spot something we missed."

"Is someone selling fake pearls on the black market?"

"We're not sure. Pearls are harder to find than most gemstones, except diamonds. But now the market is inundated with them. Even the legitimate jewelry stores are fully stocked."

"Have you asked Elita? She's an expert in precious stones." Plus, she had been very helpful since her part in the diamond incident was revealed.

"She thinks the black market ones are real, but they're different."

"In a good or bad way?"

"We've no idea. They could be from a new species of oyster and our concerns are for nothing." He shrugged. "We'll just have to wait and see if anything develops. In the meantime, lovely Opal, I will make a few inquiries and find you a castle."

I spent the remainder of the day visiting my old friend and mentor, Aydan. Working with him in his glass shop had been my lifeline while I had been a student. By the time we had caught up on news and shared a meal, it was late. My footsteps echoed in the empty streets of the Citadel as I returned to the Keep. Even more time had passed than I realized. I reached through my pants pocket, grasping the handle of my switchblade. No real reason to worry as this section of town was patrolled on a regular basis, but Valek had taught me not to trust those illusions of safety.

The night stayed quiet. A block from the Keep, a small furtive movement to my right caught my attention. I spun, pulled my weapon and froze in midyank. A little girl, too young to be out on her own at this time of night, stepped into the lantern light. She reminded me of a wild rabbit. One move and she would dash away.

I waited for her to speak. She scanned the street before she met my gaze. Her large blue eyes held fear and determination. Dirt streaked her face and her corkscrew curls hung past her shoulders in a tangled mess. She held a stuffed dog to her chest as if it were her shield. Perhaps it was. I recognized the pink bow.

"Where's my brother?" she asked in a strong, no-nonsense tone.

I inclined my head toward the Keep. "In the infirmary."

She suppressed her horrified gasp with amazing speed. Impressive.

"What did you do to him?" she demanded.

"Nothing. He pulled too much magic and almost died. He's suffering from exhaustion."

She cocked her hip and glared at me. "That's what that helper whore said. I didn't believe her and I don't believe you."

Helper whore? A thousand questions formed in my mind, but I stifled my curiosity. Instead, I challenged her. "Are you calling me a liar?"

"Yes, I am."

Bold. I liked this girl. "Then let me prove it to you. Come with me."

She stepped back as if I had brandished a weapon. "Why should I trust you?"

"Because you don't have anyone else left to trust," I guessed. "And you came to me. Why?"

"You were the only one..." She swallowed. "My brother pushed everyone out. Even me." She glanced at the stuffed dog as a glassy sheen coated her eyes.

"No one could get into the building. Except you." Stabbing an accusatory finger at me, she asked, "What did you do to him?"

"I kept him from dying." A light touch of power brushed my skin. She was too young to have magic, let alone be able to control it. I glanced around. No one was within sight. Perhaps it came from the Keep.

She nodded. "Now you're telling the truth. Can I see my brother?"

"One condition."

Instantly wary, she checked the street as if planning her escape route. "What is it?"

"You tell me your name and your brother's name."

"That's two."

I grinned. "All right, then on two conditions."

"What do I get in return for the extra condition?" she asked.

"My name."

My offer didn't produce much enthusiasm from her.

"And a bowl of soup," I added. "Do we have a deal, Miss…?" I extended my hand.

After the slightest of hesitations, she clasped it for one quick shake. "Reema." She yanked her hand away. Her long, thin fingers had felt brittle in mine. She would need more than one bowl of soup.

"And your brother?" I asked.

"Teegan."

I led her past the Keep's guards and to the infirmary. Healer Hayes stood outside Teegan's room. Concern creased his face as he whispered to Irys. The words *null shield* filled me with an icy dread. An automatic reaction. Reema sensed my unease and slowed her pace.

A null shield would be necessary to keep Teegan

alive. Waking in an unfamiliar place surrounded by unfamiliar people, he could pull magic and risk flaming out again.

Irys and Hayes ceased their conversation as we neared. No surprise touched the Master Magician's face, but Hayes stepped toward me.

"Something wrong, Opal?" he asked. "Are you ill?"

"I'm fine. I've brought a visitor."

He raised his eyebrows and I realized Reema hid behind me. I moved aside.

"Ah... It's a little late for visitors."

"She's Teegan's sister." I introduced her.

He crouched down to her level. "Your brother is gaining more strength each day. What is your clan name?"

Reema pressed next to me. "Why do you need it?"

"I can create a stronger bond between us. Teegan's been unconscious since he arrived and I can only reach him on a subconscious level. The more I know about him the better."

Hayes had said the wrong thing. I felt her stiffen. Before she could bolt, I laid my hand on her bony shoulder.

"Let's visit with Teegan first, and I promised Reema some soup." I gave Hayes a pointed look.

He straightened. "Of course. I'll send one of my assistants to the kitchen. I'll also have an extra bed brought in. It's too late for Reema to go home." He hurried away, calling to one of his helpers.

Irys had been studying the girl, and I willed the Master Magician not to scare her off. She met my gaze and nodded with approval. "Let me know if anything changes," she said before leaving.

I pushed open Teegan's door. The lantern by his bedside cast a weak light. White blankets covered a small lump on the bed.

Reema climbed up, put her stuffed dog down on his pillow and shook him hard. "Tee, it's me. Wake up."

"Easy." I tried to pull her away, but she shrugged me off.

"Come on, Tee. Wake up." This time, she straddled him and bounced.

I grabbed her around her skinny waist and yanked her off the bed. She fought me, but she didn't have the muscles or the stamina to break my hold. One benefit to the ruckus, Teegan opened his eyes.

"S'okay, Ree." He glanced at me. A wispy thread of magic grazed my face. Before I could raise an alarm, it disappeared.

"Stay with Fire Lady, Ree. S'okay." His eyes closed.

Reema had stopped struggling. I let her go. This time, she sat on the edge of his bed and held his hand. Her stubborn pout dared me to make her move. Instead, I plopped into the chair as weariness flowed through my body.

"Is this Fire Lady a friend of yours?" I asked her.

"No."

"A relative?"

"No. We don't have any relatives."

"Yes, you do. You're part of a clan, and if you dig far enough back into history, you're distantly related to all the members in your clan."

"Our mother told us not to tell anyone our clan name. She said no one would know it."

Progress. "Where is your mother? She should know about Teegan."

"She's buried under a red rock in the Courtyard of Souls."

"I'm sorry—"

"Shut up. Tee and I are just fine. Once he gets better, we can take care of ourselves."

Such confidence. With her small stature she could pass for six years old, but I guessed she was closer to eight.

"Who is this Fire Lady? I can try to contact her for you."

Reema ignored my question. Her attention was fixed on the night table. Next to the lantern was Teegan's teapot resting on top of his apron. Someone had washed and folded the garment. The girl stroked the fabric with her fingertips. "I thought they had been stolen."

"I brought them here. I thought he might want them when he woke."

She turned her gaze to me. And for the first time I saw behind her tough girl mask. It took all my strength not to wrap her in my arms. The arrival of Hayes with a tray saved me from giving in to that desire. Reema launched herself at the food, eating with a steady determination as if the soup, fruit and cheeses would be snatched away.

Hayes pulled me from the room, closing the door. "Did she give you any more information?"

I relayed the sparse details.

He sighed. "Orphans. Wonderful." He rubbed a hand along the stubble on his cheek. Dark smudges underlined his brown eyes. "Teegan's a powerful magician. If he can control his magic, he'll be enrolled in the Keep's program." He scowled.

I guessed where his thoughts went. If Teegan can't

control his magic, he would be joining his mother in the Courtyard of Souls.

Hayes returned his distant gaze to me. "Reema, however, is another story. We'll have to contact the authorities and find her a place to stay. She can sleep in his room for a couple nights, otherwise…she's yours."

"Mine? But I thought—"

"She trusts you, and I need you to find out as much about her brother as possible."

"But…"

"What? Do you have something else to do?"

Yes, but I needed to be in the Keep regardless. After Hayes left to check on his other patients, I returned to Teegan's room. Reema had devoured every bit of food. When a knock sounded, she startled. I opened the door, stepping back so Hayes's assistant could wheel in another bed. The sheets smelled of soap—a contrast to the rancid odor emanating from the little girl who eyed the assistant with distrust.

My charge. At least for the next few days. First order of business would be a bath. But when I made the suggestion, she refused.

"I need to go home," she said.

"It's too late to be out by yourself," I tried.

Reema scoffed.

"That abandoned warehouse isn't a home," I said.

She bristled. "You know nothing about it."

True. But she loved her brother. "You're right. But I do know Teegan needs you here. He hasn't woken for the healer, but he woke for *you*. Without you here, he might not get better."

A snort of derision. "You're bluffing. All you grown-ups are the same. You think I'm some dumb kid. That

I would stay here and be easy prey for the Citadel's guards to pick up." She hopped off the bed.

"At least let me contact this Fire Lady. Teegan told you to stay with her, remember?"

Reema snagged her lower lip with her teeth for a second before crossing her arms. "He's sick. He doesn't know what he's talking about."

It had been easier to stop a flameout than convince this girl. This whole situation felt familiar. I searched my memory and it didn't take long. Some recollections never fade with time. Although I might not think about my sister Tula every day, she was always in my heart.

"I'm not bluffing about Teegan," I said. "My sister needed me with her. She wouldn't wake for the healers or for Master Magician Jewelrose or for Yelena Zaltana, the Soulfinder. Master Jewelrose showed up in the middle of the night, took me from my home in Booruby and brought me here." I gestured, indicating the room. "I was terrified, worried about my sister and overwhelmed. They claimed I was the key to saving her. What if I did something wrong and she died because of me?"

The memory of those dark days surged through my body and transported me back in time. I saw Tula, not Teegan, lying on the bed, looking small and brittle. My body ached to hold my sister again. If I had been as smart and savvy as Reema, I wouldn't have let her murderer into the room. Wouldn't have gone with his accomplice, trusting them to keep their word that Tula would live if I cooperated.

"What happened?" Reema asked.

Dragging myself to the present, I said to her, "I crawled into bed with my sister and stayed by her side.

I helped Yelena coax her back to consciousness." The girl didn't need to know the sad ending to the tale. Instead I let the joy of having Tula awake and healthy shine on my face. I would always treasure those few days we had together.

"If I stay here, will you promise me one thing?" she asked.

"If I can, I will."

She nodded. "If I'm captured by the Citadel's guards, promise me you won't let them sell me to the Helper's Guild."

# 19

I blinked at Reema for a moment. Had she really uttered the words "sell me" and "Helper's Guild" in the same breath? I remembered Fisk's comments about vicious rumors, but had taken them in stride, never imagining the actual reality of them. She scrutinized my body language and balanced on the balls of her feet. Convinced of the danger, she would run away if I didn't promise to protect her.

Now wasn't the time to assure her about the true nature of the Guild. "No one will sell you to the Helper's Guild. I promise," I said.

With the slightest softening in her posture, she stuck out her hand. I shook it and she relaxed.

"What's next?" she asked.

"A bath." When her stubborn chin jutted, I added, "The bathhouse is empty right now. Unless you want to wait until morning and be there with all the students? Your choice."

"No it isn't. Don't play those games with me. You be straight with me and I'll be straight with you. Deal?"

She didn't sound like an eight-year-old. "No sugar-coating?"

"None."

"How old are you?" I asked.

"Does it matter?"

"To me, yes. You're either a child genius or older than you look."

She flashed me a grin. "I'm both."

"Humor's okay then?"

"Yes."

"All right. So naked truth it is. Do we need another handshake or maybe a blood oath just for something different?" I asked.

Another grin. "I'm ten, and my mother taught me to listen past people's words and hear their true intentions."

"Smart lady. Did she teach you to play fair?" One of my pet peeves, I believed schooling kids to play fair failed to prepare them for adulthood.

"No." Reema tucked her stuffed dog under Teegan's covers. He rolled over and curled his arm around the toy. "Let's go."

"Don't you want to know my name?"

"I know it. That healer called you Opal when we arrived."

Smart girl. The bathhouse was straight north of the infirmary. As I guided Reema, I played tour guide as we passed the dining hall and formal garden located in the center of the Keep's complex. The two apprentice wings curved around the sides of the garden like an incomplete ring around a bull's-eye. Torches lit the empty pathways. No pools or webs of magic touched me. A nice respite. I hurried Reema past the Fire Memorial. I didn't have the energy to explain its significance to her.

As predicted, we had the bathhouse to ourselves. I helped her wash her hair. After multiple scrubbings, her true color emerged—white blond. Beautiful.

Reema frowned at the long coils.

"It's lovely," I said, combing out the knots before it could dry.

"It stands out. Not a good thing where I live." She scanned the elegant bathhouse.

The arched walls and high ceiling had been decorated with colorful mosaics. Blue-green tiles lined the oval pool. In the corner, the washing area had metal spigots protruding from the walls above head level. The water would rain from one of them when the lever hanging next to it was pulled. A rack nearby held piles of clean towels. A mirror image of this half of the bathhouse resided on the other side for the males.

"I guess around here, you'd want to stand out," Reema said. "You'd want to be the best and brightest at the Magician's Keep. Right?"

"The magicians and teachers don't compare you to other students, but everyone knows who is strong and who has limited power. By the end of the first season of the first year, the pecking order has been established."

"It must have been fun being at the top."

I paused. Why would she…? Oh. She had watched me enter a building no one else could, not even a Master Magician. Naked truth sounded refreshing, but might be harder than I first thought.

"Actually, I was at the very bottom," I said.

She turned. "Really?"

I considered. "It's a long, complicated story."

"Tell me…please."

"Why do you want to know?"

"Stories help me sleep at night."

I imagined her life. Living in a condemned warehouse, no parents, no food unless she found, stole or begged for some, she had to constantly worry about predators and the Citadel's guards. Stories would be an escape from her harsh reality.

My future life may be uncertain, but I would not let Reema go back to that horror. I vowed I would find her a home.

I told her about my misadventures as a first-year student. Her light laugh spurred me to dig deeper for the humorous moments. Interesting, I hadn't considered them funny at the time. I stopped once we arrived back at the infirmary. She jumped into the extra bed in Teegan's room without reclaiming her stuffed dog. I guessed she felt safe.

Pulling the covers up to her chin, I promised to return in the morning. I turned the lantern down to the lowest setting and said good-night.

"Good night, Fire Lady," she said.

I paused in the threshold. I'd been called various names before, but that was a new one. Unable to squelch my curiosity, I asked, "How do you know Teegan was referring to me?"

"I just do."

"Why fire?"

"You'll have to ask my brother."

I'd spent time with Reema over the course of the next couple days. She mainly stayed by Teegan's side, but she needed fresh air and Hayes needed information about her and Teegan. I'd shown her more of the Keep's complex, hoping to deepen our connection. Unfortunately, she had refused to share any more details. At least her brother's strength increased every day.

When I arrived on the third morning, Reema sat cross-legged on her bed. She read aloud from a book resting on her lap. I listened for a while, glad she could read. It would give her an advantage on the streets.

Finding her a home was proving to be impossible. My visit to Child Services had been a frustrating and depressing experience. By the time I reached the correct agent, she took Reema's file, set it atop a three-foot-high pile and instructed me in a dead voice to deliver the child to care facility number two. Knowing Reema, she would be there for five minutes before escaping. When I asked if Reema had a chance to be adopted, the woman looked at me as if I was an idiot.

I also struck out with my other forays into the Citadel. Either Fisk avoided me or he had legitimate business. Hard to tell.

"Where to today?" Reema asked.

Her question snapped me back. She closed the book and set it reverently on the night table. Hayes had lent her the story to help her pass the time. Her actions gave me an idea.

"I'm going to show you the Keep's library." I led her to the student barracks.

The long building was curved like the apprentice wing, but it was three times its size. Located on the west side of the Keep, it housed the students who were in their first three years of study. The library filled half of the ground floor. The Keep's curriculum concentrated on learning from textbooks those years, while the seniors in their fourth year began a more hands-on type of learning.

Seniors shared the other long building that mirrored the barracks with the Keep's employees. The senior quarters were broken into rooms shared by five students. Much better than the rows and rows of bunk beds that lined the floors of the barracks.

When we entered the library, a few students glanced up from their books, but they soon returned to their studies. Tables and chairs occupied the space between the bookshelves. I waded through puddles of magic, wishing I'd remembered morning was a popular time.

Reema stayed by my side. Her lower lip hung open as she absorbed the sheer number of books. Rows and rows filled the space, seemingly unending. I moved instinctively, searching for the history section, but not concentrating too hard.

The stronger the desire to find a certain book the more it guaranteed a failed effort. It was an odd quirk of the library, as if over the years magic had soaked into the tomes, giving them an essence. A more relaxed, half-distracted search worked better. However, if a book didn't want to be found, you were out of luck.

I discovered the *List of Clans* tucked between *History of the Cloud Mist Clan* and *Sandseed Soil Study*. Reema wanted to explore, but I carried my find to an empty table. She followed, dragging her steps with reluctance and huddled on a chair.

Opening the book to the table of contents, I glanced at her. She had shoved her hands under her legs, and she stared at the hem of her shirt.

"Your mother told you no one would know your clan's name. Right?"

"Uh-huh."

"Maybe it's listed in here?"

She wouldn't look at me. I slid the book to her. Frowning, she scanned the page. I studied her, watching for a reaction to one of the names. After a few minutes, she relaxed.

"It's not here," she said. "Why is it so important to know my clan's name?"

I debated, but settled on the truth. "I've run out of options. I would like to find you a home, preferably with a relative."

"I don't need—"

"Reema, once Teegan is healthy he'll be enrolled as a student at the Keep. You'll be on your own, and I can't allow that."

She straightened. "You can't stop me."

"I know. That's why I need to find you a place where you'll be happy and safe."

"That's easy."

"It is?" Had I missed something?

"Sure. I'll stay with you."

I walked right into that one. A hard knot gripped my throat.

She noticed and shut down. All emotion fled and she returned to street survival mode. "Forget it."

"Reema, I—"

"Are we done here? I should get back to Teegan." She slid off the chair and headed for the door.

I followed and tried to explain that taking care of her would be impossible. That I might be called away at any time. But she ignored me or she pretended to. Either way, I lost her.

* * *

"What do you think?" Fisk asked.

I walked around the two-bedroom, furnished apartment in amazement. It was the first day of the heating season and sunlight poured in from huge windows occupying two of the four walls. "It's incredible." When Fisk had led me to the run-down factory, I had been dubious, but the inside had been renovated and broken into several apartments. "How did you find it?"

He puffed his chest out. "All in a day's work."

I shot him a look.

"What? I'm not going to reveal my secrets. I'd be out of a job."

"It's a clever location," I said. The building was on the eastern edge of the business district in the north section of the Citadel.

"And not too many people know what's hidden here. Perfect for security. Plus I thought you'd like to be close to the Keep and Council Hall."

The apartment was on the third floor, which was the same distance from the roof and from the ground, making it harder for "spiders" like Valek to climb. "You're right. I'll take it."

Before Fisk could go and negotiate a fair price, I stopped him. "What about my other request?"

"Nothing, yet."

I tried not to show my disappointment as we left the building. I shouldn't complain; it was better than Reema's future. Unless I found her a home.

"Anything else?" Fisk asked.

"Yes. I've heard a rumor about the Citadel's guards selling homeless children to your guild. What's going on?"

His pleasant demeanor dropped as anger flared. "And you believe it." It wasn't a question.

"Of course not—"

"Then why mention it?"

I told him about Reema. His anger transferred from me to those who had scared her.

"I've been dealing with these nasty rumors. The Helper's Guild is a very profitable business. After I pay my members a small allowance, I use the rest of the money to buy housing, clothes and food for them. But there is another group trying to form their own guild so they can keep the profits."

"And the children?"

"You saw where Teegan and Reema were living."

For an instant Fisk let his exhaustion show as he drooped. The responsibility of caring for his guild weighed on his shoulders and lined his face. I had to remind myself he was only sixteen.

"How can I help?" I asked.

"You can't…"

I waited.

He brightened just a bit. "You can convince Reema we're the good guys."

If she'd let me.

I moved my meager possessions to the apartment as soon as the deed was signed. Even though I spent most of my day at the Keep, it was a relief to leave at night. Teegan's heath improved and my concern about Reema grew. I kept walking into my extra bedroom and just standing there, straining to find a solution or a way to help the girl. Life in the guild was better than on the streets, but life in a home would be ideal.

But my apartment wasn't a home for me, nor was my factory in Fulgor or my parents' house in Booruby. Kade's cave? I didn't know! If my blood was recovered and if I regained my powers, everything might change.

Leif and Mara returned from their vacation all glowing and silly. Yelena also stopped by, but she picked up Kiki and was gone before I could talk to her.

"If you do that one more time, I'm leaving," I said to Mara. I sat in their small kitchen, sipping tea. They had decided to stay in Leif's quarters at the Keep for now, but when I had told them about my new place, they planned to talk to Fisk.

"Do what?" Mara asked, attempting to appear innocent.

"Get all kissy and lovey-dovey. Can you at least stop pawing each other while I'm here?"

"Jealous, Opal?" Leif asked.

"No. Nauseous."

They broke apart and sat on opposite sides of the table. "Happy?" Mara asked, but she still made moon eyes at Leif.

Newlyweds! Not fit for company for... Well, longer than the fourteen days it had been since their wedding.

"So what's going on around here?" Leif asked.

I filled him in about Teegan, Reema and the First Magician's decision not to inform the Council about my immunity.

"Bain's been under a ton of pressure lately. With Zitora's retirement and no other students showing potential to reach master level, he's been grumpy."

Leif was kind enough not to mention how both those problems were my fault. Pazia Cloud Mist had been the first student magician in ten years to be strong enough to take the master-level test. Until I had siphoned most of her magic, during an experiment. She had attacked me with all her power, intending to harm me, but I should have had more control over my response.

"Opal." Leif swatted my arm. "Snap out of it. Zitora and Pazia made their own choices—whether good or bad. *You* didn't cause Bain's problems."

"I thought you couldn't sniff my moods."

Leif's unusual magic allowed him to smell emotions, read people's intentions and determine their prior deeds. Handy for interrogating criminals.

"I don't need magic to read your mind. You get this little crinkle between your eyebrows when you're feeling guilty."

I rubbed the spot with two fingers, smoothing the skin. Even if I claimed I was among family, Valek would still fuss at my betraying body language. "I don't know how Bain plans to keep my immunity a secret. If I hang out here long enough, any magician interacting with me would discover it."

"Unless you claim you have a null shield woven into your clothes for protection. No, that won't work." Leif tugged his shirt down, looking guilty.

"Does the Council know how malleable null shields are?" A sick feeling roiled.

"No."

"Why not?"

He fiddled with the fabric of his sleeve. "The Master Magicians decided to keep it quiet for now. Plus the Councilors are protected by magicians who can create null shields when needed."

"But wearing shielded clothes would give them protection all the time."

"Yes, but…" Leif's gaze swept the room, avoiding mine.

"Eventually another magician is going to discover how to graft shields onto fabric and walls. You know it's inevitable, and once the Council finds out, they'll be upset." An understatement. They would be livid, feel betrayed and be suspicious of Bain and Irys, but if all the Councilors were shielded by Bain's magicians… I followed the logic. Those magicians reported *every-thing* to Bain. "Master Bloodgood's wading in danger-ous waters."

Leif rubbed the back of his neck. "I know. He says it's temporary. Knowing how blood magic can switch people's souls, Bain is worried another person might try to take over one of the Councilors' bodies. If they're shielded all the time, he can't tell if that has happened. With a magician guarding each Councilor, he knows—"

"Everything. The magicians are loyal to Master Bain and are spying on the Councilors for him." But Zebb hadn't informed Bain of my immunity. He cared about Councilor Moon enough to keep his bargain with me. As for the others, there would be no way to tell.

Leif grimaced. "*Spying* is such an ugly word."

"It's an ugly situation."

"I tried to explain it to him, but he threatened to assign me as a guard dog for Councilor Greenblade."

"That doesn't sound like Master Bain. Perhaps…"

"Don't even go there, Opal. Not many people know the whole blood magic switcheroo. Besides he's too strong for anyone to do that to him."

I had learned nothing was impossible. Not when it involved magic. Ulrick and Tricky were gone, and we had won the battle against blood magic. But the war was ongoing.

* * *

The next day, I took Reema shopping. She trailed behind me with her gaze on the ground. She hadn't said anything to me since the day at the library, but at least she stopped ignoring me.

When we reached the crowded market, Reema stepped closer to me. I headed in the direction of the clothing and fabric stalls, determined to purchase a few items for Reema and her brother.

"Lovely Lady, can I be of assistance?" a young girl asked.

She wore a comfortable-looking shirt over loose pants and cinched with a leather belt. I guessed her age at fourteen. Perfect.

"Yes—"

Reema grabbed my arm, digging her fingernails into my skin. "You promised," she whispered.

"I know. Relax." I turned back to the Helper's Guild girl, who had been staring at us in confusion. "What's your name?"

"Amberle." She played with a silver pendant hanging around her neck.

"I'm Opal and this is Reema," I said, pointing. "Amberle, I'd like to know where I can find clothes like yours."

She brightened and led us to a small shop near the northern edge. "Jane makes practical clothing from durable fabric. Your sister will grow out of them before she wears them out."

I didn't bother to correct her as we entered the cozy shop. The shopkeeper smiled her thanks at my guide. I paid Amberle a copper, but asked her to help Reema choose garments while I shopped for Teegan.

Reema shot me a shrewd look. She understood my real reason for having Amberle stay. By the time we were done, both Reema and Teegan had two new sets of clothes and I found a couple pairs of sturdy travel pants. Both dark brown in color. Drab, as Kade's mother would say, but the color hid stains and road dirt.

Loaded with packages, we returned to the street. Amberle flagged down two more members of the Helper's Guild. The boy and his friend ran over to us. They both wore the same pendant as Amberle's—two hands together with the fingers spread out. At first glance the design looked like wings. I asked her about it.

She touched it reverently. "Master Fisk gifted all his helpers with the symbol for the Helper's Guild. It serves many purposes. A way for our customers to know we are legitimate, a reminder to us of our tasks and as inspiration for us."

One of the boys said, "The wings mean if we work hard enough, anything is possible."

Nice. I handed the boys each a copper and the packages, instructing them to deliver them to the Magician's Keep.

Reema's face whitened. "You're trusting them? Just like that?" she asked me.

Insulted, Amberle snapped, "That's my brother and cousin. They would never steal from a customer. Master Fisk would throw them out of the guild."

"Has he thrown many out?" I asked.

"A few," she acknowledged with a sad shake of her head. Amberle touched her pendant. "Is there anything more you need today?"

"Yes." I pulled a list from my pocket.

Reema groaned, then said, "I'll meet you back at the Keep."

"No. Some of these things are for Teegan, and I'll need your opinion on them."

She eyed me with suspicion. "What for?"

"He's going to be enrolled as a student and he'll need some basic items like paper and ink." Plus I needed a few comforts for my apartment.

Not happy, she grumbled and dragged her feet. I ignored her as Amberle guided us to various stalls and stores in the market. She answered all my questions about working as a guild member, but I could tell she wondered why I was so curious. Reema, though, saw right through me. She shot me so many poisoned glares, I stopped counting after ten.

In the rug store, Fisk appeared next to me as I browsed through a collection of small remnants.

"Don't scare me like that." I had grabbed my switchblade, but hadn't triggered the blade.

"Sorry," he said, but his smirk countered any genuine remorse. "Your reflexes have improved. Been training?"

"Always. Once you stop, you lose your edge." I rubbed my shoulder, remembering Sarn's vise grip as he had tossed me to the ground.

He nodded to Reema, who sat in a corner with her arms crossed over her chest, staring at the floor. "Is that her?"

"Yes."

Amberle hustled over to us in concern. "Lovely Opal, I hope I—"

"Relax," Fisk said. "I have some business to discuss with Opal. Can you take Reema to the bakery?" He handed her a silver coin. "Buy her a dozen of those delightful cinnamon cookies Barb makes. We'll meet you there."

"Yes, sir."

As Amberle went to collect Reema, Fisk pulled me outside and led me to an empty alley. I scanned the area, remembering the last time Fisk had shown me a back door and I had walked right into an ambush.

"Looking for rats?" he asked, smiling.

"I still owe you for that."

"Master Bloodgood already paid me."

I stared at him.

"It was business, Opal. Nothing personal."

"Yeah, right." I let him fidget for a moment. "Any news?"

"Not on your boy, Finn. He hasn't come through here and no one has heard of him."

Not like it was a big surprise. Yet disappointment still welled. He waited and I realized he had more information. "Well?"

"I found out more on those pearls."

"Good or bad?"

"Depends. If you're looking to buy a pearl, the prices have dropped significantly. There are so many available, it's a buyer's market. However, if you make your living harvesting oysters for pearls, you're out of luck. And income."

"Have farms closed?"

"The smaller ones have, but a couple of the bigger ones are in trouble."

Interesting discussion, but I wondered why Fisk cared, so I asked him. "And don't tell me it smells fishy."

I surprised a laugh from him, but he soon returned to being serious. "I think someone is messing with the market on purpose, driving those others out of business. Once the supply is controlled by one farm, then they can withhold pearls and drive the prices up as high as they want."

"Again, why do you care?"

He jabbed a hand toward the market. "They're messing with *my* customers. Already a few jewelry stores are putting pearls aside, waiting for the price increase."

"How can I help?"

"Can you talk to Councilor Bloodgood? The oyster farms that are closing are along the Bloodgood coast. Maybe he can do something about it."

Remembering Bain's comments, I said, "I'm not sure the Councilor would agree to talk to me. Have you tried Master Bloodgood?"

"Yes. He has to remain impartial unless there is evidence of foul play."

"I'll try to see the Councilor. Do you have any idea which farm is harvesting all those pearls?" I asked.

"I just got a name today. They must be located close to the Jewelrose border. They call themselves—"

"The Bloodrose Clan."

"How did you know?" Fisk asked.

"When you said they lived close to the Jewelrose border, I guessed. I've been to their compound." A stark, dreary place.

"Why?"

I told him about Quinn.

"You saved another magician from flameout?"

"No. He managed to gain control of his powers, but Quinn wanted to stay so we left him there. We didn't have much choice. They weren't doing anything illegal."

Fisk considered. "Where is their compound?"

On the tip of the Lion's Claw Peninsula, but I wouldn't tell Fisk. He tried to hide his interest behind a casual question.

"Do *not* send any of your guild members to spy on them. Don't even pretend you weren't thinking it." I waggled a finger at him.

He conceded defeat. "Your observation skills have improved, as well. Who's been teaching you?"

"A friend," I hedged. I wasn't ready to tell him about Valek's training.

"What about these Bloodroses?"

What indeed? "I'll look into it." I expected a dubious look or for him to question me on how I planned to investigate.

Instead, he nodded. "Good. Let me know what you find out."

I smiled at his bossy tone. "Do I get a necklace, then?"

"You like those?"

"They're pretty."

"Unfortunately, they were necessary. This other group is becoming a problem."

"Do you need help with them?"

"No. This is my world, Opal. *I* need to deal with them."

I almost reached out to him. He should be dealing with the problems of being a teenager—girls, raging hormones, schoolwork—not rival gangs and a monopoly grab. "Fisk, when you have a few free days, find me. I have another job for you."

"Sounds intriguing. But it might be a couple months before I have the time."

"That's fine."

We exited the alley. As we searched for Reema and Amberle, Fisk glanced sideways at me. "You're not going to tell me anything about this new job, are you?"

"Nope."

"It's not payback for that ambush I organized, is it?"

"Nope. Don't worry, you'll enjoy it." I suppressed a grin. I planned to send him on a vacation. Probably the first for him.

We found the girls sitting at one of the tables outside Barb's Bakery. Crumbs littered the table and cinnamon sugar clung to Reema's chin. Packages surrounded them. When the girls spotted us, Reema jumped to her feet and shot Fisk a terrified glare. Keeping his distance, Fisk waved goodbye.

After arranging for the packages to be delivered to the Keep and to my apartment, I paid Amberle for her help. Reema kept pace with me as we followed the procession of boys to my apartment building. Once there, I gave each boy a copper. They thanked me and hurried off. As they raced down the street, calls of "you're it" and "am not" echoed. I smiled, but Reema frowned at them.

She helped me carry the bags up to the third floor. I unpacked and put my purchases away as Reema walked around the rooms. When I finished, I found her standing by the window in my bedroom. Her hair shone in the sunlight. I joined her. The Keep's tall towers dominated the view.

She turned and gestured to the room. "Are you rich?"

Reviewing our shopping trip, I shouldn't be surprised by her question. I debated. Naked truth versus it's-none-of-your-business. "Yep." I braced for her follow-up question and she didn't disappoint me.

"Then why can't I stay with you? You can afford it."

I knelt down so I was eye level. "I may have to leave suddenly for a season or more at a time."

"So? Hire a babysitter." She put her hands on her hips.

A touch of magic brushed my face.

"Didn't think of that, did you?" She dared me to correct her.

I hadn't considered a sitter, but what concerned me

more was the magic. Either a magician hid in my apartment or the power came from Reema.

"How did you know what I'd been thinking?" I asked.

She wilted a bit. "I guessed. I'm good at guessing people's moods, but you're the hardest person to read! Did you win all your money from playing poker?"

I laughed. "I wish." If she was already displaying power at age ten, then she could be a powerful magician like her brother. I needed to talk to Irys.

"Then how did you get rich?"

"Another long and complicated story. One I'm still trying to figure out. It's why I can't make any plans for the future."

"Then stop hanging around with me and go sort it out. I'll wait."

I peered at her. "Are you sure you're not older?"

"My mother hated indecision. She told us she always let others decide for her until she became pregnant with me. She didn't want us to be punished for her mistakes, so she took Teegan and ran away."

Now I understood. "That's why you won't tell me your clan name. You're afraid of them."

"Mother made us promise to never tell anyone."

"And you should always listen to your mother," I said.

"Do you?"

"No."

"And?"

"Mixed results."

She giggled, but then turned serious. "What would your mother say about your complicated future?"

"She'd tell me to stop procrastinating."

"You should listen to your mother," Reema said.

Easy to say, so hard to do.


"Come in, Opal," Irys called before I could knock on her office door.

"How did you know I was there?" I asked as I entered.

She sat on the front edge of her desk. Her hair had been swept up and she wore a green tunic and pants. "Didn't you feel my magic?"

"In the Keep, I'm always encountering magic. This place is saturated with it." In fact, a bright bubble of it pressed on me at the moment.

"When you approached my door, I felt the…absence of magic, which tells me either you or Valek are in the hallway. Since Valek was last seen in Mica…" She swept her hands out as if to say "ta da!" "Do you need something?"

"I wanted to talk about Reema." I explained about her power.

"Interesting. We've been so focused on the boy. Are you sure? She hasn't reached puberty yet."

"And how many times have we discovered a new wrinkle with magic?" Both good and bad.

"Good point."

"Can you test her?"

"Of course." She laced her fingers together. "Anything else?"

The magic in the room pulsed, but I sensed it came from behind the Master Magician. "What are you hiding?" I asked.

She sighed. "Something we were debating about telling you, but you'd find out eventually anyway."

Irys stepped to the side, revealing an orb. Magic oozed from it.

"What is it?" I asked.

"You tell me. Go ahead, pick it up."

Upon closer inspection, it wasn't an orb. Orbs were bigger, and either hollow or filled with a storm's energy. This was a solid cube of clear glass. I hefted the palm-sized object. Trapped inside was a dark thumbnail-sized substance shaped like a drop of water. "The magic is coming from inside." The shock of recognition hit me like a bolt through my chest. My legs turned to mush, and I handed Irys the glass before I dropped it. "Is it...?"

"Yes," she said in a gentle tone. "It works just like your glass messengers. Sit down."

I perched on an invisible chair. My peripheral vision had shrunk to encompass only that single item in Irys's hands. "Who? Why?" Questions formed and popped.

"This came from Vasko Cloud Mist. He says his daughter invented it."

"But Pazia has little magic."

Irys tapped the sphere. "That's not Pazia's magic in there. Vasko told us he found black diamonds in his mine."

"Black?"

"Extremely rare. The Commander of Ixia has only found two in the Soul Mountains in twenty years of mining. Vasko says he mined dozens."

The mention of diamonds triggered a memory of the time Pazia and I had tried to encase a regular diamond charged with magic in glass. It had worked as a super messenger, but the diamond had cracked after she used the magic.

I told her about the experiment.

She nodded as if that explained something. "These don't crack after the magic is used, and they can be recharged and reused, which helps when you consider the cost."

"Expensive?"

"Outrageous. Only a few people in Sitia will be able to afford them."

I motioned for the cube. She handed it to me. I studied the dark tear-shape nestled inside. "It doesn't have facets. Are you sure it's a diamond?"

"Unless we dig it out, it's hard to say for certain. But I can't deny the magic it holds."

No missing the power, but a sense of familiarity tugged at my heart.

"Besides, why would Vasko lie?" Irys asked.

Rich, powerful and well connected, Vasko didn't need to lie.

Unless he purchased it on the black market.

Unless he paid Finn a ton of gold for it.

Unless it was my blood trapped inside.

Was it even possible? Valek had said blood magic was potent.

"Irys…" My voice cracked.

"What's wrong?" She pressed a cool hand to my forehead. "Are you sick?"

"I need…" I leaned forward and drew in deep breaths. When the room no longer spun, I sat up. "Remember when I mentioned those wrinkles about magic."

A stern gaze replaced her concern. "Go on."

For a moment I transformed into a first-year student who had misbehaved, waiting for the Master Magician's punishment. Nothing I could do, I confessed my suspicions about Vasko.

She said nothing.

The silence was unbearable, and I rushed to apologize for keeping her in the dark about my search for my blood. "...didn't know he would use—"

"Opal, that is a serious accusation."

"It's a serious crime. He stole my only chance to get my powers back!" A devastating anger rumbled through me until I shook. I thought I had prepared myself for this possibility and had almost accepted it. Guess I lied to myself.

"Calm down, Opal. You don't know that for certain. He only made a few messengers. Besides, someone else may have taken your blood."

Unable to sit still, I surged to my feet and paced. She could be calm, standing there with all her powers intact. I slowed. It wasn't her fault. I had been so close and then Finn had snatched it away. I needed for this to be over. Either I find my blood or it's gone. End of story.

I mulled over our conversation. "You weren't surprised I was searching for my blood. You knew?"

"Of course. Yelena kept me informed of your progress. Plus we had Zebb's reports on your involvement with Councilor Moon." She cocked her head to the side. "We would have been very happy if you had recovered your magic."

"You and Bain or the Council?"

"You would have earned their trust...eventually. And you have a champion in Councilor Moon. She returned to the Citadel yesterday, and she'd like you to visit her. I would have told you sooner, but Vasko dropped this little bomb on us right after the Council meeting."

"Does the Council know about the new messengers?"

"Not yet. Vasko wanted us to verify them first."

I chewed on my bottom lip. Yet more information being withheld from the Council. "What happens if he is using my blood?"

"He would be arrested. However, what to do with the messengers will be problematic. If your blood is inside them, do we siphon it out? What happens if that doesn't work? Or if you can't recover your magic from your blood? Did he use all your blood? There will be a million questions to consider."

"And the Council will argue over each and every one, taking forever."

Irys frowned. "They are cautious. It's an excellent trait." She gave me a pointed look. "The Council works best when they have all the information. Bain and I will arrange to get a tour of Vasko's messenger operation."

"I should go. It's my blood."

"Undercover?"

I thought back to when Janco and I had been searching for Ulrick in Ognap. Janco considered sneaking into the ruby mines a challenge worthy of him. If I could get into Wirral, the mines shouldn't be as hard. "I could steal into the mines on my own. But why go to all that trouble? Pazia and I are friends. How about I pay her a friendly visit?"

"Vasko'll see right through that."

I shrugged. "He probably expects you and Bain to investigate. It can be an open secret, but once I'm there, I can snoop around."

She crinkled her forehead. "Vasko's intelligent. He'll ensure you don't see anything out of the ordinary."

"Vasko's also overconfident. Right now he thinks

I'm a washed-up magician with no prospects. Play it up. Hint that you asked me to visit Pazia out of pity. Tell him how devastated I was over these new messengers." I paused as I realized that one wasn't very far from the truth. "Make sure he knows you gave me this assignment to make me feel important. Ask him to indulge me. I'll act the part and he'll underestimate me."

"You believe this ruse will work?"

"No doubts."

While Irys arranged a meeting with Vasko, I prepared for my trip to Ognap. Reema was my biggest concern. Healer Hayes would discharge Teegan soon, and Irys had offered to train him until the new school year started at the beginning of the cooling season. The Citadel practically shut down during the hot season. The Keep's students returned home and the Council dismissed for their annual recess.

Reema's comments about hiring a sitter circled in my mind, but who could I hire? I was sure Fisk would know someone trustworthy, but Reema would be suspicious of anyone working for him.

The next morning, Irys stopped by my training session. She watched me spar a third-year student. I blocked his practice sword with my sais, hooked the sword with the hilt of my right sai and yanked it from his hands. Match over.

"Impressive," Irys said.

"I couldn't use that move on an apprentice," I said. Or Sarn. The big brute would have unarmed me in seconds.

"But you would have used another tactic for an apprentice."

"True."

"You've gotten quite the reputation out here." Irys gestured to the training yard. Students practiced drills and sparred each other. "Has anyone beaten you besides Captain Marrok and Sarn?"

I searched my memory. "No. But they're students. I wouldn't last long in a fight with Valek or Yelena." Or Finn. Considering how short that list was, I straightened a bit.

"Then it's a good thing they're your friends. And, speaking of friends, Pazia is looking forward to your visit."

"Great. When is Vasko leaving?"

"He isn't. He has more business to attend to in the Citadel." She met my gaze. "You were right about him. He's very confident, but he could have good reason to be."

"As my father would say, only one way to find out."

"Make sure you visit Councilor Moon before you go. And take someone with you for backup, just in case," Irys ordered. "How about Leif?"

"And listen to him moan about missing his new wife? No thanks. I'll find someone else." But Leif's name triggered another question I had for Irys. "Do you remember a student who probably came through the Keep around the same time as Yelena, maybe with Leif?" I described Finn to Irys. "He's powerful enough that I think he would have stood out among the class."

She drummed her fingers on the wooden fence. "There were a number of strong students. And with Yelena taking all my attention I wasn't as involved."

"How about a graduate who didn't stay and work for the Council? I couldn't have been the only one to branch out on my own."

"There have been a few. Vasko for one, his children and probably a bunch of his nieces and nephews. They're all invested in the family business and too rich and powerful to work for the Council. And since they're all so worried about their children being kidnapped, many of the kids came through here under different names."

"But you knew about Pazia and now Walker."

"The family informed the Master Magicians, but no one else. Pazia thought her father was paranoid and refused to go undercover. It's the same with Walker. Although the boy is keeping a low profile. Unlike his sister."

Except with me.

Irys continued, "I'll go through the records while you're gone. Maybe a name will jump out at me."

I thanked her and hurried to the bathhouse.

After a quick bath, I headed to the glass workshop to talk to my sister. Mara worked in the mixing room. She poured sand onto a scale, weighing ingredients. Her loose golden curls had been pinned back from her face.

Mara finished measuring the different types of sand. She poured them into the drum mixer. The device resembled a wine barrel lying on its side. She spun the barrel a few times, then she added lime and soda ash—all the ingredients to make glass.

"New recipe?" I asked.

She startled then admonished me for sneaking up on her. "I brought a batch of Crimson sand back from our vacation. I'm hoping it produces a nice red-colored glass."

"I'm surprised you left the cottage long enough to

notice the sand. Unless the beach was softer than the bed?" I smirked.

She threw a towel at me. "Are you here for a reason or just to bug me?" Mara returned to the mixer and cranked the handle. As the barrel rolled, the metal fins inside blended the glass components together. The mixer rang like a steady rain on a metal roof.

"Actually I have a proposition for you?"

She stopped. "This ought to be good. And it better not involve Leif running off on some crazy mission with you."

I held up my hands in surrender. "Leif stays."

"But you're leaving?"

"Yes, Irys needs me to look into something for her."

"Something. How vague. Should I worry now, or when I get the message that you're on the edge of dying and I should come?"

"It's not like that. You sound like Mother."

"No. Mother would tell you to slow down and think!" She tapped my temple with two fingers. "You do have a brain. I've seen you use it. Do you need me to introduce you to it?"

Wow. Her sarcasm was impressive and scary. "Marrying Leif has changed you. What happened to my sweet sister?"

"She was left home to worry and wait too many times."

"This trip is not dangerous. I promise. I'll be back by the hot season at the latest."

She failed to look convinced. "And your proposition?"

"Would you and Leif like to stay in my apartment while I'm gone?"

"Are you worried someone would break in?"

"Ahhh…no. Remember when I told you about Teegan and his sister?"

She smoothed the apron over her skirt. "Opal, just spit it out."

I asked her to watch Reema for me.

She opened her mouth, closed it and appeared to search for words.

"It's just a couple weeks," I rushed to explain. "When I get back, I'm going to find her a proper home. I just don't have time right now."

"I have to think about it and talk to Leif. In the meantime, please consider Mother's advice."

"Slow down and think?"

"Since you came back from Hubal, you've been different. I think you've lost your purpose, and are just dashing around looking for something to call your own. The factory in Fulgor, the apartment, Reema. Raising a child is a huge responsibility, you—"

"Forget it. I'll find someone else." I left the mixing room.

Mara knew nothing about my purpose. She didn't understand. Couldn't. On my way out, I almost ran into the first-year student I had helped.

Keelin jumped back. "Sorry."

I waved her off. "My fault."

"Opal, wait," Keelin said.

I turned.

She handed me the dolphin I had made. "It's pretty. You should display it."

Absently, I glanced at it. "Thanks. How did your paperweight turn out?"

"Like a clump of dirt kicked up by a horse." She

laughed. "But you were right, my latest one is better. And I tried to make a dolphin, too."

"Good for you. How did it look?"

"Not as sleek as yours and it didn't flash, either."

"Flash?"

Keelin pointed to the shelves filled with finished pieces from the annealing oven. "When anyone in here used magic, it would flash. I thought since you…you know…with the glass…that it was supposed…" Her voice petered out.

Odd. "Must have been a trick of the light."

"You're probably right." A queasy relief shone on her face.

I hurried away. Out in the bright sunlight, I examined the dolphin. Nothing out of the ordinary. When I encountered a few pools of magic, nothing happened, just as I had suspected.

Stopping by the infirmary, I visited Teegan. Reema read to her brother. She held the book up to the lantern light. His room didn't have a window. Teegan didn't seem to mind the gloom. He listened to the story with his eyes closed anyway and a half smile on his lips. I waited for her to reach a break.

Magic touched my cheek.

"Fire Lady's here," Teegan said without opening his eyes.

"Your control has improved," I said.

He peered at me with a sly smile. Impishness danced in his gray eyes.

"And you're feeling much better, aren't you?"

He sat up in his bed. "Yep!"

"Good. Now you can tell me why you call me Fire Lady."

He glanced at the dolphin in my hand. "Did you bring me a present?"

"You're trying to change the subject."

"Can I see it?" He reached.

"Only if you answer my question." Ha!

Holding a hand out, he said, "The dolphin will tell you."

"Tee," Reema warned. "Don't."

"Why not?"

She waggled her fingers as if communicating to him. He scratched his nose and tapped his shoulder.

Reema grunted in frustration. "She won't believe you."

Teegan smiled. "Seeing is believing." He turned to me. "May I see your dolphin please?"

He played it just right, making me curious and hitting me with a polite request. I handed him the dolphin. He placed it on the table next to his bed. Folding his hands, he closed his eyes.

Magic spread from him. It was slow and in control. Impressive. When it reached the dolphin, the glass animal blazed with light. He pulled back and the glow died.

I grabbed the statue. "Do it again…please."

The magic swelled, and the light returned. I handed it to Reema. "One more time."

She squealed in delight when fire burst from the glass.

I met Teegan's gaze. He said, "I call you the Fire Lady because you have magic trapped inside you and when you—"

"Teegan!" Reema jumped to her feet. "Be quiet!"

"Doesn't matter now, Ree." He swept an arm out. "We found a home."

"*You* found a home. I'm still too young. And you're going to scare her."

"Has Master Jewelrose tested you?" I asked her.

She nodded. "I don't have any magic."

"Not that the Master can detect," Teegan said. "I'd bet you a hunk of bread Fire Lady has felt it."

"You're guessing," I said.

"So? I'm right. Aren't I?"

"Teegan, that superior attitude won't help you make friends at the Keep," I admonished with a stern tone.

His arrogant manner remained. "Now you're trying to change the subject. You felt Reema use magic, didn't you?"

"I thought it was from her. But I could be wrong."

"No, you weren't wrong. The trapped magic burns inside you. You feel power. Even when it's a tiny bit. Even when the person doesn't even know she's using it. When you touch magic, there's a faint shimmer around you. A glow. You can't see it. Reema and I can, but—"

"No one else. How convenient," I said.

A sullen pout creased his face. "That's right. We're a couple of homeless street urchins. Why believe us?" He flopped on his pillow and turned his back on me.

His words slapped me in the face. It hadn't been too long ago that I had fought to convince my friends and colleagues about an unbelievable twist of blood magic.

I sat on the edge of his bed. "I'm sorry. It's hard for me to believe you because…" Did I really want to tell him and Reema? "I'm immune to magic. No power can be inside me. There's nothing there."

Teegan rolled over. "Then why did your dolphin blaze with light?"

"*Your* magic caused it to light up."

"Exactly."

"But I have nothing to do with that. It's all you," I said.

He hissed in frustration. "It's both of us! *You* created the magic detector. I just supplied the magic to detect."

Magic detector? Hard to believe and even harder to wrap my head around. Yet Teegan and Reema took the revelation in stride. They didn't understand enough about magic to think it odd. Who really understood it? As each generation reached puberty, new wrinkles seemed to develop.

I reviewed our conversation and remembered Keelin's comment. "If no one can see me…shimmer when I encounter magic, then why can they see the dolphin light up?"

Teegan shrugged. "Probably the glass works like a…" He cast about for the right word. "One of those… things that increases the light."

"Like a magnifying glass?" Which was also used for my spyglass.

"Yeah. The glass magnifies the glow so everyone can see it."

His explanation sounded logical. "Reema, why did you think the information would scare me?"

She shrugged and dipped her head. Her long cork-screw curls hung in her face.

Crouching down, I lifted her chin and looked her in the eye. "Worried I would leave you?"

The slightest nod.

"It's going to happen no matter what. In fact, I'm leaving tomorrow for a mission for Master Jewelrose."

Her features hardened into her tough street kid mask.

"I'm trying to find a sitter for you. And don't worry so much." I tucked a curl behind her ear. "When I'm done, I'll come back and find you a home." I straightened and picked up the dolphin, shoving it into a pocket. "And I'll figure out what this means. For now, can you keep it quiet?"

They gave me their solemn promise. As I left the infirmary, I realized my intentions for full disclosure had failed. I'd kept many things from the Council and others—my immunity, being trapped by a null shield and now the magic detectors. If I recovered my blood, those secrets would be moot. And they couldn't mourn the loss of something they never had. Right?

Or were my motives a bit more complicated? If Pazia's super messengers proved to be legitimate, the Council might think I was better off with my immunity and confiscate my blood, claiming it was illegal for me to use it.

I checked on Quartz and inspected my tack. The trip to Ognap would take nine days, including the shortcut through the Avibian Plains and a stop in Fulgor. As for my backup, the only way to reach Ari and Janco would be through a complicated series of message relays, starting with Leif. And there would be no guarantee my request would reach them in time. Instead, I planned to arrange for backup in Fulgor.

"There you are!" a girl's voice cried.

I spun to see a young page hurrying toward me. She wore a Council uniform. A finger of unease slid under my ribs.

"Opal Cowan, your presence is requested. You are to accompany me," she said.

"Requested by whom?"

"Councilor Moon."

I relaxed. "Tell her I'll—"

"You are to accompany me *now*."

"And if I don't?"

"You will be violating a direct order of the Council."

"The whole Council? I thought you said—"

"She is a representative of the Council. Her requests have the Council's power."

The page's haughty tone annoyed me. "Is it a request or an order?"

She drew herself up to her full height, which was a few inches taller than me. "The request is her way of being polite."

I suppressed a chuckle at her increasing frustration. "Oh. A polite order. Why didn't you say so? Lead on."

As I followed her from the Keep, I regretted giving her a hard time. She was a page, and had nothing to do with the Council's decisions.

Instead of taking me to Councilor Moon's office in the Council Hall, she led me to Tama's private residence. Each Councilor owned one of the town houses that had been built in a long row behind the Council Hall. All Sitia's government buildings were located in the southeast quadrant of the Citadel.

The door swung open as we approached, and Faith

greeted me with a relieved smile. "Come in, come in." She thanked the page and ushered me inside.

Before I could say a word, Faith handed me a glass of red wine and gestured to an overstuffed white chair with black spots. All the living room's furniture matched— black, white, or black with white circles. No other color had been invited. I felt out of sync in my comfortable tan tunic and dark brown pants.

Faith called to Tama before she settled on a solid black couch across from me. "We don't know what to do," she said.

"Is this about Tama's new assistant?" I asked.

"No. After a thorough background search, we hired a sweet man. My only complaint is he's a little too organized. Makes me feel sloppy in comparison."

"Wow. I didn't think there was anyone more organized than you. But you can't go by me. I thought the woman we hired before was a perfect candidate."

"We all did." She shooed my comment away. "Leia didn't have time to do any damage, and now we have Captain Alden and Zebb in charge of personnel."

"Zebb?"

"Tama has come a long way," Faith said. Her gaze slid past my shoulder.

I turned in time to see the Councilor and Zebb enter the room. Tama carried the glass paperweight I had made for her. I had forgotten about it. Zebb sat in the chair next to mine, but she set the paperweight on the table before me.

Tama remained standing and peered at me as if I had played a nasty trick on her. The desire to slouch down and avert my gaze flared. I felt like a kid caught sneaking out.

Not bothering with the niceties, she asked, "Did you know what this could do when you gave it to me?" She jabbed her finger at the glass.

"No."

She softened a bit. "It scared the hell out of me the first time it exploded with light."

"I'm sorry."

"Don't be." She perched on the end of the couch, tucking her long white skirt under her knees. "Once Zebb and I figured it out… It's a wonderful tool, but I wasn't sure what I should do about it."

I glanced at Zebb. Surely he had reported it to Bain by now.

He pressed his lips together before saying, "Too many variables. We needed additional information. Can you make more?"

Pulling the dolphin from my pocket, I placed it next to the paperweight. With a quick strike, Zebb's magic touched the dolphin. It glowed red-hot.

"That's a yes," he said.

"Opal, what do you want us to do?" Tama asked.

My thoughts scattered as shock slammed into me.

Faith smiled at my reaction. "You've done so much for us. Did you really think we would do anything without consulting you first?"

I tried to collect my wits, but they slipped away. "I didn't… I just found out."

"How?" Zebb asked.

"Two kids." I told them about Teegan's discovery.

"I've heard of him," Tama said. "Master Jewelrose was very excited. She thinks he may have master-level powers."

Not a surprise.

"Is he the one who almost flamed out?" Zebb asked.

"Yes," I said, but regretted it as three people turned to stare at me.

"You saved him, didn't you?" Tama asked. "Master Bloodgood said the boy was stopped, but not by who. The Councilors assumed it was one of the Masters."

Faith added, "That means the Masters know about your immunity. Do they know about the detectors?"

"Not yet."

"I understand about the detectors. You just found out, but why would you keep your immunity a secret now?" Tama asked.

"Bain advised against it." When spoken out loud, it sounded lame.

Zebb nodded. "She's a magician...or rather a... In any case, Master Bloodgood is her boss. He makes the decisions regarding all the magicians in Sitia."

"He also said my immunity would scare the Council."

Tama agreed. "The Council has a love-hate feeling toward magic. On one hand, they're skittish and on the other they're all protected by it. To know you could walk through their magical defenses would be scary." She picked up the paperweight. "But this could cancel it out."

"You lost me," I said.

"The Council wouldn't be afraid of you if you provide them with these detectors." Tama brandished the glass in the air.

"But it doesn't protect them from me."

"They'd be grateful for the peace of mind. With so many magicians around, who knows what they're doing. No offense, Zebb." She shot him a tender smile. "But any one of them could be influencing our Council decisions. We could have sessions where no magic is allowed and your detector will ensure it." Tama's eyes blazed with her conviction.

Before, I would have attributed Tama's antimagicians rant to paranoia, but I remembered Leif's comment about Bain's magical bodyguards. And perhaps it wasn't all Tama's idea. Her complete relaxation around Zebb was unexpected. However, the paperweight didn't flash, so she wasn't under his magical influence.

My head spun with all the potential complications and possibilities. "I need to sort it out." I stood. "I'm going to Ognap for Irys." Yet another secret. I would soon need a chart to list who knew what. Would this be my life if I worked for Valek? Keeping secrets, telling lies and half-truths. "Can we decide what to do with these detectors when I return?" No sense getting everyone excited and then not be able to make them. It would be just like the crisis with my glass messengers.

They agreed.

Tama walked me to the door. "Is this…mission for Irys dangerous?"

"It shouldn't be."

"Shouldn't?"

"I've learned to expect the unexpected."

"Does it work?"

"No." Although it wasn't funny, I laughed at the sad truth.

"Is there anything I can do?"

I opened my mouth to decline her offer, but I realized she had become a trustworthy friend. "Actually, there are two things you can help me with."

My one request was granted without hesitation, but the other took Tama a few minutes to consider before she agreed.

Carrying a backpack with her meager possessions, Reema trailed behind me. "Are you sure?" she asked for the hundredth time. "I can stay with Tee. The barracks are huge. No one would notice me."

"The barracks are filled with student magicians. They'll notice. If I'm not back by the hot season, you can move in there with him until I return." Only a handful of students remained at the Keep over the long break. A few stayed to work; others had no place else to go.

When we reached the door, Reema grabbed my arm in a panic. "You'll be back before then. Won't you?"

I had reassured her before. With travel time, I estimated my trip to last about thirty days. "What's really worrying you?"

"Nothing." She shifted her backpack to her other shoulder and scuffed her foot on the ground.

Putting myself in her place, I imagined how I would feel moving into a stranger's house and having the only adult you trusted leave. "I promise, I'll be back."

"Don't promise," she said. Moisture glistened in her eyes. "You can't control fate. If she wants you, you can't stop her."

"Did your mother—"

"Promised us everything would be fine. Don't worry, she said when we were kicked out of our apartment. Don't fret, she told Teegan when he got sick. I'll return with enough money for a season, she promised. She never came back."

Sorrow gripped my heart and squeezed. I knelt next

to her. "You're right. I can't stop fate, but I can stay one step ahead of her."

She squinted at me. "Can you really do that?"

"Already have." I winked.

Faith opened the door and welcomed us inside. She had a plate of cinnamon cookies on the table, and she addressed Reema as if she were an adult, gaining bonus points from the girl. We chatted about nothing in particular until I needed to leave.

After I said my goodbyes, I stood in the doorway.

Faith led Reema upstairs to her new room and office. "You'll be my assistant. First Adviser to the First Adviser." Faith's laugh floated down the stairs.

Confident Reema would be safe, I returned to the Keep and saddled Quartz. I mounted and patted her on the neck. "First stop, Fulgor. You know the way."

As Quartz walked to the Citadel's east gate, I enjoyed the sunny day. Only seven days into the heating season, the cool temperature would warm as the sun climbed the sky. No humidity and a light breeze kept the flies from annoying Quartz. The hot, sticky weather wouldn't arrive until late into the season and by then, I planned to be back at the Citadel. And then? No idea. I hoped this trip would be decisive.

Five days later, I arrived in Fulgor. Again. No matter how far away I traveled or what else was going on in my life, I seemed to return to this town. Mixed emotions fluctuated in my chest as Quartz navigated through the morning business crowd.

The familiar streets comforted like home and upset my stomach like a horrible nightmare. I did have friends here, and the factory, which I should sell. And Devlen was here. Why was I so… Impulsive? Confused in Fulgor? At least, this stop would be short. In other words, no visiting Devlen.

I had missed the morning training at Fulgor's Security HQ. The new annex looked complete from the outside, but various workmen carried supplies into the building. Not wanting to see Devlen, I hustled into the reception area.

The same bored receptionist sat behind the counter. Would she recognize me as the prisoner Rhea Jewelrose?

"Can I help you?" she asked.

Guess not. "I'd like to see Captain Alden, please."

"Name?"

I told her.

"One minute." She swiveled around in her chair and shouted through the opening in the wall behind her. "Collin, tell the Captain Opal Cowan's here to see him."

So much for a quiet return. Chairs scraped the floor and Nic and Eve filled the doorway.

"The Captain more important than us?" Nic asked in an unfriendly tone.

I sighed. "I'm here on business. If I asked for you first, the Captain would be upset. Besides, I thought you'd be out." I pointed toward the door. "You know, working?"

While Nic scowled, Eve cut to the heart of the matter. "What business?"

"I need to check with the Captain first," I said.

"Come on in." Eve gestured toward two desks facing each other in the back corner.

"Cozy," I said.

"Not my idea. Believe me. It's bad enough I have to work with the guy," Eve said.

"Cap's in with some bigwig from the Councilor's Hall. Take a load off." Nic pushed a chair out with his foot and patted the seat. "So… Besides the new hairdo, what have you been up to?" He acted casual, leaning back and resting his arms on his waist, but his gaze pinned me with keen interest.

"Not much." I yawned, playing along. "I went down to Booruby for my sister's wedding and then to the Citadel to hang out with the Master Magicians. Boring stuff."

"Too bad." Eve tsked in mock sympathy. "You missed all the fun here."

"Really?"

"Oh yeah. Lots of laughs," Nic said without humor. "There was a prison break at Wirral." He studied me.

I kept up the inquisitive facade. "Did anyone escape?"

"One person. And she left a mess in her wake." Hard lines formed on his face. "Five max security prisoners dead, two missing officers and one enraged warden."

"We're still dealing with the consequences and the cleanup," Eve added.

"Sorry to hear that," I said with genuine sorrow. No matter what anyone else said, Ulrick's death rested on my shoulders. It wasn't guilt. It was regret.

"Are you?" Nic asked.

"Of course," I snapped. "Spit it out, Nic. What are you implying?"

"Evidence led to one of the hotshots as the killer, but he could have taken them out at any time and made it look like suicide or an accident. I suspect the escapee planted the evidence to cover her tracks."

He thought I killed them. I glanced at Eve. She looked curious and not hostile.

"Why?" I asked.

"For someone who allegedly committed a crime of passion, she certainly knew what she was doing. She smuggled in lock picks and darts treated with a sleeping drug. The deceased prisoners had no connection to this woman, who, by the way, doesn't exist except on paper. I would bet a month's wages she was a hired assassin, paid to eliminate them, except for one thing."

"Go on, you've created quite a story."

"You."

"How am I involved?"

"You've been asking about the prison. You disappeared the same time *she* appeared. You had an excellent reason to see those men dead." Nic clutched the chair arms.

"Easy, Nic," Eve said.

I locked my gaze on him and leaned closer. "Do you *really* believe I am capable of cold-blooded murder?"

No answer.

"I've met only one person in my life that I would have gladly killed if I'd been given the chance."

"Who?" Eve asked.

"Devlen." I stood. "Good thing I don't know how to hold a grudge."

Captain Alden's door opened. He shook hands with an elderly man. Without saying another word to Nic or Eve, I crossed to the Captain. He invited me in and I closed the door behind me.

"I guess this isn't a social call," the Captain said when I refused to sit down. He stood behind his desk.

"No." I pulled Councilor Moon's letter from my pocket and handed it to him. "I've a request."

Alden scanned the document. "Shouldn't be a problem. Take Nic and Eve with you. The three of you seem to work well together."

I barked out a humorless laugh. Originally, I had planned to request them. "I don't think they would… enjoy the assignment. I'll take your two best officers."

He gave me a sardonic smile. "They are my best officers. I don't assign people based on enjoyment, but on skills. When do you need them to start?"

"Right away. I should brief them." I suppressed a cringe. This was not going as I had imagined.

Gesturing for me to take his seat, he strode to the door. "There's no privacy out there, I'll send them in for the briefing."

I sat down, placed my elbows on the neat desk and rested my head on my hands for a moment. The air thickened when they entered. A surly resentment pulsed from Nic, but Eve seemed more annoyed at her partner than at me.

Tossing a small sackful of coins across the desk, I outlined what I needed them to do. They nodded in understanding. Eve tucked the purse into her pocket, and they left to prepare for the assignment.

I had completed my business at HQ before noon. Glad for the extra time, I led Quartz to Justamere Farm and groomed her. The owners were happy to see her, but I explained she would be there for one night only. After I had brushed all the road dirt from her copper coat, I checked on my factory.

Stale air and dust puffed in my face when I entered the factory. Darkness filled the first floor and I groped for the lantern, hoping it remained in the stone alcove. I found and lit it, breathing a little easier when the soft light illuminated the kilns. Walking around, I inspected the equipment. In order to return this place to a true glass shop, I would have to tear down the boards on the windows and install shutters.

The apartment upstairs looked undisturbed. I pulled back the curtains and the late-afternoon sunlight revealed the dust motes. Valek had left a few of his belongings behind. I straightened a couple things and rolled up the blueprint of Wirral. The place echoed and I longed for company. After shaking out my sheets and dumping my pack onto the bed, I debated about supper.

I had planned to go to the Pig Pen and have a bowl of Ian's stew with my friends. The memory of Nic's accusation ruined my appetite. And I would *not* visit Devlen. Instead, I lit extra lanterns and brought them downstairs. I practiced blocks and strikes with my sais.

Concentrating on perfecting a set of moves, I almost dropped my weapons when a loud bang cracked through the air. It took me a second to realize someone had pounded on the door.

I peered through the peephole and groaned. Nic waited on the other side. This would not be fun. Wiping my sweaty hands on my stained practice tunic, I opened the door and let him and the gray twilight in.

We stood in the front room. Gressa had used this space for her store. Nic carried a package wrapped in wax paper, and I still held my sais with the tips pointing toward the floor.

He eyed them. "Planning to attack me?"

I glanced at his uniform and sword. "Depends. Did you come to arrest me for murder?"

He sucked in a breath. I waited.

Releasing the air in a rush, he said, "Damn it, Opal. I'm sorry."

"Are you really? Or did Eve make you come?"

"I am. I was mad and had jumped to conclusions."

"Heck of a jump."

"No it wasn't. You didn't trust us with your plans. Why would we trust you?"

"I trusted you with my life, Nic. Remember all those early mornings?"

"Yeah, well…I said I was sorry." He held out the package to me. "Peace?"

I sheathed my sais and took it. Warmth radiated under the wax paper. Curious, I peeled back an edge, releasing a yummy scent. Ian's stew. My stomach growled. "You're forgiven," I said.

With those two words he returned to his old self. "Are you going to tell us more about this new assignment?" he asked.

"Is Eve waiting outside?"

"No. She thought I should talk to you myself or you'd think she made me apologize."

"Did she?"

His face creased into his wounded puppy dog expression. "No. She just explained a few things, made me remember you aren't the killer type." He hooked his thumbs on his weapon belt. "When I get mad my brain turns off."

"Tell me something I *don't* know." I smirked. "And Eve's right, I'm not the type to murder my husband. He committed suicide. Poor guy had rotten aim."

I laughed as Nic sorted it out.

"I knew it was you!" He rubbed the stubble on his chin. "But if you didn't kill those prisoners, who did?"

"Finn."

"You're sticking with that?" Nic asked.

"Yep."

He grunted, but didn't comment.

The stew cooled in my hands. "Come upstairs. I'll give you a few more details about our trip to Ognap."

Nic shook his head. "Tell us tomorrow. I wasn't planning to stay."

"Oh."

He smirked at my disappointment. "I know I haven't been that supportive of your…new interests. So I brought you another peace offering."

"A mug of Ian's mulled ale?"

Nic didn't answer. He opened the door and disappeared.

While he was gone, I tried to guess—a new weapon, a bottle of Ian's house wine—but none of them came close.

Nic returned with Devlen.

# 22

I stepped back and I think I gasped. "How…? When…?"

Devlen stood in my front room. Devlen. He wore civilian clothes. His hesitant smile faded and he glanced at Nic in uncertainty.

Nic said, "We can sign prisoners out for a few hours at a time. Only the ones who have earned a ton of trust. Your guy here stopped a riot at Dawnwood. He received major points with the prison along with a nasty gash and death threats from his fellow inmates. He's being housed in protective custody—a special wing of the prison." He looked at Devlen. "I hear they have real beds in there. It's pretty nice, isn't it?"

"Yes," Devlen said, but his worried gaze was fixed on me.

My muscles had petrified. I couldn't move or speak.

"Anyway, I thought you two would like to catch up. You have three hours before he has to return," Nic said. "I'll be back then."

"Opal, are you okay with this?" Devlen asked in concern.

More than okay. That was the problem. I nodded and

forced myself to relax as Nic left. Devlen didn't move.
An awkward silence filled the air.

"Come upstairs," I said to Devlen. "I need to heat
this up before I starve to death."

A tentative smile flashed as his blue eyes shone with
hope. My insides liquefied and pure willpower kept me
from tossing the stew aside and...what? Why could I be
so rational about him when I was with Kade, yet when
he stood mere feet from me, my heart acted like a teen-
age girl with her first crush?

With effort, I concentrated on moving my feet without falling as I led him through the factory.

"Grab a lantern," I said to break the quiet. "I didn't
light a fire upstairs." Which meant Nic's peace offering would have to wait.

As expected, darkness covered the upper rooms. I
lit a couple more lanterns while Devlen crouched next
to the hearth and stacked kindling. His quick and sure
movements reminded me of his skills with a sword. A
chill zipped along my skin and I rubbed my arms. Still
damp from my workout, my practice tunic smelled rank.

I hurried to the washroom to change and rinse off as
much sweat as possible with a sponge and small bowl
of water. At least my extra tunic and dark brown pants
were clean and dry.

By the time I returned, Devlen's fire blazed on top
of a bed of coals and he had transferred my stew to an
iron pot. He sat close to the flames. The bright light illuminated his sharp features and the scar on his neck.
He wore a plain white shirt half tucked into black pants.
I wondered if he'd borrowed them from one of the correctional officers.

I perched on the edge of the hearth, joining him.

"I miss having a fire at night," he said.

"Why?" I asked.

"It reminds me of my childhood in the plains. At night, the elders would gather around the fire and tell stories. It was the best part of the day."

"Were they Story Weavers?"

"Yes."

"Did you have a large family?"

"No. My mother died in childbirth and my father was always busy. He was one of the leaders of the clan. He only became interested in me when I developed magic, which just fueled my desire to irritate him as much as possible." Devlen added another log. "Things might have been different if I had a big family like yours."

Remembering my mother's anger, I said, "I wouldn't be so sure. Upsetting family members is pretty standard." I watched the flames lick at the new log as if deciding to consume it or not. "Do you think of the plains as home?"

"No. What about you? Where's home?"

"It used to be my parents' house in Booruby."

"Used to be? What about now?"

"I don't know. No place really feels right."

"Perhaps you should fire up one of those kilns downstairs."

Surprised, I met his gaze. "I'm only here for tonight. Didn't Nic tell you?"

"No. He said you had returned, but nothing else. I was just happy you came back." He grabbed a poker and fished out a few coals. They glowed. He set the pot on top of them to heat the stew. "Was your mission a success?"

I should have kept the distance between us. But as I

had told Kade, I needed him. And Yelena had even suggested I talk to him. So I did. "It was a disaster." Once the words started to flow, everything poured forth. My immunity, Reema and Teegan, the detectors...everything.

Finally, from deep down where I had shoved it, a horrible admission bubbled to the surface. "Despite all that, I'd give anything to get my magic back. I'd do anything. Does that mean I'm addicted to magic?"

Devlen had listened without uttering a word. He spread his arms, inviting me close.

The knots already twisting in my stomach tugged harder. I remained in place. "I'm confused about that, too."

He tried to cover his disappointment by ladling the stew into a bowl and handing it to me.

"I can't—"

"Eat something. You'll feel better," he said.

"You sound like my mother before I landed on her bad side."

"I'm sure her ire is temporary."

I considered. "But how many times can you upset someone and still return to normal? Isn't there a point when the person gives up on you?"

"It would depend on the person. I think in the case of mothers, you'd have to do more than be late for your sister's wedding."

What about with Kade? I filled my mouth with stew to keep from asking Devlen that question. The warm meat tasted divine, and I attacked the rest.

"Feel better?" he asked when I finished.

"I'm not hungry anymore."

"One problem solved." He moved to a more comfortable position on the couch.

"And only three hundred more to go," I joked, but it was halfhearted.

Devlen smiled. "One at a time."

Not good enough. I wanted to snap my fingers and be done with the decisions and the problems.

"Opal, come here." He pointed to the cushion next to him. "To talk," he added, sensing my reluctance.

I sat, but couldn't relax. When I stood to pace, Devlen grabbed my wrist and pulled me back, tucking me under his arm. For a moment I stiffened. Then I leaned against him, resting my head on his shoulder.

"There're no easy answers," he said. "The only thing I can assure you of, is you are *not* addicted to magic. We both know there're many things you wouldn't do to get your magic back. Wishes and desires don't mean an addiction. I know."

"How about an obsession?"

"No. Otherwise you wouldn't have gone to the Citadel to help Teegan. You would have stayed with Valek to hunt for your blood."

"But—"

He put his fingers on my lips. "Stop second-guessing yourself. Do what you need to do. Don't apologize. When the time comes, you'll know what is important and what isn't." He dropped his hand.

"I thought you said there weren't any easy answers."

"I didn't say it would be easy. Sometimes being true to yourself is the hardest thing to do."

I straightened and met his gaze. "That sounded like a Story Weaver platitude."

"Platitude number five. My favorite," he teased.

I punched him. It was a light blow, but he winced. Before he could stop me, I pulled his shirt up, revealing a six-inch wound on his torso. It was stitched closed with black thread.

"Didn't you go to the healer?" I asked.

"There aren't any healers in prison."

"Devlen, stopping riots and becoming a target isn't necessary. You've proven your commitment."

"I did it for me."

"That doesn't make sense."

He tugged his shirt back down. "My actions earned me three hours with you here and not in a sterile visiting room. If I accumulate enough points, I could be released early. So I am being selfish."

Released early? The words hit me hard. I sprang to my feet. This time he didn't pull me back. I paced.

"What would you do?" I asked.

"Do you want the truth? Or for me to tell you something that wouldn't scare you?"

I halted. "What does that mean?"

"Right now, I think the truth would scare you away."

Unable to remain still, I carried the pot and stew bowl to the kitchen. Reema had worried about the same thing. But, damn it, I wasn't easy to scare anymore. And I was tired of avoiding uncomfortable situations.

I returned to the living area. "Tell me."

He kept his face neutral, but his gaze burned with intensity. "There's only one thing I wish to do when I'm released. Be with you."

Proud I didn't panic, I asked, "What if I recover my magic and am sent on missions for the Council?"

"I'll provide backup."

"What if I decide to join Valek's corp?"

"I'll sign up."

"What if I decide to stay in Fulgor and make glass?"

"Just tell me if you need a slug gathered on a pontil iron or a blowpipe."

"What if I decide to stay with Kade on the coast?"

He didn't flinch. "I'll respect your decision."

"And?"

"I'd find a job here. I do enjoy helping others, and maybe I can put my Story Weaver skills to use. Perhaps Nic's captain would hire me."

"He'd be an idiot not to." I wondered if I would be an idiot to walk away from someone who would be content being with me no matter what. But I didn't quite understand why. "I get that you want to make amends. But don't you want a life of your own?"

"I already did the life of my own and I did horrible, terrible things. As I said before, you inspire me to be a better person. I fell in love with you while I was disguised as Ulrick. Even through the haze of addiction, I saw your willingness to sacrifice for others. And even with your search for your blood you still gave up precious time to help Councilor Moon, Reema and Teegan. Any one of those delays may have cost you the return of your magic. Do you regret doing them?"

"No."

"That's why I want to be with you. And perhaps, someday I will deserve your kindness. And eventually I might even earn your love." Unable to wait for my reaction, he asked, "Have I scared you away?"

"It would be easier if you did." I joined him on the couch, and tucked my feet up under me. "I do admire your calm acceptance of your life and how you know exactly what you want."

He wrapped his arm around my shoulder. "You will, too, Opal. Give it time."

"I need to find my blood."

"And that will solve all your problems?"

"Yes."

"Do you really believe that?"

"Yes. But before you go all Story Weaver on me, it also isn't an excuse to avoid making decisions."

"Why not?"

"Because once I either reclaim my blood or I know it's lost forever, then I'll know who I am."

"I see." His tone implied otherwise.

"I'll either be Opal Cowan, the glass magician, or Opal Cowan, the antimagician."

"Antimagician?"

"You know…" I gestured. "Immune to magic. Yelena occasionally uses it to describe Valek."

"Interesting. But why can't you be Opal Cowan without a descriptor?"

I closed my eyes for a moment, then tried to explain. "A person's actions define who they are. It doesn't matter what he says, or what he wishes he could do. It all comes down to…"

"What she sacrifices," he said.

"I miss it, Devlen. More than Kade, more than… anything. I miss the way my glass pieces sang to me. The magic connected me to the world. I feel cut off. Isolated." All my energy fled. I had worked hard to suppress those feelings. To not admit it to myself, let alone another. I didn't want to dwell on the grief, but to focus on fixing it because there was only one cure.

"Your anger is gone. And you've filled the emptiness."

I pulled away. "Haven't you been listening? I haven't. It's what I'm trying to do."

"I've been paying attention. You haven't. But you will."

"Another Story Weaver inanity. You have it easier."

He shook his head. "Waiting is never easy."

After five days on the road, I arrived in Ognap alone. Nestled in the foothills of the Emerald Mountains, Ognap buzzed with activity. The town's main income centered on the gemstones mined from the mountains. Factories charged with transforming the raw uncut stones into sparkling gems lined the busy streets. Well-protected caravans of loose stones headed west toward the Jewelrose Clan where they would be set into various types of jewelry and goods.

Nic and Eve planned to enter town this evening and rent a room at the Tourmaline Inn. Finding Vasko Cloud Mist's extensive compound proved harder than I had expected. My inquiries were met with suspicion. Finally a servant employed by Vasko recognized my name and led me to the gate. Hidden by the rolling terrain east of the city, Vasko's manor house had been built into the side of the Emerald Mountains. The tall spires overlooked a valley filled with buildings.

Vasko trusted no one with his rubies. According to the locals, the mine entrance was in the basement of his house and all the stones were sorted, sized and cut on-site before being sold.

As I waited at the gate, I noted the thick wall that surrounded the compound on all sides. The location and arrangement of the buildings suggested someone took care with their placement. An army would have trouble invading Vasko's home. I guessed that was the point.

Pazia arrived. Genuine welcome shone on her face as she embraced me. Even though she was a few inches shorter than me, Pazia gave the impression of being taller. Her long hair had been pulled up and braided. The thick loop of hair resembled a crown on her head. Add in the way the guards deferred to her, she oozed royalty.

Pazia asked about my trip as she escorted me through her family's grounds. The well-groomed walkways flowed past ornate gardens. Flowers burst from baskets and workers tended to the landscape. Nothing within sight suggested a mining operation.

"How are you *really* doing, Opal?" she asked, raising one thin eyebrow.

"I'm fine," I assured her.

"Don't lie to me. It's quite an adjustment."

And she was the only other person besides Devlen who had firsthand knowledge of just how much of an adjustment. I shrugged. "I'm still getting used to the idea."

"I was stunned when we heard the news of your sacrifice. My father…"

Having no desire to hear about Vasko's reaction, I stopped listening until she brought the topic to the discovery of the messengers.

She practically bounced. "It's exciting, isn't it?"

I decided to be honest. "It's a little hard to believe."

"I know. We ruined that diamond we tried in the glass before, remember? But black diamonds are incredible!"

Her enthusiasm seemed genuine. "How did you know what they were?" I asked.

"We didn't at first. Our gemstone expert thought they were a hard black coal. But after multiple tests, the results matched diamonds in everything but color."

"Where did you find them?"

"Deep. That's all I know. Father is very secretive. The miners still think the black diamonds are coal."

How convenient. "It's bound to get out," I said.

"Eventually," she agreed.

Pazia didn't appear upset by this. Either she didn't think it through, or she wasn't as greedy as her father. Because if the black diamonds were real, then every Emerald Mountains mine owner would be searching for their own vein. I tried another approach. "How did you decide to try one for the messengers?"

She glanced around. The footpath remained empty of workers. "Father's still angry at me for losing my magic." She held up a hand to me. "Don't start. He's been experimenting with different *legal* ideas to recover my powers. As part of his…quest, he wanted to see if the black diamonds could hold magic like the regular diamonds. And he found out they were better. The black ones can hold twice as much magic, but using it was…painful."

"How so?"

She showed me her hands. Burn scars crisscrossed her palms and covered her fingertips. Ouch. Blood wouldn't sear her skin. Perhaps they had discovered real diamonds. I viewed that possibility with mixed emotions. It meant I hadn't found my blood at all, but it also implied my blood could still be in its original container.

"I tried gloves, but I couldn't control the power,"

Pazia said. "Then I remembered our experiment with the glass."

"I'm surprised your father let you use the black diamonds. Alone they're worth…"

"More gold than I can carry. And Father would have had heart failure if he knew I planned to encase one of his blacks in glass, so I didn't tell him until after. It worked better than I had dreamed."

"What type of glass did you use?"

"I'll show you. My workshop is over here."

The sweet scent of burning white coal reached me before I spotted the smoke curling from the chimney. Mounds of dirt and construction litter surrounded Pazia's small glass factory. Unexpected, but not surprising, guards stood beside the entrance to the building.

She gestured to the men. "Thieves will be a concern once news about the messengers spreads."

I paused in the threshold, soaking in the warmth and hum of the kiln. Pazia gave me a quick tour of her gleaming shop. Everything appeared to be in order. All the right tools hung within reach, the mixing room was stocked with the proper ingredients and the annealing ovens contained cooling projects.

But no diamonds. Black or otherwise.

She tsked at me when I asked. "You can't just leave them lying around!" Pazia led me to a windowless office in the back. A safe had been built into the wall. She spun the dial with practiced ease, opening the thick door.

Magic poured from the safe. Pulling out a drawer, she set it on her desk. Then she hefted a couple of super messengers, stacking the blocks next to the drawer. I hesitated.

"Go on, Opal. I trust you."

Being trustworthy hadn't been my concern. It was the lumps of black that caused my reluctance. No vial of blood in sight. I guess I should be happy the super messengers were legitimate except I couldn't produce the emotion.

When I reached for one of the diamonds, Pazia said, "Be careful, they're charged. You'll be okay as long as you don't try to use the magic."

I paused. "Who charged them?"

"One of my father's people."

Pushing through a thick layer of magic, I picked up a small black stone and held it up to the sunlight. It looked familiar, but as a gemstone, it failed to impress me. "Why doesn't it glitter?"

"No sense polishing and faceting them if they're going into the glass."

I replaced the stone and grabbed one of the messengers. The power felt muted. "Can you send messages?" I asked her.

"Yes." An inner excitement danced from her eyes.

"You can do more with them." It wasn't a question, but a heartrending realization.

"Can't you?" she asked. "I so hoped they would help you, too."

"No." As usual, I felt the power, but couldn't use it. "What else can you do?"

"It's…odd. It's like I have magic again, but instead of drawing from the power source through my…" She tapped her chest. "Through me, I draw on the cube. And when the power is gone, I take it back to my father and he has them charged again. My abilities from before remained the same. I can still light fires, move objects and read minds, but I have to be touching the glass."

Another thought struck me. Even if I recovered my blood, no one would want my little glass animals when Pazia's super messengers could do so much more. Except for the cost. "Has your father decided on a price?"

"No. But he plans to be...egalitarian about them. He's going to give one to each Master Magician for free, and then anyone can purchase one. He'll work out payment plans. If you think about it, you could buy one and then charge a fee for others to use. Once the messenger is paid for, you could make money. I'm sure businesses will capitalize on that."

The possibilities were endless. The richest man in Sitia would be even richer. What would he do with all that gold? I'd purchased a number of things with mine, but besides the wedding, none of them touched the emptiness inside me. Devlen's Story Weaver mumbo jumbo about it being filled had been wrong.

Pazia returned the messengers and drawer of diamonds to the safe.

Trying to see all angles, I thought if I did regain my powers, my animals would be much cheaper and they would compete with Vasko's, especially if he had only a few super messengers. Would he steal my blood to keep that from happening?

I pointed to the safe. "Is that all the diamonds?"

"No. The vein is pretty thick."

I considered. I'd never seen a black diamond before. So why did they feel familiar? "Can I see the vein?"

"I'll have to ask my uncle."

We left the factory and searched for her uncle. He worked in a building that Pazia called the command center. She explained it was an old family joke that stuck.

Hans Cloud Mist stood up as soon as we entered his large office. His resemblance to his brother Vasko was uncanny, and I wondered if they were twins. Hans insisted he was not only the younger brother but also the smarter and better-looking one, as well.

Pazia rolled her eyes. "Just humor him. He thinks he's funny."

Hans pretended to be hurt, but his pout lasted less than a second. "Did Pazia show you her factory?" he asked me. "She's quite proud of it."

She blushed and quickly changed the subject, asking about a tour.

"You'll have to get permission from Galen." He glanced out the window. "He should be overseeing checks now."

She frowned.

"Another uncle?" I asked.

"No. My father's right-hand man and I don't need *his* permission."

"Are you going to be her tour guide?" Hans asked.

Pazia shivered. "No."

"And I don't know where the vein is, so it's Galen or nothing."

She grumbled, but didn't argue. I followed her from Hans's office.

"Why can't you take me?" I asked.

"I can't stand being in the mines. I'm claustrophobic." She stopped. "Are you?"

"Afraid of small spaces?"

She nodded. "And the dark?"

"No lanterns?"

"Plenty of light, but sometimes an errant wind blows them out. We pump air down into the shafts to keep it fresh."

I thought of my various adventures, being hidden in a box under a pile of sand, swimming through a tunnel in a cave and spending a couple weeks chained in a dark cell. "I'm not claustrophobic."

"Good."

"Do you know the location of the vein?" I asked her.

"No. I think only Father and Galen do. They tend to get all paranoid when they make a new find. Both of them know every shaft below. I don't even think there are any maps." She shook her head and continued.

Pazia led me to the lowest level of the command center. Rumors about the main entrance to the mines hadn't been too far off. Instead of being in the basement of his house, the doorway for the miners was deep under the command center.

I waited with Pazia as the day shift's personnel streamed in from the large cavern. Under the keen gaze of another group, the workers stripped off their jumpers, stood under spouts of water and were searched before they donned clean clothes. The process reminded me of Wirral. Except they seemed more worried about what might be smuggled out of the mines than in. Mirrors lined the wall opposite the search area and I suspected they were two-way ones and observers lurked behind them.

When the last worker left, Pazia told me to wait while she slipped behind the mirrors. It didn't take her long before she returned.

"Come on," she said, almost running from the underground entrance. She finally slowed when we exited the building.

"I hope you're not in trouble," I said.

"Not at all. Galen just gives me the creeps. He practically lives in the mines. In fact, I haven't seen him in seasons, which is fine by me. But when I do see him, he acts like he's in charge." She smoothed her skirt. "He gets away with that attitude because my father trusts him."

"What does he do?"

"Whatever my father wants." She took a breath. "I know I shouldn't be so down on him. He's dedicated to our family, and he was the one who found the black diamond vein. And Galen promised to find someone to give you a tour tomorrow."

I accepted her offer to stay in their guesthouse, but convinced her to join me at the Tourmaline Inn for supper. Pazia made the proper appreciative noises over the large pink tourmaline the inn's owner, Carleen, wore around her neck.

Carleen remembered me, but since I had paid in full before Janco and I had made our sudden departure, she welcomed me back. She led us to a nice table and served us each a heaping portion of beef pie. Pazia and I chatted about our days at the Keep.

"How is your brother doing?" I asked.

She crinkled her forehead. "Which one?"

"Walker. Do you have another brother at the Keep?"

"No. My older brother also attended, but he graduated the season before I started. I guess Walker's doing okay. He hasn't written to say otherwise. Have you met him?"

I smiled, thinking about his attack. "Briefly."

"Don't mind him. He's a hothead like all the male members of my family. They get all high and mighty about honor and family and duty."

"Your uncle Hans seemed nice," I said.

"They're all nice as long as you play their game. Once you cross them, look out. They think it's a personal assault."

"Does your older brother work here, as well?"

"Sort of. My father calls him his secret weapon. He sends him off on missions and to strong-arm the people who owe my father money."

Interesting. He would have enough money to purchase my blood. As for motive, he could want revenge. "What type of missions?"

"I don't know and I don't care. I never wanted to be involved in the family business, but…" Pazia drained her wine, then changed the subject. "So what's new in the Keep's glass shop?"

I filled her in on the new kiln and water system. As we talked, Nic and Eve entered the inn's common room and flagged down Carleen. They rented a room and followed the innkeeper up the stairs. Eve had signaled me her room number, and after a few minutes I excused myself to meet up with them.

Nic bounced on the edge of the bed. "I think you have more pillows," he said to Eve.

"She also has the best mattress in the house," I said.

"It's discrimination. All this pink is unfriendly to men."

"At least she didn't tell you to take a bath," I offered, but he wrinkled his nose.

I tried to stifle a laugh. "She's concerned about your health."

"She's concerned about her clean sheets," Eve said.

He crossed his arms and continued to look sour. "Should I be listening for anything in particular at the bathhouse?"

"Good idea. I think there's a bathhouse over by the miners' village," I said. "They're basically barracks for the underground workers. Listen for any comments about black coal or black diamonds from the miners."

"Do they know what's going on?" Eve asked.

"They're not supposed to, but..."

"It's hard to keep something that big a secret," Nic finished for me. "I wouldn't be surprised if one of them smuggled a few stones out."

"It would be difficult." I explained about the search.

"But not impossible," he said.

I recalled what I had been able to carry into Wirral with me. "You're right. Nothing's impossible."

"We should make that our motto." Nic surged to his feet.

"This is probably a waste of time," I said. "So far, everything appears to be legitimate."

"Nothing wrong with good news," Eve said. "It would be refreshing."

I felt a small twinge of guilt as I crept from the guesthouse. My actions were not exactly proper guest behavior. Oh well. A half-moon hung high in the sky, illuminating the buildings. Even at this late hour, armed guards patrolled the walkways and a dozen guarded the main house.

Avoiding Vasko's residence—I needed more training to slip past so many watchers—I sneaked into a couple of the utilitarian structures. Conveyor belts from underground brought up crushed rock, dumping it into piles. Workers shoveled the rock into screens and sifted the material. Others watched.

Interesting how all the sorting was done inside. Even the wagons filled with rejected material were taken to another building. I found a couple of open mine shafts, but they were too small to be anything but air vents and they had protective walls around them.

From my nighttime explorations, I couldn't find another way into or out of the mines. Before stopping, I circled the command center. Guards had been stationed next to the two entrances, but no one bothered to watch the sides of the building. With no windows on the first two floors, there wasn't a reason to be concerned. Unless the thief's teacher happened to be Valek, who delighted in climbing up sheer walls. And most people didn't bother to lock shutters on windows above the fourth floor.

I kicked off my boots, tied the laces together and looped them around my neck. Using fingers, toes and a mortar crumbler invented by Valek, I scaled the side of the building. Bypassing the third and fourth floors, I found an open window on the top level and entered a dark office.

I poked around the offices on the fifth floor, read a few papers by moonlight and worked my way down. All the offices looked the same, and I found nothing out of the ordinary. Even Vasko's spacious work area held nothing incriminating.

After searching a few more rooms, I decided to exit the building through Vasko's office on the third floor. Unlocking the shutters, I pushed them wide. The light from the moon pierced the darkness and shone on the desk. Metal glinted from under the wooden top. I pulled the chair back and ran a hand along the wood. Encountering a small lock, I crawled under and used my picks. A small panel clicked open.

Inside the hidden drawer were stacks of files. I brought them out into the moonlight and skimmed the papers. About three files down, I hit the jackpot.

My name had been written on the file folder's tab, and inside was an accounting of expenses. The list included prices for forged documents, bribes, the purchase of drugs and weapons. *Damned expensive, but worth every piece of gold,* was scrawled under the total. And farther down it in big letters, *Success! Junior pulled it off again.*

23

Finally a connection! Junior had to be Vasko's son and Pazia's older brother. And from the list of prison officials Junior had bribed, he had to be Finn. He was the right age and had attended the Keep. I did another quick search of Vasko's office, but uncovered nothing to implicate him. They hadn't used my blood for the super messengers. So where was it? Locked away?

"Find anything interesting?" a male voice asked from the doorway.

I stifled a yelp and grabbed my switchblade. The snick of the blade cut through the quiet office.

"Easy, Opal. It's me."

"What are you doing here?"

"Same thing you are, looking for clues."

"I meant why here in Ognap?"

"Oh, that." Janco entered the office. He wore a skin-tight black coverall and had darkened his face.

"We linked Finn to Vasko Cloud Mist and I'm playing miner, hoping he'll show up. But no luck so far."

"And the message to me that you found Finn is en route to the Citadel?"

"I didn't find him," he said. "He's Vasko's oldest son and he has dropped out of the gossip network. None of our…informers have been able to tell us where he's been for the last half year."

I showed Janco the file of expenses. "Why would Vasko send his son undercover? It doesn't make sense."

"From what I've been hearing, Vasko doesn't trust many people outside his immediate family. And he kept his children out of the spotlight. Perhaps for that reason."

It made sense, which was unexpected, considering the source. "Since Finn's not here, maybe he's at the Citadel with Vasko."

"Then Finn's in for a nasty surprise. Valek's there, as well." He grinned. "I would love to see the two of them fight. Finn's not as good, but he'd hold his own."

Unless he cheated and used a null shield. "Where's Ari?"

"Fulgor. It's the only major city between here and the Citadel."

"Finn would avoid it. The Sitian authorities have an arrest warrant out for him."

Janco snorted. "No offense, but the *Sitians* are way out of their league on this guy."

"None taken." I returned the folder to Vasko's hidden drawer. "Any news on my blood?"

"It's not in the compound. This is my last building."

"I've been through it. No luck."

"Did you check the safe?" Janco asked.

"I didn't see one."

He tsked. "He's a paranoid patriarch with trust issues and the richest man in Sitia. He *has* a safe. Actually, I already found two in his private residence." A superior little smirk twisted his lips. "But no blood."

Even though I was impressed by his ability to bypass a dozen guards, I wouldn't say so. Instead, I tugged on all the wall art as Janco searched through the bookcases. I found a safe hidden behind an oil painting of sand dunes.

Safecracking hadn't been included in my training. Janco quickly set to work and pulled the heavy metal door open.

"Remind me never to store my valuables in a safe," I said.

"They are effective for the most part." He rummaged inside and removed a tray of gemstones. "Too bad I'm not a thief or I could retire."

"Anything else?"

"Just more files. Sorry." Janco tried to cheer me up. "We know who Finn is now. It's only a matter of time before we catch him."

I pointed at the tray. "Have you heard or seen anything about those black diamonds while working in the mines?" I asked.

He picked one up, and rolled it between his fingers. "It doesn't look like a diamond. Are you sure? It feels weird." Dropping it into my palm with distaste, Janco rubbed his hand on his shirt.

A familiar stickiness clung to the stone. "It's real. And it's charged with magic. You don't have any power, but you're sensitive to magic. Aren't you?"

Janco scratched his goatee. "I'm not sensitive. I'm allergic."

* * *

The next morning at breakfast, I asked Pazia about her older brother again. By the way she frowned, they weren't close.

"I haven't seen him in ages," she said.

"Sounds like you don't get along with him."

"He's a bully, but he stopped bossing me around once my powers came in." She smiled. "My magic was stronger than his and it galled him!" Then the humor dropped from her face. "Now I'm not worth his time. We avoid each other. It works for me."

"What's his name?"

"Phinnegan. Why all the questions?"

Yes! I kept my voice steady. "Just curious. I didn't even know you had brothers until I met Walker." I changed the subject even though I wondered just how long ages was.

Pazia escorted me to the command center, but she stopped outside the building. "Galen said a guide would be waiting for you at the mine entrance. Come to the glass shop when you're done."

When I reached the lower level, I encountered two men. They argued, but ceased their discussion as soon as I appeared. They both wore yellow helmets and orange coveralls. No dirt stained the one on the left, but mud spattered the other man's.

"I'm Opal."

Mud-spattered man said, "He'll be out soon." They entered the mines.

With nothing else to do, I explored the area, searching for another entrance. Eventually, a lanky man slipped out from behind the mirror. His black hair hung in greasy clumps to his shoulders and his skin looked as if it hadn't seen the sun in years. He wore oversize dark glasses.

"I'm Galen," he said. Instead of shaking my outstretched hand, he handed me a clean pair of orange coveralls and pointed to a privacy screen. "Regulations. Leave your backpack on the shelf. No one will bother it."

I changed. The durable material chafed against my skin, but the fabric blocked the chilly air. When I stepped out, he gave me a helmet for safety.

"Shall we?" He swept his arm out toward the large tunnel.

I glanced around. The other men were gone. "I thought you'd—"

"You're our special guest." He grinned. Black grit discolored his teeth. "I would be remiss in my duties if I assigned just anyone to show you around. Besides, you want to visit a highly restricted area."

His bulky glasses blocked his expression, but there was something…off about him. Creepy seemed mild. Why the dark lenses? Perhaps this tour wasn't a good idea, but it was too late to change my mind. I followed Galen into the mines.

At first the walls of the tunnel rose high above my head. Lanterns hung every couple of feet and a nice breeze fanned my face. The damp smell of earth alternated with the sharp tang of rock.

As we traveled, I noticed scratches and deep grooves marred the walls. The passageway shrank and the light dimmed. When the ground angled down, I imagined the dark corridor before us as the gullet of a large beast, swallowing us.

My guide grabbed one of the lanterns to carry with

us. He paused every so often and pointed out an interesting rock formation or geological feature.

If it wasn't for the current of air, I might have panicked. The tunnel zigzagged and we passed so many other branches and caverns that I was soon lost. The distant sound of machinery echoed off the hard walls. I spotted a few miners, but soon we were alone with the darkness being held back by that one lantern.

I felt the pressure of the mountain on my shoulders, reminding me about all that weight hanging over us. I asked Galen about cave-ins.

"Unlikely. This section is new. We haven't opened it up yet."

"What about along the way out?"

He chuckled without humor. "Down here, *anything* can happen."

I decided to quit asking questions. We entered a narrow shaft. My arms brushed the walls and Galen hunched over. The moist smell intensified as the airflow died. I moved closer to him and almost bumped into him when he stopped without warning. Another dry chuckle.

He held the lantern up, illuminating the end of the shaft. It widened slightly like a head on the end of a match. I moved closer as he tapped the black wall in front of us. The pockmarked surface appeared porous.

Galen pulled a small metal tool from his pocket and scraped at the black stone. A few pieces broke off and clattered to the floor.

After a few minutes, he handed me a smooth black rock. "A diamond hidden in the lava."

Magic radiated from the stone so I ran my hand along

the bumpy wall of lava, but didn't feel any power. I suspected he planted this diamond here.

Pretending to be awed, I asked him how he could see it with his glasses on.

"My eyes are sensitive to the light." He tried a smile, but it failed.

The slight catch in his voice meant he lied. A person could change his hair color and style, grow a beard, add putty to his face, put lifts in his shoes, or stuff his clothes with cotton. But one thing that was impossible to do without magic was change his eye color. Seeking a disguise, I asked if I could dig for a diamond.

He handed me the scraper. I opened up a small hole, but didn't find anything. He swept his fingers inside and pulled another stone free, using sleight of hand. Before my training with Valek I would have missed the subtle motion. That and the fact the stone pulsed with magic.

I kept quiet as we started back to the surface. Why would Vasko set up this elaborate ruse? Perhaps he didn't want anyone to know where he mined the diamonds. Then why not refuse to give me a tour? Because he wanted me to back up his claims. It would have worked if Vasko knew I could feel the magic.

Another realization hit me. Galen wouldn't have used charged diamonds if he had been warned about my immunity. Which meant Finn hadn't been here since our encounter in Hubal. No Finn. No blood.

I pulled my morose thoughts back to Vasko. Nothing illegal about hiding the source of the black diamonds. No one had reported them stolen. Unless he imported them illegally from Ixia? The Commander and Valek hadn't known about the other diamond pit in the Northern Ice Sheet at first. Why would this be different?

A rumble shook the ground under my feet. Galen cursed.

"What was that?" I asked, coughing on dust.

"An explosion or a cave-in…or both." He handed me the lantern and jabbed a finger toward the ground. "Stay here. Don't move. I'll return for you."

The panic must have shown on my face because Galen gave me the two diamonds. "Here's more incentive for me to return." He disappeared into the blackness.

If he had been joking about the diamonds, it failed to amuse me. I clutched the stones in my fist. The sharp edges dug into my palm, but the pain wasn't enough to distract me from the situation. The lantern's flame stayed steady. No breeze, but before I worried about running out of air, I remembered a fire couldn't burn without it.

Waiting was torture; I decided to continue up the shaft until I reached a junction. I reasoned that Galen would still be able to find me. The next intersection resembled all the others we had passed on our descent. At least there was a little more room for me to move. I turned a circle, searching for an airflow. Nothing stirred.

Resigned to wait, I sat on the ground, crossing my legs under me. My thoughts kept trying to imagine all types of horrible scenarios. I clung to one piece of logic. This wasn't part of Vasko's revenge for Pazia. He needed me to confirm the legitimacy of his messengers to Irys and Bain. Besides, Pazia, Nic and Eve knew I was down here. No. I wouldn't contemplate this as a murder attempt.

Instead, I examined the black diamonds. The rough

uncut gemstones lacked beauty, but held an incredible amount of magic. Too bad I couldn't use it to communicate. Then again, what would I say? *I'm stuck at the intersection of Rock Boulevard and Rock Street? Come get me.*

I was being silly, but it gave me an idea. I looked on the walls of the connecting shafts, searching for directional markings. The miners had to get lost from time to time. Wouldn't it make sense to name the shafts or at least indicate an exit? An array of scratches lined all the walls. Perhaps the miners could read them, but I couldn't.

Focusing my energy on what I did know, I mulled over a reason Vasko would lie about where the black diamonds had been found. Perhaps he discovered them in a more accessible or even public location, and didn't want his competitors to find out. Unlike my glass messengers, these super ones didn't require any special magic. Any magician could charge the diamonds and any glassmaker could encase them in glass. Therefore keeping the location secret was key.

If he imported them from Ixia, Valek might already be suspicious. Before, he had Ari and Janco investigating General Kitvivan's illicit operation. Except this time all three of them had been here in Sitia helping me.

Fisk might know if any of the blacks had gone through the underground market in the Citadel. He had been the first to discover Kitvivan's diamonds and had kept track of the pearls. Thinking of Fisk, I remembered my promise to investigate the Bloodrose Clan.

I shot to my feet as my brain made a connection. My helmet tumbled to the ground as I raked a hand through my hair, pulling all the clues together. It was a huge leap of logic. But I believed the reason the blacks looked so familiar was because I had seen them at the Bloodroses' complex.

The second building where Walsh's men had captured Quinn. Instead of oyster shells and long tables filling the space, boxes with mesh screens like the ones I had seen in Vasko's sorting building, mounds of sand and black rocks littered the area. I had been so worried about Quinn flaming out I hadn't given the strange contents a thought.

Walsh's actions against the other oyster farms made more sense. Not only could he affect the pearl prices, but he could keep the others from discovering that those black rocks were actually diamonds.

But once I considered it fully, there were more than a few holes. Those rocks could indeed be rocks. If they weren't, then how did Walsh figure out the rocks were diamonds? I remembered the sea glass Heli had found. The pieces had been scratched, and there were only a few substances hard enough to scratch glass. Diamonds being one of them.

But why would Walsh team up with Vasko? Even with these questions, a visit to the Bloodrose Clan was overdue.

One problem. Galen hadn't returned. I checked the oil level in the lantern. Half-full. I settled back on the ground. Devlen had been right. Waiting wasn't easy. And how long should I stay here before trying to find my own way?

The diamonds still clutched in my hand could scratch a mark into the wall. Perhaps I should explore—

A rumble rolled through the shaft. The lantern jiggled and small stones rained down. I donned my helmet as dust filled the area.

Then a blast of fresh air cleared the cloud. Unfortunately, the wind extinguished the flame.

The complete absence of light was a unique experience to me. Even at night there was always the moon or a distant fire or a lantern. Without any real hope, I waited for my eyes to adjust. The darkness clung and pressed, feeling tangible like magic.

Perhaps the coveralls I wore had matches in the pockets. This had happened before. Pazia had warned me about the lanterns.

Relaxing my grip on the diamonds, I opened my fist. A dim orange light glowed from my palm. I blinked a few times to clear my vision, but the weak radiance remained. Teegan had said I shimmered when I touched magic. Probably why he called me Fire Lady. Unable to see it for myself, I didn't really believe him. At least it was useful in this situation.

I searched the pockets, and only found the items I had taken from my pack—my lock picks and switchblade. Waiting was no longer an option. I turned in a circle and stopped when I felt the breeze full in my face. The air had to come from somewhere and I planned to find the source. I scratched an arrow pointing in the direction I traveled and walked into the wind.

At each intersection I marked my route. I ignored the doubts and worries bubbling on the surface of my mind. When I reached a shaft with lanterns hanging from hooks, the pressure eased in my chest. The glass was still warm, which meant these had been lit before the blast of air.

Encouraged, I increased my pace. A crunching shuffle sounded behind me. I turned. Galen rounded a corner. Thank fate! He held a dim lantern.

He slowed. "I told you to stay put. You're lucky I found you. Otherwise you'd die down here."

"Sorry. When you didn't come back, I thought the worst. What happened?"

"They were enlarging a cavern and hit a stink hole."

"What's that?"

"There're bubbles of gas trapped underground. When you drill into one, a horrible stench hits you first, then it reaches the lanterns and…boom! If you're lucky it's a flash fire and you walk away with minor burns."

"And if you're not?"

"The force blows you apart and brings the ceiling down on your head."

"Which one?"

"The explosion collapsed two quadrants. Vasko's going to be livid."

"Did many miners…" I couldn't finish.

"A handful died." Galen dismissed the loss of life as insignificant. "He'll be more upset about the time and cost to open up new shafts."

"That's—"

"A risk they're well aware of and are paid extra for. And most of them still steal gems from the mines."

Another tremor vibrated under my feet.

"Come on," he said. "Let's get out of here."

Galen brushed past me as he took the lead. When his shoulder had touched my upper arm, I felt magic. By itself, it wouldn't cause me any alarm. Vasko was a shrewd businessman, and I could understand why he would hire a magician as his right-hand man. But the texture of the power reminded me of someone. I just couldn't put my finger on who.

My opinion of Galen increased as he navigated the maze of shafts, chambers and intersections with confidence. The trip seemed never ending.

"How much longer?" I asked. My throat burned from the dust.

"A few more minutes. We have to bypass the weak quadrants."

When the shaft's incline increased, I hoped I would see blue sky soon. I would never take it or fresh air for granted again. But the passage leveled off and ended in a room. Galen set the lantern on a desk, and I corrected my initial impression.

"I thought—"

"You thought wrong." Galen rummaged around the office and found a canteen and two cups.

Pouring water into both, Galen handed me one of the cups. Our fingers touched, and I finally recognized the magician. Finn.

# 24

I drew my switchblade and stabbed, aiming for his heart. He blocked the attack, but didn't move quite fast enough to avoid the blade. It sliced his upper arm.

Finn/Galen growled in pain and I slammed into a null shield. Acting on pure instinct, I flipped my switchblade around and flung it at him. It sailed through the shield, but he deflected it with his power.

Then the shield pressed on me, forcing me back until it flattened me against the wall, unable to move.

Finn plopped into his desk chair and drank from his cup. "Too easy, Opal."

I glanced at his ripped and bloodstained sleeve. "Next time, Finn, I'll slice higher."

He pulled off his glasses and wig. "Points for following the clues and linking me to Vasko, but I'm not his son Phinnegan. I'm really Vasko's faithful dog." He didn't bother to hide the bitterness in his voice.

"Then who is Junior?" I asked, managing to surprise him.

"I didn't think you'd learn anything useful from Vasko's office. Your Ixian teacher should be proud." He watched me. "The Commander isn't the only one with a network of spies in Sitia. The Council is more aware of what's going on than you give them credit for. And Vasko's tapped into that network."

"Is Junior working for the Council or Vasko?"

"He's me. I'm not related, but I have disguised myself as Vasko from time to time. Occasionally he likes to be in two places at once."

"Why tell me all this?" I pushed against the null shield, but it remained firm.

"You're going to be a player in this game. You should understand the basics."

"What does Vasko want now?" I asked. "He already has my blood."

"No he doesn't."

"But he sent you to Wirral?"

"To gather information on blood magic. The existence of your blood was a nice surprise. One I failed to tell him about."

"Why does he...oh." I connected the dots. "He wants to use blood magic to return Pazia's powers." All my actions, whether good or bad, inadvertent or on purpose, have all spun in circles and returned with force, slamming right back into me. "Does he know about the side effects?"

"Yes, but not to worry about your friend. Vasko would never endanger his daughter. Instead he has been experimenting on test subjects, trying to find a way to increase a person's magic without the addiction."

"Should I be horrified by the mention of test subjects?"

"Oh yes. I am. And I'm not the squeamish type.

Vasko makes me look like the nice guy. Why do you think I'm so loyal?"

"For your private office?"

He laughed with genuine amusement then sobered. "If I were to betray or double-cross Vasko, I'd disappear in these mines. I'd either become a new test subject or locked in the cells below and left to die of thirst."

I reviewed his comments. "If you haven't told him about the blood, isn't that a betrayal?"

He snapped his fingers. "Smart girl, I knew I liked you for a reason. If Vasko found out what I've been doing..." He shuddered. "That's why I triggered the cave-ins. If everyone thinks I'm dead and buried under tons of rubble, no one will search for me. And I'm free to pursue other interests."

"Except I know." A rush of cold fear swept through me. "I'm a casualty, too."

"Yep. Otherwise your friends and family would tear Sitia apart looking for you. And they are way too powerful for my liking."

"They'll do it anyway. Unless there's proof of my death."

"The searchers will find your backpack and if they dig deep enough, they'll find a crushed female corpse wearing your clothes. She's approximately your age, size and weight and has the same hairstyle. Although I must admit, the short cut looked better on her."

I closed my eyes, letting grief for the anonymous woman overcome me for a moment. Then I shoved it deep. I would need to focus. "Why bother with this elaborate ruse?"

"I'm tired of playing in Vasko's sandbox. I've a new partner. He's a simple man and only wants one thing in exchange for giving me control over the black diamonds and the super messengers." Galen gazed at me as if appraising a vein for hidden gemstones. "Aren't you going to ask?"

"Who is it?"

"Aren't you curious what he wants?"

"No."

"Ah, denial. Doesn't matter, you'll find out soon enough." Galen pulled a dart from his coverall and approached me.

"You don't need that," I said, thinking fast. "I'm lost down here. I can't run away."

"Nice try, but I've a few tasks to finish before we go." He jabbed the dart into my arm. As my head spun, he dropped the null shield. I sagged forward and he caught me.

"Believe it or not, you're better off with me," he whispered in my ear.

A pounding headache woke me. I kept my eyes closed, wishing I was immune to Finn's...er...Galen's sleeping drug, since the magic immunity didn't do squat against him. Immobilized and lying on my back, I smelled the familiar aroma of damp minerals. Opening my eyes didn't change a thing. Pure blackness surrounded me.

The rough floor scratched my back as I squirmed, but I couldn't move my arms or legs, so he must have secured them. The crook of my right arm throbbed.

As the drug wore off a strange feeling of being satiated welled. Alarmed, I confirmed my coverall remained on. What had Galen done to me while I was unconscious? I yanked and pulled and tried to free my limbs, but the bands holding them down didn't budge.

I waited. The damp air seeped into my skin, numbed my hands and caused bouts of uncontrolled shivers. Keeping my thoughts on the positive, I ignored the panic building in my dry throat.

My muscles stiffened and ached. Galen had a nasty sense of humor if he thought this was better than... What? Vasko using me as a test subject? Sounded bad, but what tore my heart was my family and friends believing I was dead. What if I never saw them again?

My biggest regret was not apologizing to my mother, not explaining everything to her and not taking her into my confidence. The reasons seemed petty now. I had wanted to save her from worry and grief, but the real truth was I wanted to save myself from the hassle of having to explain my actions to her and dealing with her reaction.

And I had pushed Kade away, too. Running off after my blood, I only thought of myself and no one else. At least now, he'd be free to find someone to settle down with. What about Devlen? Would he continue his rehabilitation? I hoped so.

My thoughts lingered on all the people who would be affected by my so-called demise. Not only my family, but Nic, Eve, Yelena, Ari, Janco and Valek. The list lengthened when I added Tama, Faith, Reema, Teegan, Fisk and Zitora.

With all these people in my life, how could I whine about feeling empty? What a brat!

After an eternity of blackness, a glow pushed it back and then burned my eyes. Squinting, I peered at my surroundings. A small cave with one opening that led to a tunnel which housed the source of the growing brilliance. Boots crunched on loose stones, coming closer.

As the footsteps neared, I shut my eyes, pretending to be unconscious. The light shone on my face, stabbing straight through my closed eyelids. After a shuffling scrape, a clink sounded.

"Opal?" Galen asked. "I know you're awake."

"The light's...too bright," I said. Speaking took effort and my voice rasped as if I had gargled rocks. I thought longingly of the cup of water he had offered me before.

Metal rattled and the glow dimmed. I opened my eyes. The lantern had been placed as far away as possible in the meager space. Galen crouched down and lifted my head with one hand and tipped a canteen full of water to my mouth with the other. I gulped it down greedily, making a mess and not caring if it was poisoned or not. The water poured over my cracked lips and soothed my throat.

He pulled the bottle away and shrugged off his backpack. With a hand dipping inside the pack, he met my gaze. "I forgot to ask. How do you feel?"

"Do you want me to list my complaints? Or should I just roll it all into one big tale of woe?"

"Sarcasm aside. Do you feel like your old self?"

A little zing of... What? Fear, hope and panic zipped.

Galen withdrew a package wrapped in leather. With theatrically slow movements, he peeled the layers off. The vibrations reached me first, humming deep within my chest. He uncovered a glass tiger—one of mine! An inner fire glowed from its depths and the magic trapped inside sang to me, welcoming me. My heart squeezed with a moment of joy. Then despair crushed it. Even though my magic had returned, it wouldn't do me a damn bit of good against Galen.

He had watched my face as he sprang his surprise. "You can thank me later." Setting the tiger on the ground near my head, he reached into his pack and drew out a vial filled with a bright red liquid.

My blood?

He flourished it. "This isn't what you think it is. I already injected all your blood back into you." To emphasize his point, he touched the sore spot on the crook of my right arm. "This blood is mine." Galen set it next to the glass tiger, then retrieved a couple syringes from his pack, lining them up in a neat row.

"I told you Vasko's been experimenting with blood magic. He hasn't discovered the perfect combination, yet, but his tests have produced a number of strange results. A few of them caused the complete opposite effect—test subjects who craved even more power."

Questions formed, but they stuck to the roof of my mouth when Galen began rolling up my right sleeve past my elbow. He picked up one of the syringes and filled it with his blood. Then did the same for the second syringe.

"When you inject a magician's blood directly into another magician's bloodstream, it doubles the receiver's power. It also quadruples the consequences."

He tied a rope around my upper arm and rubbed a thumb over the crook of my arm.

Panic burst from my chest with one word. "No!" I thrashed and strained, channeling every bit of strength I had into breaking free. Nothing worked.

Galen didn't have to wait long until exhaustion swept

over me and I stilled. No food equaled no energy. Unable to watch him, I turned my head.

"You may be interested to note that injecting a magician's blood into a regular person does nothing but make them stink of magic. They remain unable to access the power source."

A prick of pain then pure fire raced through my arm. Another prick sent it rushing across my shoulders. I screamed when it engulfed my heart and magical energy consumed me as if I burned alive. Power flowed through my body, sending a healing wave. All my aches and pains disappeared. Strength returned and instinctively I knew I could pick Galen up and smash him into a wall.

The magic swirled around me, loose and messy and growing. I realized I had grabbed too much just like Teegan. Modifying my advice to him, I imagined the power as molten glass. I gathered it and returned it to the cauldron or rather the blanket of power. The effort left me shaking.

"Impressive," Galen said. "You have excellent control. You must have learned something useful at the Keep after all." Galen repacked his supplies. "With my blood, you have my skills as well as your own glass magic. I can move objects, heal and read people's emotions enough so I know if someone is lying or not. And there might be a few hybrid powers with the mix."

When he unlocked the cuffs holding me down, I puzzled over why he would give me such power, but after sorting through his explanation fear bloomed in my chest.

"You mentioned consequences," I said. "What are they?"

He shouldered his pack and helped me to my feet. I wobbled as a dizzy spell threatened.

When I steadied, he grabbed the lantern. "I'll tell you on the way."

I followed him through the mines. We encountered no one. After we navigated a series of turns, he slowed so I could walk next to him. "There are four side effects to your current condition. One. You can't harm me with your magic. Or, more accurately, *our* magic."

Icy fingers stroked the back of my neck as I remembered Galen had injected *his* blood into me. A creepy sensation flowed over me as if a million ants crawled on my skin.

He tapped a finger on his chest. "Every beat of your heart mixes our blood together."

I stopped. "I was hardly a threat to you before."

"Remember when you insisted to Ulrick you wouldn't be ruled by an addiction? That you were smart enough to avoid blood magic?"

"Yes."

"Well." He spread his hands wide. "You weren't smart enough to avoid it. As for the question of addiction, time will tell. You feel fine now, but it won't be long before you're *begging* me to give you more power."

"I—"

"That's two consequences. Do you want to know the other two now or later?"

I leaned against the wall. "Now."

"Brave girl. The third side effect is we're connected. You can block your emotions from me by using magic, but each time you use our magic, our connection grows stronger. Eventually, you'll be unable to resist my orders." He smiled. "I'm looking forward to that one.

Especially since right now you're stronger than most magicians."

Panic squeezed my insides. I panted with the effort to draw in a breath. The tunnel spun and Galen blurred. This was worse than being tortured. I reined in my swirling emotions. Think! Plan!

The obvious answers appeared first. Don't use magic. Kill Galen. Find Yelena.

He laughed. "You can try to kill me, but you lack that killer instinct." He resumed walking.

I fell behind, hoping distance would help dilute the connection.

"You should ask me about the last side effect before you get too far away from me," Galen said over his shoulder.

"Why?" I demanded.

"The test subjects felt too ill when separated more than a few hundred feet from their creators."

That one was hard to believe. In fact, the whole situation sounded ridiculous. I tried to suppress my fear and panic. I'd been in bad situations before. However, I couldn't keep the thought—that if Galen told the truth, then I was truly screwed—from my mind.

"Fear, panic and was that a hint of acceptance at the end?" he asked.

Frustration boiled. "Would you stop that!"

"Make me."

If I had any chance of escape, I had to block him. Unsure how to build a barrier, I envisioned a thick glass wall between my emotions and Galen's.

He smirked. "The first link in the chain, binding you to me."

"Why do this to me? You could have just dragged me along with you."

"True, but your glass magic is valuable to me and my partner. And I'm aware of your history. You won't use your magic because I ask nice or because I threaten you with bodily harm. I guess I could have kidnapped someone you cared for, but that would complicate things. This is a perfect solution. Once the chain is complete, you'll be my…"

Galen pretended to be deep in thought. "What should I call you? My creation? My offspring? No, they suggest a fondness between us. My victim? My dupe? My servant? No, they're not quite right. I think the best descriptor is my slave."

"How many times did you practice that speech?" Sarcasm and fury sharpened my tone.

I spent the rest of the trip imagining all the ways I would kill him. The depth of my creativity surprised and inspired me.

We exited the mines and entered the dark forest surrounding Ognap. A half-moon peeked out between clouds as a warm breeze rustled the leaves. "How long—"

"Two days," he said.

I considered escape as we hiked through the foothills. Soon the lanterns from Ognap flashed between the trees. When we reached the outskirts, I bolted for town.

Galen laughed and yelled that he would wait for me on the south road. I ignored him. Instead I debated if I should report Galen to the Ognap security forces or find Nic and Eve first. Potential power throbbed inside me. With this much magic, I could contact Yelena from here.

No. No magic. I headed toward the inn. The streets

were deserted at this late hour. I hit the wall about four blocks from the Tourmaline Inn. Not an actual wall, but the…force that slammed into me caused me to stumble. It seized my body and yanked. I stepped back before I realized what I was doing. Concentrating on putting one foot in front of the other, I managed to go two more steps. Sweat dripped from my brow and soaked my underclothes. The miner's uniform's rough fabric seemed to tighten around me.

My muscles trembled and I struggled to remain on my feet as bouts of nausea and dizziness rolled through me. Unable to go another inch, I searched the pockets of the coverall for some clue I could leave behind to let my friends know I was still alive. But my switchblade and lock picks were gone. No surprise. Instead, I called Quartz. Sinking to the ground, I rolled into a ball to wait.

When Quartz trotted into view, relief soothed. Her disappearance could be a clue for the others.

*Fire Lady safe,* she said in my mind with pleasure.

Shock at hearing her creamy voice inside my head dominated for a moment. I pulled it together and asked, *Is that my horse name?*

*Yes.*

*Why?*

Quartz was confused I needed to ask. Images of me gathering a molten slug of glass flashed in her mind. *Control fire.*

Her choice of words reminded me of Galen. I had used magic to contact her! Did I just imagine the sound of a click in my mind? Another link in the chain? How long was the chain?

Quartz nudged me with her nose. *Smell different.*

I wrapped my arms around her neck. Unwilling to break our bond, I asked, *Good or bad smell?*

*Fire brighter.*

I sensed that was a positive thing.

*Smell not herd.*

Which meant she smelled Galen's magic and didn't like it. In other words, both. Either way, I needed to stop using magic.

The need to be with Galen overcame me. I couldn't resist any longer. In a fog, I mounted Quartz. Spurring her into a gallop, we chewed up the distance between me and Galen. With each stride the horrible pain subsided until I wilted in relief.

I met up with him on the south road. Galen sat on a brown horse with white socks. Her mane had been braided. The thin braids hung from her head to her shoulders.

"I didn't think you'd reach the inn," he said, then peered past my shoulders, seeking with his magic. "Good. You weren't followed. I'd hate to leave dead bodies in our wake. Come on." He urged his horse into a gallop, heading south.

We followed. The road snaked along the Emerald Mountains foothills and ended at the border of the Daviian Plateau. Small villages and other working mines dotted the area. A tiny town called Delip was located farther south, but nothing else of note. The Warpers had lived in the plateau before they invaded the Citadel. Perhaps a few still hid there.

When the sun rose, we camped on the edge of the Avibian Plains, staying back far enough to avoid triggering the protection. Galen's saddlebags were filled with supplies, and he even managed to obtain a set of my travel clothes. As he cooked stew, I changed behind Quartz, glad to be out of the miner's coverall. I wadded it into a ball and stuffed it behind a bristle bush, leaving what I hoped was another clue.

Starving, I downed the meal without care and collapsed near the fire.

Nightmares plagued my sleep. I dreamed of Teegan and Reema. They cried for help; someone had set fire to their house. I reached and pulled magic, dousing the flames. But their clothes had ignited. The harsh scent of burned flesh spurred me to extinguish the fire on them and to send healing magic for their blisters.

The fire then traveled to Leif and my sister. Once they were safe, it spread to Councilor Moon and Faith. I kept the inferno at bay until I used all my energy. When I reached the point of exhaustion, the flames rushed in and engulfed me.

I jerked awake. My skin tingled and my bones felt as though they had been baked in an oven. Our campfire had gone out despite having plenty of wood. Fatigue weighed on me as if I hadn't slept at all. The effort to get ready depleted the little strength I had left. Unable to resist the warm sunshine, I napped as we rode, trusting Quartz to keep me safe.

We kept close to the border of the plains as we headed south. Galen avoided the small towns in the foothills of the mountains. We traveled at night and slept in the morning.

By the fourth day of our trip, we reached a deserted section of the Cloud Mist's lands. The flat land between the mountains and the Avibian Plains narrowed. In a couple days we would reach the Daviian Plateau.

When we stopped for a water break, I summoned the strength to ask Galen about our destination.

"You have enough information to figure it out on your own," he said.

I had been concentrating on finding a way around our blood connection without success. Reviewing his comments from inside the mine, I pieced them together. He desired control over the black diamonds and super messengers. If the gems had been found in Vasko's mine, then he wouldn't have staged his own death. So my theory of the diamonds coming from the Bloodrose Clan was correct.

"We're going to Lion's Claw Peninsula," I said. "How—"

"Did I find them?" Galen finished for me. "I didn't. Walsh Bloodrose came to me. Or rather to Vasko, but he wasn't home at the time. Lucky for me. Walsh and Vasko had attended the Magician's Keep together, but Walsh was just as happy to work with me."

I thought about the Bloodrose leader. Walsh preferred to live with his family in relative isolation. They harvested oysters for income. Fisk had mentioned a sudden influx of oysters. If Walsh wanted to ensure privacy, what better way than to drive his fellow oyster farmers out of business and buy their farms. That would also keep the farmers from discovering the black diamonds. But Walsh couldn't sell those rare diamonds without drawing attention to himself. So he sought a middleman.

"Does Vasko believe those black diamonds came from his mine?" I asked.

"Yes. Poor guy." Galen tsked. "Lost his most trusted

employee and the location of all those expensive black diamonds in one cave-in. He'll be desperate for more."

"But you'll just sell them to him. Why go to all this trouble?"

"All Walsh cares about is money and his family. He has no desire to wield the political power he would have by controlling the black diamonds and the super messengers. Fortunately he wanted something, and he was happy to let me run the diamond business as long as the money kept flowing in and I brought you to him."

Not for my glass magic. Those black diamonds rendered my little animals obsolete unless he was worried about the competition. But that didn't sound right.

"Okay, I'll ask. Why?"

Galen grinned. "He was fascinated by you and your powers. With Quinn's magic adding to his family's resources, he wanted more magicians. Hard to get magicians to join a cult on the edge of nowhere. And the Council tends to get involved when one of them goes missing."

He didn't wait for me to reason it out. "When I found your blood, I thought to sell it to Walsh so he could inject it into his family members and create more magicians. But then I realized he was willing to give me more than money if I brought you along. And I'll get a bonus because everyone thinks you're dead, you can't run away and you'll be incapable of refusing an order. Walsh is going to be ecstatic."

"How did you know I'd link you to Vasko?"

"I planted enough clues to frame his son. A little goodbye present to him, keeping him busy trying to explain Finn to the authorities. Also, once the Master

Magicians learned about those super messengers, any idiot would know they'd send you to investigate."

I followed the logic. "I'm going to work for Walsh." Which might not be as horrible as I expected.

"He plans to make you a member of his family. You should be honored."

"Am I going to make glass messengers for him?"

Galen dismissed the notion. "Any glassmaker can make us those messengers. You'll be needed for other tasks."

"For example?"

"You'll be required to birth more magicians in order to expand Walsh's happy family."

# 25

Birth more magicians. Didn't expect that little revelation. It was far worse than anything my overactive imagination had produced.

Galen delighted in my shocked silence. "I'm to become a member, as well. I'm looking forward to doing my part for the family. Walsh has developed this whole breeding program. It's quite impressive."

I rallied. "I'm still able to refuse orders."

"Not for long."

We continued the journey south, reaching the Davian Plateau on the sixth day. Any chance I'd have to seek help from a fellow traveler or local died as we turned west and entered the plateau. No one lived there. The Daviian Warpers had tried, but they were long gone.

The flat expanse stretched to the horizon. Brown clumps of grass dotted the cracked and sunbaked soil. A few stunted trees clung to life.

"Do you have enough food and water?" I asked Galen.

"We'll let Quartz lead us to water. As for food, I should be able to snare a few rabbits."

It would take us ten days to cross the plateau. Ten days with the sun's heat beating down on us, and we were only halfway through the heating season. At least we would be on the coast before the blazing hot season.

In order to find water, I had to communicate with Quartz, using a small bit of magic each time.

Halfway across the plateau, I felt restless and craved…action. When we stopped, I paced around the campfire unable to sit.

Food did not help. Water failed to quench the unrelenting need. Pulling my hair just to feel something different only helped for a second.

Galen watched me with a gleam in his eyes. Eventually the plateau faded from my awareness as the hunger dominated all my senses. It hurt. An ache stabbed deep within me as if a person squeezed a pressure point on my heart.

I huddled on the ground, rocking back and forth. No position eased the excruciating desire.

A cool touch on my skin sent a surge of instant relief. I looked over at Galen. He crouched next to me with his hand resting on my shoulder.

"You desire more magic. Let me—"

"No." I knocked his arm away and the all-consuming yearning flooded me. I rolled into a ball. Now that I was aware of what would relieve the pain, I felt worse.

At one point, I pulled magic to me, packing it into my body, hoping it would satisfy my hunger. It didn't. In fact, it was just another link in the chain binding me to Galen.

"Opal, let me help you," he whispered in my ear.

Shaking with an unstoppable desire, I nodded.

"Relax your left arm," he instructed.

I let him pry it from where I had clamped it around my knees. His touch no longer cooled. Through my haze of pain, I realized he straddled me. Then metal pricked my arm. A mere annoyance compared to the crushing need. Liquid fire raced through my veins, extinguishing the agonizing desire, leaving me limp and gasping.

Galen leaned over me. He held a syringe.

"Whose blood?" I asked.

"More of mine." He rubbed his thumb over the spot. I hissed in pain.

He moved away. Spent, I flopped to the ground. Now I truly understood how Devlen felt. How the addiction was to blame. Ulrick, too. He didn't know what he had gotten himself into when he agreed to switch souls with Devlen.

I considered. This "treatment" had been free. What would the next one cost? Would I be able to resist? If I kept using magic, it wouldn't matter. Galen would force me to do whatever he wanted.

Twenty-six days. The trip from Ognap to the Lion's Claw Peninsula lasted a total of twenty-six long, horrible, terrible days. Heading west, we crossed the plateau, cut through the narrow tip of Cowan's lands, bypassing my hometown of Booruby—those days had been my darkest of the trip, envisioning my family and friends gathered for my flag-raising ceremony—and we skimmed above Bloodgood's southern border. Galen avoided all major towns and cities.

We arrived at the Bloodroses' outer wall in the afternoon. Located on the tip of the Lion's Claw Peninsula, the compound was isolated from the rest of the Bloodgood lands. The narrow finger of land jutted out into the Jade Sea. Blue-green water glinted from both sides of the peninsula. The extra beachfront added to their annual pearl harvest.

The eight-foot-high stone wall contained only one gate. The wrought iron was spotted with rust. Galen called to the two guards on the other side. They opened it without hesitation. The gate's hinges creaked in protest.

The complex hadn't changed in the year since I had visited. A few stunted trees and scrub bushes grew in the otherwise barren landscape. The tangy scent of the sea filled the area with a moist mist. Even though clan members moved between the buildings, the only sounds to reach us were the constant roll and crash of the waves and the shriek of gulls as they dived and fought over the discarded oyster shells.

Beyond the massive wall, small cottages built from bamboo were arranged in perfect lines. Past them was a smattering of sun-bleached public buildings. The beaches on each side of the peninsula had a long structure built in the sand. On the northern coast, children dived for oysters, carrying buckets of them into the shade of the sorting area. Adolescents pushed wheelbarrows full of sand and hunks of black rocks on the southern coast. Armed guards watched both. The excuse for their presence had been to protect the clan from pirates and thieves.

It was quite the operation. Pearls, diamonds and breeding magic. My stomach felt as if I had eaten too many raw oysters.

After leaving the horses in the stable, Galen led us to Walsh's office. He ignored Walsh's assistant. Her protest died on her lips when he frowned at her. Smart girl. But she did hover in the threshold, lacing her hands over her bulging belly. I swallowed. She looked about fifteen years old—way too young to be with child.

Walsh's skeletal face lit up when he spotted me. He stood from behind his desk and came around with his arm extended.

"Opal, welcome back. It's so nice to see you," Walsh said, flashing stained teeth as he smiled. He wore all white. It matched his long white hair.

I clasped his hand and suppressed a cringe at the creepy feel of his bony fingers wrapped around mine. "I wish I could say the same."

He kept hold of my hand. Power swept over my skin. I fought the urge to block his invasive scan. For the last fifteen days, I hadn't needed another shot of blood magic. By not using power, I extended the time between bouts of withdrawal. According to Galen, I couldn't avoid it altogether. I sensed things would change. And not for the better.

Walsh patted my hand with his free one. "Your unique powers have fascinated me. I'm looking forward to exploring them with you. I'm sure you'll love it here with time. Even during the hot season, there's a cool breeze from the sea. No one bothers us with their petty political wrangling and backstabbing. It's paradise."

He finally released my hand and addressed Galen as if I wasn't standing right there. "She's healthy and strong. A little old. We should breed her right away. But all in all a nice addition to our family."

Even though I had been warned, I still gaped at him.

"Opal, wait for me in the reception area. I'll be right out," Galen ordered.

"Penny, fetch our new sister something to drink," Walsh said to his assistant.

She gestured for me to precede her, and shut the door behind us.

"What would you like?" she asked me.

"Nothing."

She gave me a miserable look. Her drab tan skirt dragged on the ground, and she kept smoothing the fabric of her dull off-white tunic over her stomach.

"Water is fine," I said.

Relieved, she rushed off. I pressed my ear to the door. They talked about the black diamonds and plans to make super messengers. Since I already knew greed was a motivating factor for Galen and Walsh, I wasn't sure what I had been hoping to overhear. The topic changed to me and I strained.

"How soon until she's yours?" Walsh asked Galen.

"Not long. She has a soft spot for others."

"Then finish it. She's dangerous right now. House her in the brig until we can trust her."

Footsteps sounded and I backed away from the door. Galen was amused. "Any questions?"

"What did you mean by I have 'a soft spot'?" I asked.

"You run to everyone's rescue. I'm sure you wouldn't hesitate to save a drowning child. Come on. I'll give you a tour."

I wondered when he had been here before as I trailed after him. He headed straight for the south coast. The long wooden building remained the same. Along the side open to the beach, workers wielded boxes with bottoms made from wire-mesh screens. They barely glanced at us. Using handheld spades, they filled the box with sand and then held it in the water flowing through a chute. The water washed away the sand, but left the rocks behind. After inspecting each black stone, a worker placed it in another box or tossed it onto a pile.

Galen answered my unspoken question, "Only the diamonds are kept."

There weren't many. "So not all those black rocks are diamonds?"

"Chunks of useless lava," he said.

He poured the diamonds into his hand and left. The next building perched on the edge of a dune and resembled three of the bamboo cottages stuck together.

In the front room, Quinn worked at a table. He concentrated on the black stone in his hand. When he finished, he glared at Galen through the shaggy hair hanging in his face. Unaffected, Galen smiled and handed the young man the diamonds he carried.

"More for you to charge," Galen said.

Quinn remained silent, but he turned his attention on me. With a flash of recognition he leaped to his feet. "You!" He rushed me.

I stepped to the side, dodging his attack. He hit the wall and pushed off, coming at me again. Running out of room to maneuver, I blocked and punched him. The hard muscles of his torso did more damage to my fist than to him. He wrapped his hands around my neck and squeezed.

"You bitch! You left us here!"

No air to respond, I slammed my arms down on the crook of his. Nothing. My vision turned to snow. I could be nasty and dig my thumbs into his eyes or strike his neck with a knife-hand, but I didn't want to hurt him.

"Opal, use your magic," Galen said. His voice sounded faraway.

No. Darkness claimed the edges of my world. Then with a jerk, the pressure on my neck released. Air burned in my throat. The pain didn't stop me from sucking in huge lung-filling gulps.

When I regained my senses, I looked up. Galen held the adolescent in a headlock.

"Another person to add to your fan club, Opal," Galen said in amusement. He released Quinn, but kept a wary eye on him. "You two should try and get along. After all, you'll be working together."

Quinn glowered at me as he tugged his shirt down and swept his black hair from his face.

"Working how?" My voice squeaked. Quinn was seventeen years old at most.

"There's an interesting little twist to those super messengers. If I or any other magician charges the black diamond with magic, the damn thing cracks after the magic is used."

"Like the clear diamonds?"

"Exactly. But if Quinn here charges the blacks, they work fine and he can recharge them again and again."

"Did you enhance his powers with blood, too?"

"No. Quinn's a Bloodrose. He does it for his clan."

By the young man's disgust, I knew Galen's explanation was far from accurate.

"And my job?" I asked.

"Until you're mine, you can encase the black diamonds in glass and teach Quinn how to do it," Galen said.

He opened the door to the back room. The floor was concrete instead of sand and the walls were covered with stones. A kiln and a variety of glassmaking equipment littered the room, which even had a chimney. Barrels of lime and soda ash had been stacked in the corner.

"Everything you need is here. Get started. I'll be back later." Galen paused next to Quinn and whispered something to the young magician before leaving.

I waited for Quinn to attack again. But after shooting me a venom-filled glare, he returned to his table. It was the first time in half a season that Galen wasn't with me. The hard knot in my chest eased just a bit and knowing I'd have access to a kiln gave me a tiny crumb of hope. But I'd need allies. I approached Quinn.

"Go away," Quinn said in a low growl. He kept his gaze on the diamond in his hand. "Or I might do something you'll regret."

"Then I'll just add it to my list."

He ignored me.

"I'm sorry for leaving you here, Quinn."

He continued to stare at the stone, but I sensed a change in the way he held his shoulders. Wearing a loose tan tunic over white pants, Quinn blended in with the bamboo walls and fine white sand under his bare feet.

"It was a mistake. An oversight. An inexcusable laziness on our part. Pick one. I could list reasons…or rather excuses for why we walked away, but it doesn't help you." I drew in a breath, trying to organize my thoughts. "I will fix it. And I'm going to need your help."

He leaned back as if lost in thought. I waited. Finally, he met my gaze. "You're going to need a miracle."

Progress. "They've been known to happen," I said.

"Not here. Although many of our new family members think being invited here is a miracle when they first arrive. We entice them from the streets and homeless shelters with promises of food. We welcome them in, provide them with clothing and shelter. They're happy until they learn the price of admission—working and obeying Walsh. Until they discover they can never leave."

"One woman escaped with her children."

"No she didn't. They found and killed her."

"But they didn't find her children."

His surprise only lasted a second. "Good for them. I hope they stay hidden."

"Would Walsh kill the children?" Even with all his creepiness, he didn't act the type.

"No. Just drag them back here, and force them to work magic for him."

Like Quinn. "What does he hold over you?" I asked.

"My sisters' lives."

I swallowed a dry lump, and felt it land with a thud. "Tell me what's going on."

Anger flared. "You don't know the havoc your little visit caused?"

"Sorry, no."

He surged to his feet, and I moved so the table remained between us. Instead of attacking, he ran a hand through his messy hair as if to collect his thoughts. Dark smudges under his gray eyes gave him an older appearance. His muscular build must be a result of all those years swimming and diving for oysters.

Quinn pulled the chair farther out and pointed. "Sit down. This is quite a tale."

Not wanting to upset him, I perched on the edge of the seat.

"Your glass magic fascinated Walsh," Quinn said. "Since he knew I had an…affinity for glass, he asked me to make those glass messengers. I couldn't. My magic sticks to the glass, but that's it."

"You make the cold glass!" I said.

A flash of pride. "Yeah." But then he switched to sarcasm. "More money for the Bloodrose Clan. Yippee." He kicked the sand. "At least it worked better than the sea glass. That didn't go at all like I had hoped."

The sea glass had been found by Heli and brought back to the Stormdancers' cave. Infused with magic, the glass made everyone go crazy with desire. They had fought over the pieces until I figured it out and diffused the magic.

"Was the sea glass a message for help?" I asked.

"Yes, but I couldn't control my power so it backfired."

Heli had been right. She had said she was close to deciphering the code. Mixed emotions rolled through me. If she understood the plea for help, would she tell Kade? Or rush to the rescue on her own? Knowing Heli, she would come alone and get herself into trouble. At least she was busy with the storm season.

"The issue with the messengers was resolved, but Walsh's fascination with the quirks of magic, his words not mine, continued. He decided to implement his breeding program to see what would happen."

I asked Quinn why the clan obeyed Walsh. "You outnumber the guards and he's the only one with magic."

"A few have tried, but they're caught and punished. The first offense is a beating and confinement, but after that they force you to watch them hurt someone you care about...." He shuddered. "Everyone's terrified."

Valek's lessons in strategy bubbled in my mind. "A few people won't work anyway. *Everyone* needs to be committed. If the entire clan attacks at a prearranged time, it would be hard to counter." I tapped my leg. "You'll need a leader. Someone to convince them and to organize them. You'll need captains who could be in charge of different areas."

Quinn stared at me as if I had gone insane. Perhaps I had, but as much as I wanted to fix this situation, I couldn't do it myself.

"If I'm caught helping you, my sister..." He shook his head.

"Where are they holding her?"

"She's Walsh's assistant. If I make any trouble, she's within easy reach."

"Even at night?"

He spat in disgust. "Especially at night. Who do you think is the baby's father?"

Bile pushed up my throat. "Walsh."

Bitterness rolled from Quinn. "Give the lady a prize."

Walsh already started the program, but he wasn't the only magician. "Did he—"

"He sends a new girl to me every couple of nights."

"Oh." I didn't know what else to say.

"Don't worry. He still gives me some privacy. We rumple the bedding and make appropriate noises to entertain the guards outside my door. But Walsh'll figure out what I'm not doing soon enough."

"When no one becomes pregnant."

"Yep. Then my privacy will be gone."

"Don't wait for that time. Take action. All those girls are probably grateful and their families would support you."

"Won't work. We don't have weapons. Walsh's guards can't be bribed. We can't get messages out. And now they dragged you here," he said. "Just as screwed and helpless as the rest of us. Do you *really* believe you can fix it?"

"No idea. But I'm going to try."

Over the next few days, I bided my time and worked with Quinn. With the kiln up and running hot, I created the super messengers as ordered. Galen seemed distracted and I took advantage. We experimented with the glass. In addition to creating the cold glass, Quinn could produce hot glass as well.

I dwelled on the positives. Quinn was free of blood magic. There had to be a way to capitalize on that. He could also move around the compound without causing suspicion. Each night as I slept in the brig—a large cottage with a couple of locked rooms, bars on the windows, a cement floor and an area for a guard—I planned out Quinn's next lesson.

I taught Quinn how to thumb a bubble and we made an orb. Any glass container would work, but an orb reminded me of Kade and happier times. After I cracked off the orb into the annealing oven to cool, I showed him the amazing versatility of glass.

"If you sand the edge with the flat side of a diamond, it will become sharp enough to cut skin," I said. I also instructed him on fighting tactics, and how to spot weaknesses in an opponent.

Quinn understood my hints. During one session, he rounded on me in anger. "It's easy for you to talk about a rebellion. You have nothing at stake. You have all this magic, yet you obey Galen and Walsh. You can use one of those super messengers and call for help for all of us. But you hand them over. Why should I listen to you?"

*Maria V. Snyder*

"Because, if you think fighting back now is too hard, if I use my magic to send for help, you will have *no* chance at all." I explained about the blood connection. "I'm saving my free magic to take out your two biggest opponents. In fact, if you organize a revolt, don't tell me any of your plans. Don't trust me. If Galen forces me to use my magic and I'm…lost to him, take me out first. I'll be your strongest opponent."

Quinn looked a little green, but he nodded.

Unfortunately, whatever had distracted Galen stopped after four days. Then he launched an aggressive campaign to get me to use my magic. I resisted even when the guards whipped a woman. Quinn needed more time, and I rationalized one person's suffering, although horrible, was better than the whole clan being in danger. After three unsuccessful days, Galen switched to children and I could no longer resist.

The links in my chain built rapidly. Five days later the shakes started. I ignored the initial signs of withdrawal and concentrated on teaching Quinn. But once the tremors in my muscles could no longer be disregarded, I raced to the brig and collapsed on the bed. The hunger grew inside me. I fought it, keeping my thoughts on other things—my family, friends, Kade, Devlen. In time, nothing distracted me from the need. Every single part of me craved magic and I struggled with the desire to pull it toward me. The suffering seemed endless.

I was granted a moment of clarity and relief when Galen visited. He held my orb in one hand. His other rested on my arm.

He brandished the orb. "What were you planning to do with this?"

Strung out, I couldn't produce any emotions over his discovery. "Suck you and Walsh dry," I said.

"In order to siphon my magic, you would have to sacrifice your own again."

I shrugged. "Unoriginal, but it works."

"Temporarily."

"Why?"

"Walsh and I have stockpiled our blood. Drain us now and we'll just reclaim it by injecting our saved blood. Thanks to you, we already know it works."

"Glad to be of service." At this point sarcasm remained my only weapon.

Galen handed me the orb. Potential throbbed under my fingertips. Too easy. A trap. "What if I just drain myself?" I asked.

"Go ahead."

A trick. In order to siphon my own magic, I would have to use magic. The effort would finish the chain and he would stop me. Not enough time for Quinn.

"I didn't think you'd fall for it," Galen said. "You're very resistant. It's a good quality. However, Walsh is very impatient." He removed his hand.

The longing returned full force. I trembled and shook. Sweat stung my eyes as wave after wave of raw need rocked me. At one point I realized I still clutched the orb. A survival instinct kicked in and I closed my eyes, focusing on the potential in my hands. I was desperate enough to try siphoning my powers, hoping I could do it faster than Galen could stop me.

Summoning the strength, I— The orb was yanked away.

"No," Galen said.

I opened my eyes. He loomed over me. Before I could protest, he jabbed a needle into my arm.

Instant relief spread throughout my body, smothering the craving.

Galen's gleeful voice woke me.

"Today's the day." He poked my arm.

I flinched away. "The day for what?" I asked.

"The final link in your chain. This is going to be fun and so easy." Galen strode from my room and flung the main entrance door wide-open. Heli stood on the other side.

26

I leaped to my feet. Heli! Oh no! The sunlight glinted off the blond streaks in her light brown hair. She had pulled it into a ponytail, but a few wisps had escaped and clung to her cheek. Despite being in utter shock over seeing me alive, terror gleamed in her eyes.

She wore a Bloodrose tunic. But the gray fabric had been wrapped around her, trapping her arms in the material.

I hid my dismay at her presence. It was a token effort and Galen knew it, as well.

"We found her trespassing." Galen pulled Heli inside. Two more guards entered, bringing the total to three.

"A friend of yours, right?" He didn't wait for an answer. "What I want to know is how she found you?"

"You deciphered the message on the sea glass, didn't you?" I asked her.

Her gaze jumped to Galen.

"Answer me," I snapped, drawing her attention back. "Yes."

Her voice remained strong. Good. Although I wondered why she hadn't tried to use her magic to escape.

"And you took off without telling anyone, didn't you?" I asked.

Understanding flashed in her eyes. She dipped her head as if ashamed. "Yes."

"What message?" Galen asked.

"On Quinn's sea glass collection. A generic cry for help. Right?" I asked her.

"It said he was being held against his will." She licked her lips. "I came to check it out."

"And you found a ghost," Galen said. "This must be the season for reunions. Even an old friend of *mine* showed up a few days ago. What is it about flag-raising ceremonies? Brings out the long lost. But I believe you're already acquainted with my friend." He leaned outside. "Come say hello."

Devlen entered the brig. A jolt zipped through my spine. His bare arms hung at his sides. Tattoos covered them. My heart melted, dripped into my guts and solidified. I met his gaze and saw what I needed to see.

"Let her go, and I'll cooperate," I said to Galen.

He laughed. "She knows too much. And I know who she is. She created a sandstorm trying to escape." He gestured to her. "Can't do anything now that she's wrapped up in a null shield."

The strange tunic. Only a few people knew null shields could be grafted to clothing. I scowled at Devlen.

"He's been a fountain of information," Galen said. "I also know you care about her. Maybe you care enough to use your magic to save her?"

My fears realized, I braced myself for the ultimatum.

"A simple request. Drain her powers or I'll kill her."

I silently bid my soul goodbye. "I'll need an orb."

Galen looked at Devlen. He disappeared for a moment and returned with my orb. I snatched it from his hands. Heli backed up to the wall. She shook her head no. Tears streaked her face. Her terrified gaze pleaded with me.

"Her tunic," I said in a monotone. The glass in my hands buzzed with potential.

"Devlen," Galen said.

Heli squeaked when he approached her. She looked so young and fragile next to him. He spun her around. The tunic had been tied up her back. Ripping the laces free, he stripped the shirt off her.

"Now," Galen said.

Glad I had kept my mental barrier between Galen and my emotions, I reached. I connected with Heli's mind, discovering I could communicate with her. Must be one of those hybrid powers Galen had mentioned. *Act like you've been stabbed with a knife in your stomach,* I said in her mind. Then I bypassed her to contact Devlen.

He stood behind Heli. Focusing on him, I opened my mind to him. *Don't react. Help Quinn.* Then I drew his magic into the orb, draining his link to Galen, freeing him of the addiction. And at the same time the last link locked around me, binding me to Galen.

Heli yelped and doubled over, moaning in pain. A little too much, but Galen was distracted by the ringing of diamonds filling my orb. Devlen remained impassive despite the burning pain.

*Heli, pretend to pass out. When I shout, create a tornado, blow a big hole in the wall and go,* I ordered. *Do* not *come back.*

She swooned and collapsed on the ground. The last of Devlen's magic chimed into the orb. Galen grabbed the orb, admiring the diamonds sparkling inside. Before he could issue any commands to me, I shouted at Heli to go.

A blast of wind knocked Galen over as sand spiraled into the air. The tiny grains stung my face and arms as I jumped on Galen and wrapped my hands around his neck. An explosion of sound and debris slammed against my back, but I kept squeezing.

He recovered from the surprise and peeled my fingers from his neck. "Stop." He wheezed with the effort to speak.

I obeyed. I had no choice.

"Get off me."

My muscles moved without waiting for my approval. I stood as if another worked the controls on my body.

Galen brushed sand off his shirt and pants. "Did you enjoy your last hurrah?" he asked.

I had to be honest. "Yes."

"Where is she going?"

"Away from here."

The guards had been knocked unconscious, but a couple more poked their heads into the room.

"Find the young Stormdancer. Don't get close. Use the blowpipes," Galen ordered.

They nodded and hurried off. I willed Heli to run faster.

Galen frowned. "You *will* pay for that." He glanced at Devlen's prone form. Heli's mini tornado had knocked him over and pieces of wood from the hole she blasted had pierced his skin. The tattoo ink still stained his skin, but the blood magic was gone.

"Heal him," Galen ordered me, probably thinking it would be a punishment.

When I turned toward Devlen, Galen added, "And then heal yourself. Your back is a mess."

Funny, I didn't feel any pain. I reached around and touched my shoulder blade, setting it on fire. My fingers came away sticky with blood.

I knelt next to Devlen as he struggled to sit up.

"I'm fine," he said, pushing my hands away from his bloody torso.

But it didn't matter; I plucked the splinters from his skin. He winced in pain. Galen hadn't said to be gentle and, if I was too nice, he would be suspicious.

The guards called Galen away. After ordering me to stay, he stepped outside.

Once Devlen's wounds were clear, I checked to make sure Galen was gone before reaching around and coating my fingers with my own blood.

"Opal." Devlen grabbed my clean hand. "I *need* to explain."

"Later." I smeared my blood into his cuts, taking as much from my back as possible.

His eyes widened and he seized both my wrists. "No."

"Trust me. It's to protect you."

He released them without hesitation. "How?"

"To quote Leif, you'll stink of magic, but won't have any power. You're on your own for the rest." When I finished, I traced his wounds with a fingertip. I imagined them as cracked glass and I applied the magic like applying heat to the crack. The skin melted together, leaving behind bright purple scars. Lingering over his body, I didn't hurry. He had worked hard while in prison, building muscle tone.

Devlen twined his fingers in mine, bringing them to

his lips. He kissed the back of my hand. "I knew you weren't dead."

"I *have* to obey Galen's orders. And as soon as he remembers to order me to remove the magical barrier between us, he'll be able to read my emotions as well. Understand?"

"Yes."

"Since you don't have magic, he can read your emotions now. So be careful."

"I will." He glanced over my shoulder and dropped my hand. A scowl creased his forehead.

"What's taking so long?" Galen asked, but he didn't wait for an answer. "Finish up. Devlen, help her."

He tried to be easy as he tugged the splinters free, but a few had been driven in deep. I admired Heli's strength as I gritted my teeth. The hole in the wall where one of the rooms had been could fit a grown man.

"That's all of them," Devlen said.

"I need to see the damage. Is there a mirror anywhere?" I asked.

Galen grumped. "Use Devlen."

Appearing disgruntled, I instructed Devlen to trace the cuts as I had done for him. Then, closing my eyes, I sent him the hot magic to seal the wounds. For a brief moment I tasted his torment over watching me obey Galen and not being able to help me.

*Stifle it,* I sent to Devlen.

When I finished, I marveled at the ease of healing. Even after all the magic I used, I felt energetic.

Galen ordered me to find Heli. When I moved to leave the barracks, he grabbed my arm. "With your magic."

"Oh." Pulling thin strands from the power blanket,

I sent them from me, weaving a web. He didn't specify how fast, so I moved as slow as cooling glass. I searched every nook and cranny, being very thorough. It occurred to me that I might be able to capitalize on the loopholes in his orders. Specifics would be essential.

I found Heli hiding in a cave on the north coast, east of the Bloodroses' beach. Rocky cliffs extended along the peninsula before smoothing out. The water had carved caverns deep into the cliffs. If not for me, it would have been a perfect hiding spot.

"Did you find her?" Galen asked.

I couldn't shut my mouth. "Yes."

"Tell me her exact location."

Feeling horrible, I gave him directions. He ordered me to stay put and took Devlen with him, but he returned an instant later. "Almost forgot. Don't use your magic to warn her."

Not good. Galen was catching on. However, Galen didn't know Heli wasn't alone. When I was certain they were gone, I sought Kade. A strong barrier surrounded him. I tapped on it and he opened his mind to me, welcoming me in with astounded relief.

*Opal! Thank fate you're alive! What's going on? Where are you? What—*

I cut him off. *They're coming to get Heli. They know where she is.* Galen hadn't ordered me not to warn Kade.

*How?*

*I told them.*

Silence.

*They don't know about you yet. Take Heli to safety and stay there.* Both *of you.*

I felt his resistance.

*Heli and I can fight them,* he said.

*You can, but you can't fight* me.

*Tell me what's going on,* he pleaded.

*As long as you're moving.*

*Okay. We're leaving now. We'll head—*

*Don't tell me. Just listen.* As I detailed my predicament, his emotions flowed over me. Shock. Horror. Anger. Determination.

*Send a message to Yelena and Valek. They have the best chance. Okay? You and Heli need to stay away,* I said. *I will be forced to hurt you. Do you understand?*

*Yes, I understand.* An undercurrent of misery rippled with his response. *Since we've been together, this is the third time you've told me to stay away.*

*It's for your protection!*

But Kade had severed the connection.

With nothing else to do, I changed my shirt and cleaned up the mess. The orb had dropped to the ground during Heli's escape, but it wasn't broken. Diamonds had spilled. I picked them up and piled them all on a piece of the wall.

Sitting cross-legged, I cradled the orb in my lap. The glass sizzled with potential. It sang to me, vibrating deep in my soul. I concentrated on my heartbeat, mixing my blood with Galen's. I couldn't separate Galen's magic from mine, but I could siphon it all.

Too bad Galen had stockpiled his blood. He would reclaim his powers and where would I be? Stuck here, but at least I wouldn't be able to hurt anyone. Unless he used blood magic on me, tattooing the power into my skin like he had done for Devlen. Then I would crave more power and be at Galen's mercy again. And my glass magic would be gone forever.

Right now, my powers were the strongest in the compound. I had the chance to use them to help as long as I found loopholes in Galen's orders. It worked to warn Kade.

Of course it could all go wrong, and he would use me to take over Sitia. No. I wouldn't let him. I had too many precious gems to care for. Reema and Teegan, protecting them and warning them against the dangers of magic. I hardly knew them, but I missed them more than I ever did my glass magic.

I realized dashing off to help others wasn't a distraction from my purpose. It was my purpose. Between Valek's training, my fortune in diamonds and with assistance from my friends, I could do it. I could be Opal without the descriptor. I could be an adoptive mother one day and go undercover to help Fisk with that rival gang the next. And I planned to follow up with Fisk; he shouldn't have to deal with such problems on his own.

But Galen first. I didn't know how I would stop him. I just would.

"What are you doing?" Galen demanded.

"Thinking."

"About what?"

"Siphoning your magic."

He cocked his head to the side as if curious. "You know that won't work."

"Wishful thinking. Is that better?"

Galen strode over and grabbed the orb. "In order to avoid a future hassle, do not siphon my magic and do not attack me." Finding the pile of diamonds, he poured them back into the glass. "Come with me."

We walked to Walsh's office building. His assistant quickly announced us. Her resemblance to Quinn was obvious now. The desire to tell her to run away bubbled up my throat, but I bit my lip. Now was not the time nor the place.

Walsh's pleasure at my enslavement soured on hearing about Heli's escape. He rounded on Galen. "Opal was dating the Stormdancer leader. They could attack us with storms."

A hollow thud echoed in my chest over Walsh's use of the past tense.

"They won't risk Opal's life or the children who live here," Galen said.

"I'm not worried about them, you idiot. My oyster beds could be destroyed." Walsh's icy voice cut through the sudden tension.

Their relationship could be falling apart. I wondered how I could drive the wedge in further.

"Who cares about your oysters? One black diamond equals two dozen pearls."

"And if the storms disrupt the currents that bring those precious stones to our shore? What then?"

Galen brandished the orb and poured the clear diamonds onto Walsh's desk. "We'll recapture Heli. She isn't far. Besides, if they try to attack us, they'll have to be close to us. Opal is strong enough to drain their powers from a distance."

His smug smile didn't go over well with Walsh. "She didn't siphon that young Stormdancer."

Galen's humor died. He rounded on me. "Whose magic did you siphon?"

Damn. "Devlen's."

He laughed. "That's an easy fix. Don't worry, Walsh. It was her *last* act of defiance."

I rubbed the back of my hand, reminding myself of his kiss. "How do you know Devlen?" I asked.

"We met when I funded the Daviian Clan's attempt to take control of the Council. Revolts are costly and Vasko thought their cause worthy. I befriended a few Warpers. After that disaster, I kept in contact with a couple who escaped. I've hired him for a number of jobs over the years. But when I learned he was another one of *your* victims and he was in jail, I had to pay him a visit. Did you fall for his model prisoner act?"

"Yes."

Galen tapped his chest. "My idea. When you saw him today, did it hurt? Did it feel like a slap in the face?"

"Yes." At first glance, but I couldn't mistake the pain in his eyes. But why hadn't he mentioned Galen to me before?

He gloated. "Good."

Walsh interrupted us. "What if the Stormdancer informs the Master Magicians? I didn't want to attract attention."

Galen downplayed his concerns. "She won't. You keep forgetting, Walsh. Opal's under my control. I could order her to go to the Citadel and drain both Masters dry right now."

Walsh's concern hadn't softened with Galen's reassurances. "Opal, come here." He pushed back from his desk, but remained sitting.

"Go," Galen said.

No choice. Walsh grabbed my wrist and tugged me closer. "Since you are part of my family now, we will have a celebration on the night of the full moon, five days hence. We do it for all our new members and for the children when they reach maturity. It's a special night. We have a big bonfire and clambake, we tell stories and sing songs. Every clan member attends and everyone has a wonderful time."

It was an odd speech and I braced for the bad news. He didn't disappoint me.

"There is a little ceremony where you are inducted into the clan. First your old clan name is written on a piece of wood and we'll burn it in the fire. It's all very dramatic." He smiled. "Then you marry me."

"What?" I jerked back, but his grip was strong.

"Keep still and listen," he ordered. "All the men of the clan pledge an oath of loyalty to me, and all the women vow to be my wife and we consummate the marriage following the ceremony."

Horror welled. "You've slept with all the women?"

"At least once," he said with pride. "Although, I must admit, some I favor more than others."

"But…before…when I visited there were families."

"Of course. The woman can marry another as long as I approve. And it's a source of pride for her husband when I choose his wife for a night of pleasure. He is pledged to me."

Finally, the reality of my situation sank in and I cast about for a way out. "I'm experienced. And you don't need my vow; I already have to obey."

"Relax. Many of our members have come to us experienced. For those, there is a cleansing ritual before they are inducted to the clan."

Galen's sadistic smirk didn't bode well for the ritual.

"Besides, you are in luck, my dear," Walsh said. "You will stay with me every night until you are with child."

*Lucky* would be the last descriptor I would apply.

\* \* \*

After our meeting with Walsh, Galen proceeded to issue orders. "Never tell Walsh anything I say or do. Comply with all requests for the ritual, the ceremony and with the commands Walsh makes to you in his bedroom. For any other tasks he assigns you, you must clear them with me first."

Fury simmered, but I concentrated on the wording of Galen's orders, searching for loopholes.

When I woke on the morning of my wedding, a thick fog had settled over the compound. It gave me an idea and I searched the area for a good hiding spot. If Galen couldn't find me, he couldn't order me, cleanse me or marry me. A desperate plan, but I had no other options left. I had considered every angle, but couldn't find a loophole.

I had tried running away two days ago. But since I had completed the binding with Galen, the tolerable distance between us had shortened considerably. When I reached the outer limit, the physical weakness and pain had been so intense, I couldn't move. The guards had no trouble dragging me back.

Between the north and south beaches, the tip of the peninsula extended out like a finger. The surf had dug nooks and crannies into that outcropping. I found one above the waterline big enough to fit into and not be seen. It was a little damp as a few of the stronger waves sent sea spray into my spot.

I squirmed into a comfortable position. With the low ceiling, I lay down. Crossing my arms under my head as a pillow, I reviewed everything since Galen injected me with his blood. One bright spot, I hadn't had withdrawal

*Maria V. Snyder*

symptoms since the binding. But each time I was with Galen, he added to his list of things I was forbidden to do. The most frustrating part was I felt strongest when Galen stood next to me and I couldn't do a damn thing!

Except make super messengers. Before I didn't use them to avoid being bound to him, and now I wasn't allowed to use them to call for help.

Focusing on what I could do, I created a mental list of possible ways to cause trouble.

No one came near my hiding spot until the afternoon sun burned away the fog. A few shadows crossed the small opening, but so far no one spotted it. I could use my magic to ensure my spot remained hidden, but then the power would tip off Walsh and Galen.

Finally one shadow paused. I knew it was inevitable, but I had hoped for a couple more hours. I debated if I would go quietly or kick and scream the whole trip back.

When Devlen entered, relief and fear swirled together in a confusing mixture. I had been avoiding him since Heli's escape, but now I wanted to throw myself into his arms. Must be my blood inside him calling to me. Yeah, right, and I wanted to be Galen's slave. When would I stop lying to myself? About the same time a miracle happened and I was free.

He crouched in the small space, looking downright miserable. "I didn't want to be the one to find you," he said. "But you *need* to be caught. It's important for you to be at the bonfire party tonight."

"So I can marry Walsh?"

He shook his head, but wouldn't explain. Smart.

"Is this the blood magic talking?" More tattoos stained his skin.

"No. The addiction is there, but it won't force me to do horrible things this time."

"Why not?"

"I will not hurt you or anyone else."

"Then come here." I rolled to my side and he lay next to me, curling his body around my back.

Devlen stretched his arm out so I could rest my head on it. He draped his other arm around my waist, pulling me closer. I hadn't realized how chilled I was until his warmth soaked into me.

"Now you can fill in the blanks," I said.

"At least, I don't have to convince you that I'm on your side. I was worried you wouldn't let me explain."

"It was a surprise, but there was something in your eyes…. You hadn't come to hurt me."

"You trust me." He said it as if he couldn't believe it.

"Yes."

He stayed quiet.

I nudged him with my elbow. "You still need to tell me how and why you're here."

"Galen visited me in Dawnwood soon after you did. He wanted me to get close to you, find out why you were in Fulgor. I played along so I could learn what he was up to. He also mentioned working out a sweet deal on the Bloodgood coast with some cult and that if I ever escaped he could use my help. I had no idea he was that hotshot CO Finn or that he was experimenting with blood magic. He never came back. But when Nic visited with the news…" His arm tightened around my waist as his voice cracked. "Nic mentioned that Vasko's right-hand man had also died. No way Galen gets caught in a cave-in. And I didn't believe you were… dead. I escaped and found the cult."

"What about the tattoos?"

"Test of loyalty. Plus it gives Galen the illusion of control over me since he provides the blood. That, and he's technically in enemy territory. This is Walsh's domain, and if anything happened between them, Galen would need supporters."

"Galen has me. I'm powerful." I rested my arm on his, lacing my fingers with his. "I now understand the desire for more magic. If he didn't hold my leash, I would—"

"No, you would not."

"I gave in twice to the addiction."

He laughed. "Look at my arms, Opal. Four tattoos on each. I gave in eight times and he started me with a tiny amount of magic. You were given all your own power back, plus Galen's. He was so frustrated with how you held off the withdrawal, and how you wouldn't use the magic. And he's surprised you have not gone into withdrawal since the binding."

"Not for lack of trying. I went from avoiding magic to using it all the time."

"At his command. Have you tried anything on your own?"

I considered. "When I communicated with you and Heli, but that is what put me over the edge."

He squeezed my hand. "You shouldn't have risked your freedom for me."

"What freedom? I was stuck here regardless. Plus I've felt the unbearable need for blood magic. I couldn't see you suffer, and, I'll admit it, I really didn't want you to become a Warper again."

"There's no chance I would become a Warper."

"But—"

"*No* chance. Before the addiction fueled my desire, I wanted to be powerful and to reach the highest level of the Kirakawa ritual. This time, I'm able to separate the addiction from my desire. While I give in to the physical need for the magic, my love for you has not allowed it to change who I am. Does that make sense?"

I turned to him. "A little." But did I love him? With our history, could I? A year and a half ago, he had kidnapped and tortured me, all for blood magic. I understood the addiction, but would I go to those lengths to obtain relief? No. Because, like Devlen now, I had separated the addiction from my own desires. My worry about being addicted before all this was laughable.

My sister's question from long ago echoed in my mind. *What do you regret?*

Devlen was a different man than the one who hurt me. I'd known it in my head, but my heart had been slower to accept it. And after we left this cave, I wouldn't have another chance to show him how I feel.

"One question," I said.

"Anything."

"What do the battle symbols on my switchblade mean?"

"Didn't Janco tell you?" he asked.

"No. He turned red, sputtered some excuse and bolted."

"Sounds like Janco."

"Tell me."

"The symbols are a vow. They say, I offer my heart, entrust my soul and give my life to you."

I reached up and cupped his face. His hair hung loose and it fell forward when I drew him closer to me. A hopeful joy shone in his eyes as our lips met. Long-suppressed desire for him burst through all my doubts, worries and fears. I deepened the kiss.

He held me and I wrapped my arms around his neck. But I needed to feel his skin against mine. I pulled at his shirt. He broke off the kiss, stopping me.

"Opal, I endeavor to earn your forgiveness. This is more than I ever hoped for. I do not deserve—"

I placed my fingers on his lips. "Shhh. We don't have much time and I don't want to waste it talking. Now, where were we?" Yanking off his shirt, I ran my hands over his torso and around his back.

His mouth sought mine and soon I had my wish. Skin against skin.

# 27

Wrapped in Devlen's arms, our connection ran deeper than any magical bond. The past hour an amazing reprieve from my fear and dread over this evening's activities.

We untangled to dress, which, in the small cavern, was harder than getting undressed. After one last kiss, Devlen's smile faded into a sad determination.

"We'll get through this," he said, squeezing my hand.

"I'll drain your magic and then you run away. I don't want to be forced to hurt you."

"I'm not leaving." He poked his head outside, checking for guards. "All clear. Come on."

We climbed out on the rocks and headed toward the buildings. When one of the searchers spotted us, Devlen grabbed my arm as if he dragged me along.

"Remember you hate me," he whispered as a bunch of Walsh's guards rushed over.

I struggled to break his hold, glaring at him. The men escorted us to Galen. He had been given an office in Walsh's building. His fury over my game of hide-and-seek rolled off him.

"Where was she?" he asked Devlen.

"Hiding in the rocks out on the point." Devlen released his hold. "Her clothes blended in with them, but she can't hide from me." He sneered. "I know all her tricks."

I shot him a nasty look and cocked a foot to kick him.

"Stop," Galen said. His anger eased toward amusement. "Opal, you will not hide from us again. That's an order." Then to the guards, "Take her to the hut for the cleansing ritual."

They pulled me away, but as we reached the door, Galen called for us to wait. When he approached, I knew by the sick little smile twisting his lips that this wouldn't be good.

"I almost forgot," he said. "Opal, remove the barrier shielding your emotions from me now. I wish to know exactly what you're feeling during the biggest night of your life."

The glass wall disintegrated in an instant. I blasted pure hatred at him, but he chuckled. "Love you, too."

The bamboo hut resembled one of the cottages, except it was bigger and only contained one room. Four women waited for me. They wore identical sleeveless white dresses that hung to the sand. Their hair had been tucked up into white scarves. No shoes on their feet and no softness in their faces. Their eyes held no spark.

The guards left me standing in the threshold, secure in the knowledge that Galen had ordered me to comply with these women. They resembled each other enough for me to guess that three of them were sisters and the older woman was their mother.

I scanned the room. Certain items, like the two

posts with leather straps in the middle of the room, sent queasy warning signals through my body. A large tub of water filled one corner and buckets, sponges and cleaning supplies leaned against the side wall. Despite the heat, a fire burned in the small hearth.

The mother took charge. She closed the door and ordered me to strip. As I peeled off my clothes, the girls tossed them into the fire. I watched the flames consume the fabric.

"Eat this," Mother said.

She handed me a wad of slimy green seaweed.

"All of it. Now."

I almost gagged at the taste of rotten vegetables and briny goo mixed with the gritty crunch of sand. It made me appreciate Leif's healing concoctions. They were mild in comparison. As soon as I swallowed, my body flushed with heat. Sweat beaded on every inch of my skin. The hut tilted as my head spun. The girls led me to a bed covered with towels.

They ignored my requests for water. I understood the need for towels as sweat gushed from my body. When it finally stopped, Mother gave me a brown leaf to chew. It tasted like paper and flakes stuck to my tongue. It was also difficult to swallow with a dry mouth.

The girls hovered around me holding buckets. After a few minutes, I found out why. My stomach reacted violently to the leaf, expelling its contents in painful bouts over one of the buckets. I only had a few seconds of peace before cramps hit my guts and I quickly sat on another bucket.

No dignity during the cleansing ritual, which seemed to have no end. I would have loved to spit out the purple flower Mother shoved in my mouth, but Galen's command forced me to chew and swallow. Burning pain stabbed deep inside me. I bent over as spasms seized my lower abdomen.

When blood poured from between my legs, I panicked.

Mother held me down and shushed me. "No lasting harm," she said. "It's to cleanse out a baby that might be growing. Master Walsh only wants his baby to grow inside you."

Eventually the pain subsided and the girls helped clean me.

"Answer me honestly," Mother said. "Have you taken moon potion in the last year?"

"Yes. Why didn't you ask me before you gave me that flower?"

"Moon potion is not a hundred percent effective. How many years have you taken it?"

"Two."

While she measured out a silver powder, I cursed Galen a thousand times. Moon potion prevented a woman from getting pregnant. One dose lasted a year. However, if you wanted to have a child before the year was up, a dose of starlight would neutralize the protection.

Mother mixed starlight with water and handed it to me. "Drink it. That is fresh water pumped from under our home."

Then she fed me fruits and vegetables grown in the Bloodroses' compound. I made the connection between purging all that I may have imbibed before coming here and replenishing it with substances from the clan.

My hope of being finished after the meal died when the girls strapped my wrists and ankles to the two posts in the middle of the room. My vulnerable position reminded me of my time at the prison.

Rustling sounded behind me; I craned my neck around. Mother held long strands of dried seaweed. She cocked her arm.

"Wait," I said. "What's left to cleanse?"

"Blood."

"But—"

She whipped me with the seaweed, leaving behind lines of stinging pain across my back and the back of my legs. When she moved to do my front side, I yelped more from surprise. My skin was extra sensitive on my chest. The seaweed sliced thin cuts and blood welled from the rows. After all I had been through, the wounds felt minor.

It was over as quick as it had started. The girls released me, but my relief didn't stay for long. The girls' grim frowns warned me a second before they seized my arms and legs. Lifting me off the floor, they carried me over to the tub. Time to wash the blood off. But why did they brace themselves for trouble?

They dunked me in the tub and held me underwater. Every single cut blazed. Salt water! I struggled to sit up as the searing pain dug into me and set my whole body on fire. Keeping firm pressure on my shoulders and hips, the girls wouldn't let go.

The ache in my lungs soon eclipsed my burning skin. This couldn't be a part of the ritual. I gathered magic to me, but released it back into the power blanket when my brain caught up. Acceptance was a part of this custom. Relaxing as much as possible for a drowning victim, I stopped fighting. Five heartbeats later, they let go.

I broke the surface sputtering and gasping for air.

The three girls wouldn't meet my furious glare, but Mother had no qualms.

Her unflappable manner remained the same. "You are clean," she said. "Here." She handed me a white shift just like the one she wore. "Get dressed."

"Undergarments?"

"Not for you."

Better than nothing. I pulled it on. The dress dragged on the sand.

Mother stepped to me. "My single piece of advice. Obey Master Walsh. He has a bad temper. Remember the pain you felt in the tub?"

"Yes."

"Imagine being whipped with leather and then submerged in salt water on a daily basis for a season. Master Walsh calls that pepper and salt, and that is just one of the punishments he hands out to those who upset him," Mother said. "Your presence has caused us trouble. See my beautiful daughters?" She stabbed a thick finger at them.

"Yes."

"I don't want them to suffer because of you."

As one of the girls pulled my hair up and wrapped it into a white scarf, Mother applied a colored paste to my eyelids.

Mother said, "We won't be attending the ceremony. We'll be in our cottage so we stay out of trouble. I don't want my girls involved."

A couple clues snapped together, and I guessed the reason Devlen had said I needed to be at the bonfire.

"Yet you'll allow your girls to marry Walsh when it's their turn. You'll allow them to be his slaves. You'll allow them to risk their lives diving for oysters or mining diamonds."

"You know nothing about it. You're not even a mother."

I imagined raising Reema and Teegan in this place and a whole new fury burned inside me. "*You* are doing more to harm your daughters than I *ever* will. That is how Walsh is able to control all of you with so few armed guards. You're terrified!"

"He's a powerful magician. And now this Galen is giving orders, and you." She jabbed my arm. "Galen's slave. Quinn is young and inexperienced and foolish. How can he counter three magicians?"

"He can't. That's why he needs you." I surprised her. Score one for the new girl.

"I can't—"

"Yes, you can. Who is serving the clams tonight?"

Confused, she cast about for the answer. "One of the cooks…Miranda or Lilian."

"Friends of yours?"

"Sort of. We don't form close attachments."

"Which just helps Walsh all the more." I shook my head. "Here's how you can help. Give some of that brown leaf stuff to Miranda and ask her to mix it in Walsh's, Galen's and my food. We can't do any magic while we're throwing up."

"But only temporarily." She snagged her lower lip with her teeth.

"Are you good with plants? Is there another leaf or root that would incapacitate us for a longer period?"

Fear and uncertainty flared in her eyes. "There's beach root. It causes a horrible stomachache for a few hours."

"Do you have any sleeping potions?" I asked.

"No."

"Then use the beach root if you can. See? It takes *everyone* helping, otherwise we won't be successful."

"We? What can you do?" she asked.

"My usual. Cause trouble. But first, I need a few things."

She chewed on her lip. "Things?"

I smiled. "Undergarments and pants for starters."

"Hurry," one of the girls called. "He's coming!"

Adding a scarf around my shoulders, I turned in a circle with my arms out. "Well?" I still wore the shift.

Mother inspected me with a critical eye. "It'll do for now. Don't let him rub against you."

I shuddered at the image. "That is always my intention."

When the door swept open and Walsh entered, we all held our breaths.

"Is my bride ready?" he asked Mother.

She nodded and I remembered to breathe.

He held out his hand, and I grabbed it before he could notice how nervous the women were. We walked through the compound hand in hand. The sun dipped into the horizon as fingers of thick fog stroked the shore.

"It was nice of you to escort me," I said. A few of his men followed us at a distance. Both Walsh and Galen had an armed escort at all times.

"It's to ensure no one...harms you before the ceremony. Some of my wives get jealous."

I'd bet, but he had given me a perfect opening. "I would think you'd be more worried about Galen."

"Why?"

Gotcha. Now I had to tread through the loopholes with care. "Galen has Devlen now."

He frowned. "So? Devlen knows quite a bit about blood magic."

I cringed. "Did they tell you how addictive it is?"

"Of course. I've seen it for myself."

"Last time Devlen's addiction consumed him, he wasn't content to wait for others. He's clever and intelligent. Unparalleled with a sword..." I let the information sink in.

Walsh stopped. "Is Galen planning to double-cross me?"

"I can't say."

"Even if I order you to?"

"Not even then."

He dismissed my concerns. "I have my guards, my clan members and my own considerable magic. There are only two of them."

"Three of us."

Alarm filled his thin face. In the twilight he resembled a ghost. "Why are you warning me?"

"I hate Galen and Devlen. If you kill them, I would consider it a perfect wedding present."

He laughed with a harsh bark. "Nice try. I almost fell for it."

Shoot. Time for a different angle. I silently thanked Mother and shrugged. "As long as you don't mind sharing me."

"What do you mean?" he demanded, yanking me close. "You've been ordered to *my* bed every night."

"And to Galen's every day." I rubbed my belly. "I wonder who will give me a baby first?"

"You're lying. Galen loathes you. He would never

take you to his bed." Walsh considered. "You shouldn't
be able to lie to me. He assured me of your coopera-
tion." His hard eyes bored into me. "Kneel."

Since I wasn't in his bedroom and this had nothing
to do with the ceremony, I remained on my feet.

He grabbed my shoulders and shook me. "Did he
order you to obey me?"

Magic blocked me from answering, but he already
figured it out.

"Son of a bitch!"

Walsh didn't waste time. "Take her to the bonfire, I'll
be there shortly," he ordered one of his guards.

As the guard marched me to the beach, I hoped I
hadn't ruined anything Quinn might be planning by
tipping Walsh off to Galen's deceit. If Galen had been
tired of playing in Vasko's sandbox, he'd never put himself in the same position again.

On the beach, bright flames as tall as a man pulsed
and flickered. A pit had been dug in the sand and the
pile of driftwood snapped and popped. The firelight illuminated the fog, creating a fuzzy softness around the
bonfire. Clan members had brought blankets to sit on.
A few kids played in the gentle waves and others made
sand castles. If I didn't know any better, I'd think this
was a large family picnic.

A dais had been set up with three ornate chairs. Purple silk screens boxed in the dais on three sides, leaving the one facing the sea open. My guard led me to the
chair on the left.

"Sit," he said, before taking up position nearby.

From this position, I spotted a couple tables filled
with food and more armed guards patrolling the pe-

rimeter. Not all the clan members had come, and I remembered what Mother had said about staying in their cottage. A breeze blew onshore, pushing the fog in thickening swells. One minute I couldn't see past the fire, and the next it was clearer.

Galen bounded onto the dais with Devlen a step behind.

"Where's the groom?" Galen asked me.

"I don't know."

"What happened?" he asked.

I jerked a thumb at the guard. "Told him to escort me and said he'd be here soon."

Galen glanced at Devlen, who gave him a slight shrug. Settling into the chair on the right, Galen inquired about my afternoon. "Did you have fun with the women?"

"No."

He chuckled. "Come here."

Devlen moved to stand behind Galen.

Although I wished to remain in my seat, my body complied. Galen yanked at the scarf, uncovering my arms. Lines of red welts striped my skin.

I glanced at Devlen. Anger flashed in his eyes.

Galen admired the damage. "Is it still tender?" He rubbed his hands along my arms, inflaming the cuts.

I jerked back and grabbed the scarf.

"Keep it off," Galen said, pulling it away from me.

Walsh arrived with six guards. It seemed the guards outnumbered the clan. A couple followed Walsh. He introduced them to us as Minister Heath and his wife, Nancee.

I wasn't the only one confused by the Minister's presence.

Galen asked about them. "Don't you usually use a Bloodrose member?"

"Yes I do. But I wanted this one to be official and legally entered into the record books."

Bile rose in my throat.

"When did you decide on that?" Galen demanded, his ire evident.

I wondered if Walsh had already suspected Galen, and the couple was his insurance nothing would happen tonight.

"As soon as I set eyes on my bride." Walsh took my left hand and brought it to his lips. "I sent the Minister a letter right away." He turned back to his guests. "I'd also like to get married first then have our meal."

Galen smoothed the annoyance and suspicion that had creased his face. "Of course. It's your night." He shouted for everyone's attention, and when silence descended, Galen gestured to the Minister.

He moved into position, standing to face both the clan members and us with his wife by his side. The dusting of gray along his temples and the fine lines around his eyes gave him a distinguished air. Nancee opened a book and held it for him to read. Minister Heath loomed over his wife. The way they moved in unison and the image of the two of them side by side felt...right. This couple belonged together. Unlike Walsh and I.

Walsh pulled me close as the Minister began the ceremony. Heath's young voice didn't match his older face. With the fog and firelight and the magic forcing me to kneel with Walsh in front of the Minister, the whole situation felt surreal. My mother would be livid when she found out I was married without her.

I glanced at the gathered crowd. Wouldn't this be

the ideal time to revolt? No one moved. The Minister reached the part where he solicits objections to the union.

Dead silence. No revolt. No outcry. Even Devlen didn't speak. Just when I lost hope, one voice said, "I object."

Unfortunately, the voice was Galen's.

"What do you think you're doing?" Walsh demanded.

"Taking over your little family." He whipped out a knife and before anyone could even blink, he stabbed it into Walsh's throat.

Blood gushed and I reached to help him, but Galen ordered me to stop. None of the guards moved a muscle.

"Any objections?" Galen asked everyone.

Walsh's family stood there in silence, watching their leader die. A few nodded as if they witnessed justice. The Minister and his wife gaped with horror.

"I—"

"Be quiet," Galen said to me.

No one else objected.

Galen motioned to Devlen to drag Walsh's body to the side. Devlen kept a neutral demeanor as he carried out the orders.

Galen knelt next to me. "Please continue with the service," he said to the Minister.

Nancee clutched her husband's arm in a death grip.

He opened his mouth and closed it, searching the crowd for anyone who was upset by the murder.

"Please continue," Galen said again.

I marveled at how fast Heath recovered. Although he rattled off the vows in a rush. Galen allowed me to speak again and my mouth betrayed me, saying all the right things at the right time. In a matter of minutes I was married to Galen. No revolt. No rescue. Nothing but the creepy fog.

The rest of the evening passed in a blur. I hoped to get a moment alone with Devlen, but Galen kept me close to him. At the end of the night, Walsh's body was thrown onto the fire without ceremony. A couple of the clan members added wood to the bonfire, stabbing the branches into the flames as if they could pierce his heart.

At the end of the evening, Galen escorted the Minister and his wife to the guest cottage. I stayed behind them, but through our connection I felt him draw magic, seeking the couple's emotions. Fear, horror and the desire to keep something from Galen reached us. I sensed Galen planning to interrogate them with his drugs, but for now he tugged at their emotions. Drawing magic from me, Galen erased the horror and fear over Walsh's murder from their minds and replaced them with fondness and joy for the happy couple, masking the bad memories.

They said good-night with wide smiles. When their door closed, Galen looked pleased with himself.

"What was that all about?" I asked.

"I knew I could control a person's emotions, but I never had enough power to do it. With your added magic, I have more than enough strength."

My head spun with how much havoc he could cause with his new ability. I bumped against him.

"I feel dizzy," I told him when he shot me a nasty glare.

"That's what you get for not eating."

We swung by the kitchen. The woman cleaning the counters stopped and prepared a snack of bread and cheese for us. I avoided the cheese, but ate a big portion of the bread, taking my time, delaying the inevitable. Galen ate absently.

"How long were you planning to assassinate Walsh?" I asked.

"Not long after I met him. His little kingdom was just too tempting. Black diamonds, pearls and an in-house workforce that's not going to cry foul about anything. Not a squawk from them when I murdered their leader in front of their eyes."

True. No love lost over Walsh's demise. Not even his guards. "Did you bribe his bodyguards?"

"Oh yeah. Devlen's been working on them since he arrived. That man has a golden tongue."

I bit my lip, dredging up memories of long ago when Devlen had twisted my words. When I had wanted to sink my switchblade into his heart.

Galen laughed. "Do you hate him more than me?" he asked.

"No."

"Good." Then Galen added, "You already know I hold all the power. And tonight the Bloodrose Clan has realized the power had shifted to me. Three against one. Quinn's magic is minor, and Walsh wouldn't let me increase the boy's strength with blood." Galen ripped off a piece of bread. "Worked out in my favor, and now I can turn him into another slave."

That was *not* going to happen. Not while I lived and breathed.

Galen watched me with amusement. "You haven't asked the big question."

"Maybe I don't want to hear the answer," I said.

"Doesn't matter what you want. Not anymore. Ask me why I married you."

No choice. I repeated the question.

"You were mine in all ways but one. And the thought of you sleeping with Walsh galled me. I don't like to share. Now you're legally joined to me." Galen stood. "Come."

I followed him to a cottage near the office building. The fog obscured most of the compound. We encountered no one, and the moist air dampened any sounds.

Dread slowed my steps and I lingered outside, peering into the dark fog. At this time, I would welcome a distraction. Perhaps a backup plan would be put into action. Something must have gone wrong during the bonfire. Surely, Devlen didn't plan for me to marry Galen.

"Opal, come here now," Galen called.

Despite my mind's frantic screams, my body complied. He had lit a lantern and waited for me in his bedroom in the back. Galen lounged on the bed, but he sat up as soon as I entered.

"I can taste your fear. It's an unexpected addition to the excitement. Don't you agree?"

"No."

"Doesn't matter anyway. Take off your dress," he said.

I peeled it off.

"I thought you were supposed to be naked underneath."

"I wasn't comfortable," I said. I wore a sleeveless shirt and white short pants. A knife, compliments of Mother, was tucked into my waistband.

"What were you planning to do with that weapon?"

"I was hoping an opportunity to use it on Walsh would present itself on our wedding night."

Galen laughed. "You're full of surprises." But then he stopped abruptly. He clutched his guts as his face paled. "Did you poison me?"

"No. How many clams did you eat?"

He blanched, turning green. "Don't talk about food." Galen groaned and curled into a ball. Sweat dampened his clothes.

I suspected his food had been spiked with beach root. If the clan members planned to revolt while he was incapacitated, I shouldn't be close enough to hear Galen's commands. I moved to leave, but Galen ordered me to stay in the cottage. At least he was too sick to do anything besides shiver and moan all night.

The gray fog still clung to the compound in the morning. Galen felt better, but he dropped into an exhausted sleep. I had spent the night on the couch in the living area.

When a soft knock sounded, I rushed to open the door before another knock could wake Galen. Even when sound asleep, Galen could rouse in an instant. In that regard, he reminded me of Valek.

His guards had taken up position next to the door, but Devlen waited.

"Where's Galen?" he asked.

The bodyguards seemed interested in the answer, so I crossed my arms and frowned at Devlen. "Sleeping."

"He asked me to report to him this morning."

"You'll have to come back later. He had a strenuous night."

The guards chuckled, but Devlen pushed his way inside. "I'll check for myself."

He peeked into the bedroom then pulled the divider between the rooms closed. He returned to the guards. "He's fine. I'll wait here until he wakes."

This time the guards leered as Devlen shut the door. He leaned against it as if he would collapse without its support. Wearing the same clothes as yesterday, he gazed at me as if I might explode. Deep lines of weariness marked his face. His hollow, bleary eyes a sign that he hadn't slept.

"I'm sorry I couldn't stop Galen from killing Walsh and marrying you," he whispered. "Did he…have time…." He averted his gaze. "…have time to…"

"To rape me?"

He flinched as if I had slapped him.

"Why couldn't you stop the wedding?" I asked, keeping my voice low despite my desire to scream at him. "Was it part of your plan for me…for him to consummate the marriage?"

"No." He slid to the floor and dropped his head into his hands. With pure misery in his voice, he said, "He was *supposed* to get sick."

Regret immediately bloomed in my chest. I knelt next to him. "Nothing happened. He did get sick."

He gathered me into his arms and held me close. "Thank fate."

"What's been going on?" I asked.

"I can't tell you."

Gritting my teeth to keep from yelling at him, I tried another question. "Why did you let him kill Walsh and marry me?"

"A tactical decision."

And then I knew. His answer was classic Valek. Last night was all part of a grander scheme that I knew nothing about. Which kept everyone safer except for the clues I'd already put together.

"What can I do?" I asked.

Devlen closed his eyes for a moment. "When the fog burns off, keep Galen busy."

"You're not serious. Are you?"

"I am. It's critical that he is distracted when the fog lifts."

"The fog…Kade's here."

He wouldn't say anything. I understood, but for sand's sake it was so frustrating. I had already guessed Valek and Kade were nearby. "Why doesn't someone just assassinate Galen? Valek could—"

Devlen covered my mouth with his hand. "Don't speculate out loud. I know this is difficult for you. Waiting and trusting others are not your best qualities." He whispered in my ear. "There has been some discussion over Galen's death. We're worried his demise would also cause yours."

I shook my head, planning to argue, but he continued. "Your and Galen's blood are mixed. Your souls are intertwined. If one of you dies, we believe the other will, as well."

"Yelena—"

"She won't return a soul to a dead body."

"Oh."

"I can't exist without you, so killing Galen is not an option. I would rather lose you to the Stormdancer than lose you to the sky."

"But what about curare—"

"Please. Stop. Trust us to have considered all the angles. Just keep Galen busy."

"How distracted do you need him?" I asked, dreading the answer.

"It would be best if he wasn't walking around the compound until nightfall. Going between buildings is okay as long as he's busy with a specific task."

"You do understand the longer I stay with him, the greater the chance he'll force me to consummate the wedding." It needed to be said. Although stating my fears out loud didn't alleviate them one bit.

He squeezed me tight. "I'm *painfully* aware of the danger. This would be an ideal time to use that clever brain of yours. You have gotten out of more difficult situations than this."

But I hadn't been bound to a sick bastard. I buried the doubts deep and promised to try. I nuzzled his neck, inhaling Devlen's distinctive scent. My connection to Devlen seemed stronger despite Galen's hold. Just like my glass animals, I felt his song deep inside me. A desire to repeat yesterday's liaison flushed through me.

I lifted my head and he turned as if he read my mind. We kissed and I moved so I straddled his lap. I ceased worrying about my situation and was just satisfied to be with him.

Eventually, Devlen broke off. "Too dangerous."

He was right, but I didn't have to like it. When he left, all warmth fled my body. I shivered and planned different ways to distract Galen. If I was lucky, he would sleep all day.

I wasn't lucky. Galen woke when the sun burned through the fog. Grumpy and irritable, he ordered me to fetch him something to eat with a specific request to make sure the food came from a container that served everyone. I hustled to the dining room, trying not to search the faces of the clan members I passed. If I spotted a disguise, I could endanger the person, who would most likely be a good friend or a relative.

Without the fog, the entire compound was visible. Sunlight sparked from the blue-green waters of the sea. We were a few days into the hot season—my favorite time of the year. Kade and I had promised to visit his parents and we were going to return to Booruby, as well.

My heart ached when I thought of Kade. I still cared for him, but the fire had died.

By the time I returned to Galen's cottage, he had washed and dressed. He ate without saying a word, then ordered me to follow him to Walsh's office.

"Until I'm certain the Bloodroses won't do anything stupid, you're to stay with me at all times unless I say otherwise," Galen said.

Quinn's sister jumped a foot when we entered. I feared she would go into labor, but she pulled it together and helped Galen find Walsh's files and important documents. More armed guards stopped by, reporting on the evening's patrol and on a few minor incidents.

Devlen arrived a couple hours later. He had changed into fresh clothes. Ignoring me, he said, "You were right, Galen. No problems. The Bloodroses have accepted your leadership."

"We'll keep things as is for now, but once they're

comfortable, we can start implementing our changes," Galen said.

"What should I do next?"

"Take a contingent and sweep the coast. Make sure no one is hiding in the rocks. Damn fog is a pirate's best friend. And then find the woman who worked in the kitchen last night. She put something in my cheese to make me sick. Pepper and salt her and put her out to dry in a very public location."

Devlen nodded and left. I hoped for the poor woman's sake he didn't follow all of Galen's orders.

"Opal," Galen said, jerking me from my thoughts. "Tell Penny to fetch the Minister and his wife. I want to speak with them before they leave."

Happy for a break, I hurried to the outer reception area where Penny worked and relayed Galen's message.

She stood, but instead of dashing off, she inclined her head as if she wanted me to follow her. I couldn't go far, but she stopped near a file cabinet. Opening the bottom drawer, she withdrew a small package.

"Master Walsh told me to give this to you if anything happened to him," Penny whispered.

"What is it?" I asked.

"No idea, but don't let Galen know about it."

"I'll try."

Penny put her hand on my shoulder, comforting me. "You can endure. I pretended I was lying with my boyfriend when Walsh ordered me to his bed." Then she hurried to run her errand.

Her concern touched me. I let the guilt over not recognizing the horrors going on here consume me for a moment before I used it to motivate me. I glanced at the office door. It was ajar, but Galen couldn't see me.

Unwrapping the package, I uncovered two syringes filled with blood and a note. I pocketed the note and rewrapped the gifts from Walsh, returning them to the drawer. Hoping I would have a chance to read the letter later, I returned to my post.

Penny soon arrived with Minister Heath and Nancee in tow. They smiled at Galen and inquired about Walsh.

"We hope his illness isn't serious," the Minister said. "We're honored to be here. This is the first time he invited us to officiate a wedding."

Nancee beamed at us. "You two must be a special couple."

"We are," Galen said.

The Minister flourished papers for us to sign. Nancee brought them to Galen first, pointing out where to write his signature. She gestured me over, then handed me the pen.

The air in the room clung to me like a thick syrup. My lungs strained to breathe. Nancee's short fingernail marked the proper spot. Her nails had been cut short and lacked polish. For a well-dressed woman who had spent time arranging her hair in a neat style and putting on makeup, her hands didn't match. Then I spotted the scar along her index finger. One of my worries floated off my back, but it was immediately replaced with a different concern.

"Sign it Opal Bloodrose," Galen said.

I scrawled the name under Galen's.

Nancee marked the papers and handed one set to Galen. "For your records. We'll send the other to the Bloodgood capital, Vein Ravine."

As they made small talk, Galen drew power, seeking their deeper emotions. The ones they hid under the polite small talk.

I moved between Galen and the couple. "It's getting late. If you plan to be home before dark, you should go soon."

Galen kept his smile, but it didn't reach his eyes. "They're welcome to stay as long as they'd like. I was about to offer them some refreshments."

Heath thanked Galen. "Opal's right. We should go." He tsked. "The heating season's foggy weather just won't quit, putting a crimp in travel."

We did the polite goodbyes.

"I'll escort you out." Then I said to Galen, "I'll be back. Okay?"

Outmaneuvered, Galen's grin strained as he agreed.

The three of us kept silent until we were far enough away not to be overheard.

"How did you know I was here?" I asked them. When they acted offended and confused, I cut in. "Valek did another excellent job with your disguises, but you can't fool me anymore. I saw Eve's scar. The one I gave her the last time we did knife defense."

"Ah, hell," Nic said. He pulled a silver coin from his pocket and gave it to his partner.

"Always a pleasure taking your money," Eve said.

"We don't have time for this," I said.

"We followed Devlen," Nic said. "Along with that big Ixian."

Ari was here, too. I didn't know if I should be glad or scared. "Leave now. Galen's suspicious of you."

But Nic wouldn't budge. He engulfed me in a hug, squeezing the breath from me. Then he rested his hands on my shoulders and peered at me in concern. "How are you holding up?"

I stifled the desire to punch him. "Better now that I know I'm not legally married to Galen, but if I'm forced to reveal your identities and harm you then I'll be sick. Go, so I don't have to. Please."

"Okay, okay. Settle down. We'll leave. Our job's finished anyway," Nic said. He hugged me again and Eve squeezed my hand.

"Stay strong," she said.

I watched them cross to the stables, wishing Nic was a better liar. The big lug had no intention of leaving. I wanted to cry and cheer at the same time.

Before I reached Galen's office, I read the note from Walsh. He suspected Galen would attempt to take control of the family. Even in his warped mind, Walsh loved them and didn't wish to see them subjected to Galen's harsh leadership. Explaining what was in those syringes, Walsh hoped I would aid his family. I tore the letter into small pieces and threw them in the trash.

When I returned to the office, Galen didn't wait to unleash his anger over my little trick. "You are to remain silent unless I ask you a question or give you permission to speak. You've been taking advantage of my inattention to details. I'm going to rectify that right now." He read from a list he had written.

My loopholes disappeared with each command. All but two and I clung to them. They were all I had to keep me from giving up.

He slammed the paper down on the desk. "I've been too nice to you. I don't think you really understand how nice." Galen stood. "Don't move."

My mind yelled to run away, but my feet remained planted.

He approached me and slid his hands under my shirt, fondling my breasts. I bit my tongue, hoping the pain would distract me.

"I can feel you're repulsed and afraid," he said. "I order you to relax and enjoy my touch."

Heat spread across my body, igniting desire.

"Better or worse?" he asked.

"Worse."

"Now do you understand how nice I've been?"

"Yes."

"Good. I think it's time to consummate our nuptials. You will get pleasure from everything I do to you even if it hurts. Consider it a wedding gift." He yanked my shirt off.

I shivered in delight as he ran his hands over my back and again when he finished undressing me. A distant corner of my mind recognized the horror and humiliation, but I was powerless.

A knock sounded before Galen could do more. Thank fate! Irritated, he strode to the door and opened it a crack.

"This better be important," he said.

Devlen's voice replied, too low for me to discern his words.

Galen glanced at me. "Get dressed."

More than happy to oblige, I pulled my clothes on in record time. Galen swung the door wide and returned to his desk.

Devlen entered, leading a dozen guards.

"Show Opal what you caught on your fishing trip," Galen said.

The guards parted, revealing two figures wrapped in null shield jackets.

29

My legs refused to support my weight any longer. I dropped into a chair. This nightmare would never end.

"Heli has returned and she brought a friend," Galen said. "Is he your Stormdancer, Opal?"

I met Kade's gaze. "Yes."

"He came to rescue you. How sweet." Galen rubbed his chin as if considering. "And despite Devlen's assurances that the Bloodroses have meekly accepted me, I've been picking up an undercurrent of unrest from them. Which is concerning. Opal, has Devlen been lying to me?"

"Yes." The word burned my throat.

"Is he planning on helping you?"

"Yes." I tried to catch Devlen's eye, but he kept his attention fixed on Galen.

Galen said to him, "You were worried Opal would endanger her own rescue so you kept her out of the loop. But all this time, you've been a wonderful source of information. Your blood magic isn't strong enough to block me from your emotions." He gestured to the guards. "You believe they are loyal to you, when in fact they are still mine. And I know all about the fog. How many people have you sneaked into the compound?" He didn't wait for Devlen to reply. "I counted six—the Minister and his wife, two disguised as guards and the Stormdancers."

The small bit of hope clinging to me kissed me good-bye. Listening to Galen gloat was like watching someone burn to death and not being able to throw water on the poor soul.

Drawing power, Galen concentrated on Kade and Heli. "The jackets aren't tied. They're supposed to rip them off and cause problems when given the signal," Galen explained to me. "Go ahead, Stormdancers, take them off."

Kade and Heli shrugged free of the jackets. They exchanged a look.

"I'm more than capable of producing a null shield. Everyone was so worried about Opal's power, you disregarded mine." He tsked. "And is she really worth six lives? If she's so devoted to her Stormdancer, then why did she sleep with Devlen?"

Dead silence. No one said a word. Beyond horrified, I stared at the floor.

Finally, Galen ordered his guards to wrap up Kade and Heli in the jackets and to secure Devlen.

As if on cue, Kade, Devlen and Heli fought the guards. But they were outnumbered, and Heli didn't know how to defend herself. She was the first to be subdued and tied into a jacket, followed by Kade and then Devlen.

"Announce a mandatory clan meeting to start in one hour," Galen ordered his guards. "Escort the three of them to the dining room. I'll join you there after I finish."

I returned my gaze to the rug until the rustling sounds of movement faded.

Galen crouched in front of me. "Feel terrible?"

"Of course."

"You're going to feel worse after you kill your friends."

Before we left, I used the washroom near Penny's area and was alone for a few precious minutes. Opening the drawer, I took out the syringes Walsh had left me. I shoved them deep into my pocket as Galen stepped from his office.

He grabbed my hand and we walked to the dining room. All the clan members sat around the tables. Armed guards ringed the large space and lined up along the front wall were Nic, Eve, Kade, Heli, Ari and Janco. My friends. My family. My reasons to stop Galen.

Unfortunately having reasons gave me no power. I couldn't meet anyone's gaze.

Their disguises had been ripped off and they were either manacled or wrapped in null shields. All had been secured to the wall. At least Valek wasn't among them. I'd like to think he remained off-site to call in reinforcements. A valiant gesture, but they wouldn't arrive in time.

Galen stood with his back to the prisoners and made a speech to the Bloodroses. I scanned their faces. Quinn sat next to Penny, but his attention was on Galen. I opened my mind to them. Anger and resistance simmered, but worry and fear also churned. And if I dipped deeper... No. I wouldn't invade their privacy.

"...the outside world has forgotten you," Galen said. "Do you think these people are here to help *you*?" He swept an arm out, indicating the prisoners. "They came to rescue Opal. They're professionals and powerful magicians and they *failed*. Now you can witness what I do to those who try to upset my plans." He handed me my switchblade. "Kill Devlen," he ordered.

I triggered the weapon and the blade shot out. The Ixian battle symbols Devlen chose for me marked the steel. I ran my fingertip along the flat side of the blade, feeling the ridges of the etchings. *I offer my heart, entrust my soul and give my life to you.*

"Now, Opal."

I turned toward Devlen, but stopped. He had given me his heart, soul and life. Therefore, in order to kill him, I would have to kill myself. Without hesitating I put the blade to my own throat, and pulled.

"Stop!" Galen ordered.

Too late! Warmth gushed down my neck, soaking into my shirt. I smiled until he ordered me to heal the wound. As I used magic to seal the skin, I realized the cut hadn't been deep enough to finish the job anyway.

"What the hell was that?" Galen asked.

"Magic is very literal. Devlen had given *me* his life. I was following orders."

"I take it back," Devlen called, trying to protect me.

No! Unable to speak, I appealed to Devlen. He remained stubborn, but his eyes were wide as if he had been scared.

"Opal, don't—"

Before Galen could finish, a puff sounded. A strange clear dart struck my biceps. I teetered and Galen caught me as I collapsed.

"Heal yourself," he said. "Push the drug from your arm. Now."

I envisioned a little butterfly sucking the drug as if it were nectar. Liquid trickled down my arm. The Bloodroses didn't wait to see if I was successful. They surged to their feet and chaos erupted as they attacked the guards.

Galen yanked me down as he crouched low. "Protect us from objects."

I covered us with a glass barrier. Darts ricocheted off it and from within, I watched the fighting. Bloodroses wielded glass knives, glass darts and bamboo spears tipped with glass. The weapons might not be as strong as steel, but they were razor sharp and a slash across an unprotected neck did the job as well as a sword through the heart. I silently cheered them on.

Quinn threw glass balls that seemed ineffective at first, but must have been charged with heat. They ignited clothing and tablecloths.

"Idiots," Galen said. He pulled me through the melee and we exited. "Secure the doors," he ordered.

They slammed shut, trapping everyone inside. I looked away as black smoke poured from the chimney. The flames spread. Horrified, sick and disgusted weren't strong enough to describe my torment. I huddled on the ground in misery. The black clouds overhead matched my mood until I realized they were thickening.

An explosion rocked the ground as the roof of the dining room blew apart. Then rain teemed from the sky. The incredible deluge soaked me in an instant and I choked on water, but I didn't care as the fire sputtered and died.

"Damn Stormdancers," Galen said.

He would soon have another problem. I spotted Valek approaching us. The clan members streamed from another hole in the dining room, but they kept their distance from us.

"Can you sense the Stormdancers?" Galen asked me.

"Yes."

Kade and Heli worked to free the others.

"Stop them from helping the Bloodroses. Now."

I projected my magic. As slow as possible, I smoothed it over Heli and then Kade, erecting a null shield around them. The rain lessened into a drizzle and ceased. But by this time, Valek had arrived.

Galen appraised the assassin with a critical eye. "Am I supposed to be scared of you?"

"With my reputation, you should be terrified," Valek said.

"Because of your immunity? Didn't Opal tell you about the null shields?"

"She did." He flung a succession of darts at us.

Galen easily batted them away. His magic was strong enough for a few missiles. Then Valek withdrew glass balls from his pockets and lobbed them. They crashed around us, but the breeze carried the sleeping gas away. Valek stopped moving when Galen encased him in a null shield. Valek looked furious. But by then, Devlen, Ari and Janco had joined the Bloodroses outside, which, I suspected, had been Valek's intent.

Before Galen reacted, a battle cry rose. As one they rushed us, screaming loudly. Galen shouted my name, but the noise from their attack drowned out the rest of his words.

Pushed and shoved, I was hustled along and up a

slight dune of sand. I bumped into Quinn. He gave me a wild grin and thrust glass into my hands. An orb.

"We're doing it, Opal," he shouted. "Fighting together!"

Even outnumbered, Galen had magic and the skills to defend himself. He had cleared a space around him. From my position, I had a good view despite being boxed in by Bloodroses.

The mob shifted and I stumbled. A strong arm encircled my waist, steadying me.

Devlen pointed to the orb in my hands. "Can you drain him?"

I shook my head no.

"How about a null shield?"

Frustrated, I grabbed Quinn's arm. *Can you hear me?*

He blinked in surprise. "Yes."

*Tell Devlen I can't erect a null shield, but you can.*

"I can't. I don't know how!"

*I'll help you. We can only do this together. All of us.*

"But my magic is weak and it only sticks to glass."

*Stick it to that glass ball you made and use the black diamonds for a power boost.*

"Oh. Okay." He plowed through the crowd.

"Where is he going?" Devlen asked.

I waved him off, too tired to explain with gestures. Exhaustion tugged and I sagged against Devlen. Galen must be tapping my power to protect against the Bloodroses, and to keep Valek trapped.

"He's big and bad, but don't get me mad," Janco sang out.

I glanced over at Galen. He fought Janco. The Ixian had donned a null shield jacket and had found a sword.

Their swords clashed with a clang and I noticed Janco held his weapon with two hands. It was Valek's broadsword. Why hadn't Ari taken it? He could wield it one-handed.

But then Janco attacked with a flurry of strikes. Even with the heavy sword, his speed was impressive. Too bad Galen was the better swordsman. The match wouldn't last long. I willed Quinn to hurry.

The young magician's feet pounded on the sand. He wasn't even out of breath. We found a quiet spot away from the crowd. I sat cross-legged in the sand and Quinn plopped next to me. Loophole number one— Galen never told me not to help Quinn.

Touching his arm, I said, *Hold the glass in one hand and the diamonds in the other.* Since he had worked with glass, I used his experience to explain how to build a shield. It had worked for me. I hoped it would for him.

*Using the power in the diamonds, expand the bubble so it's big enough to fit a man and attach it to the ball like you had applied the heat earlier.*

"And almost fried the entire clan."

*You didn't. Focus!*

Quinn was quick to catch on and after a couple heart-stopping mistakes, he erected a shield.

*Do you have good aim?* I asked Quinn.

"How far?"

*No closer than that dune we stood on. Any nearer and he would feel you coming.*

"No."

*Ask Devlen.*

Quinn relayed my question.

"I'm not accurate at that distance," Devlen said.

We returned to the dune and I searched the crowd.

Unable to get to Galen, the Bloodroses watched the match and kept the noise level high. Valek could do it if he wasn't trapped. Ari and Janco exchanged places in one sweet move that they had to have practiced before. Ari had also donned a null shield jacket. He slashed and cut with one hand, trying to get close enough to use his strength to his advantage. Nic and Janco stood together, encouraging Ari. Janco's arms and torso sported multiple cuts and he breathed heavily.

Kade and Heli watched the fight, staying out of the way. I still couldn't break the null shield around them. Eve hovered nearby.

Eve! She could kill a fly on the wall with her knife.

*Tell Devlen to send Eve over to us, and then stay there. He'll only have a second to knock Galen out. Does he have curare?*

"No curare," Devlen said after Quinn explained. "Our weapons and supplies were confiscated by Galen's men."

Devlen lifted my chin and kissed me before releasing his hold. I hung on to Quinn as Devlen weaved his way toward Eve. Ari kept Galen busy, but blood streaked down his face from a cut above his eye. Janco gave Nic his jacket and I would have laughed at the way the fabric strained over Nic's broad chest if the circumstances were different.

Nic stepped next to Ari and grabbed the sword, freeing Ari to retreat. Nic wasn't as strong as Ari nor as fast as Janco, but he had a certain finesse and he wasn't tired from fighting two other opponents. Teamwork at its best.

Galen sucked more of my energy. If it wasn't for Quinn's support, I would have buckled. By this time,

Devlen had reached Eve. She didn't hesitate, plunging into the crowd.

When she joined us on the dune, she asked, "What do you need?"

Quinn handed her the ball, filling her in on the plan.

She hefted it, testing its weight. "One chance, right? Near his feet? Do or die?"

"Yes."

Eve smiled. "I like a challenge." She lobbed the glass. Sunlight glinted off its surface as it sailed through the air. It landed a foot short.

I felt the thud in my chest. Out of ideas, I watched the fight with numb dread. Devlen donned Ari's jacket and switched places with Nic. I had forgotten how adept he was with a sword. His smooth and sure movements flowed with dead precision. I could appreciate his skill now that he fought on my team. Devlen used an effective combination of speed, strength and tactics, forcing Galen to take one step back. And into range of the null shield!

But Galen still had his weapon and needed to be unarmed. Using a last resort move, Devlen blocked Galen's sword with his body and trapped it against his torso with an arm. He yelled, "Now!"

Nic, Ari and Janco moved, rushing Galen together. Ari and Janco seized his arms and Nic punched him in the face. Galen crumpled. If I had any energy I would have jumped for joy. The crowd cheered.

Eve and Quinn helped me down to my friends. Even though Galen was unconscious, his orders to me still applied and I couldn't speak. But the null shield around Valek had dissipated. I could drop the one around the Stormdancers. The Bloodroses no longer needed help.

We gathered near Galen. Nic, Janco and Ari slapped each other on the back and discussed the fight in an excited play-by-play. Boys.

But Devlen remained on the sand, gasping for air. Galen's sword wedged between his arm and side. I knelt next to him. Color leaked from his face as fast as the blood gushed from his torso. The blade had sliced deep into his ribs and had pierced a lung.

He reached for me. "Opal...love...you." Devlen passed out.

30

I grabbed the sword, intent on pulling it from Devlen's torso, but Valek stopped me. The joviality died as the others realized one of our teammates was injured.

"Can you heal him?" Valek asked me.

I shook my head. My energy had been depleted. I cast about for a solution. *Come on, Opal, use your brain!*

Quinn! I latched on to his ankle. *I need charged diamonds.*

He opened his hand. "These are the only ones and they're spent."

*The super messengers?*

"If there're any here, they'd be in Walsh's office. Locked in the safe, but I don't know the combination."

*Take Janco. He'll open it.*

"Which one is Janco?" Quinn asked.

"The handsome gent with the superior safecracking skills," Janco said.

Quinn turned to Valek. I would have laughed at Janco's outraged expression, but Devlen's blood soaked the sand, making a puddle.

I shook my hands in impatience.

"Lead on, Puppy Dog," Janco said. "I fear time is an issue."

They bolted for the office building. Valek studied the darkening sky and began organizing the Bloodroses, setting watches for the night. They dispersed. Nic and Ari carried Galen into the half-burned dining room. I motioned, making sure they understood that he had to be kept unconscious.

Eve followed them, bringing the glass ball, but she soon returned with a wad of towels. We packed them around Devlen's wound. I held his hand, willing him to live.

What would I do if they couldn't find a messenger? Quinn's power wasn't enough to even seal a cut. Would Kade and Heli be willing to help? They had kept their distance. I met Kade's gaze. Anger and pain flared and he looked away. Did I have the gall to ask him? To save Devlen's life, I would do anything.

Valek returned. He sat next to me and said, "Since you can't talk, let me tell you a story."

Eve seemed a bit awed by Valek. She asked, "Should I go?"

"No need. You already know most of this." He squirmed into a more comfortable position. "Devlen was well aware of Galen's eavesdropping on our plans to rescue you. In fact, he purposely kept them on the surface of his thoughts. We had another way to free you. Easier by far. Quicker. We would have been gone from this horrid place days ago. I liked that one very much. But it included only you and Galen, and would have kept the status quo. The Bloodroses would have continued to be passive sheep." Valek shrugged. "If they give him the power, they're equally at fault."

I would have argued the point, but Valek continued. "Devlen wished to guide them. To help them help themselves. He claimed it was what you would do. He understood the risks were significantly higher and reduced the chance of success. Counting on people who have been repressed for decades isn't a sound tactic. But he convinced everyone it was the right thing to do. Even me. Don't tell anyone." He pushed his sleeves up, showing me his forearms. Tiny cuts crisscrossed his skin. "I never thought I would be sick of teaching knife fighting." He paused. "Is it a knife if it's made of glass?"

I made a slicing gesture across my throat.

"Yes, it does have a deadly sharp edge. No worries about it dulling with use, either. Just with it shattering." He mused, staring off into the distance.

I nudged him.

"Oh yes. And the moral to this story is Devlen is good people. I'm always leery around the so-called reformed, but I trusted Devlen with my life and my team's lives and he came through."

But not without paying a price. How high? Too high in my mind if he died, but I was sure Valek would see it as one life given in exchange for seven—or rather an entire clan's lives—a bargain.

Devlen struggled to breathe. I hovered over him, not knowing what to do. Should I ask Kade and Heli? A shout cut through my panic. My name. I glanced up in time to see Janco running full out.

He skidded to a stop. "Is this what you're looking for?" Opening his hand, he revealed a bottle of ink.

I punched him in the leg.

"Ow! That's payback for letting us all believe you were dead." He dropped a super messenger into my lap.

Magic flowed through me, energizing me.

Valek grabbed the sword's hilt. "Ready?"

I nodded and he yanked. The injury was extensive, but I ignored the jagged flesh and broken bones. Concentrating on repairing the damage, I gathered magic and pretended I fixed a glass statue. I drained the messenger dry, healing him until nothing was left but a nasty purple scar along his torso.

Too tired to stand, I snuggled next to Devlen in the warm sand, letting the day's heat soak into my bones. Truly happy for the first time in seasons.

The next few days ran together. We were moved to one of the cottages to recuperate. Valek poured endless amounts of Leif's teas down our throats. Devlen had lost a lot of blood and needed to drink the one that tasted like dirty wash water.

"You can laugh. *You* don't have to drink this stuff," Devlen complained.

I grunted and pointed to my cup. My tea smelled like moldy mushrooms. I sipped. Compared to the slimy seaweed Mother forced on me, it was actually quite good. I glanced at my nightstand. Mother had visited, bringing me a single purple flower in a white vase and a dose of moon potion in a sealed vial. I had set both aside for now.

"Where did Valek get all these potions?" Devlen asked.

"From Leif," Valek said from the doorway. "Are you feeling well enough to discuss what must be done with Galen?"

I picked up a tablet and wrote: *No need to discuss. We drain him dry and kill him.*

"I thought you couldn't siphon his magic," Devlen said.

I slid from the bed and reached under it. Pulling the orb and the two syringes out, I showed them to Devlen.

He understood. "Are they filled with your blood?" he asked.

I nodded.

"Are you sure?"

I tapped on the tablet, circling *drain him dry and kill him.*

"What's going on?" Valek asked.

Devlen explained.

Valek met my gaze. "Is this what you want?"

I wrote YES on the paper in big capital letters.

"Sounds like a plan," Valek said.

Claiming prior experience, Devlen offered to inject my blood into Galen. He wobbled a bit when he stood, but he shooed away my efforts to help him change clothes. I handed him the syringes.

"Are you sure?" he asked for the tenth time.

I pushed him toward the door.

"Okay. I believe you." He kissed me and followed Valek.

I changed, as well, and visited the small stable. Quartz's happiness at seeing me almost knocked me over. I had been avoiding her since I was bound to Galen, trying to hide my shame and the taint of him.

Feeding her a handful of peppermints, I scratched behind her ears.

*Fire Lady smell good.*

*Really?*

*Smell Changed Man.*

Devlen's image filled her mind.

*Do you like him?* I asked.

A series of her favorite things flashed, including Devlen.

*Even before? When he was mean?*

*He needed herd. Our herd. Changed Man.*

Interesting. I found a currycomb and groomed her. Just being with her helped me deal with those last days as Galen's slave. I mulled over Quartz's comments.

*Who is in our herd?* I asked.

Loving images floated one after another. Me, Devlen, Kade, Valek, Yelena, Irys, Ari, Janco, Nic, Eve, Leif, Mara, my parents, my brother, Heli, Ulrick, Fisk, Pazia, Quinn, Reema, Teegan and all the Sandseed horses.

*Big herd,* I said.

*Good.* She nudged my stomach with her nose. *Make bigger. Plenty of room.*

I laughed.

"I haven't heard that sound in a long time," Kade said from behind me.

*Stormy Sea Man.* Quartz turned to nuzzle his ear.

*Stormy Sea? Who came up with that one?*

*Smell like rough sea.* Offended, she flicked me with her tail.

Certain I would see anger and betrayal and pain all caused by me, I met Kade's gaze with reluctance. His sad acceptance shot right to my heart and I bawled. Big racking sobs shook my entire body. A distant corner of my mind wondered, why now? I had stayed dry-eyed and stoic through the horrors of Galen, yet Kade's understanding unhinged me.

He held me while I soaked his tunic. Eventually the sobs dwindled and the rock in my throat dissolved.

"I know I'm being unfair by coming here when you can't talk," Kade said.

I shook my head no. Pointing to my chest, I tried to tell him if anyone had been unfair it was me.

He held my hands so I couldn't gesture. "Listen. Even before I found out about you and Devlen, I realized we couldn't be together. Now brace yourself, I'm going to use a weather analogy."

I groaned.

He quirked a smile. "You're all energy and excitement and then you blow away. Being with you is like being on the coast, dancing in the storms. Breathless activity, followed by calm. I have that with my job." He brushed my hair from my eyes. "After you sacrificed your magic I thought you would be content to stay uninvolved in Sitian affairs and be with me. But you rushed off, jumping right back into the maelstrom. I don't have the energy to deal with storms on both fronts—pun intended. I need someone steadier."

Tears ran down my face.

He hugged me. "And I'll offer to render aid whenever needed because I know you wouldn't ask. After all, I don't want to miss out on all the fun." He kissed my forehead and walked away.

Devlen hovered near the stable's entrance and Kade paused next to him and said something. I held my breath, but Devlen nodded and Kade left.

When Devlen came closer, I raised my eyebrows, inviting him to explain. He peered at me in amazement. "I never dreamed you would forgive me. Would want to be with me." He cupped my cheek, wiping away my tears with a thumb.

I covered his hand with mine, pressing it against my face.

"Kade asked me to be the voice of reason when you dash off into danger. Note he said *when*."

Valek arrived to escort us to Galen. It had been a full day since Devlen injected my blood into him. They had chained him in one of the cottages. Quinn's glass ball/null shield nearby. Valek had also gagged him so he couldn't order me to free him.

A deep hatred consumed me when I saw him. I gripped the orb hard. Devlen stood behind me. He squeezed my shoulder in support. Quinn's parents acted as witnesses. Since the revolt, Quinn's father, Lane, had been unofficially voted as the new clan leader. According to Valek's report, he planned for a more democratic society where everyone shared the work and the profits. Since Quinn was the only Bloodrose with magic, I had asked him to stay away from me just in case I accidentally grabbed his magic.

I started with Devlen, draining the blood magic from him. Then I nodded to Lane. He moved the null shield away from Galen. Without hesitation, I concentrated on the orb, siphoning our magic. Galen's eyes widened in surprise. The steady ring of diamonds filling the orb sounded. Between the two of us, our power was considerable.

Controlling the pull of magic, I drew it all. Galen bucked and screamed. But for me, the burning sensation of the magic leaving felt purifying, cleaning Galen from my body and soul. The pings of diamonds slowed and I closed my eyes, reaching for the last bit. A heavy fabric of magic settled on my shoulders and I instinctively pulled it as well.

When no power remained, I opened my eyes. The effort had sapped my energy, but I stayed on my feet.

Able to speak for the first time in days, I said to Galen, "A good friend told me that criminals get caught because of greed and stupidity. Loophole number two, Galen. You ordered me not to siphon *your* magic, but not *our* magic. And you underestimated Walsh, who took steps to protect his family before he died."

I turned away. Valek had taken Devlen's place behind me. He pulled the fabric from my shoulders and the significance of its presence finally sank in. It was a null shield jacket. I glared at Valek.

"I thought it was worth a try. Did it work?" He gestured for Lane to approach.

Lane held Quinn's glass ball. The null shield's magic pushed me back. It did work. My immunity had returned. Damn it! I sputtered. "You... How... I don't want *magic!*"

"Being immune isn't magical. There's no magic involved," Valek said in a flat voice.

"Save that speech for the Commander of Ixia. *I* know and *you* know and the *horses* know better." And Reema and Teegan, but I wasn't going to tell him. He'd try to recruit them to our team. And they were too young to decide if they should join or not.

"Before you start lecturing me, I have a present for you." Valek handed me a spyglass.

"Is this—"

"No. Yours was crushed in the cave-in, but I thought you'd like a replacement."

"Thanks."

He waited.

I pulled the spyglass's sections out and peered at Devlen through the barrel. "You're right. I can see the future."

"And?" Valek asked.

"And if you need *our* help for any future missions, just ask."

"A package deal?"

"Yes," Devlen answered.

"Good thing, I brought another." With a dramatic flourish worthy of Janco, Valek presented a spyglass to Devlen. "Now you need to leave so I can finish our business with Galen." Valek showed me one of the glass knives. "I thought it fitting."

"It is." I took the knife from Valek. "You once told me Galen was my problem and I should deal with him."

"You're not a killer, Opal," he said.

Devlen agreed. "You'll regret it."

But they didn't know what it felt like to be magically bound to another. To feel helpless. "This isn't about murder. It's about justice. We know the Sitian Council will discuss the situation until the subject is exhausted. Anything could happen during that time. They're already backing away from charging Vasko." He claimed Galen had engineered the blood magic test laboratory and he had no knowledge of it.

Fire flashed in Valek's eyes. "Vasko's due for a visit."

"I'll let you handle him, but Galen is mine." I spun and sliced the sharp edge of the glass knife deep into Galen's throat, drawing a line from ear to ear. Blood spurted. I watched until he died. No regret.

I paused on the doorstep. Was she still disappointed? Would she be upset over my delayed visit? Would she be able to accept all the changes in my life? So much had happened, she might be overwhelmed.

"Opal, the door is not going to open by itself. She's your mother. How bad can it be?" Devlen asked.

Sweat dampened his tunic. The bright sun blazed. It was midafternoon in the middle of the hot season. The humid air felt hot enough to melt sand into glass. His skin had darkened as we traveled south, but our paler traveling companions hadn't fared as well.

Grabbing Devlen's hand for strength, I knocked and entered the kitchen, pulling him in with me. As expected, my mother prepared the evening meal for my father and brother. She gaped at me as if seeing a ghost. Considering that I hadn't seen her since she learned I was alive, I shouldn't be surprised.

I braced for recriminations or for her to ladle on the guilt for not rushing home as soon as possible. Instead, a smile lit her face and she ran to me.

"Opal!" She embraced me and held me like only a mother could.

All my worries dissipated, and any hard feelings between us had been forgiven and forgotten in an instant.

"Your letter asked us to wait. That you'd be visiting us at the start of the cooling season. Why didn't you tell me you were coming sooner?" she asked. She finally noticed Devlen standing by my side. Stepping back, she clutched her hands to her chest. "And you brought a guest?"

"Yes. Mother, this is Devlen, my…" All moisture fled my mouth. My tongue refused to work.

"Her betrothed." Devlen extended his hand.

Shocked, my mother stared at him for a moment. I

fiddled with the ring on my finger, spinning it around and around.

And then my mother pulled it together and shook his hand. My emotions flipped from being terrified of her reaction to being impressed.

"Nice to meet you," she said then addressed me. "Are you planning on staying with us for long?"

Time to drop my final surprise. "Yes. We hoped to visit for the rest of the season. All *four* of us. If that's okay?"

My mother brightened. "Of course! You know me. I love a house full of friends and family." She peered behind us. "For sand's sake, Opal. Did you abandon them outside in the hot sun?" She tsked. "Where are your manners?"

"They're giving the horses water," I said.

Devlen offered to check on them.

When he left the kitchen, I said, "Before you fuss about not having enough to eat, I also brought plenty of food."

"Thoughtful of you," she said in a flat tone. "But you can't bribe me. You *will* tell me everything, including what was so important at the Citadel that you had to go there *first*."

I hung my head. "Yes, Mother."

Devlen returned with Reema and Teegan in tow. The siblings hovered near the door, one shy and uncertain and the other getting a feel for the situation.

After a few seconds of silence, my mother grinned at the kids. "Come in, come in. Nothing to be afraid of in here. Unless you don't like my cooking. Then you have to do the dishes!"

Teegan laughed. "I'll *never* have to do the dishes."

Reema stepped closer to her brother. She would be harder to win over. Spirals of blond curls hung down from a once-neat knot on top of her head. Being out in the sun had reddened her cheeks.

My mother put her hands on her hips. "You sound pretty confident, Mr...."

"Teegan," he supplied.

"Mr. Teegan. What would you say if I served spider soup and dung beetle pie?"

He glanced at me before replying. "Opal's been telling us how yummy your cooking is. So I would say, 'give me extra helpings please.'"

Mother chuckled. "And what would your sister say?"

"Reema would tell me to eat it first. Then she'd wait to see if I got sick before trying it."

My mother nodded in approval. "A smart girl and a brave young man. Your children are wonderful, Devlen."

"They are," he agreed.

I drew in a deep breath. "They're not his or mine. Well, not yet. We're still waiting on the official adoption papers."

Again my mother showed impressive restraint over her emotions. Her voice only squeaked a little. "Adoption?"

Teegan answered in a rush. "Our mom died and we were on our own, which was okay. I mean, we were doing fine, but then I had trouble with magic and Opal saved us."

"She did?" My mother wiped her clean hands on her apron over and over—a danger signal.

I jumped in before Teegan could expound. "Actually, they saved me. And they're the reason I went to the Citadel. I'll tell you all about it during supper."

The mention of a meal propelled her into host mode.

"Where are my manners? You're hot and thirsty from your trip. Go relax in the living room. It's cooler in there and I'll bring drinks and a snack." Mother shooed us out of her kitchen.

The room was ten degrees cooler. I sprawled on the couch, propping my feet up on the ottoman. Reema and Teegan explored the space, found the bookshelf and happily sorted through the selection, making a pile to read. Devlen settled next to me and automatically tucked me under his arm.

"That went well," he said.

"I'll suffer for it later. Her interrogation techniques would crack a hardened criminal in seconds."

"I think you're exaggerating. She's very sweet."

"Uh-huh. Then why didn't you tell her you're my husband?"

He had the decency to look chagrined. "I didn't want to overwhelm her. She just met me and the children. It's a lot to absorb. We'll explain it to her later."

"Uh-huh."

"Besides, I'm going to ask her to plan and organize a big beautiful wedding for you."

"Interesting strategy. Bribe her first, then blindside her. Good luck with that."

He laughed. "I'm sure she will be thrilled since she missed our tiny ceremony. And I want your family and friends to be able to share in our joy."

I rested my head on his chest, remembering what had led to the simple service in the Keep's formal garden with Reema and Teegan. Leif and Mara acted as our witnesses. In order for both of us to adopt the children legally we had to be married. I still marveled at Devlen's instant acceptance of the siblings in our lives.

He had meant what he said before. To be with me regardless. Although he wouldn't let me procrastinate and delay this trip to introduce everyone to my parents and brother.

Once Nic and Eve sorted out the paperwork and officially released Devlen from Dawnwood, Devlen had asked me to marry him.

My left hand rested on his lap. Smiling, I played with the ring on my finger. The proposal hadn't been a surprise, but his betrothal gift had brought tears to my eyes. Set in an elegant gold band, the two-carat black stone glinted with flecks of red and orange. A fire opal.

We married in the early morning to avoid the heat. Master Irys Jewelrose officiated the ceremony near the Fire Memorial. She wore her formal robes made with purple silk. I wore a simple cream-colored gown. Devlen chose to don the Sandseed's ceremonial attire—a long-sleeved black tunic with animal shapes and geometrical symbols embroidered in silver thread, a black leather belt, gray pants and black boots.

After we exchanged vows, I presented Devlen with my wedding gift to him—a scimitar with a simple leather hilt and Ixian battle symbols etched into the blade. The symbols matched the vows we had just spoken aloud. *I offer my heart, entrust my soul and give my life to you.* And they matched the marks on my switchblade.

He beamed at me and presented his gift. A vial full of blood. Magic clung to the glass, preserving the contents.

Shock ripped through me. "Whose?"

"Yours." He curled my fingers around the barrel. "Blood is very powerful, I only needed to use one of your syringes on Galen. The other I saved for you."

"But I don't—"

"It's yours. Use it, keep it or throw it out. It's your choice."

After the ceremony, our little family celebrated by having a picnic in the garden. We left soon after for my parents' house in Booruby.

Having no desire to reclaim my magic at this time, I placed the vial in a box and secured it. Then I gave it to Irys, asking her to lock it in the Keep's safe. I might need it someday.

But not today. Not as I sat next to Devlen with happiness welling inside me. I pivoted and kissed him deeply. Reema and Teegan made yuck noises. Devlen and I hadn't had any privacy during the trip to Booruby. I was about to suggest to my husband a private tour of the guest room upstairs when my father and brother burst into the living room. Loud and welcoming and full of questions, they embraced my new family without hesitation. My mother followed them, carrying a tray overflowing with enough food and drinks for twenty people. She appeared to be recovered from the shock of our arrival and beamed at Reema and Teegan. Probably realizing they would soon be her grandchildren.

After the kids, Ahir and Devlen went to bed and after a marathon conversation with my parents—yes, I loved Devlen with all my heart; no, we weren't going to settle in Booruby, but live in my glass factory in Fulgor so I could make magic detectors and he could use his Story Weaver skills to help reform prisoners; yes, we would visit as often as possible; no, we didn't plan to work for Sitia or Ixia, but to help Valek when he needed us; yes, they could watch the children when Devlen and I were on assignment—I climbed the stairs exhausted.

I checked on my charges. Reema slept in my bed and

*Maria V. Snyder*

Teegan was next to her in Mara's old bed. She wouldn't let him stay in Ahir's room as he had wished. The two "boys" had bonded within minutes of being introduced. They had already gotten into trouble twice for rude and obnoxious behavior during supper.

Devlen slept in the guest room. He roused when I slid into bed with him. He rolled over and molded his body to my back, draping an arm around my waist.

"How did it go?" he asked.

"Like expected. I cracked after an hour and spilled my guts."

"Did you tell them about me?"

He had insisted that I inform my parents about *all* his past misdeeds. "Yes, and it triggered another two hours' worth of questions and reassurances."

"And the marriage?"

"That, too. My mother had heart failure, or so she claimed, but she instantly forgot all about your colorful past when I asked her to plan us another wedding."

I realized more rounds of questions and assurances and explanations would be required to reach normalcy with my family. It would be crazy, exhausting and probably involve a lot of laughing and tears. With Devlen's love and support, I could easily handle all of it.

Devlen intertwined his fingers with mine. "What are you thinking about?"

"The future."

"And?"

I turned to face him. "Welcome to our herd."

\* \* \* \* \*

# ACKNOWLEDGEMENTS

A huge thank-you to my husband, Rodney, and children, Luke and Jenna. Their encouragement and support never wavers.

During the writing of my books, I'm thankful to have a wonderful network of supporters. My critique partner, Kimberley J. Howe, is always willing to read and comment on my first drafts. My friend Judi Fleming has encouraged me in many ways. Our contest to see who could write the most words in a day was what I needed to finish the story. Thanks for the incentive and the wine!

After visits to Harlequin's Toronto, New York City and London offices, I was amazed to learn how many people are involved in getting my manuscript transformed into a published book. I'd like to thank them all for their hard work and effort on my books!

My excellent editor, Mary-Theresa Hussey, thankfully continues to give me invaluable advice and inspiration. Thanks to Elizabeth Mazer, a vital member of our team.

The art department has done a fantastic job with this bright cover. Many thanks to all the talented artists, designers and photographers for your creative efforts.

A special thank-you to my friend Kathy Flowers. She arranged for me to take a tour of a maximum security prison and then played tour guide for the day. It was an enlightening experience and a bit scary as we mingled with the inmates. And a shout-out to the Black Sergeant, visitor number one-three-six-five thanks you for your time.

And a huge thanks to my massive army of Book Commandos! Your efforts have helped in spreading the word about my books. Special mention to those who have gone above and beyond the call to duty: Louise Bateman, Justin Boyer, Elizabeth Earhart, Michelle Gottier, Jane Gov, Jimmy Grogan, Jen Grzebien, Kelley Hartsell, Kate Ladd, Heather Lloyd, Denise Löchtermann, James Pellow, Kelly Plaia, Erica Rowe, Greg Schauer, Laura Schibinger, Jessica Scott, Larry Smith, Ashlen Stevenson, Julie Walsh and Sarah Weir. Valek may try to recruit you to his team.

# REQUEST YOUR FREE BOOKS!

## 2 FREE NOVELS FROM THE PARANORMAL ROMANCE COLLECTION PLUS 2 FREE GIFTS!

**YES!** Please send me 2 FREE novels from the Paranormal Romance Collection and my 2 FREE gifts (gifts are worth about $10). After receiving them, if I don't wish to receive any more books, I can return the shipping statement marked "cancel." If I don't cancel, I will receive 4 brand-new novels every month and be billed just $22.76 in the U.S. or $23.96 in Canada. That's a savings of at least 17% off the cover price of all 4 books. It's quite a bargain! Shipping and handling is just 50¢ per book in the U.S. and 75¢ per book in Canada.* I understand that accepting the 2 free books and gifts places me under no obligation to buy anything. I can always return a shipment and cancel at any time. Even if I never buy another book, the two free books and gifts are mine to keep forever.

237/337 HDN F4YC

Name _____ (PLEASE PRINT) _____

Address _____ Apt. # _____

City _____ State/Prov. _____ Zip/Postal Code _____

Signature (if under 18, a parent or guardian must sign) _____

### Mail to the Harlequin® Reader Service:
**IN U.S.A.:** P.O. Box 1867, Buffalo, NY 14240-1867
**IN CANADA:** P.O. Box 609, Fort Erie, Ontario L2A 5X3

**Want to try two free books from another line?**
**Call 1-800-873-8635 or visit www.ReaderService.com.**

* Terms and prices subject to change without notice. Prices do not include applicable taxes. Sales tax applicable in N.Y. Canadian residents will be charged applicable taxes. Offer not valid in Quebec. This offer is limited to one order per household. Not valid for current subscribers to Paranormal Romance Collection or Harlequin® Nocturne™ books. All orders subject to credit approval. Credit or debit balances in a customer's account(s) may be offset by any other outstanding balance owed by or to the customer. Please allow 4 to 6 weeks for delivery. Offer available while quantities last.

**Your Privacy**—The Harlequin® Reader Service is committed to protecting your privacy. Our Privacy Policy is available online at www.ReaderService.com or upon request from the Harlequin Reader Service.

We make a portion of our mailing list available to reputable third parties that offer products we believe may interest you. If you prefer that we not exchange your name with third parties, or if you wish to clarify or modify your communication preferences, please visit us at www.ReaderService.com/consumerschoice or write to us at Harlequin Reader Service Preference Service, P.O. Box 9062, Buffalo, NY 14269. Include your complete name and address.

PARA13R

# Maria V. Snyder

As the last Healer in the Fifteen Realms, Avry of Kazan is in a unique position: in the minds of friends and foes alike, she no longer exists. Despite her need to prevent the megalomaniacal King Tohon from winning control of the Realms, Avry is also determined to find her sister and repair their estrangement.

Though she should be in hiding, Avry will do whatever she can to support Tohon's opponents—including infiltrating a holy army, evading magic sniffers, teaching forest skills to soldiers and figuring out how to stop Tohon's most horrible creations yet: an army of the walking dead.

War is coming and Avry is alone. Unless she figures out how to do the impossible…again.

## Available wherever books are sold.